In the Company of Shadows

The Night's Road: Book Four

When the Walls Fallt

Andy Monk

All rights reserved. No part of this publication may be reproduced, distributed, or transmitted in any form or by any means, including photocopying, recording, or other electronic or mechanical methods, without the prior written permission of the publisher.

Copyright © 2024 Andy Monk
All rights reserved.
ISBN: 9798322847434

Three Weeks Later

Part One

Possibilities

Chapter One

Ettestein, Principality of Anhalt-Dessau, The Holy Roman Empire - 1631

The sun dazzled through the steam of her own breath. Her narrowed eyes remained on the Elbe, cutting through lands dead in more ways than one. A few birds, no more than black dots, flitted in the distance. Crows. They thrived while everything else died. Otherwise, all remained still.

Her gaze followed the river as far as the tower's height permitted. East, towards Magdeburg.

She shivered despite the thick wool-lined cloak around her shoulders.

"I must confess..." Lucien continued, "...'tis not the soundest plan I have ever heard, and Lucien Kazmierczak has heard some bloody stupid plans in his time..." he sat on the battlement between two crenelations, facing away from the view, boots scuffing back and forth over worn stone.

Behind him, the long drop to the rocks far below.

Falling, falling, falling...

She touched her throat. Torben's lion still hung from a thong, but a second cord had joined it, from which a leather pouch dangled. Her fingers itched for it, but Renard

1

was watching her closely. He disapproved, so she let the hand fall away.

Cloud crossed the sun. The temperature dropped further in an instant, but she made no move to leave the tower. At least Morlaine could not come up here in the daylight. One less person to nag her.

Renard and Lucien exchanged a glance.

They were worried about her. She didn't need the *sight* to tell her that.

"I have been in cities when they have fallen," the mercenary went on when she said nothing, "'tis never pretty. Lucien Kazmierczak is seldom troubled by sleepless nights, but when he is... those memories are usually why."

One way or another, the two men and the vampire sheltering in their rooms had been trying to talk her out of going to Magdeburg for weeks. At some point she assumed they would decide to save their breath.

"You do not have to come," she said.

The two men shared another look.

"I release you both," she added when neither replied.

"I stand with you, my lady," Renard said without hesitation, "always."

"As do I," Lucien said a heartbeat later.

She knew why Renard said that. His honour. His oath. And the price he felt he must pay for breaking them the night The Wolf's Tower fell. But Lucien?

Renard thought the mercenary followed Morlaine not her. Perhaps he was right. Men were strange, after all.

"But there must be another way..." Lucien held out his hands, palms up, towards her.

"I don't believe Cleever was trying to trick us," Renard said, "Wendel's life was the proof of that."

She again resisted the urge to touch the pouch around her neck.

Lucien shook his head, "It will be hard enough to destroy these demons wherever we face them. In a city teeming with thousands of soldiers slaughtering the population..."

"We will find a way. We have months to prepare," the assurance in her voice sounded decidedly hollow to her, but both men showed the good grace not to comment on its emptiness.

What am I going to do?! How can I do this?!

Her hands wanted to move to the pouch hanging from her neck again. Instead, she tightened them both to fists beneath her cloak.

"You are looking better," she said to Renard before either man insisted on telling her anything else she didn't want to hear for the hundredth time.

"I am, my lady?"

She found a false smile; it was the best she could do.

They enjoyed regular meals and warm beds here, but she had eaten little and slept less since killing Wendel. By the look of him, Renard had benefited more from the *Markgräf's* comforts.

He'd put on weight, whether from Ettestein's thin food or drinking with Lucien, which he seemed to be doing quite a lot of, she couldn't say, but he looked much better for it. The dark bags under his eyes were receding, the red, sore rings around them had all but gone. He still was not the strong, handsome young man he'd been before Saul the

Bloodless destroyed their lives, but he looked less like a wraith than he had. And less like the one she felt.

"'tis good," she said with a nod, "we need to summon our strength for what lies ahead."

"What does-"

"I have no bloody idea!" she snapped at Lucien.

Her eyes returned to the Elbe just as the sun found a break in the clouds, its alchemy turning the river's thread from grey to silver. Then she twisted away and walked briskly towards the doorway, "I am not my brother!"

As soon as her back turned, her hand clamped around the pouch.

It brought neither comfort nor contentment as her boots clipped the stonework.

But it did bring a smile to her face, albeit a bitter one.

And few things did that anymore...

*

The maid – he didn't know her name – hurried by.

Lucien sat up straight. If she noticed the imbecilic, near-on drooling grin as the oaf's eyes followed her, she did a respectable job of not showing it.

"I think she likes you," the mercenary slumped back into the chair, reaching for his ale.

He ignored the comment and concentrated on the bottom of his own pot.

How many emptying ale pots did my father stare into over the years?

"You should introduce yourself," Lucien suggested.

He raised his eyes to the even more disagreeable sight

sitting across the table from him.

"To whom?"

"To Hilde, of course," Lucien nodded in the direction the passing maid had disappeared in.

"Oh... I don't think so..."

"Whyever not? A fetching lass might cheer you up a bit."

His eyes fell back to the ale pot.

"I was fond of a maid back in Tassau, Erna; she had no feelings for me, but... she died, her throat ripped out by one of the Red Company. In Madriel, I met Madleen and was fond of her. I think she might have been fond of me. I don't know, though. She died as well... so..." he sighed.

Lucien looked sympathetic. For all of two seconds. Then he reached over and patted his shoulder, "Lucky for us, I am not a maid. Lucien Kazmierczak has no intention of dying any time soon!"

"You have nothing to fear. I am not fond of you."

"Pah! Lucien Kazmierczak is a friend of all. Well-liked by men and adored by women," the mercenary leaned across the table and lowered his voice, "which, in truth, can be a tad awkward when the man who likes Lucien Kazmierczak is married to the woman who adores him but still..."

Lucien sat back with a look suggesting he thought he'd said something profound. It seemed a direct correlation existed between Lucien's pride in what he'd said and the actual inanity of whatever garbage he'd just spouted.

Draining the froth and fumes from the depths of the ale pot, he pushed himself to his feet.

Lucien's eyes rose with him, "Where are you going?"

"I should check on Lady Solace."

"Why?"

"She might need me."

"What for?"

"I have no idea. That's why I am going to check on her."

"She'll be too busy being wooed," Lucien flashed one of his many infuriating grins.

Before anything suitably scathing came to mind, a group of Gothen men-at-arms passed their table. Several called out greetings; they all smiled and nodded. One even had the temerity to slap his back and wish him a good day.

"I think I preferred it when they thought we were witches…"

"Nonsense," Lucien snorted, "'tis much preferable to be a hero than a witch."

"I am not a hero."

"'tis not what I hear. You put a dozen Imperial soldiers on the ground, cut to ribbons by your flashing blade," Lucien raised his ale pot in mock salute, "the finest swordsman in Europe!"

He muttered something choice under his breath and span away. As he crossed the castle's dining hall, eyes swivelled to follow him. He'd exchanged the dark suspicion of witchcraft for the hollow fame of heroism.

He found the fit even less comfortable.

His heart sank further as Lucien came bounding after him, "Clear the way, good fellows!" the mercenary cried towards a couple of men-at-arms loitering by the door, "You don't want to get on the wrong side of this lad's blade!"

The Gothens grinned and shuffled aside while he cringed, especially after Lucien slapped a hand onto each of his shoulders.

"Do you have to keep doing that?" he hissed at Lucien once they were in the corridor.

"Do what?"

"You know damn well what, I'm no bloody hero..." his voice dropped to a whisper "...it was Morlaine who-"

"Pah," Lucien waved a hand in front of his nose, "trust me, history is full of men who, despite shitting their pants and hiding under the bed, ended up being remembered as heroes. 'tis a lot better than being thought of as a coward or fool."

He tightened his lips and lengthened his stride.

"Besides, Pastor Wilhelm swears he saw you cutting those men down with his own eyes, saving his church from those idolatrous papists. Who are we to doubt the word of a man of the cloth?" Lucien said, continuing his pursuit.

"I suspect Wilhelm's eyes are as old and decrepit as his mind."

"Seems sharp enough to me..."

The maid who'd passed their table earlier – what was her name? Hilde? – appeared around the corner carrying a stack of empty baskets towards the kitchen. She smiled at Lucien; it grew more fulsome when it swiftly moved on to him.

Her footsteps were still echoing on the flagstones when the bony end of Lucien's elbow dug into his ribs.

"Told you she liked you," a salacious grin inevitably accompanied the elbow.

"She does not *like* me. And even if she does *like* me, I do not *like* her. I have no time for foolishness."

"You have something better to do while we wait for Lady Solace's ribs to knit? Pray tell what it is. Frankly, I'm intrigued..."

He ignored the question. As usual, it didn't put Lucien off.

"If we go to Magdeburg, there's a fair chance you will die. Might as well make the most of life while you can."

"If we go to Magdeburg, there's a fair chance *we* may die," he corrected.

Lucien found that funny for some reason. When the oaf stopped laughing, he slapped him on the back.

"You are a hero! All the obliging maids swoon for a hero. Enjoy yourself!"

"I am not a bloody hero," he pulled up, "I'm a damn fool; if I'd locked the castle gates instead of chasing after one of... *them*, a lot more people would have lived to see Christmas!"

"The Imperials would still have got through the outer gates and into the village. Maybe they would have burnt the lot of them as heretics. Who knows what would have happened? Maybe you saved more lives than those lost in the fight? Regrets aren't worth spit, Ulrich."

"Either way, I'm still no hero."

"There's no such thing as heroes, lad; that's the truth of it. We're all fools drunkenly staggering through life trying to dance to a tune we can't hear whilst pretending we know what we're doing."

That pleased-with-himself look settled on Lucien's face again.

When he said nothing in reply, Lucien just patted him on the arm and turned away.

"Where are you going?"

"To make the most of being a hero," the mercenary winked.

"Oh..."

"Life's for making the most of..."

"What about Morlaine?" he asked before he could stop himself.

Lucien's grin faded, and the expression that flitted across his face was one he couldn't rightly find a name for.

"Life's for making the most of..." he said again, then mercifully headed off in the other direction.

Chapter Two

She wanted to be alone.

The desire for solitude could be frustrating when entombed within a castle's walls, even more so in winter when people only ventured outside when they had to. The air always had teeth at this time of year.

So, she went outside.

The *Markgräf* had barred the world beyond the outer walls until the ribs Wendel had broke healed.

After that?

She supposed she would see in time. Her ribs still ached for now, and despite the protests writhing within, she was not yet ready to continue her pursuit of the Red Company.

Besides, other matters here remained unresolved…

Beneath Ettestein's long winter shadow the air cut deep.

Some dark magnetism drew her to the same spot every day. Craning her neck, she squinted to make out the battlements of the Grace Tower soaring far above her.

Then her eyes descended the grey, monumental blocks of stone, flecked with moss here and there, darkened with moisture elsewhere, chipped, cracked, eroded by countless forgotten winters. Imagining them rushing by. The freezing air tugging at her as she tumbled and spun, ripping the scream from her lungs. Clawing at nothing, trying to grab hold of salvation with the bloody stumps of a fingerless hand.

Down, down, past the tower, past the castle's wall, past the colossal stonework and the scars of time, down, down onto the rocks of the bluff on which Ettestein had stood for centuries.

Down, down to damnation.

Every day, she scanned the rocks without ever finding any stains darkening them to mark where Wendel's foul existence ended. Tufts of grass, scraps of refuse, loose scree, the brittle bones of dead scrub awaiting spring to burst back into life.

Had his head cracked open like a rotten egg? Had his body bent and contorted in impossible directions? Had he been-

She stopped herself.

She was smiling.

She didn't know why.

She felt nothing.

The smile bled away.

A crow's distant caw disturbed the silence.

How many people lived within Ettestein's walls? She didn't know. Less than there had been before Christmas, but still a good number.

Tugging at her cloak as the wind toyed with it, she looked around. No one was in sight.

Good.

She still wanted to be alone.

Her eyes returned to the rocks. Worn and rounded rather than jagged and sharp, but what they would do to a body falling from atop the Grace Tower... the possibilities turned constantly in her mind.

Still, she felt nothing.

She'd seen Wendel's body, of course. Despite everyone's disapproval, she'd demanded it through gritted teeth and hot flashes of grinding pain.

The mangled, bloody wreckage she'd hoped to see had proved a disappointment. Despite Renard's warning that it was more like a thing from a tomb, she'd expected the sight of Wendel's corpse to spark something within her; satisfaction, fulfilment, joy, glee, peace. *Something.*

This was the first slice of the revenge she'd dreamed of every night since the Wolf's Tower fell.

As she'd wrapped herself around Renard's freezing, broken body to still his shivering, she'd warmed herself with thoughts of destroying the Red Company, of exacting vengeance one slaughtered vampire at a time.

And that had stayed with her through those long empty months scratching a living within the pitiful shell of her home. It had not abated after Morlaine arrived and they had set out after the demon along her Night's Road.

However, by the time she dragged herself down to the catacombs where Wendel's corpse was locked away from prying, god-fearing eyes, little remained beyond ashes and dust.

Although not a surprise, it jarred her all the same.

But not as much as the emptiness inside her.

Why do I feel nothing?

The crow cawed again in a mocking refrain.

Again and again, her eyes rose and fell. Imagining Wendel. Spinning, falling, flailing, screaming.

Had he been scared?

Had Wendel known the same terror he'd inflicted upon so many people?

How long had he fallen?

Once more, her eyes traced his trajectory from the Grace Tower.

A few seconds.

How long had her father lived when they'd roasted him alive?

How long had the women and children of Tassau lived during Saul's satanic feast?

She didn't know. She didn't want to know.

But longer. It had to have been much longer.

Was that why she felt nothing? Because no justice came with a quick death? No recompense? Did the scales of suffering need to balance?

She stroked the bag around her neck.

It had once contained Wendel's fingers, the ones she'd sliced from him atop the Grace Tower to send him to Hell. Now, only grey, arid dust lay inside.

Her hand dropped. Fascination and disgust momentarily troubled the void but soon faded.

Is anything left of me?

For a year, hatred and the thirst for vengeance had kept her alive, kept her moving, kept her from curling up on the floor and waiting to die.

Now she'd hacked off a taste of vengeance along with Wendel's fingers and felt... nothing. If vengeance couldn't bring her life back, what else was there?

Perhaps if he'd suffered more, begged more, wept, cried,

and pleaded, justice would have been better served, and she'd feel some measure of restitution, a salve upon her soul.

But it had been quick. A mercy, almost.

Was that it? She-

"I have always thought this a melancholy spot."

She turned with a start.

"My lord..."

Lebrecht had something of a knack for appearing unexpectedly. Not as good as her uncanny ally, Lord Flyblown, but, under the circumstances, still quite impressive.

"I didn't mean to startle you," he said, coming to her side.

His face retained the ghosts of the bruises earned in the battle against the imperial force that had tried to seize Ettestein for his cousin, Gottlieb, the *Freiherr* Geiss.

"You didn't," she flashed a quick but empty smile while she played with her lengthening hair; she forced her hand back to her side.

"When a boy," Lebrecht said, staring at the rocks above them, "I used to escape my tutors to play here. I thought this some distant mountain to explore, full of nooks and crannies where I could hide from my cares like some rascally hermit."

"You had many cares to escape, my lord?"

"It seemed so at the time," he snorted a little laugh and shook his head, "I know better now."

"The world is a far crueller place when we no longer view it through the eyes of a child."

His gaze returned. Catching her playing with her hair

again. A silly habit. One she intended to stop.

"You should not come out here," he said after a long pause.

"'tis not so cold, and my ribs are much eased."

"I was not talking about either the weather or your injuries."

"Am I a prisoner here, my lord?"

"No."

"Then I assume I am free to go wherever I choose, for whatever reason."

A strained smile pulled Lebrecht's battered but still handsome face, "That is not what I meant. You come here because..."

"Are you following me?"

"No, of course not!"

"Then how do you know how often I come here?"

Lebrecht shuffled his boots and avoided the question, "This is where the demon died; 'tis not a healthy fascination."

"'tis no *fascination*."

"Then why?"

"I am sorry, my lord, I do not see how I spend my convalescence is of any concern of yours."

His lips tightened and thinned, "My father has... *feelings* for you, which makes it my business. Or at least a matter for my family."

Feelings.

An interesting way of putting it. She suspected Lebrecht's brother would have an earthier way of describing it, though Joachim generally restricted himself to baleful glaring.

Sophia seemed to have adopted her as a big sister and forever wanted to embroider, gossip and whisper about boys with her.

She wasn't sure whether it was the *Markgräf's* feelings, Joachim's dislike, or Sophia's friendliness she found the most unsettling thing about the family.

Or perhaps it was Lebrecht's... whatever it was? *Concern?*

The young man's eyes were blue, sharp, and rather dazzling. Her gaze bounced away.

Concern. Yes, that was it...

"Marriage is not a matter of feelings for those of noble birth; I assume you know this, my lord?"

Again, the young man's lips tightened. His eyes remained on her. Unwavering.

She didn't know how much of her proposal the *Markgräf* had shared with his children, but clearly some of it, given the lack of surprise on his son's face.

"My father is not a man given readily to feelings. But you... you have stirred something within."

"I look very much like my mother..." she said. Was boldness the right path? Perhaps not. Although she didn't need Lebrecht's approval, the desire to explain squirmed inside her.

Lebrecht stared at her blankly.

So, the *Markgräf* had not told his children everything then.

Would he be angry if she did? Would he cast her from his home? Would the possibility of marriage burn like so many other things in her life if she told his eldest son just why his father was considering taking a new young wife to replace Lebrecht's dead mother.

A hundred men-at-arms.

I need a hundred men-at-arms...

In truth, a thousand would be a lot better, but she would take what she could get. And if the price was sharing a marriage bed with Lebrecht's father, so be it.

"You look like your mother...?" Lebrecht tugged her mind back.

"As I am sure Sophia looks like her mother," She smiled at him and then twisted away.

The smile evaporated the moment hers was turned.

What on Earth would he make of her?

What did that matter? It was the *Markgräf* that mattered, not his son. Wasn't it?

She hurried away as fast as sense and civility allowed.

She hoped Lebrecht would not follow.

Yet she also hoped he would.

How strange...

*

He wanted to be alone.

Whenever he wanted to be alone, however, he often ended up in the company of the dead.

Fifty-six graves sat in reasonably orderly rows in the cemetery behind Pastor Wilhelm's little wooden church. There were others, some old, some more recent. But it was the fifty-six freshly dug ones that concerned him.

How many of them are dead because of me?

Fifty-six graves. The *Markgräf's* men-at-arms for the most part. The Imperial dead had gone into a mass grave outside the walls.

If I hadn't pursued Wendel...

The thought had buzzed around his head like an insistent bluebottle ever since the battle for Ettestein.

A lot of those men would still be walking today. Not the men of the household guard Wendel killed to leave the *Markgräf* unprotected. That had happened before he'd followed the demon's bloody footsteps as he wore Iskra's face, but everyone who died after.

The tubby sergeant, he could chalk that death off his conscience too. Although perhaps if he'd protested more vehemently that they needed to keep searching the castle...

More ghosts.

He walked the rows slowly, the wind tugging at his cloak, head lowered, muttering his apology to each grave, as he did every time his boots brought him here.

At least these men had graves and a wooden cross to mark their passing from the world. The women and children of Tassau didn't even have that.

He could only apologise and beg forgiveness to the disembodied weeping and screams that punctuated his nights for the sins he'd committed nearly a year ago.

Some crosses bore names crudely chiselled into them, but most did not. A couple of graves had dried flowers laid on top of them. Most did not.

Fathers, brothers, sons.

All swept from the world because he'd pursued a monster he could never stop with sword or shot.

So, why had he?

"Master..."

He whispered the word, then immediately lifted his face towards the winter sun. It offered neither warmth nor comfort, but it dazzled, forcing his eyes shut. Perhaps it cleansed. The one enemy the vampires could never defeat.

When he released a steamy breath, lowered his face and opened his eyes, he found himself no longer alone.

A mangy dog stood in the graveyard's mud, head raised, brown eyes fixed on him, one ear flopping forward, the other half torn away. A skinny, sorry-looking thing with a long snout and a sad face.

He crouched down.

The dog backed away. When he held his hand out, it pawed the ground, sniffed his fingers, and then barked.

He laughed and tried to scratch the mutt behind its good ear, but it growled and edged away.

"Not the friendly type, huh? Sorry, boy, I don't have anything to eat. Food's hard to come by these days..." Judging by the ribs visible beneath its tangled fur, a fact the dog understood well enough.

When he straightened, the mutt came and sat at his feet, head raised, expectant look on its face. It wasn't buying the no-food thing.

He held out his hands to show his empty palms.

"Sorry, friend..."

The dog licked its chops and kept on staring up at him.

"An optimist, huh?" he scratched his head, "not many of them left around these days."

The wind picked up, and he thrust hands deep into his pockets to protect them from its bite.

"I came here to be alone, you know?"

The dog tilted its head. Perhaps trying to look sympathetic?

Nobody else ever did.

He narrowed his eyes and glanced at the castle, stark and brooding on its rocky outcrop. He was looking forward to the day he'd never have to suffer it again. Or the graves of those who'd died because of him.

"Do you have a master?" he asked the dog.

The mutt was still doing its tilted head, sad-eyed sympathy routine, presumably hoping he might have a titbit after all.

"'tis best not. Better to be your own man... erm... your own dog."

The dog whined. It didn't seem to agree.

"I suppose the food is better if you have a master... Do you have a name, dog?"

Unsurprisingly, he didn't get an answer.

It was a mongrel, not one of the lord's hounds. Maybe he belonged to someone; maybe he just scavenged and killed rats to survive.

He bent down again, "What happened to your ear?"

The dog shuffled forward for a sniff.

"Lost a fight?"

The dog barked.

"Right. I should see the state of the other fellow, eh?"

He scratched the dog's damaged ear; it growled again but didn't back away this time.

"I lost a fight," he shrugged the shoulder of his bad arm, "I've lost a lot of fights..."

He sighed and stood up, "Best I get back to the warm; the

dead make for poor company."

The dog shuffled forward as he turned to go.

Animals and children.

He supposed at least this sorry hound wouldn't cost Lady Solace any silver.

"C'mon, boy," he said, patting his thigh, "maybe I can pilfer a bone from the kitchen when no one is looking. What do you say to that?"

The dog jumped up and barked.

It was the big, mournful brown eyes. The mutt probably used the same trick on half of Ettestein.

He grinned. Still, it would be nice to have a friend.

He started back towards the castle, and when the dog remained staring at him, he slapped his thigh again.

"C'mon. Bone. For you."

The dog barked.

Then walked to the nearest grave, cocked a hind leg, and pissed over the cross. When done, it gave him a smug look before running off in the opposite direction.

Which, he thought, summed his life up nicely.

Chapter Three

Lebrecht followed her.

She did not wait for him.

Part of her was pleased, but she thought it best not to show it. She didn't know why the sound of him hurrying after her made her heart beat a little faster.

She said nothing. That seemed best, too.

"You should go inside," he said when he caught up and matched her pace.

"Why?"

"You are not well."

"I am very well, my lord. My ribs are healing nicely. 'tis what bodies do. I do not wish to lull in my bed, growing fat and weak. I have a long road ahead of me."

"You still intend to pursue your demons, then?"

I will be pursuing them until the day I die.

The thought echoed, distant and ominous, but she did not give breath to it.

"Yes."

"My father…" Lebrecht started.

Your father is a means to an end.

She didn't say that either.

It seemed they both had things they thought it better to keep to themselves.

So, they walked in silence.

Everyone they passed lowered their head and said, "My lord," to Lebrecht.

The castle's inhabitants lauded Renard and Lucien as heroes for their parts in fighting the Imperials, but they ignored her. Tolerated, perhaps whispered about, she suspected. A woman who'd fought alongside the men. She'd likely have been denounced by now if she wasn't under the *Markgräf's* protection. A woman taking up arms! A woman who killed men! An unnatural abomination. At least no one gave her the evil eye or crossed themselves. Not until she turned her back, anyway.

"May I ask what your intentions are, my lady?"

"Pursue my enemies and destroy them," she said without hesitation.

"I meant in respect of my father."

She stopped and stared at him, "You need not worry about the *Markgräf's* honour, I am not a harlot."

His eyes widened, "I never-"

She intended to say something withering. Instead, she laughed.

Lebrecht appeared unsure whether to smile, frown or blush and ended up trying to do all three at the same time.

"I don't know what to make of you, my lady. I do not believe I have ever met anyone quite like you."

"I should hope not. But I will take it as a compliment," she took a step, stopped, and looked back, "was it meant as a compliment?"

"I think so..."

"If I might be so bold. Perhaps you need to practice your flattery a little."

"There are few people to flatter here."

"Men gave their lives defending your home a couple of weeks ago. Are they not deserving of flattery?"

"Well... erm... yes, I suppose..."

She walked on, leaving him floundering again.

Had she ever flattered Renard?

No. But she doubted he would appreciate it. He was too obsessed with honour to have much capacity for anything else.

Lebrecht caught up with her once more.

"Have you ever considered... another life?"

That didn't sound like flattery. Which was for the best.

"Another life, my lord?"

"One that does not involve pursuing your enemies?"

"Not since they murdered my father, slaughtered my people and destroyed my home, no."

And abducted my brother.

But that was one of the things she would not discuss.

Partly because she was not at all sure *abducted* was the right word.

"'tis no life for a woman."

"'tis no life for anyone, but I will know no rest until I have my... justice."

She'd almost said vengeance, but justice sounded less grubby, less brutal, less corrosive.

It was a word she intended to use more often.

"I think-"

"Save your breath, my lord. You will not talk me from the road I follow. Your home was invaded, and some of your people killed. How would you feel if, instead, you stood here alone in the rubble of Ettestein, every person, every man, woman, and child who lived within its walls dead, many slaughtered, not in battle, but for despicable pleasure and depraved lust? How would you feel? What would you do?!"

She didn't remember whirling to face him, and she didn't remember moving so close to him their noses might have been touching if she was taller. She hadn't expected her voice to soar to virtually a manic screech. Things like that seemed to be happening more often, she realised, as she stood panting, staring up Lebrecht's nostrils.

Lebrecht kept his ground. In fairness, more fearsome sights had probably confronted him recently.

"Forgive me, my lord," she said.

"There is nothing to forgive..." Lebrecht replied. Still not backing away.

Perhaps she should? However sensible, her feet appeared to disagree.

Curious.

Steaming breath rose to mingle with his. A heat had risen within her despite the frosty air and clawing breeze. Not dissimilar to the way Flyblown's mark sometimes glowed hot on her skin, but more profound and more consuming.

Walk away, now!

She didn't.

"I cannot imagine your suffering..." Lebrecht said, his voice quiet and, somehow, twisted, "...but your life would be better if you can find a way to make that suffering end."

"It ends only in blood. Mine or there's."

Wendel's eyes falling, falling, falling away...

"There are always... other possibilities?"

Emptiness, nothingness, a void vengeance should fill but hasn't.

The words were soft, the expression on his face winning, the suggestion beguiling. The girl she'd once been had dreamed of a handsome Prince of the Empire coming to whisk her away, of course. Although she might be dead, that Solace's ghost still roamed the lonely corridors of her soul from time to time.

Other possibilities?

Perhaps. But not for her.

"Just because something is possible, my lord, it does not mean it can happen..."

With that, she found the will to turn away from the young prince.

This time, he did not follow.

And the only thought that came was one that often whispered to her from the dark nothingness within.

The price of vengeance is not paid in silver...

*

Lady Solace was not in their rooms. Perhaps Lucien had been right, and she was busy being wooed.

The thought made him uncomfortable.

He didn't know why. It should give him hope, even if only a fool's hope, but it didn't.

Perhaps if she married the *Markgräf,* she'd put aside this folly. Somehow, he doubted it, but the prospect of the spoilt life of a lord's wife might be enough to pull her away from the Night's Road. It was the life she'd been born to, after all. The one she'd expected to live, the one her father had groomed her for from the moment she'd come kicking and screaming into the world. And then he'd be free of this madness. Perhaps he could find himself a good woman, live a life worth living, have sons of his own, ones he would bring up properly, not drag across Europe from one war to the next. Sons who would not have to watch their father squander their honour and drink themselves to death. Perhaps-

"Ulrich?"

His head jerked up.

He hesitated but could hardly pretend he wasn't here.

He crossed to the door to the *maid's* room, hovering outside for a few more heartbeats before going in. He closed the door after him, blocking out the world's light.

Shutters barred the room's sole window, and blankets hung over the shutter to further keep out the sunlight. Still, a little managed to creep in. Enough to make out the small bed and chair that were the only furnishings. Morlaine was on neither of them.

The vampire sat on the floor, hunkered in the corner, knees drawn up to her chest. She wore a dress, which still seemed odd. She was Solace's lady's maid. Officially. He wasn't sure if anyone believed that, but as far as he knew, no one had asked who the demon really was.

"Morlaine..."

He felt dark eyes upon him.

"Do you need... anything?"

"Need..." the demon shook her head; the rest of her body trembled with it.

He'd never thought of Morlaine as verbose, but the rare

times he'd seen her in the last few weeks, she'd barely said a word.

The only person who regularly came in here was Lucien. Whenever the mercenary came out, he looked sickly but happy. Morlaine, however, always looked healthier but sadder.

"Are you unwell?"

He took a step forward.

"Unwell?" Morlaine laughed. The shaky titter did not sound like her at all.

The demon wrapped her arms around her knees and shivered. Like the rest of the castle, the room was cold, but nothing that should trouble such a creature.

"You do not seem... yourself?"

"It has been a long time since I knew who I was. Now... now I feel like I am no one and everyone." Another jittering laugh rolled from the shadows.

"Is there anything you need?" he swallowed, "should I fetch... Lucien?"

"Lucien?"

He always left when the Captain came to her room, but he guessed well enough what happened here.

"Blood..." he whispered.

The demon raised her hands to her temples, "I do not need blood, I need... silence."

"I see..." he moved towards the door.

"I didn't mean you, Ulrich. You, I do not hear."

"Hear?"

"The voices..." she tapped her head, "...in here. I gave my blood to too many people... during the battle..."

"And now?"

"Now they whisper in the wind. I can live with it. But... sometimes... sometimes it is hard. So very hard."

"Is there anything-"

"No... but sit with me. For a while. Please."

He eyed the solitary chair warily. The demon would not harm him; he already owed her his life, but he still did not want to stay in the dark with her. She made him even more uncomfortable than the thought of the *Markgräf* wooing Lady Solace.

Still, he pulled the chair over and sat. When someone saves your life, you owe them something. Even when the person who saved your life was a monster.

He turned hand over hand. Only the demon's breathing troubled the room's silence. Quiet, elongated gasps, interspersed by long, drawn-out silences. Two realisations came together. He'd never noticed Morlaine breathe before, and no one breathed so slowly.

"Talk to me," she said.

"Talk?"

"You know how to talk. I've heard you do it. On occasion."

That almost sounded like a joke, but, of course, Morlaine didn't tell jokes.

"I thought you didn't want to hear any more voices?"

"If I can hear your voice, it might drown out the ones in my head. A little."

After a long pause, he managed, "'tis very cold today. But bright."

Morlaine laughed.

She really was not at all herself.

"I am not much of a conversationalist. Lucien is good at talking..." he suggested.

"I hear Lucien in my head. I hear the words he will not say. I do not wish to hear them. I am using him. I should not, but... he is just another voice I do not wish to hear."

"Lady Solace then."

"She talks only of vengeance. It reminds me of what I used to be. She saddens me, too. But you, Ulrich, you are just a man."

"I am less than that these days," he tried flexing the fingers of his bad hand, winced, and let it flop back into his lap.

"You do not want-"

"No."

Those eyes lingered; their weight palpable even though he could not see them clearly in the shadows. He stopped himself from squirming.

"You are a strange man."

"You are a monster."

"Yet you walk the Night's Road with me?"

"I walk at Lady Solace's side..."

"Are you scared of me, Ulrich? Or is it something else?"

"I am not scared of you."

"You should be."

"You saved my life. More importantly, you saved my lady's."

"Yet part of me wants to kill you both."

This time, he couldn't prevent the squirming.

He thought the demon smiled, "But that is the part of myself I keep in chains. I do not think she will ever escape them, but I can't stop her howling from time to time."

"Another voice in your head?"

"The worst of them all."

He filled the following silence with another squirm.

"Who are you, Ulrich Renard?"

"Who am I? I am no one."

"I think you are more than that."

He shrugged and wrung his hands.

"You will follow Solace to Magdeburg?"

He nodded.

"We should not have told her."

As best he could recollect, he'd been the one who'd recounted what the demon Henry Cleever had told them, but he didn't correct her.

"What should we have done?"

"Said Cleever told us Saul was somewhere far, far away from here so Solace and the rest of you can go off safely chasing geese while..." Morlaine's head lolled backwards, eyes fixing on the shadowy ceiling, "...I go to Magdeburg alone."

"That would have meant lying to my lady..." which his honour forbade, though he had to confess that as a plan, it was a vast improvement on the one they currently had.

"Not a thing someone who is *only a man* would struggle with."

"I have my honour. I have my father's sword... and I have my lady. I have nothing else."

"And because of this paucity of possessions, you will follow her to your death?"

He nodded without hesitation.

"If you were free to choose, where would you go?"

"I will go wherever Lady Solace chooses to go."

"You *are* a strange man, Ulrich."

"Not as strange as bloody Lucien."

Her lips might have curled a little at that.

"I will go to Magdeburg on my own," Morlaine said.

"You will?"

"It would be madness for you three to go. I might as well slit your throats myself."

"Would it not be madness for you too?"

"Of course. But my life has been madness for... an exceptionally long time."

He hunched forward, just a fraction, "If what Cleever told us is true..."

"Saul must be stopped."

"But a city being sacked. A woman alone..."

"I am not a woman."

"You are strong, Morlaine. And fast. But even you cannot stand against a marauding, pillaging army. And that's before you even find Saul and the-"

"Are you concerned for me, Ulrich?"

He sat back. Sharply.

When he didn't answer, she laughed, just a soft snort, but she rarely laughed. The sound made her seem more human, enough to remind him he was in a bedroom with someone the ill-advised might mistake for a beautiful woman.

"I'm sure you know what you're doing," was all he finally trusted himself to say.

"When my mind has settled, I will leave. Do not tell Solace.

Or Lucien."

"Going to Magdeburg alone will not stop Solace from following."

"I know..."

His hands were turning in his lap. With an effort, he stilled them.

"How long will it take for your mind to... settle?"

The demon swallowed, "I do not know. Perhaps tomorrow. Perhaps in a year. Perhaps never."

"Never?"

"One day, my mind will snap. The voices are like the wind, the rain, the snow, like ice and sand. They erode. They wear down my will until it can no longer support the burdens I place upon it."

"And what will become of you then?"

"All vampires are mad... it is only a matter of degree, a matter of time. The wind will reduce a mountain to dust, and the voices will do the same to me... eventually."

"I... am sorry."

"Talk to me... just talk to me."

"Of what?"

"Of anything, Ulrich. Anything at all. Please, just ease my burden for a little while..."

He swallowed. Coughed to clear his throat, all the time staring at the woman hugging her knees in the corner of the darkened room.

He began to talk.

Chapter Four

The prospect of confronting Saul and the Red Company during the destruction of Magdeburg in four months seldom strayed from her mind. It both terrified and elated her. This strange, unsettling combination sometimes spun inside her with sufficient force to physically manifest itself in bouts of giddy nausea.

Still, it remained enough into the future for her to find it far less unsettling than dining with the *Markgräf* and his children. A horror she had to endure every evening now her station had risen to that of Gothen's *honoured guest*. Twice she had actually vomited out of sheer terror before dinner. A feat the prospect of facing a company of demons in the midst of a bloodbath had yet to achieve.

Whilst her mind desired only to work on the various possible schemes for killing a company of demons amongst the destruction of a city housing more than 20,000 people for entertainment, she instead had to suffer polite conversation, trawling her memories for the kind of witty and charming things Tutor Magnus and her father had insisted a young woman of quality should recite, particularly when attempting to charm Princes of the Empire.

Of course, Father and Magnus had expected her to use her charm to gain a husband rather than a hundred men-at-arms in return for her virtue. Still, she thought the principle remained the same.

What she hadn't expected was it to be both so boring and so unnerving.

She'd dreamed of princes courting her when she'd been a young and foolish girl (nearly a year earlier), but the reality was proving somewhat different.

Each evening, they would gather around the table, the *Markgräf* at one end, her at the other, and his three children between them.

A man wooing you in front of his children was surprisingly awkward.

Joachim tended to lounge, silent and sullen, hand never far from his goblet. Sophia laughed a lot, even when nothing obviously funny was afoot, eyes continually darting between her and her father, while Lebrecht often looked like someone had left an inconvenient nail in the seat of his chair.

The *Markgräf's* eyes repeatedly lingered on her. He wasn't overtly expressive, but whenever anything did ripple across his face, it made her think a unicorn might have wandered into the room behind her.

Despite the food shortages in the Empire and the gaunt-faced inhabitants of Ettestein, she found each meal a sumptuous affair. She'd been born to wealth and privilege; the knowledge that most did not share such fortune had never much bothered her previous life, but a year of scarcity, cold and hunger had changed her enough for guilt to distantly gnaw.

Still, she made herself eat. Even when her mouth still

tasted of vomit. She needed to be strong for the dangers and misfortunes that undoubtedly lay ahead. And tried not to think about how the *Markgräf*'s bed might be one of the greater ones.

For the most part, unsuccessfully.

I can do this...

This was the life she'd been born to, after all. If she could face the Red Company and kill demons, she could do anything. Surely?

She tried hard not to fidget.

When not playing with the lace cuffs of her dress, she tugged at the collar or squirmed at the pinch in her waist. It was one of Sophia's. A seamstress had altered several for her, and the *Markgräf* had promised her as many sumptuous dresses as she wanted. Silk and lace. The absolute best available. A famed dressmaker worked in Magdeburg; when the Emperor lifted his blockade, the *Markgräf* would make arrangements. She hadn't told him that in a few months, the city would be a smoking ruin and most of its inhabitants, dressmakers included, dead. It wasn't the sort of thing you mentioned over a fine dinner. Even if you waited until after pudding.

She'd said she didn't need them.

Sophia's uncomfortable dresses were better. Reminding her she did not belong here, in this castle, in this life.

The *Markgräf* had smiled indulgently. He hadn't patted her on the head, but she thought the temptation might have turned within him.

That night, Joachim excused himself as soon as he'd finished eating. Eating, drinking, and glaring, to be more accurate. The *Markgräf* excused his daughter soon after, probably to save the girl from talking herself hoarse.

"Father!" she complained.

"We have business to discuss. The kind not suitable for a young woman's ears."

"Very well," Sophia huffed to her feet, "Come, Solace, I have something I want to show you."

It would likely be a book about princely love. If not, it would be a poem about princely love; if it wasn't a poem, it would be a song about princely love. Otherwise, she would just talk about princely love. Sophia was quite single-minded. Her cousin, Gottlieb, seizing her and threatening her with his marriage bed didn't appear to have sullied the prospect of love in the slightest.

The *Markgräf* held up a hand, "The matter concerns Lady Solace."

"But you said-"

"I said you should go to your rooms, Sophia..." The *Markgräf* arched an eyebrow behind his goblet.

Sophia dusted a kiss upon her father's cheek, before leaving the dining room with a high head and heavy feet.

"That girl becomes more troublesome by the day," the *Markgräf* sighed once his daughter left the room.

She wondered what he'd say if Sophia ever doused soldiers in oil and set them alight against his wishes...

Her hand rose to find her cheek before she could stop it.

"Business, my lord?" she asked, forcing her hand back down below the table to pluck at the damnable lace out of sight.

"Indeed. Somewhat... delicate business," the *Markgräf*'s

eyes flicked to Lebrecht, but, for once, the young man's face was as expressionless as his father's.

"Delicate business?"

Delicate business sounded very much like something that would be about her. Her heart sank. Was the *Markgräf* about to commence marriage negotiations? In front of his son? As his heir, she supposed Lebrecht had an interest. She worried the lace cuff some more; it was starting to fray from the attention. She really should stop bothering it. The dress, after all, wasn't hers.

"Yes... about your maid."

Her eyes shot up, fingers pausing their lace tormenting.

"What about my maid?"

The *Markgräf* shuffled in his chair. He suddenly looked like he wished he had put on some lace cuffs so he'd also have something to fidget with.

When he turned to his son again, Lebrecht cleared his voice before saying hesitantly, "There's been some talk..."

"Talk?" she laughed, though it came out as more of a titter, "Of my maid? I know 'tis midwinter and there is little to do, but really!"

Another titter. If anything, even more high-pitched and nervous sounding than the first.

"Of witchcraft," Lebrecht said, refusing to meet her eye.

Her heart plumbed new depths. There were few things she wanted to speak of less than her possible marriage. But witchcraft was one of them.

So, she refused.

"tis late, my lords," she climbed to her feet, "and I have no desire to listen to such nonsense. My maid is not a witch.

My men are not witches," she glared at both men in turn, "I am not a witch. We have had this conversation before."

"No one is accusing *you* of witchcraft," the *Markgräf* began. She didn't let him finish.

"But you did, my lord. You wished me stripped and examined for Satan's mark."

"Yes, well-"

She raised an eyebrow the way Morlaine did when the demon wanted to make a point, "Do you wish me stripped now, my lord?"

A heat filled her, not the kind that burned out from Flyblown's mark, but one stoked by her own furies.

"Perhaps I should do it now," she tugged at her collar, "and you can examine me yourself? The light is not ideal, but good enough for you to discover the Devil's teat on me if you check me intimately. Perhaps-"

"Solace!" the *Markgräf* slapped a hand on the table, "Enough!"

She dropped her hand, "Yes... my lord."

"We just wish to know more about this woman," Lebrecht jumped in, "we don't believe the things whispered about her, of course. Just prattling nonsense, but we have... an obligation... to..."

"Find witches and burn them?" Neither man seemed comfortable meeting her eye.

"She is a maid, nothing more. You will examine her for marks no more than I will. If you try, I will no longer consider myself a guest of Ettestein," she glowered at the *Markgräf*, "I will no longer consider Ettestein has anything to offer me at all."

The silence was long, and it was Lebrecht who broke it.

"Where was your maid when we met you at Enoch the Miser's farm?"

"Hiding."

"We searched the farm."

"She is good at hiding. A woman must be in order to survive..." she nodded towards the window "...out there."

"Why did you leave her there when you knew we posed no danger?"

"No danger, my lord? You were taking us to question about Enoch's murder. About witchcraft. I decided the young woman was far less likely to be burnt at the stake if she stayed hidden."

"And yet she is now here?"

"She is exceedingly loyal. You know how some servants are."

"I-"

"Excuse my rudeness, my lords. But it has been a long day. My ribs are nagging me. I am tired. 'tis time I went to my bed."

"Why does she never leave your rooms?" the *Markgräf* asked before she could turn for the door.

"She suffers pains of the head. 'tis best she stays in the dark whilst she endures them. With your leave, my lord. I will answer your questions tomorrow if you insist. But she is no witch. In these times, strangers always attract suspicion. However, I would have hoped the actions of my men and I have earned us some... familiarity. Some trust..."

"Of course, my lady. But these are the days in which we live."

"Cursed are we..." she lowered her head to each man. When the *Markgräf* smiled, nodded, and bade her a good night, she swept out of the room. Heart thudding and face still flushed.

In fact, she left so quickly she almost knocked Sophia from her feet.

Which would have served the girl right for listening at the keyhole.

"It wasn't me!" the *Markgräf's* daughter protested after she'd grabbed her arm and marched her down the corridor, "I haven't said anything! To anyone! Not about-"

She silenced the girl by pressing a finger hard against the *Markgräfin's* lips, then ushered her to her rooms.

"Do not speak of these things, Sophia."

"I haven't," the *Markgräf's* daughter slapped both hands over her heart, "honestly!"

"Then where is this coming from?"

"Gottlieb."

"Your cousin? The one who tried to steal Ettestein from your father and hired demons to help him?"

Sophia nodded.

"Why would anyone believe him?"

"He is a Prince of the Empire. He has written letters denouncing Father as a harbourer of witches. Word of his accusations has reached the castle. Now people are whispering..." Sophia leaned closer, "...that there is a woman here with unnatural abilities..."

"Morlaine."

Sophia nodded again, "He saw the same things I did..."

She rolled her bottom lip between her teeth.

"No one will believe him," she said, as much to herself as Sophia.

"Apart from the Emperor, the Catholic League and anyone else with an eye for Gothen's lands and holdings or a grudge against Father."

She found a wan smile, "No one we need to worry about then..."

*

He looked up at the sound of approaching feet.

"Why are you loitering in the corridor, Ulrich?"

"'tis Lucien and Morlaine... they are..." his eyes bounced to the door and back, "...in there... doing... whatever 'tis they do... when they are... together."

"Ah, I see..."

"Should I go and ask them to... stop?" his cheeks flushed, and he felt ridiculous.

With anybody else, he would have just said he didn't want to listen to two people fucking. Even less when one of them was a demon who drank the blood of the other. But with Solace...

Sometimes being alone with her was the easiest thing in the world. Other times, it was the hardest. The peculiarity was that he never knew which it would be at any given moment.

"No, let them conclude their business. Come with me; we need to talk."

Talk?

He nodded and fell in at her shoulder as she headed down the corridor.

He'd spent hours talking with Morlaine earlier.

Never normally a talkative man, he'd been surprised at how the trickle of words had rapidly become a torrent.

In truth, he couldn't quite remember much of what he'd said. Was that normal when a man became unexpectedly garrulous? Or was some spell involved? He didn't think Morlaine cast spells, but he doubted any of them knew the depths of her demonic talents yet.

He'd talked a lot about Old Man Ulrich and his childhood, spent mainly on the roads of Europe as his father trudged from one drunken disgrace in search of the next. He'd talked of honour and betrayal, fear of the future and regrets of the past. But there had been other things. Intimate things. Feelings and fears. He'd talked about women.

On reflection, was that appropriate?

Telling a blood-sucking demon anything was likely inappropriate if you were keen to avoid the pyre.

He'd talked about Erna and the stillborn feelings he'd had for her and how, amongst the many horrors of The Wolf's Tower's fall, he'd felt absolutely nothing about her death, as if her choosing another had washed the possibility of grief from his soul. Of Madleen, who Morlaine had killed, and how, briefly and tantalisingly, he thought he'd glimpsed another future. He even talked about Edna and Gerty, the two plump whores at *The Bear Pit* back in Tassau, one of whom had taken his virginity and both his silver.

It had all poured out of him. A sinner before his confessor, though he was not a Papist and Morlaine was no one's priest.

He glanced at Solace as they walked amongst the dark,

silent stones of Ettestein Castle.

He'd talked of Solace, too. Hadn't he?

He knew he had. But what, exactly?

His mouth, already parched from hours of unaccustomed talking, dried further.

Perhaps better he couldn't remember.

Best Morlaine couldn't either. All those memories crammed into that head of hers. Centuries and centuries of them. She must have forgotten more than he'd ever know tens of times over. A hundred. A thousand!

Yes, she would forget as quickly as he had.

"You seem a long way away?" Solace asked, her voice soft but startling.

"I often am these days, my lady."

"You and I both."

"Where are we going?" he asked as she opened a door onto one of the castle's numerous spiralling staircases.

"To take the air. It will clear our heads."

He didn't ask where she intended to take the air. One place kept drawing her back as if she was subject to some malign magnetism.

The Grace Tower.

Lucien, who was much more enamoured with questions than he, had asked a maid (who was coincidently pretty and heavy-chested) how it came by its name.

She'd told them one of the *Markgräf's* ancestors, known as Roland the Round, had been something of a fickle despot. He showered his counsellors and lieutenants with silver, gifts, and all manner of favours when they pleased him. But when, as always happened, they disappointed he discarded them ruthlessly. His preferred method of disposing of unwanted underlings being a convenient shove from the top of one of Ettestein's highest towers.

How quickly, the maid had said with a sly smile, the favoured can fall from grace...

He hadn't told Solace that story.

The night sucked the breath from his throat as soon as they stepped out upon the frost-glistening stonework atop the Grace Tower. A fat moon teased the world from behind a hazy veil of thin cloud.

Have I fallen from Solace's favour?

What a stupid thought. Solace was not Roland the Round.

No, not yet.

The stupid thought replied.

She crossed to the battlement, placed two petite, pale hands on the pitted, moss-flecked stone of the battlements and stared at the moon. Which he supposed was better than down towards the rocks where Wendel had died. And all those long-ago counsellors who'd fallen from Roland the Round's favour.

"You wanted to talk, my lady?" he ventured.

"Morlaine," she said without looking at him.

"She is suffering."

Now Solace looked.

"Suffering?"

"The Imperial soldiers she... exchanged blood with. Too many at once, they're all... whispering to her."

"That must be quite a thing."

"I suppose."

"We can sympathise, can we not, Ulrich? The dead

whisper to us too, after all."

The dead didn't whisper to him. They wept and howled. In the depths of the night, the women and children cried, demanding to know why he, who had always considered himself such an oh-so-honourable man, had fled and left them to the mercies of Saul the Bloodless and his demons.

"The Imperial soldiers are not dead..." he said, wrapping his good hand around the bad one and squeezing it hard till he felt something, "...that is the problem for her..."

"Perhaps she should have let them die then," the words were spoken as coldly as the air upon her lips.

"'tis to her credit she did not. She has more humanity about her than many I've met."

She looked at him out of the corner of her eye, "Are you warming to her, Ulrich?"

"She is... complicated."

That made her laugh, "She is supposed to be; she is a woman."

"To the casual eye," he admitted.

Solace turned and put her back to the crenelation. The diffuse moonlight conjured a halo of silver about her roughly cut blonde hair. It was growing. He wished she'd let it grow long again. He wasn't sure why.

"They are asking questions about her?" the subtle smile dusting her lips faded.

"They?"

"Apparently, Gottlieb has made accusations of witchcraft."

"Gottlieb, that idiot? Why would anyone listen to him?"

"He is a Prince of the Empire. If he can persuade the Emperor Gothen is a nest of witches, he might provide more men to stamp it out."

"Gottlieb was the one who hired the demons!"

"Quite..."

"What did you tell them?" he asked.

"That she is not a witch, and if she is denounced he can forget about marrying me."

"Really?"

"Hopefully, that will buy us some time. But if word spreads through the castle..."

"What do you want to do?"

"Leave before it becomes a problem," her hand ran down her ribs.

"You are strong enough to ride, my lady?"

"Soon. I think."

"'tis no more than gossip. Morlaine is your maid. No one here knows differently."

"Apart from Sophia."

"Yes... of course... but she promised..."

"And I believe her. But young girls..."

He raised an eyebrow. There were many things in life he knew nothing about, and young girls were one of them.

"Would you trust your life to a fifteen-year-old girl's promise of silence?"

When he said nothing, she added, "What did she see of Morlaine?"

Sophia had seen Morlaine's unnatural strength and speed when they'd captured the *Freiherr* to make him call off the Imperial attack on Ettestein.

"Not her true face... but... enough."

Enough to see them all burn if something Sophia babbled

reached the wrong ears. Pastor Josef might be dead, but there were plenty more like him in the Empire. Probably in Ettestein, too.

Solace nodded.

"And... the marriage, my lady?"

"What of it?"

"If we leave now... It would not happen, would it?" When Solace remained silent, he said, half to himself, "I doubt he has enough men now anyway."

"Perhaps. But he has silver and gold aplenty..." she turned her eyes towards him, a chilling smile twisting her lips, "...enough to buy a bride whatever she wants."

So, she hadn't abandoned that madness any more than any of her other lunatic plans.

He fought a sudden urge to grab her hand, pull her close and scream in her face.

"You do not approve, do you?"

"My approval is irrelevant, my lady."

Her eyes returned to the night. Her right hand caressing a spot on the battlements.

He knew why. In the daylight, the marks and scores exposing fresh stone beneath the lichen were clearly visible.

Solace leaned forward and stared over the edge into the darkness.

He didn't need to ask what she was looking at.

The expression on her face told him well enough.

Part smile, part sneer, part horror, part confusion. Part... something he couldn't name but didn't like.

She was not just staring into the darkness but allowing the dark to seep into her through wide eyes, flared nostrils, and parted lips.

Another urge came. This one harder to resist. To grab her shoulder and yank her away from the edge, away from the darkness, away from whatever was worming its way inside her.

In the end, however, he did nothing.

Pulling her away from the darkness would achieve nothing.

Not when it was always with her.

Chapter Five

"I shall leave."

"We shall *all* leave," she replied.

"You are not well enough."

"My ribs have all but healed."

"You are still in pain. Nothing heals quickly upon the Night's Road."

From the way Morlaine's strange, dark eyes held hers, she suspected the demon was not solely referring to knitting bones.

Behind her, feet shuffled. Was Renard always so restless?

Over Morlaine's shoulder, Lucien was not shuffling. In fact, Lucien looked like shuffling was quite beyond him. Eyes darkened by livid rings; his pallor could have passed for a corpse's. One might have thought he'd been drinking for days if one did not know what he had been doing with Morlaine. As well as drinking for days.

Actually, she had no real idea what he had been doing with Morlaine. Let her drink his blood, for one. But other things, too. Things she knew even less about than drinking blood.

Still, that would come. And at least with the *Markgräf,* there would be no blood.

Well, she supposed there might be a little, given-

"Solace?"

Her attention snapped back up. Her mind was wandering a lot. Much like Renard's feet.

She found a smile.

"We leave together," she repeated.

And... your marriage, my lady?

Renard's question from atop the Grace Tower floated distantly by.

Oh good. Something else to practice her ignoring on.

"There is no need," Morlaine said from the other side of the small table, "Saul will not be in Magdeburg for months... if we believe Cleever. You have plenty of time to recover fully here before then."

She waited for the demon to again try and persuade her she should not go to Magdeburg and that Saul and the Red Company were things best left to her. But she didn't. Perhaps Morlaine had finally realised she was wasting her breath.

"No, I intend to put the time between now and the 20th of May to good use."

Morlaine asked the question with a twitch of an eyebrow.

"*Graf* Bulcher."

Three sets of eyes weighed upon her, but no words.

"He is as responsible for what happened as the rest of them. He must pay, too."

"How must he pay?" Morlaine asked.

"With his life. How else?"

"I will have no part in murder."

She vomited a laugh. The sound, harsh and unexpected, "He is no innocent!"

"No, I would assume not. But he is not a vampire."

"He is still a monster."

"No, Solace, he is a man. An evil one, perhaps, but if I set myself to rid the world of every evil man that walks in the sun as well as the monsters I have created..." the demon's smile was thin and far away, "...then I will never know peace."

"That is your choice. Mine is to bring Bulcher to justice for his crimes. He had my father murdered. He must die."

"There are other ways to bring a man to justice," Lucien offered.

Her eyes flicked to the mercenary, "Bulcher is rich and powerful. Do you think any court would convict him? Do you think any accusation against him would even see him stand trial? Even if the empire was not tearing itself apart? I know you are not that naïve!"

"Rich men have been denounced. Rich men have burned in the pyre. I have seen it."

"Not so many as poor women, though, I would wager."

He conceded the point with a weary nod.

"If a rich man is denounced, 'tis usually by someone who is richer, or at least more powerful," Renard said, feet shuffling again.

"So, we are agreed," she sat back, "we must kill Bulcher."

None of the three faces in the uncertain candlelight brimmed with agreement. No matter.

She'd kill Bulcher on her own if she had to. Preferably hog-tied above a fire with an apple in his mouth, but any method would do. So long as it wasn't too quick.

Falling, falling, falling...

He needed to suffer.

Suffer a lot more than Wendel had.

Morlaine's dark eyes, so beautiful and deep you could topple into them as easily as Wendel had fallen from the Grace Tower, fixed upon her.

"Evil men fall, Solace," the demon said, "it is their nature, the same as the apple falls from the tree to rot in the dirt. It is inevitable."

"So, I should wait for God to punish him for his sins then?"

"There is no God to punish anyone. It is just how the world works, the natural order. Sin catches up with you in the end."

"Then why don't you leave Saul and the rest of them to their *inevitable* fate?" she snapped.

"Because vampires are not part of the natural order. We are something else."

She rolled her bottom lip between her teeth. Then remembered she had decided she no longer indulged in that childish habit and forced herself to stop.

"So, while we leave Bulcher to fall, how many more young women will he decide should be his, how many more men who slighted him will end up roasted alive, how many more children will be slaughtered because he sets demons to do his dirty work? 'tis the problem with leaving things to resolve themselves. The natural order works slow..." she leaned forward to hiss at Morlaine, "...I have less patience..."

"People will die whatever you do."

If her rhetoric and passion were unsettling the demon, Morlaine was doing a decent job of hiding it.

"Then why do anything? Why not let the world fall to ruin about your ears and do... something else?"

"That's a question I often ask myself..."

She puffed out her cheeks and ran fingers through her lengthening hair.

"How do we even know where Bulcher is?" Lucien asked, eyes darting between them as if ready to stop them from coming to blows. Not that Morlaine was displaying any particular passion in their argument.

"He's in Magdeburg, I told you before."

"All roads lead to Magdeburg..." Renard muttered behind her.

"You said that when we left Madriel over a month ago. Why would Bulcher still be there? The city is under Imperial blockade. Maybe no one else knows what will happen on the 20th of May, but men like Bulcher don't linger in a city likely to come under siege..." Lucien cast an eye around the room, "...they leave folly to the poor, the stupid and the fanatical."

"Which are we?" Renard asked.

Nobody answered.

"Bulcher is there," she insisted. She didn't know why he would be. The man was a slug, a toad, and an evil stain upon the face of the world. But he was not a fool. He'd grown his wealth and power proportionately alongside his enormous, ever-swelling stomach. He played every side against the other, betrayed everyone when to his advantage, and followed whatever path was most profitable without principles or morals.

She doubted she was the first person in the Empire to

want him dead, and nobody else had yet managed to rid the world of *Graf* Bulcher.

So why *would* he be in Magdeburg?

"Bulcher is there..." she said again, as much to herself as her companions this time.

"Well, we're heading for Magdeburg anyway..." Lucien leaned back against the wall and crossed arms over his broad chest.

"We are not going to be in the city on the 20th of May," she announced.

"We're not?" Renard moved around the table to stand next to Lucien.

"It would be suicide."

"It would!" It was rare for Renard to say anything brightly, but the way he spoke reminded her of a momentary shaft of sunlight breaking the gloom of a winter sky.

Or someone's reaction to hearing a lunatic enjoying a moment's lucidity.

"But they will have to travel to Magdeburg. There are only a limited number of ways of reaching the city. We will lie in wait and take them by surprise," she slapped a hand on the table, "an ambush!"

If she'd expected applause and pats on the back for her cunning plan, she'd have been disappointed.

Instead, Morlaine said, "Vampires are hard to surprise."

"And the approaches will all be guarded by Imperial troops if the city is under siege," Lucien added.

She glanced at Renard and waited for him to throw a turd into her bucket as well. He said nothing, though, from the expression on his face, it was clear the sun had disappeared behind gloomy clouds once more.

"Which is why we need to go to Magdeburg now. To prepare the ground, familiarise ourselves with the land and fine-tune our plan. And while we're doing that, we kill Bulcher."

"So..." Lucien grimaced, "...after we murder a rich and powerful Prince of the Empire, we shall remain in the vicinity of our crime, in a city about to fall under Imperial siege to await the arrival of the band of murderous demons with inhumanely acute senses, who we will ambush before they can join in the slaughter of Magdeburg's population?"

"Yes," she said, despite her plan failing to sound half so attractive the way the mercenary described it. She threw out her hands, "Has anyone got a better idea?"

The demon nodded.

"I shall leave..."

*

Do you see the darkness in me?

Ulrich, I see the darkness in everyone...

Sleep had come but briefly.

He'd awoken with a start, certain a wailing child stood at the end of his bed. After he'd sat bolt upright and blinked a few times, all he could hear was Lucien's snoring. In truth, if there had been a wailing child at the end of his bed, he doubted he would have even heard it over the mercenary's infernal racket.

So, it had just been a nightmare.

This time.

He'd slumped back into bed.

But sleep refused to return this time.

Despite everything, he'd been sleeping better these last weeks, but it would not come tonight.

Ulrich, I see the darkness in everyone...

After hours of recounting all he could dredge up about his short and largely insignificant life, he'd asked the demon if she saw the same darkness in him Saul had claimed.

Her answer hadn't eased his mind.

He bundled on his clothes and crept from the room. He wasn't worried about waking Lucien; if the fool could sleep through the roar of his own snoring, not much this side of whacking things with Old Man Ulrich's sabre would disturb the oaf. Outside their little bedroom he took more care. He did not want to wake Solace or Morlaine.

Hours remained till dawn. The castle dark and silent. Down in the kitchens, there would be life. The fires burned all night, cauldrons boiled, maids scrubbed and cleaned in preparation for the coming day. Elsewhere, there were only shadows.

Several times, in the deep distance of the night a child's crying seemed to ripple the silence's edge.

He thought of Seraphina and wondered about her in Madriel's orphanage. It was the least depressing thought he could conjure about a child. The rest...

He hurried on. Skulking from one shadow to the next. Pausing to look over his shoulder every now and then without knowing why.

Would Saul send more demons when Wendel didn't return? Cleever would presumably invent some tale to account for the demon's death. Still, every possibility is more plausible during the dark, small hours when reason is as distant as sunlight.

Saul sees the darkness in you...

Wendel's taunt accompanied the echo of his nailed boots along the castle's deserted corridors.

It meant nothing. A meaningless nonsense to unsettle and disturb.

Yet he could not chisel it from his mind. Even telling Morlaine hadn't loosened its grip.

You left women and children to slaughter; of course you have a darkness in you...

The words beat out in rhythm with his boots.

"That makes me a coward, not a monster..."

What if Cleever's offer of help was just another game? A trick by Saul to lure him back into the fold? To make him bend a knee and whisper the word he dreaded to hear upon his lips more than any other.

Master...

"You think yourself so important, eh? You're a conceited fool as well as a dishonourable one!"

He walked faster and checked over his shoulder again. Nothing to walk into, nothing to run away from. He was alone. Apart from the ghosts, of course.

The ones he'd carried from The Wolf's Tower to join those he'd created here. Fifty-six fresh graves hacked out of half-frozen mud.

He should leave. That's what any sane man would do. Certainly, a sane coward like him. There was no dispute about his cowardice, so staying at Solace's side must be due to insanity of one kind or another.

He paused as he reached the end of a corridor, looking again over his shoulder before turning into another. No demon stalked him. The only vampire in Ettestein didn't need to. He'd already confessed his sins to her.

Pursued by things best forgotten, his eyes remained turned inwards.

Until he realised someone was talking to him.

He blinked.

He was down in the kitchens. He didn't remember descending any stairs, but he must have.

A round pale face looked up at him, chestnut eyes, a few licks of red hair escaping a cap to rest on chalky skin. A full mouth, an upturned nose. Petite, slim-waisted. Heavy-chested. He found himself noticing with a start.

Hilde. The Maid. Who Lucien thought smiled at him a lot.

"I'm sorry?"

"Are you lost, sir?" Hilde, the maid, smiled.

"No, erm..." he looked around; nobody was about, "...why would you think that?"

"You always look lost, sir," Hilde smiled. Again. Then she lowered her head whilst keeping her eyes on him. An expression Lucien would no doubt consider flirtatious. But then Lucien considered everything a pretty maid did, from breathing upward flirtatious.

"I do?"

"Like a little boy in the woods. Which is not what one would expect of such a fearsome swordsman as your good self, sir."

"I am no fearsome swordsman, truly."

"But everyone says so. Pastor Wilhelm saw you best a

dozen of the Emperor's men. He is a man of the cloth, so he would never make anything up. Would he?"

"Well, no... but he is mistaken; I simply-"

"Saved the castle. Single-handed. Captured the *Freiherr* Geiss, rescued the *Markgräfin* Sophia and got the *Freiherr* to pay the Imperials to leave with his own money!" she clapped her hands and beamed at him.

"Well-"

"If it wasn't for you, Gottlieb would have taken the castle, and the Papists would have done lord alone knows what with us..." she leaned in and rested a hand atop his, "...we're all so grateful the Lord sent such a hero to save us."

Fifty-six graves, sitting in the half-frozen mud...

"I didn't really save anyone, Hilde, I-"

"You know my name, sir?" Hilde's eyes widened. She bobbed up on her toes as she squeezed his hand and beamed all the harder.

Her touch was quite warming, he noticed.

I wonder how warming her-

He stopped that thought from sending his eyes southwards of Hilde's face.

"Yes, erm, sorry... we haven't been introduced, of course, but... erm..." his face flushed as his tongue thickened. Why was he always such a fool around women?

Hilde giggled, then glanced over her shoulder.

The corridor was empty; a few distant clanks and bangs floated out of the kitchens. But, otherwise, they were alone.

She stepped closer to him. When he edged back, she took another one. Eyes, big and wide, staring at him quite fixedly. He swallowed, his tongue not the only thing in danger of thickening.

"Don't need no introductions, sir. Everyone knows who you are..." she pressed herself against him, "...you're a hero. The hero who saved us all!"

"Really," he laughed (far too shrilly for any hero), "I'm not!"

"Modest too... that's a virtue that is..."

He found himself back to the wall. He wasn't quite sure how. Her fingers ran down his bad arm. Despite the sleeves of the thick coat he wore (and the limb's dead flesh numbness), the touch sent sparks arcing across his skin.

"...hope you haven't got too many other virtues, though..."

She pressed herself hard against him. Up close, her breasts really were rather large.

He dragged his eyes away from hers to check the corridor. This wasn't at all seemly. If someone were to come along now, they might get quite the wrong impression.

"I'm not a hero!"

A hand, warm and soft, curled up and around the nape of his neck. Fingers tightened; nails pressed into his skin as she pulled his lips towards hers.

"But you're my hero..." she stretched to breathe in his ear, "...you're my pretty thing."

Then her lips were on his. His eyes widened. Unlike the fingers caressing his neck, her kiss was cold. Not just cold, but frozen, as if his lips were not against a lovely maid's but a stagnant pond skimmed with January ice.

He tried to pull away, but the fingers became bands of iron, her body a crushing weight squeezing the breath from his lungs as it ground him into the wall. Something slithered into his mouth, something wet, foul, and dead that couldn't possibly be Hilde's tongue.

It couldn't be because it felt and tasted more like a rotting fish; it couldn't be because Hilde was still talking. Talking and giggling.

"Pretty thing... my hero... pretty thing... my hero..."

"No!"

He sat bolt upright, sweat slickening his chest yet shivering almost as severely as he had after hauling himself out of The Wolf Tower's icy moat.

A dream. Just a dream.

Lucien's blubbery snores rolled out of the darkness to confirm he'd never left the bedroom.

Of course. Just a dream. How could he have thought it anything else? What fetching maid would ever think the dishonourable coward Ulrich Renard was a hero?

He slumped back into the sodden pillows.

"Oh, bollocks..."

Chapter Six

"Lady Solace, would you do me the great honour of becoming my wife?"

The urge to scream and run for the door was almost overwhelming.

They had been discussing this, one way or another, for weeks. Still, stiffly and formally put to her from the other end of the dining table, the question took her by surprise.

She had expected the *Markgräf* to interrogate her about Morlaine, about witchcraft, about her mother, about why moss tended to only grow on one side of a tree or her opinion on choral music. She had expected any question other than the one she had been expecting ever since she had suggested it.

Or, to be entirely accurate, she had passed on Flyblown's suggestion.

It had never been *her* idea. It would never have occurred to her. Such a mad idea. An insane, lunatic idea! Not her first recently. No, not hers, *Flyblown's!* But she had. For reasons she could no longer recall. And now, here she was. At one end of a table groaning with food in a starving empire, wearing the ill-fitting dress of the man at the other end's daughter. The *old* man at the other end of the table. A man well over forty. Maybe even fifty. Maybe older than Father! Who sat staring. Awaiting her answer. With no expression on his face whatsoever. Should a man not boast an expression at moments like this in their life? Perhaps she had misheard him?

Perhaps he had merely enquired about the fish sitting untroubled on her silver plate?

There had never been silver plates before. She realised. She should pay more attention. The meaning of so many things hid in plain sight amongst the insignificant details.

Such as when a man - a man, good God, nearing fifty! – intended to propose to you.

It probably explained why his children were not with them.

She wondered if Sophia had her ear pressed against the door again tonight.

For some reason, that made her want to giggle.

Although woefully uninformed about so much – particularly anything involving a man and a woman *together* – she felt confident giggling was not a suitable response to a marriage proposal.

Her hand found her wine glass. She managed not to knock it over. She took a sip and forced herself to put it back again before she could throw the lot down her neck in one giddy, gurgling gulp.

The *Markgräf* continued to stare at her, face flat, eyes unblinking. Was he so expressionless on the inside? Had he been so expressionless when he had courted her mother all those years ago? Had he-

"Solace?"

Why was she so afraid? She had pursued a demon through teeth-shattering, gut-wrenching pain and sent the

The Night's Road IV – When the Walls Fall

foul creature to its doom a few short weeks ago. Surely, this had to be less terrifying. Didn't it?

Yes, much less terrifying.

Perhaps unsettling was a better word?

"I am sorry, my lord, your question took me a little by surprise."

She was *almost* certain it hadn't been about the fish...

"We have been discussing the matter for some time..."

"Yes, indeed."

"Are you having second thoughts...?"

Only if you cannot furnish me with a hundred men-at-arms...

The voice, cold, calm, and clear, was one she had come to know well enough.

It was not Flyblown, it was not the *sight*, it was... something else.

She had yet to give it a name, but it was part of her, or part of what she had become, was becoming. The thing that turned and rallied against all that had befallen her and her family. A thing that demanded vengeance, and insisted she meet whatever price necessary, in whatever currency required.

In other words, it was the part of her she thought might be going insane.

Strange that she always found its lunatic whisper calming.

"No, my lord," no doubts or tremors troubled her voice, "I have not."

"Then...?"

"There are other matters we must agree first. As we have

discussed. For some time."

Out of sight, beneath the table, she tugged and worried at the borrowed gown's lace sleeve. Above it, she remained as expressionless as the *Markgräf*.

He nodded and reached for his own glass.

A negotiation. This has never been more than a negotiation. Treat it as such...

Yes, of course. That was all it was.

"Are *you* having second thoughts?" she asked when he continued to study her over the rim of his glass.

It took him a long time to answer. When he did, he lowered the glass but kept hold of it, thumb running up and down the stem.

"With every day that passes, you remind me more of your... of my... of Elenore. That stirs things within me, things I had considered... gone..."

"Do you love me?"

That got his attention. His thumb froze, his Adam's apple bobbed up and down. Something akin to an expression skidded across his face before darting away.

It quite got her attention, too. Her stomach rolled in the wake of the words. But her stomach, like the lace cuff to Sophia's dress, was below the table and so out of his eyeline.

"That is a bold question, my lady?"

"I would have thought it pertinent when a man asks for your hand."

"Princes of the Empire do not always marry for love."

"Indeed. But that does not answer the question."

"The fact I have asked for your hand wo-"

"Say it."

"I am sorry?"

"I want you to say it to me."

She did?

"You do?"

Her words, it seemed, were as much of a surprise to her as to the *Markgräf*.

A particularly vicious tug partially ripped the cuff she was torturing out of sight below the table. She took a long, slow breath and rearranged her hands so she could worry the cuff of the other, so far, less molested sleeve.

"If I am to give myself to you, I require several conditions met."

"The means to destroy your enemies?"

She nodded, "That is one. Another is that you love me. If I am to spend my life with you, 'tis the least I require. I will rid the world of the Red Company, but if the price is to give myself to a man who does not love me..."

It will be a price I am well prepared to pay.

Then why am I saying this?

She didn't know.

"I love you," he said without hesitation, "I always have."

"'tis an easy thing for a man to say."

"Indeed."

"Actions are far more eloquent than words, I believe."

Again, he nodded. Then, a rare smile, "And you wish me to confirm my love by..."

Ah, that was why I said it...

She mirrored his smile.

"By giving me all I desire."

"But the things you desire are not those shared by most young women, are they?"

"I am not most young women, my lord."

"Therefore, we reach the same impasse."

"My lord?"

"If I give you what you desire, to prove my love, to seal our... bargain... then you will ride away and likely not come back."

She arched an eyebrow, much as Morlaine sometimes did.

"You doubt my word?"

"No, I doubt the likelihood of you surviving these demons you seek."

She sipped her wine. She was no longer smiling, "Wendel, the demon who opened Ettestein's gates to your nephew and killed your personal guard, doubted me too. Doubted me until the moment I sliced off his fingers and watched him fall to his doom."

Falling, falling, falling...

The *Markgräf* shifted in his chair. Perhaps he found the idea of her slicing off a demon's fingers unsettling. Not a common womanly virtue, admittedly. Was it the sort of thing Mother had done?

She resisted reaching for the bag hung around her neck. Partly because it was becoming an unhealthy fascination but mainly because she had taken it off. The cut of tonight's dress was too low for her to tuck it away anywhere.

The realisation a man was asking his first love's daughter to marry him whilst she wore the dress of his own child struck her. Did the Bible have anything to say on such things? Nothing came to mind, though she imagined it was probably frowned upon.

The *Markgräf* rose to his feet and came down the table. For a moment or two, he stood, looking down at her. Perfectly still, save for the rise and fall of his chest. Then he crouched till at her eye level. He didn't wince, and nothing cracked alarmingly. Impressive for an old man of nearly fifty.

"Stay with me, Solace. God returned you to me for a reason. Surely that reason is for me to keep you safe and make you happy?"

"Perhaps God returned me to you to smite the demons plaguing this land. Perhaps *He* thinks that more important than my safety and happiness."

"You are not a warrior; this is not work for you."

That rankled, but she kept her face impassive. He had no idea what she was.

For a hundred men-at-arms, she would suffer far worse without complaint.

"Perhaps God sees things differently," she leant a fraction towards him, "I have it on good authority he is known for working in mysterious ways after all, my lord."

"I see Elenore in you. So much 'tis hard to believe you are not the same woman, returned to me, untouched by the passing years, untouched by death itself."

Candlelight danced in his eyes, lending him a fervour alien to his usual demeanour.

Or maybe he did have something burning fiercely inside him. Just because he was not expressive, it did not follow that he was passionless.

That was what she hoped...

"I want an army, my lord. You know this. That is my price. Nothing more, nothing less. I will destroy my enemies, and once I have cleansed them from the Earth, I will return and be your wife. For the rest of our lives."

Given how old you are, that should not be too long...

She strangled that thought before it stirred too many unworthy feelings within her.

She had plenty of those already.

"And if I refuse?"

She conjured a smile. Aiming for winning but with a hint of sadness, though what actually twisted across her face, she couldn't say.

"Then I will leave. I will pursue my enemies. You will never see me again."

The *Markgräf's* lips thinned, and eyes narrowed. Something troubled his usually impassive features. It looked a little like pain.

She had not hurt Wendel enough. She was hurting this man too much.

But no matter. The price of vengeance...

He reached out as if to find her hand, then perhaps thought better of it.

"I understand this is difficult for you. I am old enough to be your father, and I expect you see nothing more. But I do love you. As with your mother, from the moment I saw you... this road you follow... nothing good will come of it. But here, you can be safe, can be happy. You will have comfort, you will want for nothing, you will have love and companionship. And I will worship you until my dying

The Night's Road IV – When the Walls Fall

breath. Please, my lady…"

It would be easy, wouldn't it?

To take his hand, his ring, his title, and live a life of plenty and privilege again. The life she had been born to, the life she had expected.

But that life had been ripped from her.

She pushed her chair back and rose to her feet. The *Markgräf's* eyes followed her. The rest of him remained where it was.

"An army, my lord. Nothing more. Nothing less…"

With that, she left him crouching by her chair and walked out.

*

"What's its name?"

"I call it Dog."

"Dog?"

He shrugged.

Lucien eyed the raggedy, one-eared mutt before them, then crouched in front of it.

"Careful, he isn't very friendly," he warned.

After Lucien started scratching Dog behind the ears, it licked his fingers and then rolled over playfully for its wiry-haired, muddy belly to get more of the same, "So I see…"

"For fuck's sake."

"Animals love Lucien Kazmierczak almost as much as women. I'm surprised you hadn't heard, 'tis well known from Cordoba to Cairo!"

Yes, even dumb animals liked Lucien bloody Kazmierczak more than him. He wasn't sure why he found that annoying, but he did. He supposed it shouldn't surprise him. Pretty much everything about Lucien annoyed him to a greater or lesser degree. Hilde would undoubtedly roll gladly on her back for the oaf to tickle her belly, too.

As fortune would have it, Hilde wasn't around, so he only had to contend with a scruffy one-eared mongrel displaying its preference for belly scratchers.

"He's only after food."

"Everybody is after something; if we weren't, nobody would bother getting out of bed," Lucien pulled a long, thoughtful face, "and the world would be a better place for it."

Dog yapped at the mercenary to stop slacking with the belly scratching.

They were outside, arses plonked on a small pile of timber, sitting in the mud for no apparent reason. They came here each day for sword practice, and his breath still rattled in hard, steaming pants. Lucien, needless to say, was not the slightest bit out of puff.

Their practice had settled quickly into a familiar routine. He would do his damnedest to chop Lucien's irritating, ugly head off while the mercenary side-stepped his blows or turned them harmlessly aside with a casual wrist flick. Each action accompanied by a bellowing laugh or some variety of wit at his expense. Which just made him try to take the fool's head off all the harder.

This would continue until he collapsed onto the log pile in a sweaty, gasping heap.

Still, it took a little longer each day to collapse into the sweaty, gasping heap.

And he hadn't vomited for over a week.

He was getting stronger. Just a little, day by day. The food and sleep helped, too. His bad arm was no better and never would be, but he was starting to hope the rest of him might one day be able to get back to something like the man he'd once been.

Not that he intended to articulate that hope. The world had a way of shitting on your hopes, after all.

The clouds sagged low, cold and grey. Their mood leaning increasingly towards the ill-tempered. Rain was on its way, and they should head back inside before it arrived, but for now, at least he was grateful to escape Ettestein. It was just imagination, but the more time they spent here, the smaller it seemed to become. As if the castle walls were slowly closing in about him.

Sometimes, it felt like a tomb whose entrance was gradually being bricked up.

"I'm starting to hate this place."

"Why don't you try scratching his belly? He might like it."

"Not because of the bloody dog!"

Lucien sat back up, "I've been in worse places."

So had he. But that wasn't the point.

"I wish Lady Solace would make her mind up so we can leave."

"Women for you..."

Dog, who had snarled ferally a couple of the times he'd tried to stroke him, stretched up to plonk his hairy snout on Lucien's lap and whined, looking up at the mercenary with large liquid eyes.

"Dogs for you."

"I'll let you in on a secret," Lucien winked, "if you want

someone to love you, you have to give them what they want."

Lucien dipped a hand into the pocket of the long coat he wore.

Dog's one good ear pricked up, and he licked his wiry chops.

Lucien produced a twist of dried meat.

Dog whined.

Lucien held the morsel between thumb and forefinger above Dog's snout. At least until the hound plucked it free with his teeth and gobbled it down with lip-smacking relish.

"I suppose the same applies to women, does it?" he asked in response to Lucien's expression of insufferable smugness.

The mercenary ruffled Dog's dirty, matted coat.

"Well, keeping a big piece of meat in your pocket helps with them, too..."

Oh, for God's sake.

He jumped off the pile of lumber and struggled back into his coat.

"Where are you going?"

"For a walk."

Lucien was on his feet before he could add *alone*, "Excellent idea..."

He headed for the Gate Towers, lengthening his stride as Lucien caught up with him, Dog padding at his side like any long faithful hound.

The urge to get outside the walls of Ettestein arrived sudden and overpowering.

He hadn't been through the gates since they'd entered the

castle three weeks earlier. A lot had happened since then. He resisted glancing towards Wilhelm's wooden church and the recently expanded graveyard beyond.

A lot of people had died since then.

"Probably going to rain..." Lucien glanced at the darkening clouds.

"Do you keep a piece of meat in your pocket for Morlaine?" the words rushed out of his mouth without expectation or thought.

Lucien's eyes snapped from the sky to him.

"What do you mean?"

He looked at Dog and then the mercenary before shrugging.

Lucien snorted, "Morlaine is no man's hound..."

"But she lets you scratch her behind the ear, so to speak, doesn't she?"

"And this is your business, how?"

"Because she is a blood-sucking demon, and if the rest of this place discovers that, we'll all be for the pyre no matter how much Lady Solace looks like her mother."

"Best nobody finds out then..." no flashed grin accompanied Lucien's words, "...keeping your big mouth shut will likely help with that somewhat."

Mud squelched around his boots as he pulled up and turned towards the mercenary, "Do you love her?"

In their time together, which seemed much longer than it was, he'd never seen Lucien lost for words. However, the look on his face didn't give him the sense of satisfaction he might have expected from the feat.

He wasn't sure how to describe it, and when Lucien did

nothing but glare back at him, he turned and concentrated on squelching through the mud down towards the Gate Towers.

However, he was disappointed if he thought he'd done enough to shake off the mercenary's company.

"'tis complicated..." an uncharacteristically subdued voice said at his shoulder.

"You always make it sound so easy."

"I do? What?"

"Women."

"Morlaine is not just a woman; she is..."

"A blood-sucking demon?" he offered when Lucien faltered.

"'tis complicated..."

It struck him as a barrel best left unstirred. Listening to Lucien's usual oafish nonsense was bad enough; listening to him moon about *complicated* things could only be worse.

"Maybe you should stick to fucking maids and whores then..."

He didn't often have a problem leaving barrels unstirred...

When the mercenary didn't reply, he risked a sideways glance. Lucien trudged beside him, head down, staring at his muddy boots. Dog still padded at his side, tail wagging, a hopeful glint in its brown wet eyes as it looked up at Lucien.

"Would make life less... complicated," Lucien agreed.

"Why did you leave Madriel with us?"

"I told you. Lucien Kazmierczak has no taste for burning old women."

"You didn't just ride away from a town; you left your

company behind."

"The mercenary's life had dulled for me. Responsibility? Listening to all that whinging? Keeping fools in order? Pah! Was time for a change."

"So, you are in love with her then?"

Lucien went back to silently staring at his boots.

Did he like this Lucien better? He wasn't sure. But if he could find a way to stop his snoring too...

They made the final approach to the Gate Towers in rare silence.

Yes, this really might be an improvement.

"Gentlemen!" Usk greeted them. A big ugly lug of a young man who'd survived the attack on Ettestein without a scratch but drunk so much the next day celebrating, he'd fallen down the stairs and broken his already unfortunate nose. The remnants of two black eyes still haunted his misaligned face.

"Usk," he grunted. The soldier was one of those fellows so indefatigably cheerful he was clearly yet to realise the world was mostly just one enormous steaming bowl of shit.

"What you about?" Usk grinned. Had he lost another tooth?

"Need some air," he replied.

"Walking our new dog," Lucien pointed at Dog almost proudly, "he's called Dog."

"Dog?"

Lucien hitched a thumb in his direction, "Ulrich thought up the name. He currently has a lot of spare time on his hands..."

Usk laughed so hard he risked losing a few more teeth.

He forced a smile and made to walk by the young soldier leaning on his pike in the shadow of the open gates.

"Can't let you outside," Usk said, making no move to stop him.

"Trouble?" he peered through the gate towards the deserted remnants of the Imperial camp down the track.

"No more than usual. But 'tis the *Markgräf's* orders," Usk swivelled about his pike like a child around a maypole.

"No one is to leave the castle?"

Usk shook his head, "Nope, just you two, your lady and her maid, the one no one ever sees..."

Chapter Seven

She swept into the *Markgräf*'s study without knocking.

He looked up, quill poised over parchment.

"My dear-"

"Why have you given orders that we are not to leave Ettestein?"

The *Markgräf* returned his attention to the document in front of him, adding his signature before sliding it across the desk to his steward, "That will be all for now, Tamburro."

"Yes, my lord."

The Genoese bowed to the *Markgräf,* then floated off with his nose raised, acknowledging her no more than the cat curled by the fire.

Only after the door closed behind Tamburro did the *Markgräf* turn his eyes back to her.

"For your safety, 'tis not safe beyond Ettestein's walls."

It had not proved safe inside them either, given she'd almost been raped and killed recently. But there was no need to split hairs.

"Is that the only reason?"

"Yes."

"Then I am free to leave Ettestein whenever I choose?"

"Of course," the *Markgräf* said, opening his palms towards her, "once 'tis safe..."

"And when, exactly, will it be safe?"

He leaned back in his chair, making a long face of his usually expressionless features, "tis hard to say."

"Hendrick, let me warn you..." she rested her knuckles on his desk and bent forward, "...if you start playing silly games with me, they will not end well."

Neither her familiarity with his given name nor her unladylike pose provoked a reaction. The *Markgräf's* face returned to its usual placid mask.

"I am playing no games, Solace," he said, returning the familiarity, "I have reports of brigands making merry towards Eisennitz. There may also be Imperial forces lurking, looking to cause mischief, even more so if Gottlieb still carries the Emperor's authority. I ordered no one is to leave Ettestein unless 'tis in force..."

Renard and Lucien had received the impression the *Markgräf* had aimed his edict very much at them alone. And she trusted them a lot more than she did anyone else.

"My men can look after themselves."

"I have no doubt. But I wish to lose no more lives to the lunacy enveloping the world..." he nodded towards the greyly lit windows "...out there."

She glared at him. Which had no more apparent effect than if she'd glared at one of the portraits of his ancestors on the wall behind him.

"Please, let us not argue..." he opened his hand and indicated the chairs opposite.

Slowly, she straightened her back but did not sit.

"We are not arguing, my lord. Simply... clarifying."

"Well, everything is resolved then."

"Not everything."

"No?"

"Your proposal..."

"I am still awaiting your response."

"I rather thought I had given it, my lord. I will wait until I receive a final answer..." she turned to the door, "...but be advised, I will not wait forever."

"How is your maid, Solace?"

She stopped and looked over her shoulder, "Still suffering from a poor head."

"Perhaps there would be less suspicion about her if she showed herself more."

"That is no concern of mine, my lord. She is my servant. And she is not well."

"If these allegations persist, I may have to speak to her. To settle my mind."

"Your nephew's allegations are laughable, my lord."

"Perhaps. But justice must be seen to be served. Especially with witchcraft suspected."

"She is not a witch."

"You know that, and I know that, but the world..." his eyes moved to the windows again.

I wonder if he would want to talk to Morlaine if I simply agreed to marry him...

"An army, my lord, I require an army..."

His head swivelled back towards her. No expression, no reaction.

"Good day, my lord."

She hurried from the room.

Once outside, she started tugging at the cuff of her dress.

She was getting through Sophia's wardrobe at an impressive rate of knots.

Tamburro hovered in the dim antechamber to the *Markgräf*'s office.

Dark, beady eyes followed her. He offered a shallow nod. She ignored him.

Out in the corridor, she began working on her cuff properly with a vicious twist. She doubted it would survive the journey back to her rooms. Then she could tear the rest of the damn thing off.

"Love can make men do the strangest things; don't you think?"

The voice startled her enough to release her tortured sleeve.

"My Lord Flyblown..."

The pale apparition at her side moved his head in acknowledgement no more than Tamburro had, though without the commensurate disdain.

She continued along the corridor, Flyblown a shadow at her heels.

"I thought you might have forgotten me, my lord?"

"Forgotten? Good heavens, no! My Lady of the Broken Tower rarely strays from my thoughts. No, I have simply been busy."

"Busy, my lord?"

"Schemes, plots, machinations, shady assignations. You know. The usual humdrum business of everyday life..."

She glanced sideways but found his thin, pale lips bereft of a smile.

"The *Markgräf* of Gothen does not seem inclined to give me

an army."

"No small talk then? No greetings, enquiries about my health or best wishes to my family?"

"You have a family?"

"Not in the conventional sense."

She hesitated at the sound of approaching voices. Flyblown did not appear unduly concerned. A moment later, two gossiping maids hurried around the corner. They faltered at the sight of her and performed perfunctory curtseys before picking up speed again and flashing by in silence, eyes cast upon the floor.

Neither acknowledged the tall, pale figure at her side.

"No one else can see you, can they?"

Flyblown shook his head, "Fortunately for you."

"I have enough problems with my *maid*..." she stared at him, "Is it a problem?"

"Given the lamentable age we find ourselves in, if anyone saw her do anything a woman should not be doing..." he pulled a long face, "...then you have a problem."

"She beat several Imperial soldiers senseless and killed a couple more. In front of the *Markgräf's* daughter and the idiot nephew who tried to take Ettestein."

"You have a problem."

"Would the *Markgräf* use Morlaine as a lever to keep me here? Or just lock me-"

"Of course he would."

She was rolling her bottom lip again. She forced herself to stop.

"I thought him an honourable man."

"Honour only gets you so far in life. The aristocracy

understands that better than anyone. When it stands in the way of what you truly desire..."

"It seems your advice was somewhat flawed then."

"Flawed? I do not see how. You need an army to fight an army."

"But I am not going to get Gothen's army, or anybody else's, if the *Markgräf* intends to keep me locked up here as his... whatever!"

Flyblown wagged a long, bloodless finger at her, "Do not concede defeat so easily..."

"All I can do is leave, I-"

"You have what he wants."

"My mother's face?"

Flyblown smiled. Which she found as vaguely unsettling as always.

"Among other assets. Hendrick, *Markgräf* of Gothen wants you. Not as a damsel locked away somewhere. One he visits to sate his sordid fantasies upon when his blood gets the better of him, before collapsing into a ball of self-loathing for the thing his love has turned him into..." Flyblown tilted his head toward her, "...although that is a possibility."

"How appealing."

"Indeed. But let us not dwell on the disheartening possibilities, not whilst paths to the sunlit highlands still exist, at least."

"And how might one find these sunlit highlands when the man you are attempting to marry in order to obtain an army is flirting with the possibility of locking you up and doing..." she wrinkled her nose, "...the things you suggested?"

"Well-"

"Is he thinking about doing that?"

"I cannot read minds, My Lady of the Broken Tower."

"Then-"

"But I have some experience, stretching back over many, many centuries, concerning how men behave when... shall we say... their pecker is up..."

"Pecker...?" she asked, tugging at the cuffs of her dress again.

Flyblown's lips twitched, "Their manly desires."

"Oh."

"Which can, when handled correctly, be of great advantage."

"It can?"

"Most men are not greatly blessed with brains in the first place. When the pecker becomes involved, well, they are even less likely to fully utilise that smidgeon of intellect."

"I really don't think I understand."

Flyblown stopped and turned towards her, "You are a woman, Solace. I suggest it is time you started deploying that weapon."

"I thought I had?"

"No... you have not. Offering yourself for the marriage bed is... but a start. You must do more."

She was fairly sure the blood was draining rapidly from her face. She tugged at the cuff again. Harder.

"More?"

"More."

"What does more involve... *exactly?*"

Flyblown managed to find an even more unwholesome

smile.

"You need to show the *Markgräf* what you are really worth..."

*

"Why are you blushing?"

"I'm not blushing."

"You're not sitting close enough to the fire to be that red-faced. And you certainly haven't drunk enough beer yet. You're blushing."

"I'm bloody well not!"

He fixed his attention on Lucien rather than Hilde, who kept glancing over and smiling as she cleared the table behind the mercenary.

It was making him uncomfortable. And a little hot under the collar, if truth be told.

But he definitely *wasn't* blushing.

The more he tried to ignore the maid (and he'd been trying to ignore her even more studiously since his dream), the more she took an interest, the more she smiled, the more she popped up around him.

Women were a most peculiar breed.

Lucien grinned at him. An irksome and knowing grin it was, too.

He muttered something impolite, drained his tankard and shot to his feet.

Hilde, bent over the scoured wooden table and scrubbing furiously, grinned at him too.

Why was everybody grinning at him!

He hurried out of the dining hall before Hilde completely

succumbed to his indifference and threw herself at him.

Quite why he found the idea of a woman throwing herself at him so unpalatable was one he couldn't articulate. Save the habit women he took an interest in had of dying soon afterwards, of course.

He headed back to Solace's rooms. With the short day already over, little remained but to eat, drink, talk or sleep. He'd sated the first two, had no desire for the third and doubted the fourth would come easily yet.

I dare say Hilde might be able to think of another way of passing the long, dark, cold hours of a winter's night...

He swore at himself and walked faster.

He didn't want to go to their rooms, but it appeared the least worst option. And he should be at Solace's shoulder as much as possible. If they had to fight their way out of here...

Usk turning them away from the gates had made Ettestein even more oppressive. He was in no hurry to return to the Night's Road, but the dangers they faced seemed far more intangible here and, thus, harder to fight.

Besides it was unlikely anyone on the Night's Road would be looking to marry Lady Solace.

Another rankle he could neither name nor understand.

He found her in their rooms. Most evenings, she dined with the *Markgräf* and his family. Tonight, however, she was pacing back and forth alone. And ripping the lace cuffs of her dress to shreds, by the state of it.

She paused as he closed the door behind him. She said nothing and didn't acknowledge him. Instead, returning to her pacing and pulling the remnants of her cuffs from the dress.

She had several, all borrowed from Sophia and adjusted by the castle seamstress. Solace was older and larger than the Markgräf's daughter. In several ways. Part of him wondered if the *Markgräf* had instructed the seamstress not to enlarge the garments sufficiently with respect to certain dimensions.

So much so, Lucien had once leant in close and asked out of the side of his mouth, "Have her tits got bigger?"

If it hadn't been for the fact the oaf was taller, wider, stronger, had two good arms and was a much better swordsman, he would have given him a damn good thrashing for such impertinence.

As always, he did not stare.

He did not think of Solace in that manner anyway. She was not a woman. She was his mistress. He didn't sully their relationship by thinking of her in the kind of lewd, base way Lucien talked about women.

Admittedly, his mind occasionally wandered to when they shared a bed. In her father's hunting lodge after they'd escaped The Wolf's Tower and on arrival in Madriel. But necessity had driven that intimacy; he'd nearly been dead the first time and exhausted the second.

No, his mind might wander to those memories, but no other parts of his blighted, misbegotten body ever did, in fact-

"Renard?"

Solace had stopped pacing at some point. To stare at him. In her dress with shredded cuffs that was just a little too tight in *certain* places.

"My lady?"

"You look somewhat... distant?"

"I am sorry... 'tis nothing. How did matters go with the *Markgräf?*"

"Not well."

"We're leaving?"

"I..." her shoulders slumped.

They stood silently, each mirroring the other's awkwardness. Solace looked like she thought she should say something but didn't know what. He felt he should do something but didn't know what.

The urge to wrap her in a hug surged through him. An absurd and inappropriate thought. Clearly, he'd been spending too long around Lucien.

As much to ensure he didn't throw his arms about her, he crossed the room, poured some wine, and returned to hand her the glass.

"This won't help with anything, my lady."

She accepted the glass after only the briefest hesitation and a wry smile.

"My father always claimed a drink helped him think better."

"And did it?" she asked.

"No, it just turned him into a drunk."

She laughed. Then looked like she thought she shouldn't have and tried to stop.

He smiled, too. He liked the way she laughed, the way it made her nose wrinkle and eyes sparkle. Not that there had been many opportunities for merriment in their time together.

In the Company of Shadows

As with all the previous occasions, it never lasted long.

Sipping the wine, she retreated to the fire. He stayed where he was until she summoned him to join her.

"Ulrich, I do not know what to do..."

Putting the wine aside, her right hand immediately moved to the remains of her left cuff.

"What do you *wish* to do, my lady?"

"Destroy the Red Company," she told him without hesitation. A not unexpected response, but it dragged upon his heart all the same.

"And to do that-"

"I need an army."

"But the *Markgräf* doesn't want to give you his."

"He still hasn't said no... but... I fear he may be considering... other options."

"Other options, my lady?"

"Keeping me here regardless."

"I see."

And what would that mean for the rest of them? The aristocracy was usually very efficient in removing inconveniences...

"So, we need to leave."

"I... don't know."

"There's another option?"

"I... try... *harder*."

He blinked. Decided he had heard her correctly and shuffled in his seat.

"My lady?"

He should have poured himself some of the *Markgräf's* wine, too.

"My...erm... willing participation in... erm... a marriage must be more desirable than keeping me locked up as some kind of...erm...pet. Wouldn't you say?"

He suddenly found it difficult to look at her. Or speak.

Nodding he could just about still manage.

"So it was... I mean... I thought... if I could... somehow... show him the value of... what I have to offer."

She flashed a faltering smile. Then ripped her left sleeve completely off.

"Oh..." she peered at the tattered piece of lace dangling limply from her hand as if wondering how it got there.

He wasn't entirely sure what she was talking about, but whatever it was, he didn't like the sound of it.

"Ulrich," she looked up from the lace, "you're a man, aren't you?"

He settled for nodding again.

"What would make you want a woman so much you'd give her whatever she wanted to... to have her?"

He assumed he looked as blank-faced as he felt.

"I... don't really know, my lady."

"But... you're a man of... experience, are you not?"

He wasn't sure which one of them was blushing the most furiously.

His experience was limited mainly to the two plump whores in *The Bear Pit* back in Tassau, who'd ended up hanging from the rafters by their ankles for the Red Company's demons. They'd been a few chaste fumbles with Erna before she decided dour, dull Kaspner was the better bet, but Alms had ripped her throat out in The Wolf's Tower's library. And Madleen, of course, whose hand he'd held and grown stupidly fond of in an equally stupidly short time. But she'd gone to sell herself so she could feed her child and had been turned into a demon by the Man from Carinthia. Morlaine had then chopped her head off.

"I've had some experiences..." he said, not meeting her eye.

"Well then? What would you say?"

At that moment, he was quite prepared to say almost anything to get out of the room.

He swallowed.

Despite Old Man Ulrich's pursuits of women, which had led to as much disgrace as his drunkenness, his father had never been overly taken with the fairer sex outside the bed chamber, blaming them for most of the world's ills. When he'd still been young enough to believe what came out of his father's mouth amounted to wisdom rather than horse dung, he'd done his best to avoid girls in spite of the curious stirrings that came upon him with increasing urgency as he turned from boy to man.

It wasn't until after he'd arrived in Tassau following his father's death, however, that he'd ever let them get the better of him.

And now everyone he'd let his urges get the better of him with was dead.

Apart from Solace.

Not that he thought of her like that!

"I'm not sure I understand, my lady?" he finally managed. He thought he understood but sometimes claiming ignorance was the safest tactic.

The skin between her eyes furrowed. She probably

thought he understood, too. But that wasn't enough to let him slip the hook.

"I need to make myself more alluring. So much so the *Markgräf* will give me everything I want. As a man, what would that be for you?"

Someone with a nice smile who won't die as soon as I start liking her...

He – just about – choked that answer off. It would sound glib, though, in truth, it was anything but.

"I cannot imagine, my lady."

Solace straightened her back and deepened her frown. She reached for her left cuff, but on finding she'd already destroyed it, started pulling on the right one instead.

"You are not being helpful."

"Perhaps you should ask Lucien? Or Morlaine? I'm sure they have greater experience of such things."

"But I am asking you?"

"I do not know, my lady. To my eyes, you're already quite perfect, I cannot imagine why any man would not want you as you are, whatever the price!"

She stopped tugging at her cuff.

Bugger.

She considered him for a good long time while his heart thudded with terrified abandon. Probably loudly enough to wake Morlaine. If not the wholly dead.

"Perhaps I will ask Lucien and Morlaine," she said before rising and going to her room.

Once the door clicked shut, he reached over, grabbed her unfinished wine, and downed it in one.

Chapter Eight

"Wear the lowest cut dress you can find and sit on his lap."

"Seriously?"

"Works on me every time," Lucien raised his cup, "Lucien Kazmierczak is famed from Turin to Toledo for all the times he's made a complete arse of himself after a pretty lass in a daring dress plonked herself in his lap."

"Did you ever give a woman your army?"

"Once stole an entire set of silver tableware for a woman."

"Had she sat in your lap?"

"Oh yes," Lucien's grin stretched almost from one ear to the other.

"But that's not an army?"

"No..." Lucien's face crumpled in concentration, "...once sailed to Tangiers to buy an elephant for a woman. Couldn't find an elephant. So, I bought her a monkey instead."

"How did she take that?"

Lucien winced as he shook his head, "Not so well. The monkey died on the journey back... surprisingly few women are impressed by a dead monkey."

"Still not an army."

"I ambushed the Gandolpho brothers for a woman, stripped them naked and tied them to a tree in Livorno's main square, each with a pithy witticism daubed across their chests in liquid manure."

"Who were the Gandolpho brothers?"

Lucien pulled a face, "Not the kind of men you should strip naked and tie to a tree in Livorno's main square, with a pithy witticism daubed across their chests in any medium. The Lucien Kazmierczak of those bygone days was a headstrong young man yet to develop the almost divine wisdom for which the oracle now sitting before you is so justly famed..."

When she just stared at him, he shrugged, "...although that particular young lady did wear *very* daring dresses..."

"So, I believe your advice, if I've translated it correctly, is if a woman acts *provocatively* enough, a man will do any damn stupid thing she wants him to do in the expectation she will reward him by... delivering on those *provocations*?"

"Exactly!" Lucien beamed, "Though, despite Lucien Kazmierczak's renowned wisdom, good sense and thoughtful nature, he does suffer from occasional moments of recklessness."

"Really?"

"Indeed. Such as the time I hoisted the Mayor of Mainz's wife's Sunday best dress atop the spire of *St Martinsdom*," Lucien reached for his drink, "although that was for a bet rather than at the behest of an immodestly dressed woman."

She pushed herself to her feet, accompanied by a thin smile, "Thank you, Lucien, that's been... illuminating."

"You're most welcome!"

Before she could turn to go, he said, "Men are simple, weak-willed creatures who live in the thrall of their desires.

A lion is a simple, weak-willed creature too. You might think giving the lion what it desires will make it your friend and bend it to your will... and maybe you'd be right..." Lucien opened his palms towards her, "...until it decides it wants to bite your head off..."

Later, she visited Morlaine, still ensconced within her tiny room, window barred against the day.

She decided a direct approach the best one with the demon.

"Have you ever seduced a man?"

"Yes."

"For your own purposes?"

"Why would I seduce a man for someone else's?"

She frowned and sat in the room's only chair. Morlaine remained hunkered in the corner.

"I mean to gain something from the man."

"You've seen me do that, Solace."

"I have?"

"With Lucien."

"Oh..."

"He has blood; I have my sex. It is a trade. Seduction works like that. Unless all you want is intercourse."

"That isn't the kind of seduction I'm interested in."

"You want your army."

"Yes."

"I've never seduced a man for an army..." the demon pursed her lips, "...as far as I can recall."

"As far as you can recall?"

"I have more memories than other people..." Morlaine tapped her temple, "...I also have a lot of other people's memories too... some get lost over the centuries..."

She was tempted to ask whether Lucien ever really had hoisted the Mayor of Mainz's wife's Sunday best dress atop the spire of the town's cathedral but decided that amounted to prying.

"So, what should I do?"

"Run as far away from the *Markgräf* as possible. Naples would work."

"I am not going to Naples."

"Pity."

"I'm going to destroy the Red Company... *we're* going to destroy the Red Company."

"And if doing that destroys you too?"

She raised her chin, "I know what I am doing is dangerous. I am prepared to die doing it."

Morlaine's dark eyes held her in their regard. She was aware of their beauty and weight even from the other side of the room.

"There are far worse ways of destroying yourself than dying, Solace."

"Do you intend to lecture me about them?"

The answer she got was not the one she expected.

"You remind me of who I once was."

"Before you became...?"

"Before and after. Before, I was a privileged child with little understanding of the world beyond my childish wants and desires. After, when hatred consumed me, and I allowed vengeance to break me, to turn me into a monster."

"I have seen the work of monsters. I am not one. Nor will I ever be," she insisted.

"Yet you wish to seduce a man; use his love for your mother, his broken heart in your pursuit of vengeance. To sell yourself."

"All women sell themselves, do they not? I simply desire a different metal from other women; steel instead of silver."

"No, Solace..." Morlaine finally dropped her eyes, "...only the broken ones sell themselves."

She stood up, "It seems I am wasting my time if you are not prepared to help-"

"I am helping you!" The demon rarely raised her voice. It was enough to keep her from charging out of the room.

"If you wish to help me, answer my question," she ran her hands down Sophia's old dress, "I am but a girl... I know nothing of men... of seduction..."

"The best help I can give you would be to stop you walking down the path you seem so intent on following. No good will come of it. You are trying to play with a man's love and desire for your own ends. That fire is difficult to control; it has burned many before you, Solace."

"I have not deceived him. Not told him untruths. I will be his wife and perform all the duties of a wife. If he gives me the means to fight the Red Company."

"And yet, he has not agreed to your bargain, has he?"

"No."

"Instead, he has barred the gates to this castle to you. He is asking questions about me. He has talked of witchcraft. Hasn't he?"

"Yes. So, I must make him want me more."

"You think him not wanting you enough is the problem?" Morlaine made a perfect dark arch of her eyebrow.

"If you want something enough, you will be prepared to give anything for it. If he wants me enough, he will give me an army."

The demon leaned forward as her voice dropped to a hiss.

"No, Solace, you're wrong. If a man wants something enough, he will *do* anything to have it... and that isn't the same thing at all..."

*

"Why, 'tis the most feared swordsman in Europe!"

The men with *Markgräf* Joachim mostly laughed.

He found a smile to accompany his bow, "My lord," he said before making to go around the group of soldiers.

"I understand you've been practising," Joachim said, moving to stand in his way.

"Yes, my lord," he let his eye sweep the half a dozen men with the young *Markgräf*. They seemed good-natured and light-hearted, which he took as a sign to remain calm. Joachim, however, looked like he'd quite like to rip his head off and piss in it.

As Joachim always looked like that, he tried not to read too much into the belligerent eyes and jutting chin.

"Perhaps you could show me a thing or two?"

"I doubt I could teach you anything, my lord."

Though a good beating might do you a world of good, you arrogant jumped-up arse.

He smiled, mirroring the good-natured grins of Joachim's companions.

"But you're the finest swordsman in Europe!" Joachim leaned in towards him, "'tis the talk of the castle."

"'tis the middle of winter, my lord. A time for tall tales and exaggeration. It helps pass the long cold nights."

Pastor Wilhelm, the only person who'd heard Morlaine's quip after she'd downed the imperial soldiers outside Wilhelm's church, was a man with a loose tongue. Fortunately, the Pastor hadn't seen whose sword work actually had dealt with the imperials.

"Tomorrow, at noon. I'll come to join you and your friend. We'll see who can teach who something, eh?"

He clenched his teeth behind his grin, "You honour me, my lord."

Joachim's smile faded. The young lord stood there, back to his men, the look in his eyes, half closed against the low winter sun, so close to murderous he expected a fist in his face.

Instead, Joachim clamped a hand on his bad shoulder and squeezed it.

"Good man!"

He managed to neither whelp nor twist away. Somehow.

After Joachim and his men sauntered off, he rubbed his shoulder. The young nobleman's fingers hadn't quite felt like daggers when they'd squeezed his ruined shoulder, but it was close enough.

"Fuck..." he lurched towards the nearest wall to put his back against until the nausea rising from his guts eased.

He staggered down the shallow ditch at the foot of the castle to lean against Ettestein's pitted stonework and sucked in frigid air tainted by woodsmoke.

He'd been looping around the castle when he'd run into Joachim. As well as sword practice with Lucien, he liked to walk as much as he could. It made him stronger and freed him from Ettestein's increasingly oppressive interior. As he wasn't allowed beyond the outer walls (for his own safety, of course), he found himself stalking circles around the castle.

Circles that invariably brought him back to the graveyard behind Wilhelm's church (and the fifty-six fresh graves).

He kept his eyes closed, waiting for the pain and nausea to fade. Winter sun lit this side of the castle, the orange light that made it through his eyelids felt cleansing, and he concentrated on that. Floating with it until his shoulder and arm felt as good as they ever got. Which meant numb and dead rather than hot and agonising.

When he opened his eyes, he found a young woman perched on a tree stump at the top of the ditch, a thick woollen shawl pulled tight about her shoulders.

"What you doing?" Hilde asked.

He shot out the first word that popped into his head, "Resting."

"Funny place to rest."

"Why are you sitting out here in the cold?"

She answered by opening her shawl and showing him the russet apple in her hand. She grinned and took a bite.

"To eat an apple?"

"Isn't my apple," she said, looking to see if anyone was about. Nobody was.

"You stole it?"

"Perk of the job. Everybody here steals something."

"But you'd be in trouble if you were caught."

She shrugged and took another bite, "Haven't been caught yet. Not going to tell, are you?"

"No."

He walked up the bank.

"Why come here?"

"Not many do. And this side gets the sun in the afternoon," another chunk of apple disappeared, "I like the sun."

He squinted into the sunlight, "No warmth in it today."

"Still better than the dark. Always gloomy in there. Don't like it..." she stared up at him, still chewing, then thrust the apple towards him, "...wanna bite?"

"No, thank you."

Something was burning out of sight, the only sign anyone else was about. Even on bright days, most people still stayed inside to keep warm. The January sun didn't blunt the edge of winter's blade much.

Hilde gave him an as-you-like shrug and ripped another chunk out of the apple.

She kept looking up at him, though.

Her eyes were lovely.

He looked away.

"I should be-"

"Don't say much, do you?"

"Should I?"

She swallowed before replying, "Most men like you got plenty to say. Especially to us maids. But you look like you wouldn't bother a goose."

"Men like me?"

"Fighting men."

The few times he'd spoken to Hilde, she'd always deferentially referred to him as *sir*. Out here, however, she was being very informal.

This made him think he should be getting away from her all the more.

Still, despite the itch in his feet, his legs stayed planted in the scrubby grass crowning the ditch.

She might not be calling him *sir*, but as she sat, head turned up towards him, she deployed the same sunny grin she often did when he caught her looking at him. Apart from her mouth being full of apple, of course.

"I'm not much of a fighting man, truth be told..."

"Best swordsman in Europe, I heard."

Pastor Wilhelm and his big mouth. Again.

Thanks to Morlaine's quip and the Pastor's tongue, the men of Ettestein wanted to fight him, while the women wanted to...

Hilde was still looking up at him. The apple rapidly reduced to a core as she took careful little bites of the remaining flesh.

"I really should be going."

"Wait!" she took a couple of final nips before tossing the skinny core into a scrubby, winter-shorn bush, "you can walk me back."

"I-"

"A girl should not be on her own out here," she held out a hand for him to help her up, "the *Markgräf* says so."

"He means outside the outer walls," he said, staring at the fingers reaching up towards him.

"Nowhere is truly safe for a woman."

Hilde wiggled her fingers.

Reluctantly, he took her hand with her good one and

pulled her up. Her touch was soft, warm, and slightly sticky with apple juice.

Annoyingly, he didn't want to let go once she was on her feet.

"Thank you kindly," Hilde beamed.

They should start walking at some point, but she really had lovely eyes.

Ulrich...

He managed a smile and ushered her in the direction of the castle's entrance.

"May I ask you something?"

"Of course," he said. He expected she wanted some explanation as to why he always ran like a scalded cat every time she smiled at him or perhaps was curious about his withered arm.

Instead, she asked him something else.

"Is your mistress a witch?"

Their walk ground to a halt.

"No."

"Is her maid a witch?"

"No."

"Has she cast a spell over the *Markgräf?*"

"No! Where is this coming from?"

"Just what people are saying. I don't believe it, just tongues wagging when hands grow idle, I say, but... well..."

"The same wagging tongues that prattle I'm the finest swordsman in Europe?"

"Mostly," Hilde admitted.

"My lady is not a witch, neither is her maid. We are merely refugees fleeing the war. Nothing else."

Hilde pursed her lips and nodded, "That is what I hoped."

"Hoped?"

"'tis not wise to consort with witches..."

They walked a little further in silence. He was trying not to frown.

"I saw you with *Markgräf* Joachim...?" she asked before he could work out if her last statement meant what he thought it did.

"It was not a witch's council."

She did not laugh.

"You should be careful around *Markgräf* Joachim; he is an angry man."

"More gossip?"

"More than gossip. Servants see a lot. He has a temper and a grudge against the world. Sometimes he can be... unkind."

"A grudge?"

"Being the second son."

He snorted, "Strange the nobility can be so much more discontent with their lot than those with nothing."

"I don't think he likes you. Or your lady. Be careful around him, please."

They neared the corner of the castle, marked by a jutting, bulky tower flecked with lichen; once they rounded it, they would be in sight of Ettestein's gatehouse.

"I will, thank you. Are you sure you want to walk the rest of the way with me."

"Why not?"

"An unaccompanied young woman with a strange man, tongues might... wag..."

She threw her arms towards the castle, "Half of Ettestein thinks I'm a slut already."

That stopped him in his tracks again.

Hilde tossed her head back and laughed so hard a few ringlets of red hair escaped her cap. Which reminded him of the dream where he'd kissed her, and she'd turned into Alms, one of the Red Company's demons.

"Your face..." she said as her laughter subsided.

"Well... erm... I..."

"Thank you for caring about my honour and reputation; few men do..." she took a backward step away from him, eyes holding his, "...I suppose it would be better to keep the other half of the castle from thinking the same."

She smiled, returned to him, stretched up and kissed him on the cheek before gathering up her skirts and heading off around the tower, heady laughter lingering after her like intoxicating perfume.

Once she'd disappeared, he threw back his head and stared at the winter sky.

"Fuck, bollocks, shit. Fuckety fucking arse shit wank bastard! Fuck! Fuck! FUCK!!!"

Chapter Nine

The city burned.

Cackling flames competed with the screams eddying around her. Orange light danced in manic pirouettes across the throughfare's sticky cobbles. Blood gathered in gaps between the stones, in every depression, in every crack. Puddles and pools now, later it would flow in streams and rivers.

Twenty thousand people. That was a lot of blood.

And that was why they were here, why they'd come, to feast upon what her brother had promised, to witness the World's Pain in all its dreadful agonies.

When the walls fall...

A group came towards her. Of course, they didn't see her because she wasn't here.

Soldiers, half a dozen, faces flushed and sooty. They carried flagons of ale and a young woman. Two men had an ankle each as they dragged her over the cobbles. The woman, dress torn half open, was screaming, they were laughing.

She stood in the devilish light of a dying city, hating the helplessness binding her as the soldiers carried the thrashing woman away. This might be the future, but death and terror always resuscitated her past. She could not save her father, she could not save the people she'd loved, she could not save the women and children of Tassau, she could not save this young woman, even if her life was still months away from ending in rape and murder.

Eventually, she uncurled her fists and walked on.

Further along the street, where the ravenous fire had yet to reach, furniture flew out of a fine townhouse's window to shatter on the stones below. More scruffy, soiled soldiers hauled each piece away, pulling them apart and smashing them to sticks with hatchets and hammers.

Some of the furniture was valuable but far too big for soldiers to cart away as plunder. The men were searching for smaller loot hidden behind drawers and in upholstery. A shower of dresses floated down from another window. A young, toothless soldier scooped one up and pressed the gown to his chest. His comrades hooted and told him how pretty he was. Another man, tall, sunken-cheeked, hollow-eyed, grabbed the young man's hands, and they danced a jig together as the detritus of someone's life rained upon the street around them.

Out of the next window, a man's naked corpse hung from a noose of bedsheets. He hadn't died easily from the state of his body. The owner of the house? Who hadn't revealed where he'd stashed his valuables? Perhaps.

She walked on.

Smoke drifted in patches the length of the street, languid ghosts playfully revealing each new horror before shrouding it again.

Corpses littered the street, feeding the rivulets of blood accumulating between the cobbles. Few were soldiers, some were completely naked, and most stripped to some degree.

Good clothes were valuable. Tonight, A man's life was worth less than a sturdy pair of boots or a well-made jacket.

As for a woman's life...

Another scream rang out, from inside one of the houses this time. A woman. The sound cut a night already dripping with terrors. The doors of every building hung open, some off their hinges, some shattered, each broken by the tide of soldiers that had washed down the street.

She could, if she wanted, go in to find the scream's source. But what was the point? There was nothing she could do. None of this had happened yet. That woman was still alive, unaware how her life would end on the 20th of May 1631.

She walked on.

A figure lurched out of the smoky gloom, bare-chested, hands outstretched. A scrawny old man with wild, white hair. Mouth a gaping black circle and bloody pits where his eyes once were. He was wailing, something incoherent, though it might have been a name.

She stepped aside and let him stumble on. She needn't have; he would have walked straight through her. She only here to bear witness to the things yet to come.

She walked on.

Behind her, the wet thwack of metal on flesh and an anguished cry. Then braying laughter. She didn't look. The blinded man's suffering had ended. But the city's would continue throughout the night.

A boy sat against a wall. The hands he had clamped across his stomach, unable to keep his intestines from spilling into his lap. Glassy eyes stared from a waxy face.

He was fourteen. Maybe. His blood, pooling around him, ran to join the rest.

She walked on.

A soldier argued with a group of comrades. A woman cradling a baby cowered behind him. Was he trying to protect her, or did he want her for himself? Perhaps some humanity survived whatever had turned these men into beasts. But she didn't wait to find out.

She wasn't here for this.

She didn't know why she was here, but it was not to simply bear witness to horrors yet to come.

Surely?

Though, she'd always suspected her *sight* was a whimsical, maliciously playful fellow whose motives it was better not to even try to guess.

An alley splintered off the main thoroughfare. One of many. This one no different from the rest, save her feet had chosen to stop in front of it.

No fires burnt here. Yet. It would in time. Too many buildings burned already, and no one was trying to prevent it spreading. The attacking soldiers were too busy looting, raping and killing, the city's inhabitants too busy trying to stay alive.

She walked into the shadows.

Someone cried nearby. A young woman or child. They should keep quiet. The sound would attract soldiers.

The alley was dank and narrow but short. It opened into a secluded courtyard dominated by a church.

A place of sanctuary.

Would soldiers ransack a church and slaughter those

inside? Not normally, even one belonging to the heretics you were fighting. When it came to God, most erred on the side of caution. Just in case God took a dimmer view of murder and rape in one of His churches than he did when it occurred in the rest of the world.

Many would seek refuge in a church; the invader warned of the consequences of defiling a house of God from behind a locked door. The door to this church, however, hung open.

As she approached, screams and laughter rolled out of it.

Not everyone erred on the side of caution when it came to God, it seemed.

Blood smeared the steps of the church.

She hesitated. Screams and shouts echoed but distantly. Inside, it had fallen silent. An orange glow haloed the buildings around the courtyard as the fires spread. Smoke haunted the air and hazed the moon. But nothing moved.

I want to wake up now...

She didn't.

Instead, she gathered herself and crossed the threshold.

Nothing could hurt her. Not this time.

Figures stood in front of the altar. A few candles burned, and a diffuse, unsteady orange glow pressed against the stained-glass windows, but the shadow remained thick.

She walked on. Along the aisle of the church, like a bride approaching her groom. Save the only congregation sitting amongst the mostly overturned and shattered pews were corpses.

The corpses of old women and men...

Those who had come to seek the protection of God as their

city fell. But God held no fear for those that had broken down this church's door.

She walked on.

Down an aisle of the dead.

Another body sprawled over the altar, a woman, naked, face down. Bloody handprints stark upon the milky skin of her exposed behind. Young. Very young. Blood dripped from her neck and from between her legs.

A couple swung before the altar, blocking some of the view. At first, she thought they were kissing, but, of course, they weren't.

Other figures moved beyond the altar, but the shadows hung too thickly to see them clearly. That was a blessing. Sounds echoed around the high vaulted ceiling.

Crying. Weeping. Sobbing. Sniffing. Pleading.

A choir of the damned.

The young women and children who'd sought sanctuary here, herded into the back of the church.

Awaiting their turn.

Like the women and children of Tassau and The Wolf's Tower.

The ones that haunted Renard because they had ran and left them to Satan's Banquet.

But these women and children weren't dead. Not yet. They still lived; they *could* be saved...

The orange light pressing against the windows grew. The fires destroying the city were either racing towards them, or perhaps the whole church was descending through the earth to an even greater inferno. The very fires of Hell itself.

Both seemed equally likely.

She walked on.

There was nothing to fear. No one could hurt her. Not this time.

A tall man with a slim waist and broad shoulders stood before the altar. He wore a wide-brimmed hat with a peacock feather in the brim. A dandy hat, indeed.

He bore a young woman in his arms, her torn dress exposing one large, pale breast.

He was not kissing her, although his face pressed hard to her neck. Blood trickled in twisted rivulets over the exposed flesh of her breast.

Behind them, other figures danced, other figures writhed, the Choir of the Damned sang louder and blood flowed down the steps in a slow, dark waterfall.

She walked no more.

"I will destroy you..." she said, coming to a stop as the blood swirled around her feet.

The light grew, more red than orange now, pushing shadows back, turning everything to the colour of the blood at her feet.

She kept her eyes from the horrors of the Devil's Banquet. Concentrating only on the figure before the altar. The font of all this evil.

"I will destroy you..."

Slowly, the man raised his head, bloody lips poised over despoiled flesh. The girl's head slumped to one side. Cap falling free, her hair, turned to flame by the light, tumbled to her shoulders. In less than a heartbeat, the monster's thin, pale face became one she recognised from all her memories and nightmares.

"I will destroy you!"

Saul the Bloodless frowned as if hearing something peculiar on the wind.

He shifted towards her, peering, but eyes, bright as blue lanterns, did not focus on her. The girl would have fallen to the bloody floor but for Saul's arm around her waste. Instead, she swooned backwards like an overcome lady of delicate manners. Blood continued to pump from her neck. Her lips moved, but nothing came bar dark bubbles.

"Is somebody there?" Saul asked good-naturedly. A grin that would have been warm and dashing if his face were not dripping with blood and gore spread wide enough to reveal bright, white teeth.

He twisted fully around to face her, the young woman still hanging over the arm slung about her narrow waist.

Every part of her wanted to run. Every part of her wanted to run steel through this monster's heart.

Instead, she walked up the slick, wet steps and stood before him.

Saul was a head taller than her, and those blue eyes swung back and forth over her, searching the dead congregation.

"A problem?"

Another demon approached. The giant, Jarl. Bare-chested, blood and tattoos writhed across his flesh.

"Thought I heard something... someone..." Saul said, still looking over her head.

She stretched on tiptoes to see into those bright, intensely blue eyes. Even in the dancing blood-light, they held a rare beauty. A charmer's eyes. If you didn't know better.

How had Renard described them? A liar's eyes? Yes. Oh, yes, that's what they were alright.

"I am going to destroy you!" she spat in his face.

His head twitched, frown deepening.

Jarl came to the side of Saul a half-dead young woman wasn't hanging from to stare back along the aisle.

"No one living out there," he said.

"No," Saul agreed, still staring.

"Still a few back there, though..." Jarl hitched a thumb over his shoulder.

"Excellent..." Saul glanced down at the girl hanging over his arm, "...this one's just about done."

He dropped her to the floor. She rolled down the steps, coming to rest in the bloody stream, lips still moving, trying to say something.

"And when they're done?"

Saul patted Jarl's back, "There'll still be a few hours left to enjoy the World's Pain..."

"Shame the fuckers didn't take the city in December. Hate these bloody short nights."

"Don't fret, my friend," Saul chuckled and swept a hand towards the back of the church, "one day, the whole world will be like this..."

She tried not to follow his hand toward the twisting, coupling, writhing forms, tried not to hear the screams, the weeping, the Choir of the Damned.

To the things that had not happened yet, to the things that had happened before, to the things that would happen again.

Towards the World's Pain.

The world Saul the Bloodless wanted to create.

A world that would not have to hide its horrors beneath the cover of a falling city or perpetrate them only in far-flung little backwaters like Tassau. A world where demons rose, and men fell.

And the innocent became nought but a feast at the Devil's Banquet.

Saul and Jarl sauntered off around the altar.

She sucked in a breath she didn't need and made to follow. She had to know, to understand, to comprehend. How else could you defeat evil? How can you hold back the darkness unless you're prepared to step into it?

The girl at the foot of the steps groaned as blood pooled around her, matting the hair spread across the floor.

"If I can stop this happening to you, I will..." she said. An empty promise, most likely. Even if she could stop the Red Company, the girl would just die at the hands of the men sacking the city rather than the monsters who came to delight in the slaughter. But at least against men, she might have a chance.

The girl was still trying to say something; it seemed familiar but couldn't be. She didn't know this young woman. And never would.

A movement caught her eye before she could push her legs after Saul and Jarl.

Above her and to the left, a shadowy figure stood in the pulpit, hands resting on the edge. No light fell there, but she knew who it was.

"Torben..." her voice wavered.

The figure shifted, head tilting in her direction.

Sister...

The word slapped her as hard as Father's hand had her cheek the last time she ever saw him.

"You can see me?"

Of course.

Her brother's voice, as deep, guttural, and ill-fitting as when she'd first heard it, when she'd dreamt of him in the Grey Plains, echoed inside her head.

A scream, more awful even than any of the others so far, dragged her eyes towards the debauched slaughter desecrating the rear of the church.

They recoiled.

Could you vomit in a dream?

She didn't know, but she had to fight her gorge down all the same.

"Why don't you stop this?" she demanded once her stomach was under control.

None of this has happened yet.

"But it will. I don't understand how you can be part of this?"

'tis but one possibility, sister. No more than that.

"So... we can stop this from happening?"

Another scream. This one a child's. And laughter, cackling gales of side-splitting merriment. She didn't look. She forced herself not to look.

There is no we. You are not me; I am not you.

She stepped towards the pulpit. Her brother had been mute before he gave himself to Saul the Bloodless. She'd never imagined his voice would have sounded like this. A deep resonating thrum, like something plucking thick, taut, bleeding bass strings.

Something not quite sane.

"You sent Cleever to us. He told us you wanted to stop Saul. You knew I would kill Wendel. You didn't warn him you-"

Possibilities, sister, all just possibilities...

"What does that mean?!" she was at the foot of the pulpit, craning her neck to make out the tall figure looming above her. The glow in the windows grew brighter. Maniacal, gibbering light, pressing against the glass like fiery claws, eager to rend, burn and destroy. To join the slaughter.

It means nothing is ever real. It means nothing ever lasts. It means... Torben leaned forward, letting the light kiss his face *...all vampires are mad!*

She backed away.

His face was more familiar than her own. She had spent her whole life loving him, caring for him, fighting for him, seeing what nobody else could in his soft, gentle eyes and flickering smile.

But now it dripped with blood, the eyes were not gentle, and the smile didn't flicker at all.

"Torben! Torben!" she sobbed *"Torben!!!"*

*

Hilde slapped her plate on the table and jumped onto the bench next to him.

Lucien's spoon paused mid-air and his eyes rose from the watery stew he hunched over. The eyes moved from Hilde to him, back to Hilde again, before finally returning to settle on him.

Although gristly chunks of fatty meat filled his mouth, it didn't stop a knowing grin spreading over Lucien's face,

"How's the stew tonight?" Hilde asked.

"Shit," Lucien told her, gulping down another mouthful.

"Well, look on the bright side," she said, "'tis going to get a lot worse."

"I've heard the rumours..." Lucien nodded.

"We'll get by..." Hilde cracked open a coarse bread roll, showering the table with shrapnel. She tried softening it in the stew.

He wasn't sure whether he should be asking what the rumours were or why Hilde and Lucien acted like it was totally unremarkable for the maid to join them at their table in the dining hall.

"You don't mind me joining you, do you?" Hilde asked as if hearing his thoughts. Or possibly seeing the look on his face.

"Not at all!" Lucien beamed before he could think of a polite objection, "nice to have something pretty around rather than his sour grumpy visage."

"Does he always look like that?"

"Oh, he's usually much worse. Been a veritable beam of sunshine today..."

Hilde giggled.

He scowled at the pair and returned to playing with his stew, pieces of fat floating in greasy brown water alongside slithers of a vegetable of indeterminate origin. It might have been turnip, but he'd never been a betting man.

"I'm sure the food was better when we first arrived," he said, stirring.

"Nope, you're just not as hungry now," Lucien said between slurps.

"The stores are getting low," Hilde explained, "more mouths keep arriving in dribs and drabs and the *Markgräf* isn't turning people away yet."

"Enough to get through the winter?" Lucien asked.

"The meals will get thinner, but yes. Unless there's another big wave of refugees..."

Well, I did my bit to help with that. Fifty-six fewer mouths to feed now than before Christmas...

"Next winter?" he asked.

Hilde's shoulders twitched as she munched bread now soft enough to eat with minimal risk of slicing her tongue open, "Maybe the war will be over by then..."

Lucien snorted without looking up from his bowl.

"What was it like before the war?" Hilde asked. He doubted she was yet twenty.

"Much like it is now," Lucien said, "just with a bit less killing."

It was Hilde's turn to snort, which made her nostrils flare. She had a cute nose.

Fuck! Fuck! Fuck!!!

"I can just about remember," she said, stirring more bread into her greasy stew, "used to go and play in the woods with my siblings and children from the village when chores were done. No one seemed worried we'd come to any harm..."

"What happened to your family?" he asked, guessing Hilde's answer even before the light dimmed in her eyes.

"All dead. Farm burned. Village burned. No children play in the woods anymore..."

"I'm sorry..." he said. The words as hollow and useless in his mouth as they were familiar.

"And you? Your family?"

"None," he said quickly, "My father died a while back. A soldier. I travelled with him. Plenty of work for soldiers. After he died, I got a posting in... a *Freiherr's* castle. Just a little backwater place. Then... the war came there. Now..." he puckered his lips and shrugged before forcing another lump of gristle down his throat.

Always empty your plate, next time the world might not put anything on it.

Another of Old Man Ulrich's homilies. One of the better ones, he'd always thought.

"A wife...?" she asked, looking out of the corner of her eye at him. He ignored Lucien's smirk.

"No. No one. The war... perhaps afterwards..."

If by some immensely unlikely fluke, I'm somehow still alive, and anyone wants whatever remains of me.

"And you?" Hilde asked Lucien before he could stop her.

"The world is Lucien Kazmierczak's family, and he has more wives than he can remember. Not quite one in every town..." he raised his cup in salute and winked, "...so I'm always on the lookout for more."

Hilde laughed and lifted her own cup in return.

Why do women find this arse charming?

Lucien drained his cup. Which was usually the signal to immediately go and find more. Instead, he threw his arms out wide and engaged in possibly the longest and most unconvincing yawn in the history of Christendom.

"Lucien Kazmierczak is famed from Le Havre to Lesbos for

his vitality and ability to carouse the night away..." he leaned across the table and put his finger to his lips, "...so, I'd be obliged if you kept it quiet that I'm going to bed early."

"Well, maybe I should-"

Lucien clamped a hand on his shoulder and pushed him back down onto the bench, "No, no! Stay and finish your meal. First rule of soldiering that is, my friend."

The mercenary winked, nodded at Hilde, and sauntered off, shooting greetings and insults to all and sundry in equal measure.

He returned to his dinner and tried to ignore Hilde. The quicker he finished eating, the quicker he could escape before he did something stupid. Such as starting to like her.

Her eyes followed his spoon.

"Hungry then?"

He nodded between mouthfuls.

It wasn't a lie. His appetite had been growing since they'd arrived at Ettestein, as if his stomach, which had shrivelled on a diet of forage during those long, bleak months in The Wolf's Tower, had finally remembered what food was for.

"I can steal a few apples for you..."

"No need," he said, not looking at her, "wouldn't want you to get into trouble."

She found something funny about that.

"Should you be here?"

"Why shouldn't I be?" she laughed. She laughed a lot. She had a good laugh, too. Warm and infectious. Obviously. Bellowing like an unmilked cow would just have been too easy.

"Haven't you got work to do?"

"The *Markgräf* lets us eat from time to time. Sleep as well, though not too long, just for a bit. He's not all bad..." she slurped up a spoonful of watery stew.

"Is he... bad?"

She rolled her shoulders and dropped her voice, "There's worse lords around."

"You do not sound... impressed with him?"

She made a figure of eight with her spoon in the bowl.

"We get this shit while he feasts every night. Table groaning with food. Half of it they don't even eat. In the kitchens, we fight over their crumbs and scraps like hungry dogs..." those big, chestnut eyes darkened, "...clean the master's plates with our tongues, we do..."

The masters...

He swallowed.

"That's the way the world is..." he said finally.

"Eat shit and be grateful we're not starving like half the Empire, eh? Because of *their* bloody war. Arguing over the right way to worship God..." she spat the last words out, then looked around. The dining hall was busy, but no one was close enough to hear her over the hubbub of voices and clanking plates.

"That's the way the world is..." he said again.

"Shouldn't have to be. All supposed to be equal before God, aren't we?"

"Not sure the Princes of the Empire see it like that."

"No. They don't. Especially when they're trying to impress someone."

"Impress someone?"

"Your mistress."

His spoon hovered in mid-air.

"Lady Solace?"

"Ever since she's been eating with them..." Hilde tapped the table, "...they've all been scoffing like kings, while the rest of us make do with gristle and water."

"Plenty of beer, though," he picked up his cup and drained it.

"Men will suffer most things, but not running out of beer."

He didn't want to smile. Smiles encouraged people, but he couldn't help himself at that truism.

"Lady Solace is not demanding to be fed like a king."

"Don't suppose she's complaining much."

She didn't complain much when they had to live on berries and skinny rabbits either, but he kept that to himself.

"What is she after?" Hilde asked over the top of her own cup.

"Think she tells me?"

Hilde sipped beer and kept watching him.

He shrugged and chased the last piece of sinewy meat around the bowl.

"Don't like me much, do you?"

He looked up, "I don't know you."

"Easy enough to change that."

"Is it?"

She drained her cup, "Drinking more beer helps..."

He stared at her.

I wonder what her hair looks like under that cap?

He stopped staring.

Fuck! Fuck! Fuck!!

She jumped up. Relief and regret surged in equal measures.

Hilde scooped up both their cups and headed off towards the kitchens.

A few heads turned; curious eyes followed her. Hungry ones, too. She was a pretty lass. A couple of glances came his way as well. A wagging tongue's work was never done, after all.

Part of him wanted to sprint out of the hall to spend the rest of the night enduring Lucien's snores. Another part of him wanted to spend the night doing something entirely different.

A weariness descended on him, similar to the one he'd endured as he recovered from his injuries in The Wolf's Tower. Similar to the one that had accompanied him every exhausted step in the endless trudge behind Styx's swaying arse as they'd walked to Madriel. Similar to the one that had almost dragged him down into the mud as he'd run back to the Gate Towers with Morlaine, Sophia and Gottlieb.

Similar. But not quite the same.

He couldn't put his finger on the difference but thought it had something to do with the spark of hope rather than its complete and utter absence.

And in the end, of course, hope always cuts the deepest.

Chapter Ten

"Torben!"

She was on her hands and knees in the dark and had just thrown up over one of the *Markgräf's* rugs.

She wiped away acidic drool hanging from her lips with the back of her hand. Still prone on the floor, she didn't trust herself to move. Her mouth tasted foul. She spat a gob of something vile out. The rug was probably past caring by now.

"My lady?"

Renard's head and a rushlight appeared around the door. It wasn't appropriate for him to enter his lady's chamber, but her honour was currently the least of her worries.

Trembling and head swimming, she managed to lever herself up onto her knees.

Renard giving her a hug would be even more inappropriate, but right then, she might have struggled to think of something she wanted more.

She tried waving him away and telling him she was alright, but nothing comprehensible escaped her. Then she burst into tears.

I am not a silly little girl!

Renard managed to scoop her up and carry her back to bed. Either he was getting stronger, or she was getting lighter; the Ulrich Renard of even a few weeks ago would not have been able to pick her up.

He was still dressed. Scents of sweat and beer tickled her nose. Tantalisingly, the coarseness of his beard grazed her face. Her skin tingled in its wake.

After laying her down with only the barest of grunts, he retrieved his rushlight to put the flame to one of the candles by her bed.

"My lady?" he asked again.

"Why?"

Renard frowned and leaned closer.

Why would my gentle, lovely brother do such terrible things?

She stayed the question and concentrated on trying to stop shivering.

Renard reached out, placing a hand against her forehead. It both warmed and cooled her.

"You are burning, my lady? You have a fever?"

"No. A dream."

"Just a dream?"

She shook her head once his hand slipped from her skin and then pulled the blankets over her again. She wore only a night dress; it was not seemly for Renard to see her dressed so, to be here, in her chamber, by her bed.

"Don't go," she said when he looked like the same thought was galloping across his mind.

He eased himself onto the edge of the bed.

"I saw what they do… what they will do, in Magdeburg."

"What did you see?"

She shook her head sharply, "I don't want to speak of it

yet. Too real. I can still smell the smoke, the blood... I'm frightened, Ulrich..."

She found his hand and held it tight. He squeezed back.

"We do not have to go to Magdeburg," he said, the words both soft and heavy in the flickering candlelight.

"You do not want to stop them? Destroy them? Avenge those they killed in The Wolf's Tower?"

His lips twitched, trying to form a response several times before his eyes slid away and his shoulders sagged.

"I am frightened too, my lady."

She wanted to say something brave and inspiring about how overcoming your fear was the first step in defeating your enemies. But her mouth tasted of bile, the stink of blood, piss and shit of the dying haunted her nostrils, and demons writhed with their victims in each shadow the candlelight teased.

So, she said nothing and did nothing.

Other than keeping hold of Renard's hand.

Possibilities...

She ran her thumb across his knuckles, feeling the hard bone beneath the skin.

Torben had said something about possibilities.

Or rather, the monster he'd become had.

She closed her eyes.

He was still her brother. The kind and gentle soul he'd been before Saul the Bloodless took him was still there, somewhere. Rescuing him would involve more than saving him from the Red Company. She would have to save him from the terrible thing he'd become, too.

That sounded much like climbing to the moon. But

Morlaine had done it. She was no longer a monster despite... being a monster. So why not Torben?

He just needed... her.

"We will go to Magdeburg..." she said, not opening her eyes.

She felt his fingers stiffen, just for a second or two.

"You do not have to come, Ulrich. I will release you from your oath. I have offered before. I will offer again."

"I will give you the same answer, my lady," he replied instantly.

"The things I saw are just possibilities," she said, forcing her eyes open again. No demons haunted the shadows. Only Renard's face crumpled with concern.

"Cleever said something like that."

"If we can stop them, that possibility won't happen, and the people I saw die might survive, might not be slaughtered and despoiled and... not suffer so..."

"Yes..." he agreed with little evident enthusiasm.

"Then that is the only possibility that matters..."

She squeezed. He squeezed back.

Then she let go, pulled her hand away and rolled over.

*

"You shouldn't have agreed to a duel."

"'tis not a bloody duel!"

"Well, I certainly hope 'tis not a *bloody* duel. If you kill him, it could be awkward. What with him being the *Markgräf's* son. I expect he isn't the *Markgräf's* favourite son, but still, he might be a bit pissed if you kill him."

"I'm not going to kill him."

"Well, that isn't likely. He's almost certainly a better

swordsman than you but do try not to cut anything significant off him. Even by accident. That'd likely not go down well either."

"I'm not going to kill him or chop anything off, significant or otherwise. 'tis not a duel!"

Lucien wrinkled his nose as the approaching group of men made their way down from the castle, "Then, of course, he might kill you," the mercenary glanced sideways at him, "and that'd be a tragedy."

"I didn't know you cared."

Lucien shrugged, "I'd have to find someone else to drink with."

"You like drinking with me?"

He shrugged again, "Your miserable, hangdog expression makes me look even more cheerful, amiable, friendly, and attractive than I already am. 'tis not easy to find so many benefits in a single drinking companion."

"You're trying to make me feel better about myself, aren't you?"

"Easier than cooking you a hearty last breakfast. Fucking hate cooking."

"I am not going to die, 'tis not a duel."

Lucien nodded at the approaching men, "Does young *Markgräf* Joachim know that?"

Admittedly, grim-faced, furrow-browed, and hunch-shouldered Joachim did not have the air of a man strolling towards a little light sword practice to warm himself on a blustery January morning. The men with him, a collection of brown-nosing lickspittles from the little he knew, were equally stony-faced.

Lady Solace's sight would have warned her if I was going to die so pointlessly.

Assuming his life merited enough cosmic significance for her uncanny ability to foretell the future to notice it.

"Is there anything you'd like me to say to Lady Solace if... things don't turn out terribly well?" Lucien asked.

"Oh, do shut up!"

"I've never considered her an excessive talker for a woman, but if you're sure that's what you want me to tell her..."

He shot the mercenary a venomous look.

"Behold! The greatest swordsman in Europe awaits!" Joachim bellowed as he drew close, still no smile sullying his brooding features.

Lucien nudged him with his elbow, "He's talking to you, not me. In case you're a tad confused..."

"My lord," he ignored the fool standing next to him and bowed fulsomely to the one in front.

Lucien chuckled and bowed somewhat less fulsomely.

"So... are you going to teach me a thing or two, lad?" Joachim asked, the words not *quite* accompanied by a sneer.

He tried not to find being addressed as *lad* irritating. Joachim was no older than him and maybe even a year or two younger. Either way, after the last year's hardships, he *looked* a damn sight older than the young *Markgräf*.

"I am sure I have nothing I can teach you, my lord."

"But you are the best swordsman in Europe. If I am better than you, what does that make me?"

"The best swordsman in the world!" one of the brown-nosing lickspittles piped up. The rest of Joachim's entourage cheered. And all looked like they wished they'd thought of saying it themselves.

Joachim pulled off his coat and tossed it to one of his companions without looking, "Come, 'tis too cold to stand about. Let's get to it!"

Another ragged cheer rippled through the young men with Joachim. Did they cheer everything he said?

The sons of lesser local nobles and gentry come to Ettestein for their martial education and as an act of fealty by their fathers. Spoilt, stuck up, worthless arseholes as far as he could see. He'd done his best to avoid them since they'd arrived in Gothen. Though, to be fair, he'd tried to avoid almost everyone since they'd arrived in Gothen.

They'd managed to survive Gottlieb's attack, so he supposed they must have something about them. Presumably, they'd fought at Jochim's side as he'd held the Imperial force in the First Hall. Or maybe they'd hid under their beds.

He ignored them. They weren't the ones he needed to worry about.

The one he needed to worry about drew his sword and cut the air a few times, grinning at him all the while.

He found his own, less convincing, smile in return before pulling off his coat and holding it out for Lucien.

When the coat continued to dangle in the air, he looked around to find the mercenary had retreated to the timber pile, where he'd plonked his arse to swig out of a water skin. Dog sat next to him, scratching his face with a hind leg.

He tried not to be annoyed.

He walked over and tossed his coat onto the wood pile while the lickspittles shuffled about and did their best to work out how to stand in a circle.

"When faced with a superior enemy, you have two options, assuming you don't want to die..." Lucien said after wiping the back of his hand over his lips.

"Yes...?" he watched Joachim continue to slice the air. The boy had fast hands; he couldn't help but notice.

"Run away or fight dirty."

"Thanks."

"You're welcome. But 'tis never a good idea to show your back to the enemy once a fight has started..."

"So, that's your advice? Fight dirty?"

Lucien took another swig from the skin, "*Always* be prepared to fight dirty. First rule of soldiering, that..."

He turned back to Joachim, who was waiting for him, a sour grin still plastered across his face.

He drew his father's blade and walked out to meet him.

It was an overcast but dry day, the air cold enough to make faint plumes of their breath. The grass underfoot was damp but without standing water or sticky mud clumps. Distant sounds floated up from the village, chopping wood, creaking wheels, voices, a cawing crow.

"You favour the sabre?" Joachim asked, staring pointedly at his withered arm held half across him. He clenched the fist and forced it to fall to his side.

Last night he'd managed to lift Solace from the floor. It hadn't been far, and she didn't weigh a lot. Still, it had surprised him he'd been able to do it. He probably wouldn't have tried if he had taken a moment to think about it. But seeing her down on the floor, drool dripping from her mouth and shaking from head to foot, had chased all thoughts from his mind.

He gripped Old Man Ulrich's sabre tighter as if trying to exorcise the memory of Solace holding his hand with the coarse, familiar leather binding wound around the weapon's grip.

There was a time to think about women. Facing a man wielding a wickedly sharp-looking blade who didn't like you very much wasn't one of them.

He shook thoughts of how vulnerable and alone Solace had seemed away.

The ones about how much he'd wanted to hold her he'd already spent most of the night quashing. And when the quashing had failed, he'd thought about how pretty Hilde was instead.

It had been the worst night's sleep he'd had since *Freiherr* Gottlieb had dropped in early for Christmas.

"I trained as a cavalryman."

"Who trained you?"

"My father."

"Was he the greatest swordsman in Europe as well in his day?"

The onlookers, save Lucien, guffawed and tittered.

"No."

"Are these things not passed from father to son?"

"The only thing I inherited from my father was this sabre."

Plus, an inconvenient sense of honour and a dislike for the nobility.

Joachim pursed his lips, nodded a few times, then leaned

in towards him a little.

"Have you ever considered the possibility your mother fucked a great swordsman behind your so-called father's back?"

More laughter. Apart from Lucien.

"I can't say, my lord. I never knew my mother."

"Were you found under a bush then?"

Joachim was trying to rile him. An old trick. An angry man is likelier to make a mistake than a cool-headed one. Perhaps Lucien hadn't been far off the mark after all. You didn't need to make a man you wanted to practice swordcraft with angry.

A man you wanted to hurt, however...

"No, my lord. In a whorehouse."

Joachim blinked and frowned.

"My father bought me from the owner, where I swept the floors and helped wash the whores' spunk-stained clothes until I was six. He wanted a son but couldn't have one, mainly because he was so ugly no woman would ever let him fuck them unless he paid her. He took a shine to me for some reason. Perhaps because we had the same Christian name. I never knew which one of the whores was my mother. They never said. My father took me around Europe and taught me how to be a soldier. How to ride and fight with sword and pistol. He taught me about honour and always striving to do the right thing despite being a drunken fool who could never keep a master for more than six months. So, my lord..." he tried to make his grin as good-natured as possible, "...my real father really *could* have been the greatest swordsman in Europe..."

He turned his back on the young lord and gave Old Man Ulrich's sabre a couple of practice swings as he walked a few paces away, "...even if I am not."

Lucien watched him intently, hunched forward on the lumber pile, waterskin swinging between his hands. Dog had started licking his bollocks.

When he turned to face Joachim again, the *Markgräf* looked thoughtful. Still sneering, but definitely a more thoughtful sneer than previously.

He grinned at the little prick. His bad shoulder was still throbbing in protest at lifting Solace off the floor but damned if he was going to show this arsehole a grimace.

"A colourful life, by the sounds of it," Joachim briefly raised his rapier to his face in salute.

"I sometimes think I'd have been better off if he'd left me in the whorehouse..." he lifted Old Man Ulrich's sabre in return, "...probably would have earned a decent discount by now."

Laughter rippled around the watching circle of men. Even Joachim's sneer momentarily flickered into a smirk.

"Do you wish me to fight with a rapier, my lord?" His sabre was a heavier slashing weapon, the rapier a lighter, predominantly thrusting one. It was a mismatch, although both weapons could kill quite satisfactorily.

Joachim shook his head, "No, I want you to show me how you put down those imperial bastards outside Wilhelm's church."

He shrugged, despite the pain it inflicted on his bad shoulder, "We were all heroes that night..." he scanned the surrounding men, "...weren't we?"

The onlookers responded with nods and affirmative cries.

An expression of mild irritation replaced Joachim's short-lived smirk.

"Still..." the young *Markgräf* began circling him, rapier held out before him, the tip angled towards the grass, "...I am curious, how you, a cripple, bested so many men?"

"The answer is a simple one, my lord. They underestimated me. 'tis always foolish to underestimate anyone with a sword..." as much as he wanted to spit, he found that good-natured grin again, "...even a cripple like me."

"Best I don't underestimate you then, eh?" Joachim winked. And then came at him.

The young lord had quick feet to go with his fast hands...

Chapter Eleven

"Who are you?"

The girl staring back at her from the looking-glass tilted her head and ran fingers through her hair.

The flowing locks she'd once taken such delight in combing were long gone. But enough had grown back since the last time she'd hacked her hair off with a knife that she didn't look quite so boyish anymore. She glanced down at the breasts restrained within Sophia's dress. No, there were times when she was not at all boyish.

She was still pretty. Though the thought brought her no reassurance. Once, it was all that mattered. Her purpose in life. To be the desirable daughter a rich, powerful (and handsome!) young prince would want. Now... now it amounted to nothing but a means to an end.

Thinner in the face, harder in the eyes maybe... but still pretty.

Pretty enough to make a man give her an army?

She didn't know. Was that enough? Men were strange. She suspected she needed more but had no idea what that more might be. Her conversations with Renard, Lucien and Morlaine had just deepened her confusion.

She was going to dine with the *Markgräf* again tonight and felt ill-prepared. Things were coming to a head. One way or another. She couldn't linger here forever. She had to be beautiful, alluring, captivating. Show him she was worth whatever it took to have her.

In the world she grew up in, she'd had a clutch of maids to pamper and prepare her for an audience with a Prince of the Empire. Now... she had no one.

She had Renard, Lucien and Morlaine, but none of them made for a passable maid.

Sophia would no doubt be delighted to help make her beautiful. But the idea of using a girl to help her seduce her own father made her uncomfortable.

Or rather, added to the list of things that made her uncomfortable.

She sighed. The girl in the looking-glass, who was not anywhere near as beautiful and alluring as she would like, did the same.

She reached for the wine on the mantle.

She'd been drinking a lot lately.

The girl in the looking-glass shrugged and told her it didn't matter.

"Who are you?" she asked again, this time over the rim of the wine glass.

The girl staring back at her was also sipping wine. As usual, she didn't answer the question.

"I wanted to take Ulrich to my bed last night..." she said, swirling wine around the goblet.

The girl in the mirror did the same. She did not appear shocked at the confession.

"Do you think he would have if I'd asked?"

You are pretty, and you are his mistress. Why wouldn't he?

"Honour."

You think that would have kept his britches on?

She laughed. The girl in the looking-glass did the same.

She was trying to seduce a *Markgräf;* giving her virginity away to another man... would not make anything easier.

It's had been a foolish thought. She'd been scared. Disorientated. All she'd wanted was comfort, reassurance, security... but although there were still things she did not fully understand about the world, she knew enough to know men always wanted something in exchange for such gifts.

She held up her chin and gave the girl in the looking-glass an imperious stare, "I have no feelings for Ulrich Renard..."

Of course you don't. How preposterous!

"He is... my retainer. We have shared much together. But that is all he is. Or ever will be."

Nothing else, the girl in the looking-glass agreed wholeheartedly.

Her eyes dropped from the sceptical face staring back at her. They came to rest on the hand Renard had held when she'd been frightened. He'd told her he was frightened, too. A man was not supposed to say such a thing. A man was supposed to be strong, resolute, defiant. A rock against which the world itself might break.

But she didn't think less of Renard for saying it. In fact, she suspected she thought more of him. Sharing your vulnerability was a form of intimacy, wasn't it?

She raised her eyes to discover the girl in the looking-glass' opinion on the matter.

And found Torben's blood-soiled face resting on her shoulder.

She screamed and dropped the wine glass to shatter on the floor.

Staggering forward towards the mantle, mirror, and fire, she twisted around.

The room was empty.

She stood, panting, hand over her mouth, heart scrambling up her throat.

"Torben...?"

The shadows didn't answer.

Lord Flyblown could come and go out of thin air. As far as she knew, her brother couldn't. So, it was just imagination. A remnant of the previous night's dream. Or her *sight* trying to tell her something.

She touched her shoulder, half expecting her fingers to come away sticky with blood. They didn't.

"I have nothing to fear from my brother..."

She didn't know who she was saying that to. She didn't want to turn towards the girl in the looking-glass again. Who else might she glimpse in that other world?

"Solace?"

Once more, she jumped and turned around. This time the shadowy figure in the corner was flesh and blood. Sort of.

"Morlaine..."

The demon crossed to the room, dark eyes narrowing a little against the light of the fire.

"I... dropped my wine... clumsy..." she looked down at the splintered shards reflecting the firelight. The demon was barefooted.

"You are troubled?"

How much had the demon heard of her conversation with

the girl in the looking-glass? In truth, she'd forgotten Morlaine was in her room. Which was foolish as the demon hardly ever left it.

"No... just... clumsy!"

Morlaine raised an eyebrow. Which she'd come to recognise as the demon's way of saying she knew when someone was lying through their teeth.

She left the remains of the glass and retreated to a chair in the corner away from the fire, suddenly hot and itchy in her skin. She started tugging at the lace cuff of her dress again.

"Tell me," Morlaine said, crouching to pick up the broken glass.

"You don't have to do that."

"I'm supposed to be your maid. I should do *something*."

Morlaine collected the fragments and placed them on the mantle. When done, she came to stand over her.

"Tell me," the demon repeated.

"I had a dream last night..."

"A dream?"

"Vision..." she shrugged, "...of Magdeburg. Saul. The Red Company..." she raised her eyes to meet Morlaine's, "...of things to come."

Morlaine folded her knees to crouch, "What did you see?"

"Men and monsters..." she breathed, "...where do you draw the line between them?"

"Sometimes, there isn't one... what did you see?" Morlaine snatched her hand. Her touch smooth and cool. So different to Renard's.

In a hesitant voice, kept low for fear of being overheard

even though no one else was in their rooms, she told the demon everything she could remember.

"This couldn't be *just* a dream?"

She shook her head, "No. It was too real, too vivid. It was the *sight*. It doesn't usually show me the future so clearly... but Saul and his fellows will be in that church when the walls fall. And they will do such terrible things."

The agonised bodies twisted and writhed on the far side of the shadows haunting the room; their screams echoed in the cracks and crackles of the fire. But she kept her eyes open. If she closed them, she'd see Torben's blood-stained face. Which was worse than anything.

She concentrated on Morlaine's eyes. Despite being the darkest part of the room, it was the only place she couldn't see the monsters.

"Why do they do those things?"

"Because they are vampires, Solace."

"So are you."

"Yes."

"But you do not."

"I do not now. But I did once..."

Morlaine still held her hand, she realised. She tightened her grip as if it were something that might keep her afloat.

"Torben... he was covered in blood. I think... I think he took part in the things I saw. The Devil's Banquet..."

Morlaine nodded.

"I don't want to believe he did. Or will. Any more than I want to believe he killed Enoch the Miser and his family. Or if he did, it was only to fool Saul he is one of them. He is trying to help us, after all."

The demon's eyebrow raised again, "Is he?"

"You said-"

"Cleever said. Has your brother contacted you, spoken to you, in your visions, to suggest he is helping us?"

Her throat tightened. She shook her head.

"Then-"

"Could he step away from it, like you did?"

"It?"

"Evil."

"Solace... the world is not black and white, good and evil. Neither are the beings that walk upon it. We all make our own choices. What labels are attached to those choices..."

"But can I save him? *Can I?*"

"The only people you can ever save are the ones who wish to be saved."

"I am not going to give up on him."

Morlaine found a rare smile, thin and unconvincing.

She pulled her hand free. Whatever comfort Morlaine offered was even more transient and unsubstantial than Renard's.

"Can we stop them?" she asked.

The demon stood up, "You said we should find them before they entered the city. It's a good plan. I do not believe the future is already decided."

"Then the people I saw... the people dying in the church... we can still save them?"

"Those people are in a city that will be sacked and razed. All we can likely alter is the method of their deaths."

She jumped to her feet. Morlaine moved aside, dark eyes following her across the room.

"Where are you going?"

"To do whatever is necessary to find an army so those people can know kinder deaths than the ones I saw..."

*

Hilde winced. She peered at him closely. Then winced some more.

"You should see the other fellow," he said, or more accurately mumbled, through his swollen lips.

"Although the other fellow was a lot better looking to start with," Lucien offered as helpfully as ever.

"Who was the other fellow?" Hilde asked.

"*Markgräf* Joachim," Lucien shot her a knowing grin.

Hilde winced again.

They were sitting outside. Hilde had come to find them. That was likely significant, but he hurt too much to consider it. Still, hurting proved he was alive.

"Why do boys always feel the need to fight?" the little fold of skin at the top of her nose creased as her eyes bounced between them.

"'tis how we prove who has the biggest cock without the need to drop our britches," Lucien took a swig from his waterskin, "if you start dropping your britches and getting your cock out too often, people can get the wrong idea entirely. Fighting is much more straightforward."

Hilde gave the mercenary a look that suggested she wasn't sure if he was being serious or not. Almost everyone got that look when they met Lucien, he'd noticed.

Meanwhile, Lucien grinned and looked pleased with himself as he offered the waterskin. He'd already discovered it didn't hold water. He took a swig. It had the same effect as before. Though maybe his eyes watered a little less this time.

"What's in that?" Hilde asked.

"'tis medicinal."

"You didn't get it from Cowmeadow, did you?" Hilde's nose wrinkled at the very idea.

"Is Cowmeadow a toothless old goat with one eye and a huge pus-filled sore on his neck?"

"Yes, that's him."

"No," Lucien shook his head, "Got this from some other chap."

"Be warned, Cowmeadow's concoctions have blinded men before now."

Lucien shrugged and took another sip.

"Don't suppose it makes your tongue swell up so much you can't talk, does it?" he asked, hopefully.

"I don't think so."

He spat. He expected there to be blood in his gob, but there was nothing.

Hilde held her hand out for Lucien's waterskin.

"I thought you said Cowmeadow's concoctions could blind a man?" Lucien asked, staring at her hand.

"I thought you said it wasn't one of Cowmeadow's concoctions? Besides...." the accompanying smile was, somehow, both sweet and steely, "...I'm not a man."

Lucien's eyes flicked up and down her. He shrugged and passed the skin, "Right on both counts..."

Arthur Cowmeadow was a sour-faced, short-tempered Englishman, who, for reasons no one seemed able to explain, himself included, had washed up at Ettestein and now did nothing but conjure hideously strong brews and obtain pretty much anything anyone wanted regardless of scarcity, season, or the laws of the land. For the right price.

"Why did you fight Joachim?" she asked, "He is a bad enemy to have."

"It was a duel," Lucien said before he could get his swollen mouth to work.

"It was not a bloody duel!" he managed to splutter.

"There wasn't a lot of blood," Lucien conceded, "which is surprising, really. As the two of you did rather go at it."

"So, tell me..." Hilde asked, glancing between them, "...just out of interest, who had the biggest cock?"

Eyes widening, he wondered if the ringing in his ears had affected his hearing somewhat. However, as Lucien started rocking backwards, roaring with laughter, he suspected he'd heard her just fine.

While he was deciding whether he should be shocked, offended or amused, Lucien regained enough control to lean in towards Hilde, "In truth, it was a piss poor display..." he lifted his right hand and wiggled his little finger and eyebrows in unison, "...both of em..."

Hilde giggled, eyes moving to his. And staying there.

His cheeks warmed despite the air's January bite.

He wanted to tell the pair of them to piss off, but he didn't like to use vulgar words in front of women. Even ones who said *cock* aloud.

Anger replaced embarrassment, and he found he'd jumped from the pile of lumber, grabbed his father's sheathed sabre and belt, and stomped off towards the outer walls before he realised what he was doing.

Acting like a petulant child was what he was doing; the realisation dawned within a few strides, but it was too late to stop by then.

He'd kept his anger in check during the *sword practice* with Joachim. It soon became apparent as they sparred that the young *Markgräf* had no intention of killing him. Why would he? Even in these times, murdering a man in broad daylight would make life tediously awkward for a nobleman for a day or two. No, Joachim hadn't tried to kill him.

He'd tried to humiliate the one-armed, broken weakling instead.

Joachim had jabbed, parried, and attempted to pierce him with his tongue as much as his rapier. When that hadn't had any noticeable effect, the young lord endeavoured to put him down in the mud as often as possible. Preferably accompanied by the laughter of his friends.

He'd like to be able to say he let him. That he sucked it up because Joachim was a nobleman, and beating the arrogant prick to a pulp would cause problems for Solace. Better to lose face than gain an enemy. So, he'd stumbled on purpose. His handwork had been deliberately stiff, his feet purposefully heavy and ponderous. For good reason, he'd let the young lord make him look like a fool.

Except, he hadn't.

He'd made himself look a clumsy fool without any effort whatsoever.

"The greatest swordsman in Europe?" Joachim had snorted, walking backwards with a shake of the head after putting him on his arse again.

Laughter had rippled around the onlookers, apart from Lucien, who'd sat hunched atop the lumber pile. Stony-faced and silent. Dog had given an eloquent reaction to proceedings by concentrating on licking his arse.

He'd smiled and laughed, too. Praising Joachim's skill through gritted teeth. Tongue pushing between the gaps Captain Bekker's boot had left. The Red Cloak's Captain had laughed at him, too. Hadn't laughed so much when he'd slit the bastard's throat though.

Anger squirmed within him, like a trapped beast in a pit roaring at a tormentor too far above to reach with claw and fang.

Never show your anger, boy...

Old Man Ulrich had taught him many lessons. Most of the ones given from behind a foaming mug were worthless; the ones on the practice ground, however, were not.

His father had been a drunken fool. But he'd known how to fight.

The greatest enemies you'll ever face are fear and anger. They'll always make your opponent's sword sharper, hand faster, arm stronger, heart braver. Fear and anger, boy, strangle the bastards, strangle em at birth...

He hadn't feared Joachim, but his anger strained upon a leash.

Which is what Joachim wanted.

So, he'd brushed off the mud, climbed back to his feet and taken it.

A couple of times, he thought irritation flickered behind the young *Markgräf's* icy eyes. That he wanted him to lose control, to lash out, to try and take the bastard's head off.

Perhaps Joachim had wanted to kill him.

He just needed an excuse.

Feet padded on the damp grass. He didn't turn around. The steps were too light to be Lucien's and too heavy to be Dog's.

"I want to be alone."

"You're in the wrong place for that," Hilde said once she caught up with him. He thought she was grinning, but he kept his eyes fixed on the wall ahead of them, "hard to be alone in a castle."

He'd lived in castles. He'd lived in all kinds of places as he'd trooped across Europe at Old Man Ulrich's side, a squire and apprentice to a drunken fool. Wherever they'd lived, he'd always felt alone.

"Maybe I'll keep walking then!"

"You'll go nose first into the wall then," she giggled.

He stopped and turned towards her. Looming over her. She didn't take a step backwards. Just held his eye. Or stared up his nostrils. It was hard to be sure which.

"Why are you following me?"

"Maybe I want to be alone, too?"

"We can't be alone together."

Her shoulders twitched. So did her lips. He couldn't see anything funny.

Old Man Ulrich had taught him to keep his anger in check when fighting. Not to listen to his opponent's taunts and stay rational. Focus on the blade and keep calm.

Old Man Ulrich had taught him nothing about women other than they eventually always made you miserable and were best avoided.

Which he'd begun to suspect was a bit of an oversight.

"We could be…"

He whirled away before his mind could try to work out what that meant, "I need to think, woman!"

After a few strides, he realised he *would* walk straight into the wall if he carried on much further. He veered left and started walking parallel to the castle's outer ramparts. The scent of damp stone, mud and decomposing leaves filled the air.

Hilde caught up with him again. She might have only short legs, but she could move them quickly enough.

"What do you need to think about?"

"Nothing!"

"That shouldn't take long then."

"Nothing I need to talk to you about."

"Only trying to help."

"I don't need your help!"

"Are you always this tetchy when someone beats you up?"

He stopped again, "Nobody beat me up."

"That's not what your face says…"

He resisted the temptation to touch his swelling lip. Joachim had put him down by smashing the guard of his sword into his face. Well, one of the times, anyway.

Their swordplay had had more than a hint of the brawl about it.

He flexed the fingers of his bad arm. A deep, dull ache from shoulder blade to fingertips had replaced its usual numbness. It didn't much care for being thrown around anymore.

"I decided it best not to take his head off..."

Empty bravado.

He'd been lucky in Wilhelm's church. Luckier still that Morlaine had shown up when she did. And the problem with luck was that it never lasted. Joachim had shattered any illusions he might still have harboured that he was the man he'd been a year ago.

Any half-competent swordsman would make mincemeat of him in a real fight.

Next time, or the time after. And if not, definitely the time after that, luck or a vampire wasn't going to show up to save him.

And he was going to die.

He busied himself strapping his weapon belt back around his waist. He didn't want to see scorn in Hilde's eyes at his childish boast or the reflection of his own shame and embarrassment.

His left hand's fat, numb, clumsy fingers made the task harder than it once was. Like most of the tasks he'd taken for granted before Saul sliced a rope and sent him crashing into the ice of The Wolf Tower's frozen moat.

He fumbled the buckle and swore.

"Here, let me help..." Hilde moved towards him.

"I can buckle a damn belt," he hissed at her.

"Don't be such a horse's arse," she said right back.

She took the buckle from him and started fixing it.

Part of him wanted to push her away and demand to know what she thought she was doing.

Part of him felt the warmth of her hands as her scent teased his nose, curls of red hair bobbed from under her cap. She barely came up to his chin.

His hands fell away.

Her breath, rising in clouds of steam, warmed his cheeks.

He bit his lip and hoped she didn't take too long with the belt...

She didn't. But once finished, she didn't step back. Her face raised to look up at him.

She was, he couldn't help but admit, pretty as well as annoying.

"You should go inside, 'tis cold," he said, wishing she would stop looking at him like that.

"I am not cold."

"Then... we should walk because I am."

They continued walking under the wall, side by side.

"You should not be around me," he said after a long silence interrupted only by distant birds.

"Why? Is it improper?"

"No..." well, it probably was, but that had not been his meaning, "...people tend to die around me. 'tis better if you keep away."

"Your friend Lucien seems very much alive to me."

He raised his good hand to put his forefinger a hair's breadth from his thumb, "He is often this close to not being..."

Hilde laughed and gave him another look. One of those that carried significance. Or at least thought it did. For all he knew of women it might just as well be due to a disagreeable reaction to breakfast.

"I feel safe enough..." her pale cheeks developed a rosy flush. Due to the cold, he assumed.

"You shouldn't," he lengthened his stride.

Her little legs kept up with him.

"You should tell me why you think people die around you?"

"Why?"

"So I can decide if I want to be around you."

"You shouldn't."

"That's for me to decide."

"'tis?"

She nodded, "Men don't usually run away from me."

"I am not most men."

"Perhaps that has something to do with it."

"With what?"

She gave him a serious look, *"It…"*

"Oh."

She pursed her lips, "Exactly."

Despite having no idea what Hilde was talking about, he strongly suspected that unlike with Solace, whatever it was, it had absolutely nothing to do with killing demons.

Which at least made for a change.

Chapter Twelve

"You are early?"

"I wanted us to be alone. We have matters to discuss... matters not suitable for your children's ears."

Matters not... suitable?

Ooh... how flirtatious, how romantic, how alluring you are, Solace von Tassau!

How could any man resist?

She ignored the whiny little voice. Voices in your head rarely said anything worth listening to.

The *Markgräf sat* in his study, papers spread across the desk. Three candles burned in a brass candelabra; others flickered around the room. However, no matter how many candles you lit in a room, it was never enough to keep the shadows at bay.

"You will weaken your eyes reading in candlelight," she said.

The corner of his mouth turned up, but he said nothing. He put the quill aside and indicated one of the chairs on the opposite side. Most businesslike. Most formal.

Most... not suitable.

He had a glass of wine beside him.

She floated around to his side of the desk. Then scooped up the glass and plonked her arse on top of some of his, no doubt, especially important papers.

His eyes widened as she sipped the wine. It was a lot better than the stuff in her rooms.

The *Markgräf's* face suggested he was not at all used to young women helping themselves to his wine or plonking their arse on his especially important papers.

"I cannot give you an army," he said.

"You have my word. I will return."

"I believe you give it sincerely. But... these creatures you pursue. Truly, what are the chances you would not return?"

"High," she admitted.

"And my men?"

"Equally so."

"My idiot nephew's antics have weakened Gothen. At the very time it needs to be strong to survive. I cannot... even for... you to be my wife... I am sorry, Solace."

She nodded and sipped more wine. It was helping. A little.

"I understand. Am I free to leave?"

"Of course. Truly. Once 'tis safe."

"How long might that be?"

He held her eye, then took the glass from her hand, "A few days, and we will have the brigands cleared or moved on. I promise."

He filled the glass from a bottle and handed it back to her.

She drank. More than a sip this time.

"How much am I worth, my lord?"

"Worth?" he frowned.

"If not to be your wife. Then... for a night?"

The *Markgräf's* frown stretched into surprise. He plucked the glass from her hand and drank deeply himself.

"Please, excuse my bold speaking, my lord. My situation demands it. How many men-at-arms would you give me for a night in your bed?" she took the glass back again, "And yes, in case you are wondering but are far too polite to ask, I am a virgin."

The *Markgräf* swallowed. His mouth opened; his eyes widened. Nothing else happened.

He was typically expressionless. Assured. Confident. A man who understood the world. A man who knew how the levers and gears operated. A man used to sitting in a high chair.

Now, he suddenly looked like a little boy being shown a new rocking horse or wooden sword that he might be allowed to play with if he was *very* good.

Is this how little it took?

She reached out with her free hand and held his. For a moment, she stared over the glass' rim.

Then she placed his hand on the top of her right leg.

Of course, she was wearing skirts and petticoats, but still, it was a shamelessly wanton gesture. One, she had no doubt, many a whore, when touting a wealthy customer, would have recognised.

She tilted her head, the glass still poised on her lips, hand atop the *Markgräf's*. It was warm but not sweaty. Hairs, surprisingly downy, pressed into her palm. She could feel veins, tendons, the hard ridge of his knuckles. His fingers were longer than hers. Beneath her hand, it looked like she'd trapped some huge, deformed spider. If you used a little imagination. Or drunk enough.

"How many men..." she dragged his hand a fraction

higher, "...my lord?"

"Solace...?"

Indecision played across his face.

Was he wavering? Or disgusted by the love of his life's daughter offering herself like a whore. Albeit not a cheap one.

"Tell me, did my mother go to her wedding bed a virgin?"

The *Markgräf* pushed her hand away but did nothing else.

"Did she?"

"As far as I am aware."

"You must have often wondered what it would have been like..."

He shot to his feet. She thought he was going to strike her. She didn't flinch.

Instead, he went to the nearest of the study's small windows. There was nothing to see but his reflection. Darkness fell early in January.

Winter was for the vampires...

"I loved your mother deeply..." he said, studiously not looking at her.

"I have never doubted it. But she is dead. I am not."

"And how would she feel about this... offer?"

"I cannot say. I never knew her."

He looked over his shoulder, "Take a guess."

Her shoulders moved up and down, "I am sure she would understand."

"Really?"

"She saw the future. *My* future. She gave her life so I could be born. Perhaps if she had become the Mistress of Ettestein, she would not have died so young and would have spent a happy life with a man who loved her. But she didn't. She chose to go to my father, knowing she would give birth to a child who would kill her. She made that choice for a reason."

"What reason?"

"So that I could destroy the Red Company. So I could stop Saul the Bloodless..." she took another long draught of wine before concluding, "...so I could save the world."

Hendrick, *Markgräf* of Gothen, stared at her like he suspected she was more than a little mad.

"Save the world? You think most highly of yourself, my lady."

"These demons, these vampires, will not die. Not like we die, at least. Their lives are long. Saul the Bloodless is upon a path. A dark one. He is mad. I have it on good authority all vampires are. But he has a particularly virulent manner of insanity. Many years hence, long after you and I are forgotten, perhaps centuries, maybe even millennia, that path, if he is allowed to walk it, will lead to the fall of the world, I must stop him. I believe that is why my mother, the love of your life, walked away from you and to her own death. I will do whatever is necessary to honour her sacrifice. And I will make whatever sacrifices I need to in return. For none will ever match hers..."

He turned to face her but remained by the window.

"Perhaps you should take your concerns to the Emperor?"

"I fear that would be more likely to earn me the pyre than an army. There is only one way to know the future, is there not?"

"The *sight*..." he said, but quietly.

She nodded.

"But you know the truth of things. You know my mother's *sight* was real. You know mine is, too. You have seen these monsters are no figment of my imagination. Gothen has suffered from their evil. Not so much as Tassau, but they would have delivered this castle and your head to Gottlieb. A great wrong. But, trust me, it's nothing compared to what they are capable of. Or what they will go on to do..."

Of course, her *sight* had told her no such thing. Not directly, anyway. But her brother, via Henry Cleever, had. Lord Flyblown had intimated the same. Saul was disrupting the natural order of things. And it felt right, felt true. And that was down to her *sight*, she had no doubt.

However, there was no need to muddy the *Markgräf's* waters with detail.

"I do not doubt you. I have seen the remains of the thing you killed, that killed my men, that Gottlieb sold his soul too, rotting to ashes before my very eyes..."

He returned to the desk and took the glass. His hand shook ever so slightly. She didn't know whether the fact a man like the *Markgräf* of Gothen was capable of shaking was a comfort or a concern.

"You are asking me to weaken my lands and risk the lives of my people for others whose great, great grandparents may not yet have been born?"

"Yes," she said.

"I love you, Solace," he said. Which wasn't quite the response she'd been expecting.

He seemed sincere, but it wasn't easy to be certain. Nobody had ever told her they'd loved her before. Not even her father.

Her throat tightened at that unwanted thought, which unnerved her far more than the tremor in Hendrick of Gothen's hand.

It was, of course, nonsense.

He loved her mother, not her. He loved the ghost he painted upon her face.

Still, that was something she could use.

That she might use a man's love, however ill-placed, for her own ends was something that only turned her stomach ever so slightly.

She returned his stare. Would he believe her if she said it in return? No, he wasn't a fool. Not that big a one anyway.

"And you can have me," she sloshed the remaining wine around the glass," for a night or for life. Or you could try to lock me up regardless. But that would be... ill-advised."

His expression suggested he wanted to protest no such idea had ever crossed his mind. His eyes told a different tale.

She placed a finger on his lips to still the lie.

"Or you let me leave and face the demons alone."

She added two more fingers to the first on his lips.

"Three choices, my lord. Which shall it be?"

He kissed her hand. Gently, like you might kiss a baby. She fought off the compulsion to snatch it away and wipe it on her skirts.

"I will leave tomorrow night," she said, removing one finger, "or I will stay one more night and leave with some of your men..." she withdrew a second, "...or I will stay a week and marry you. And leave with all the men you can spare after our wedding night..." she withdrew the third finger.

So all that remained touching his lips was her fist.

*

"Do you intend to leave soon?"

"I go where my mistress leads."

"And if she stays here?"

"She won't."

Hilde pursed her lips and turned her eyes to the horizon. He followed her gaze. A few curls of smoke twisted upwards in the distance to merge with the low-slung clouds. It was far too thick to be chimney smoke. Every day, it seemed, something was burning...

They had climbed to the battlements of the outer walls.

A couple of patrolling soldiers gave them sour looks but hadn't told them to piss off. So they remained, taking in the view; skeletal trees, muted colours, hazy patches of mist softening the edges of an unmoving world. The air was sharper up here, even with little wind to bite. Hilde looked cold. He certainly was. Yet he had no desire to return to the dark, smoky innards of Ettestein. She stood at his side, leaning slightly towards him. He'd noticed he was leaning in towards her, too.

"Haven't you got work to do?" he asked before she could throw any more questions his way.

"Oh, yes. Loads. A maid's work is never done," she said, making no move whatsoever to go back to the castle and start doing any of it.

Bright chestnut eyes looked sideways at him, "Haven't you?"

"Loads..." he nodded.

Getting drunk with Lucien and trying not to let his infernal jokes irritate him too much, trailing around after Solace, wondering how long it would be before she became as mad as the demons they pursued, trying not to let Morlaine unnerve him. Not to mention being humiliated by arrogant aristocratic pricks.

He barely had time to catch his breath.

He resisted the impulse to glance over his shoulder towards Wilhelm's little wooden church and the fifty-six fresh graves behind it.

Yes, he had been very busy.

"You won't get beaten for not doing your job, will you?".

"Not as badly as you got beaten for doing yours today," a mischievous and sparkling grin danced over Hilde's face.

It very nearly made him smile, but he managed to stop himself. He shouldn't be encouraging the girl.

"Why did you become a soldier?"

She asked as if he'd had a choice.

"My father..." his shoulders twitched; the bad one didn't thank him for the gesture, "...the possibility of being anything else was never discussed."

"Did you ever *want* to be anything else?"

Her eyes bore into him. She had a bold regard for a maid.

"No... as a boy... I just wanted to be my father..."

As a boy, he'd been somewhat blind to Old Man Ulrich being a drunken fool.

"And now?"

"Now?"

"Do you still want to be your father?"

His smile was as distant as the mist-softened trees, "As a boy, you want nothing more than to be your father; as a young man, you want nothing less... the irony, of course, is that all men are destined to become their fathers regardless."

She raised an eyebrow.

"The fools with feet of clay that they actually were, rather than the gods we saw through childish eyes."

She stared up at him with large, liquid eyes, "My father was a complete cunt."

He tried not to laugh.

Something about the cast of her face, the turn of her lips, and the sparkle in her eyes demanded a smile in return.

This really wasn't good at all.

He should go. This was not going to end well.

Leave her, go back to your mistress. Only the Night's Road beckons. Only death.

Good advice. Instead, he unbuckled the clasp on his cloak and draped it around Hilde's shoulders.

"You look cold," he said, hoping his words did not sound as lame to her as they did to him.

"Not anymore," she pulled it about her, "but aren't you?"

"Freezing."

"You should let me warm you..."

Her words warmed him immediately. His cheeks, anyway.

"I am not a whore..." when he stared at her, Hilde added, "...neither am I a virgin."

Strangely, the winter's day suddenly did not feel anywhere near so cold.

She tilted her head, smiled another of those smiles he was

struggling not to find endearing and returned her gaze to the horizon, "I just thought you should know that..."

"I..."

"When you leave Ettestein, I want to go with you."

He frowned. He wasn't sure what he'd expected her to say, but that certainly wasn't it.

"That isn't possible."

She nodded, "I thought you'd say that."

"Where we are going... you cannot... 'tis not safe!"

"You said you would go wherever your mistress takes you?"

"Yes."

"So, if 'tis safe for your mistress, why would it not be safe for me?"

Because you are not mad.

"Trust me, it isn't."

"Where are you going?"

"I cannot say."

"How mysterious you are, Ulrich," another of those teasing, flitting smiles briefly lit her face.

"I am not being mysterious. I am just thinking of your safety."

"How can you think of my safety if you are not with me to protect me?"

She blinked rapidly several times.

Is she fluttering her eyelashes at me?

"There is no safety out there..." he nodded towards the horizon where the distant tails of smoke still twisted heavenwards.

"There is no safety anywhere, so I might as well be with

whom I choose to be. Regardless of the danger."

He thought about this. For a moment. Possibly two.

"You want to be with *me?*"

She nodded.

"Why?"

She shrugged.

Which was a little light by way of explanation to his way of thinking.

Then she kissed him.

Only lightly and quickly. When she stepped back, she was blushing.

"I don't understand..." he said. Which possibly wasn't the most romantic of things he could have conjured. Not that he was any kind of expert when it came to romance. Or wanted to be.

Hilde, however, had other ideas.

"Why?" the question seemed to bear repeating.

She looked serious, her lips tightening. He thought she would give a deep and reasoned explanation as to why she wanted to be with him. Instead, she shrugged, "Dunno..."

"You barely know me?"

"No. I don't..." her hand ran fleetingly down his; despite the leather gloves he wore, his skin tingled, "...'tis rather strange, don't you think?"

"Women are peculiar."

She laughed. He smiled, mostly to cover the fact he hadn't been speaking in jest.

"What if I don't like you?"

She laughed again. He had to confess he found it a fetching sound, "I've seen the way you look at me..."

As far as he could remember, he'd been doing his absolute best not to look at her.

He turned and rested his back against the battlements. Smoke rose from the castle's chimneys and those of the village within the walls, hazing the air and scenting it with woodsmoke. Unlike the smoke souring the horizon, these were comforting things. Signs of life, civilisation, security,

"You cannot come with us," he said, refusing her gaze.

She leaned in towards him, shoulder touching his arm, "Then I will follow you."

He bit his bottom lip. What kind of madness was this? Did she have some sickness of the heart or mind? Was she playing a game? He shook his head. No matter what, she could not come with them.

"Where are you going?"

Solace would not approve of telling a serving maid anything of their plans. Still, he doubted Hilde was a spy of the Red Company.

"Magdeburg."

"And what will you do in Magdeburg?"

Her eyes were wide, beguiling, full of promises. He kept his own on the grey, expressionless bulk of Ettestein upon its grim crag.

"Die, most likely."

"You go to help the city fight against the Emperor?"

"No... my lady has... other enemies."

"Then they are my enemies, too."

His head snapped around, "No!"

Her hand slipped into his, regardless.

"They are now..."

Chapter Thirteen

"You offered him... *what?!*"

Morlaine generally displayed even less emotion than Hendrick, *Markgräf* of Gothen, but the demon's eyes widened and back straightened. She didn't look at Renard or Lucien, though there would no doubt be plenty to see there, too.

"A night. With me. If I can't have an army for my vows, I'll take as many men-at-arms as I can get for my..." now she did glance at Renard, and she let the words fade. She didn't need to finish the sentence. Everybody knew what she was offering.

Renard looked even more glum and miserable than he usually did. In fact, he'd been looking even more glum and miserable all evening. She wasn't sure if that was due to his newly bruised face or something else but had no intention of asking. She had problems of her own.

"Solace, you can't..." Morlaine shook her head.

"Why not? You do," she dropped her voice, "for a room in Madriel, for blood..."

"That is not the same."

"'tis not? Why?"

"Do not sell yourself so cheaply. Not-"

"My virginity? A valuable commodity, no? I am a woman,

Morlaine, I have nothing else to sell but my Mother's silver. And that will not buy me enough men-at-arms to fight the Red Company."

Renard shifted uncomfortably. He might have been blushing. Lucien remained stony-faced and silent.

"It is worth more than that, Solace."

"Really? How much did you get for yours?" the words came out more sharply than intended. Morlaine, however, did not react.

"Nothing. It was taken from me. I was raped. I can't say how many times, I think I passed out after the first dozen or so. It was the last night of my life…"

Morlaine talked little of her past. Saul formed part of it and that she'd once been no different than that monster, or so the demon claimed, but she'd said little else. She wished the vampire had kept it that way.

They sat around the table in her rooms. The hour was late; her eyes hung heavy. She had not been sleeping well.

"Then it would seem I have a better deal…"

Morlaine said no more.

"Good," she nodded, "we are decided. We will leave tomorrow, the day after, or in a week, depending on what the *Markgräf's* answer is."

Three unblinking faces stared back at her. None of them appeared convinced anything was decided.

Morlaine rose first; she turned her back and walked off to her room.

The demon's discontent lingered in her silent wake.

"My lady-"

"Do you wish to tell me how you lost your virginity, too?"

"Mine was to a cobbler's wife," Lucien said before the red-faced Renard could get his tongue to work.

"Really?"

"I got the shoes repaired, but didn't get so much as a pfennig for my virginity..." the mercenary pursed his lips and wrinkled his nose, "...though as the cobbler didn't know I was fucking his wife while he repaired my shoes, I suppose I shouldn't grumble..."

"Well-"

"Actually, they were my Pa's shoes. I was just running an errand..." a crooked smile broke out beneath the long moustaches, "...great value for money when you think about it..."

Her eyes moved to Renard.

"Is there anything you want to add to this conversation, Ulrich?"

He quickly shook his head.

"Excellent," she pushed herself to her feet, "Be ready to leave tomorrow on the off chance I am not so highly valued by the *Markgräf*."

"And if the *Markgräf* continues to refuse to let you go..." Lucien circled a hand in the air, "...because of these *brigands*...?"

"He will keep his word."

Lucien looked like he had a few things to say about the words of noblemen, but she was in no mood to hear them. In truth, she had her own concerns about what the *Markgräf* might do. She'd uncorked a bottle without having any clear idea about what would come out of it. But what was done was done. What other choice did she have?

You need an army to fight an army...

"Goodnight, gentlemen."

She headed for her room, head held high, hoping to affect the air of a confident woman who knew what she was doing rather than a child running away because she didn't have any more answers.

Morlaine returned before she reached the door to her own room.

The demon was carrying her gear, a sword strapped to her thigh once more.

"It is time I left."

"Where are you going?" she demanded.

"If Saul is going to Magdeburg, so am I."

"He won't be there until May."

"In the meantime, there are other ways to find Saul. I will continue searching for the man who loves songbirds too much, for one."

The vampire Morlaine had been searching for when she found them in The Wolf's Tower, the one the *sight* had whispered Morlaine believed might know how to find the Red Company. And that knowledge had persuaded Morlaine to take them with her to Madriel.

"Then we should travel together."

"I walk the Night's Road alone, Solace. I always have. I always will. Some of the things you are doing, plan to do, I want no part of."

She didn't ask which, even though there were a few to choose from.

"Very well, thank you for your help."

"My lady..." Renard shot to his feet. Lucien remained

sitting; eyes fixed on Morlaine.

"We all walk our own path. Sometimes we share it, sometimes we don't..." her gaze flicked across the two men, "...I've told you before, neither of you have to walk mine."

Morlaine paused on the way to the door.

"Solace, speaking as someone who lost their humanity a long, long time ago, you should be very careful about the choices you make over the coming days, weeks, months... vengeance is a greedy god. Once it has its claws in your soul..."

"Your counsel is always welcome, Morlaine..."

Something that wasn't quite a smile twisted the demon's perfect features, then she continued to the door. She offered a nod towards Renard and Lucien before leaving.

"My lady..." Renard, still on his feet, said, "...we need her."

"All I need is an army, Ulrich. I will do whatever I need to get one..."

It was a poor answer, but it was all she had. Part of her wanted to run after Morlaine and beg her to stay. The demon was worth more than Ettestein's entire garrison. But she would not beg her any more than she would waver from what needed to be done. Be it selling her virginity or cutting the toad Bulcher into strips.

And to hell with the consequences.

She thought Lucien would go after Morlaine while Renard sat down and stayed with her.

As with many things, she was wrong.

*

"Morlaine, wait!"

He expected the demon to ignore him, to walk into the thickest patch of shadow at the end of the corridor and disappear.

Instead, she stopped, looked over her shoulder, and waited for him to catch up.

Which meant he had to think of something to say.

He hadn't considered that when he'd hurried from their rooms. Solace hadn't called him back, and Lucien hadn't followed him. He wasn't sure why he'd run after the demon.

They were not friends, after all.

She was a demon. An abomination before God. A fiend that couldn't walk in the sun. A creature that drank human blood. The same as Saul the Bloodless, Alms, Cleever, Jarl, Wendel and the other vampires of the Red Company. A monster.

A monster who had saved his life. And Solace's.

Which made his feelings about her... less straightforward.

In the end, he used the same words that had worked so well on Solace.

"We need you."

"I know you do."

"You do? Then..."

Morlaine placed her bag on the floor, "If I can find Saul before he gets to Magdeburg, I can end this before it begins..."

"She has seen him... there."

"The road I have walked is dark. It still is. But the one Solace is walking... I fear is darker still."

"What happened to her-"

"I know. I understand. It was terrible. And it is in such

burnt ground that hatred and vengeance thrive. These things are a crucible in which one's soul can be transformed into something... less... I have seen it in others... and in myself. I cannot bear to watch it again..."

Something flashed across the demon's face he couldn't remember seeing before, something uncertain, frightened, tortured, something... almost... *human?*

She placed a hand on his arm. As when Hilde touched him earlier, the flesh beneath tingled, but this time with cold rather than heat.

"You are her only chance, Ulrich. You know that, don't you?"

"Me?"

The look on his face was enough for a rare smile to chase away whatever had contorted Morlaine's normally flawless features.

"You have no desire for vengeance, do you?"

He resisted the temptation to look over his shoulder before shaking his head.

"Then you can still save her."

"Save her from...?"

"Herself."

It was his turn to smile, "Someone once told me if I saved her, I would save myself."

Her fingers remained on his arm, his good one, and gently she squeezed.

"That is what love can do, even when all else fails, if that still holds... then hope remains."

"Love?"

The squeeze tightened further. Then her fingers sprang

open.

"If you can find a way to persuade her to stop this, do it. If you can't, try to help her keep hold of her humanity. It is an easier thing to misplace than you might think."

"I will... but what do you mean about love?"

The demon scooped up her bag, "I think you need to work that one out for yourself."

When she turned to go, he called after her, "What about Styx?"

"What about him?"

"You can't carry him over the wall..." when she continued to stare at him, he added, "...can you?"

She puckered her lips, "It would be tricky."

"And they won't open the gates to let you out. Not at this hour."

"You've seen how persuasive I can be, Ulrich..."

That made him shuffle his feet.

A rare laugh escaped her.

"You're not-"

"No, I'm not going to hurt anyone."

"Oh."

"Look after Styx; I'll collect him when you get to Magdeburg."

He frowned, "So, we will see you again?"

"I don't have the *sight*, but I think so. I just can't be with you for a while. If Solace gets her army, even a small one, I can't ride with you. The three of you knowing my true nature is a risk and one I rarely take; letting more know would be folly. Besides, people are asking questions about me here. I need to go."

Morlaine stepped back towards him, adding, "I want to stop Saul on my own and free you all from Solace's mad quest. But if I can't..."

"I understand."

"And while I am trying to stop Saul..." she raised a finger in his direction, "...you must try and stop her."

"If I save her, I save myself..."

"All things are possible," the demon nodded.

Then walked down the shadow-choked corridor.

He stood and watched her till she was gone.

Once she was, he felt strangely alone.

Chapter Fourteen

The *Markgräf's* message said to meet him atop The Grace Tower at noon. She was to come alone.

"What if-"

She'd waved Renard's protests away, "We are in his castle; we will not be able to fight our way out. I will go."

Renard had looked unhappier than usual, Lucien remained as uncommonly quiet as he had since Morlaine left.

"Where would you normally be at noon?" she'd asked.

"Sword practice," Renard had told her, touching his bruised lip.

"Act as you have every day. But ensure you have everything you'd want to take with us at hand. In case we must leave in a hurry."

Renard had nodded his understanding. A moment later, Lucien did the same.

"Perhaps we should cut the sword practice short to check on the horses...?" the mercenary suggested. She'd agreed.

"If you notice anything outside the ordinary, more attention from the *Markgräf's* men than you normally enjoy, for instance, you can take it the outcome of my negotiations have been... particularly unfruitful."

"And we should come and find you?"

"I assume I will retain the liberty of Ettestein regardless; just be prepared to get us out of here. By whatever means necessary. Understood?"

Renard nodded again; Lucien had muttered something about how escaping the castle would be much easier if Morlaine was still with them.

"But she isn't, is she? She made her choice. I will make mine," she'd said, before retreating to her room to fidget the morning hours away.

When she arrived atop the Grace Tower at noon, only a sharp wind and smeary silver-grey sky awaited her.

Not an auspicious sign.

She paced to keep warm, but her feet soon returned her to the spot where she'd killed Wendel. And her fingers to the leather pouch hanging between her breasts.

There was nothing much to feel through the leather. The finger bones had long since turned to dust, like the rest of Wendel's corpse. Only fine grey powder remained. She wouldn't be surprised if one day that was gone, too, evaporated like morning dew.

Still, she could feel the demon-ash inside when she pinched the leather. One day, a finger of all the Red Company's demons would reside in that pouch. All reduced to fine, grey dust like the monsters she'd cut them from.

The thought gave her comfort. It was but a drop within the emptiness inside her, but it was something. And she needed to have *something*. Whatever Morlaine feared for her soul. She didn't care how hungry Vengeance was. Wendel had been right about one thing: she would turn the Empire to dirt to sate that hunger and fill that emptiness.

What else was there?

To spend the rest of her life listening to the screams echoing in that vast, bleak emptiness that now resided inside her?

She resisted leaning over the battlements to gawp at the rocks below. Given all the hours she'd spent up here, she knew them well enough now.

Instead, her eyes slid to a nearby wood, reduced to bones by the winter's breath. How far had Morlaine managed to get without a horse? Had she been able to find shelter from the daylight? Had she-

Behind her, a door opened. Old hinges creaked.

She pushed Morlaine from her mind.

Her hands rested on the battlement; on either side of the spot Wendel's ruined hand had slipped over the precipice, and the monster had tumbled to its doom.

She thought her heart was beating as hard now as it did then.

Footsteps crossed the roof.

Just one set.

The *Markgräf* hadn't brought soldiers with him then. Most women would no doubt consider that promising...

She sucked in a breath of sharp, winter air, steeled herself and turned to discover whether she was going to get the men-at-arms she needed. And if she was going to lose her virginity to Hendrick, *Markgräf* of Gothen, in the process.

"Lebrecht...?"

"My lady."

She frowned, "I was expecting your father. Has there been a change of plan?"

The young nobleman offered a twitch of a smile, "Please accept my apology for the subterfuge."

"Subterfuge?"

"My father did not send for you. He will tonight. Currently, he is... making arrangements."

"I see, I-"

"Excuse me, my lady, but I must speak bluntly. Time is short."

"Time is a precious commodity; we never get it back."

Lebrecht took a step forward, towering over her.

"My father's plans... will not be to your liking."

Lebrecht's blue eyes moved from hers to the forest of towers, turrets and spires soaring around them. Some even higher than the Grace Tower.

He fixed his gaze on the tallest, topped with a conical roof.

"The Sparrow's Tower, the highest point in Ettestein Castle," he said.

"What of it?"

"Father instructed me to prepare it..." his eyes slid back to her from the Sparrow's Tower, "...for your stay with us. He told me to make it as comfortable as possible for you."

"I am getting new rooms...?" her hand slipped beneath her cloak to where her long dagger rested.

"The Sparrow's Tower is where Ettestein houses its prisoners. The important ones the *Markgräf* of the day would rather not expire in the dungeons. It has not been used for some time... from tomorrow, Father plans it will be."

Her fingers tightened around the dagger.

"You are telling me this because...?"

"Because I want no part of it."

"And what has your father told you of his reasoning?"

A thin, distant smile crossed the young man's face, "Because he loves you."

"That-"

Lebrecht stepped forward and grabbed her wrist.

"Leave your blade where it is, my lady. I have seen what you can do with it."

She thought about kicking out at his groin. She'd heard that deterred men from touching you most effectively. Instead, she let go of the dagger's hilt and allowed Lebrecht to pull her hand into the daylight.

He nodded but didn't let go.

"My father has told me everything. He thinks he loves you because you look like your mother. A woman he once loved. You have offered to marry him in exchange for our men so you can pursue the demons who destroyed your home..."

"But he will not give me the men I need, will he?"

Lebrecht shook his head, "He cannot weaken Gothen further than Gottlieb already has. And he fears you would never return, even if you destroy your enemies."

"If I give my word, I will honour it."

"Perhaps. But what if your quest takes years to fulfil? Will my father still be alive when you return? Will he still be the same man? Will you still be the same woman? He is tormented and torn. His head cannot give you what you want; his heart will not let you go."

"I had not fancied your father a man to allow his heart to win..."

Lebrecht's grip on her wrist tightened, and he pulled her

close to him.

"How can you do this? You do not love him?"

"Love?! I am a Princess of the Empire. An asset for my father to trade. I never expected to marry for love!"

Though I did once hope...

She tried to yank her hand free, but Lebrecht's grip was too firm. Perhaps she would need to use her knee after all.

"I doubt you expected to give yourself to an old man for a few dozen men-at-arms either!"

"I don't need your approval."

"No, you need my help!"

She tugged away from him again. This time he released her, forcing her to take several steps backwards to avoid the indignity of landing on her arse at his feet.

"Why would you help me?"

"Because if my father locks you in the Sparrow's Tower, it will drive him mad."

"You think so?"

Lebrecht bit his lip. He was trembling, not from the cold either.

"He is a good man. But love... it has a dark side too."

"And what do you know of that?"

"I saw what my mother's death did to him. I've heard what your mother's rejection did to him. I can see what locking you in a tower and forcing himself upon you will do to him. You do not love him. You will not love him. But by making you his prisoner, you will end up hating him, and that will destroy him. I have begged him to let you leave, but he cannot. 'tis like some dread sickness has gripped both his heart and mind. You have offered him the chance to regain what he lost decades ago. You have opened a box long since locked and cast aside. And you have released all its miseries and furies into the world."

When Lebrecht came towards her again, she retreated until her back pressed against the stone battlements of the Grace Tower.

From which Wendel had fallen...

"What do you intend to do, my lord?"

"Intend?"

"You sound like a man with... *intention?*"

Eyes hooded and cloudy, he looked down at her, close enough for his steaming breath to moisten her skin. He pulled off his right glove.

"My intention is to ensure my father is not driven mad... is not destroyed... by the furies you have released..." he peeled off his other glove and stuffed them both in his belt, "...the difficulty is in choosing the best way to seal the box you so wilfully and selfishly opened."

"I am prepared to give your father everything he wants. To make him happy. For the rest of his life. That is neither wilful nor selfish."

"And all he has to do in return is leave his home and lands defenceless in a war-torn world, where my cousin wishes to seize our *Markgräfschaft* from us, where an imperial army is heading for Magdeburg, where brigands and mercenaries roam, plundering, burning and raping at will," Lebrecht sneered in her face, "What fucking manner of deal is that?"

"The best one I can give him. If a deal not to his liking is offered to an honourable man, he walks away from it," she sneered right back, "he doesn't lock the woman offering it up in a tower, tie her to a bed and rape her!"

The retort of Lebrecht's hand on her face sent a startled crow flapping and squawking skywards from the other side of the Grace Tower.

"I'm sorry, I must have misunderstood. Is he going to lock me in his tower, treat me like a princess and try to win my heart with sweetmeats and sugar fancies then?"

Lebrecht's lip curled back in a snarl. Suddenly, he wasn't half so handsome. In fact, she half expected his next blow to be with his fist rather than his palm.

She stuck out her chin, daring him.

"My father," he finally managed, "is not a monster."

"We all have a monster inside us. And we don't all need to become a demon for that monster to escape. All the horrors of this war should tell you that. I'm sure a lot of the killers, rapists and thieves tearing the Empire apart were *good* men once..."

"If you had never come here, he wouldn't be doing this."

"So, 'tis my fault? As I recall..." she jabbed a finger into his chest, "...you brought me here. If you'd let us go like I asked, your father would never have... opened that box."

"If I had but known..."

"I didn't know he loved my mother any more than you did."

"No, but you have played upon it. Using his long-broken heart to gain the men of Gothen to your damn cause."

"My cause is worth more than any broken heart. You've seen what these monsters can do. You should thank God only one of them came to Ettestein; if it had been the whole

Red Company, you'd be as dead as everyone in Tassau!"

She neglected to mention more than one demon *had* come to Ettestein, and they'd come because of her. She doubted either fact would placate the young man's anger.

They stood there, virtually nose to nose, panting steaming breath over each other. She had the strangest notion Lebrecht couldn't decide if he wanted to kill her or kiss her.

After what seemed like an eternity, a deep, almost animal, growl gurgled in the depths of Lebrecht's throat, and he took two sharp steps away from her. As if the part of him that wanted to kill her had been yanked back like a rabid dog on a chain.

"Come with me," he said, half turning away as if nothing remained to discuss.

"What are you going to do?"

"Do? Get you out of my home before you destroy it. What else can I do?"

She swept a hand about the deserted roof of the Grace Tower, the wind tugging at her hair.

"Why did you need to see me up here?"

"There are no ears up here."

"Ettestein has many quiet corners. Why here? Where I killed Wendel?"

"'tis as good as anywhere..." he started walking back towards the door, refusing to meet her eye.

She kept her feet where they were.

"You thought about killing me, didn't you?"

He stopped and looked over his shoulder.

"My father isn't a monster, neither am I."

"Not all men who do murder start their day as a monster,

my lord."

Slowly, he turned back to face her, "The thought crossed my mind. The easy solution. Killing a man can haunt the soul. Even a demon. Maybe enough to make you kill yourself the same way you killed him, to be free of the pain..."

"My men would not have believed that. Neither would your father."

"Possibly. But, as I am not going to kill you, we will never know."

"What made you change your mind?"

"Your engaging personality."

She almost smiled. He looked and sounded more like the Lebrecht she knew. But how much could you ever know about someone? The monsters always lurked in the shadows, and if you ever cracked open a box with something inside they liked...

She nodded and followed him, pushing aside any thoughts about all the boxes she had opened in the last year...

*

Styx appeared pleased to see him.

The brute snorted, snarled, and tried to bite him, which was as close to a friendly greeting as anyone save Morlaine got from the foul-tempered beast.

The stable lad didn't question them when they told him they wanted to rub down their horses. He just looked relieved and scampered off. He got the distinct impression caring for Styx was not the boy's favourite job.

Lucien's mount whinnied and rubbed her head against

the mercenary, who laughed and whispered in her ear. The idiot's inexplicable popularity with females apparently extended to the equine variety, too.

His horse, whom he'd named Plodder during their journey along the Night's Road from Madriel, didn't pay him any heed. He didn't take it personally; the gelding was probably too busy concentrating on not dropping dead to notice him.

They had decided to stick to their normal routine, heading to the log pile for their sword practice before Solace went to see the *Markgräf*. Thankfully, no one else had taken a leaf from Joachim's book and joined them so they could have a go at kicking the shit out of a one-armed cripple too.

They brought as much of their gear as they thought they could without provoking suspicion, but if things went badly with the *Markgräf*, they would leave a fair bit behind.

After thirty minutes of sword clattering and curses for the benefit of anyone who might be watching them, they headed for the stables.

Of course, someone was keeping an eye on him.

"Where you off to?" Hilde asked as they made for the stables as casually as two men toying with the possibility of scarpering could.

She greeted them with rosy cheeks, a dazzling smile, and a large basket with nothing in it.

"Looking for somewhere to hide from all the women who throw themselves at my feet begging for a kiss..." Lucien boomed without breaking stride, "...it gets surprisingly tiresome after a while."

"I can imagine," Hilde fell in step. She winked, "So, where *are* you going?"

"To check on our horses," Lucien told her, "make sure none of you lot has eaten them."

"We're not quite that low on food... yet."

"Where are *you* going?" Lucien asked.

"To help you check on your horses."

Lucien exchanged a glance with him. He offered a shrug. He'd been trying to get rid of the girl for days with ever-decreasing success. Part of him was even glad to see her. The stupid, wilful, selfish part, admittedly, but he couldn't deny she was growing on him. As if he didn't have enough problems.

They'd skirted the village and made for the stable buildings on the far side. Few people were about making the most of the brief, watery daylight. They did see Pastor Wilhelm, who quickly scampered off without acknowledging them. For a man who'd told all and sundry Ulrich Renard was the greatest swordsman in Europe and he'd saved his little church from Imperial soldiers, the old preacher had never shown much in the way of gratitude.

So, something to be thankful for, at least.

"Haven't you got work to do, girl?" Lucien growled at Hilde.

"Yes, lots," she nodded and carried on at their side.

He could have already told the mercenary he'd tried that line without success. As Hilde believed she was leaving Ettestein shortly, she probably wasn't giving her chores the priority they deserved.

Despite considering several ways to tell her to bugger off (some more polite than others), in the end, he uttered none of them. By the time they reached the stables, he'd convinced himself this was because he knew very well she'd ignore all of them and come along regardless, rather than the possibility he wanted her to.

"He's a beauty," she said when she clapped eyes on Styx. "Is he yours?"

"No, that one's mine," he nodded at Plodder.

"Oh..."

They busied themselves with the horses without making it look too obvious they were preparing to leave while Hilde cast her basket aside and sat on a bale of hay to watch them.

"You're preparing to leave, aren't you?"

He glanced at Lucien, who gave him a *you-can-handle-this-one* look and continued brushing down his mount.

"We await our lady's instruction... we need to be ready for every eventuality. 'tis the soldier's way."

"Be prepared. First rule of soldiering, that..." Lucien bobbed up to nod approvingly from behind his horse's arse.

"Why-"

"Can you find us some oats for the horses," Lucien cut Hilde off, "that lad seems to have made himself scarce."

Hilde puckered her lips, knowing full well the request was more for the sake of getting rid of her than the horse's benefit. Still, she slid off the hay bale and went off without complaint.

"That girl really likes you," Lucien smirked once she was out of earshot.

"Don't know what life has brought her, but that wouldn't be her best choice."

"No? You're a good man, Ulrich. I think she's smart enough to know there aren't too many of those left in this world of ours."

He let the compliment slide off him, "Good or not, I will be dead soon. If she stays too close to me, she'll likely end up the same way."

Lucien rested an arm across his mount's flank as he peered over at him, "None of us know what tomorrow will bring. So, make the most of today. Every moment is a long time coming, and a long time gone. Drink, sing, make merry... and don't look a gift horse in the mouth. Especially a pretty one."

"You have a simple worldview, don't you?"

"I'm a simple man. I leave the complicated stuff to the lords and bishops. A strong beer, a lovely lass and something that makes you laugh so much you want to piss. If you get all those things in one day..." he shrugged, "...really, what more do you want?"

The sound of approaching feet prevented any critique of Lucien's horseshit philosophy.

"My lady..." he stepped away from Plodder as Solace rushed in, cheeks flushed red from the cold. His words dried as *Markgräf* Lebrecht followed her inside.

"We are leaving," she announced.

"When?" Lucien asked, eyeing Lebrecht.

"Within the hour would be ideal," Lebrecht answered for her, "before sunset is essential."

When Lucien raised a questioning eyebrow, Solace explained, "My lord is kindly helping us leave Ettestein."

"My father has forbidden you leaving Ettestein; you won't get through the gates without my help."

"The *Markgräf*...?" he asked quietly.

"Is busy preparing the highest tower in the castle for my comfort. He envisages me being his guest there for some considerable time," Solace said.

"For now, you are all free to move around Ettestein," Lebrecht cast an eye across the three of them, "but once he has told Lady Solace of his decision this evening..."

"We are ready to leave?" she asked him.

"We have our weapons, shot, and some provisions and clothing. The minimum we need," he said.

"But our bed rolls and the remainder of our food would make for an easier journey," Lucien offered.

"'tis not long from here to Magdeburg..." Solace said, as much to herself as them.

"You could be there by tomorrow evening if you rode hard and late..." Lebrecht said, "...and you don't run into trouble."

"I'm loath to give up the rest of our gear," Solace said, "but we need to be out of here. Returning to our rooms for it might draw attention and reveal we are leaving."

"I can get them for you."

Hilde stood behind them, a bucket of oats in hand.

"Who are you?" Solace frowned as she turned to face the maid.

"I'm Hilde," she shook the bucket, "I'm good at fetching and carrying. Do it all the time. If any of the guards notice me, it'll only be to ogle my tits."

He filled the awkward silence with a cough before offering, "She's a friend... erm... of mine..."

Chapter Fifteen

"You trust this girl?" she demanded.

It wasn't the first time she'd asked the question, but it earned her a different answer on the third or fourth time of asking.

"Do you trust *Markgräf* Lebrecht, my lady?"

On balance, she'd preferred the mumbled and ever so slightly unconvincing "yes," she'd received before.

"I don't see what he has to gain by lying; besides, I think he seriously considered killing me earlier..."

Renard frowned, "And that makes you trust him?"

"You have to go with your instincts."

"I suppose, my lady."

"Your instinct is to trust this Hilde girl?"

"I don't see what she has to gain by lying either."

"Other than a reward from the *Markgräf* for betraying our intentions to leave?"

"Then you should not have let her go."

"We need those provisions. And I am prepared to trust your judgement."

Renard's face crumpled deeper into its mask of doubt and concern.

"What do you think?" she asked Lucien, leaning against a wooden pillar doing something to his blackened teeth with a piece of straw.

"Never trust a woman. Contrary, dishonourable, double-crossing minxes the lot of em. As likely to sell your soul for a pretty ribbon or a glass of cheap wine as they are to slap your face in return for a harmless fondle of their arse," he grinned, "no offence intended, my lady."

"None taken."

They sat in silence, nostrils serenaded by horse sweat and dung, ears teased by the patter of rain on the roof while they waited for Hilde. Lebrecht had gone to gather a few men he trusted to escort them out of Ettestein. He'd assured her riding alone with them would only raise suspicion.

It seemed she had little choice but to trust them. The alternative would be to saddle up and try and trick, cajole, or fight their way past the guards on the Outer Gates.

She just hated having to rely on other people.

Lebrecht, she at least knew. He'd fought at her side and had no reason to betray them. If he wanted to honour his father's wishes, he only needed to do nothing. If he wanted her dead to save his father, he could have thrown her off The Grace Tower. He hadn't, so she would trust him.

But this girl, Hilde?

Something about her gnawed, but she couldn't put her finger on it. Perhaps it was the way she looked at Renard. Perhaps it was the way he looked at her. Perhaps...

Not that any of that mattered to her. Renard was her retainer, not her slave. She didn't own his heart and had no right to tell him where he could put his affections.

If he wanted to give it to half-witted scullery maids with

overdeveloped chests, that was fine with her.

Wasn't it?

She slid off the bale she was sitting next to Renard on and moved to Lucien's side. Putting her back to Renard, she asked, "What do you know of this girl, Hilde?"

"She's taken a shine to young Ulrich, so, I suspect, poor eyesight and questionable judgement..."

"Do you ever-"

"We can trust her," the familiar grin faded from the mercenary's lips, "she isn't going to betray us to the *Markgräf's* men. Lucien Kazmierczak is famed from-"

The sound of a door creaking open stilled Lucien's words.

Despite his assurances, Lucien still put one shoulder in front of hers and a hand on his sword's pommel.

Hilde appeared, basket filled and covered by a blanket.

"You've got a lot of gear," she dropped it at Renard's feet as he slid off the haybale.

"Were you seen?" she demanded, pushing past Lucien.

"Schiff the Stiff whistled at me," Hilde shrugged, wiping hands on her apron, "but he always does. He thinks it's funny. Does it to all the maids."

"Nobody else?"

"No..." Hilde's grin faded as she performed a rudimentary curtsey, "...Ma'am."

She stared at the girl.

What was it about her? Whatever it was, it made her skin itch like sleeping in a dog blanket.

Still, it didn't matter. She'd brought their gear, hadn't betrayed them, and would soon, like the rest of Ettestein, be left far behind them.

"Thank you, Hilde, we appreciate your help. I hope it doesn't cause you any trouble later."

"Oh, no, it won't cause me any trouble, my lady," Hilde shook her head, "as I'll be leaving with you."

She looked at Renard.

"I've told her she can't. Several times. I don't think she's good at listening."

"There's nothing wrong with my ears!"

"Well, Hilde. I'm telling you the same thing. You can't. 'tis far too dangerous. And we have no need of you."

"Heard your maid left. I'm a good maid."

"No."

Hilde's smile faded as her chin went up.

"Yes, I am... my lady."

"Is that so?"

"Yes. If you don't take me with you, I'll go straight to the *Markgräf* and let him know what you're planning," she glanced at Lucien, "perhaps he'll give me a pretty ribbon or some cheap wine for that bit of gossip..."

"Or I could slit your throat and leave you under the hay pile?"

"You're not that kind of woman, my lady," Hilde replied, not backing down a fraction.

"Trust me, Hilde, you have no idea what I'm capable of. In truth, I don't have much of an idea either these days..." she took a step towards her, "...shall we find out?"

"My lady," Renard stepped between them, "I've told her no, I've told her 'tis too dangerous. She won't listen. 'tis her choice and not worth the fight to refuse her."

She glared at Renard, then Hilde and then, for no other

reason than completeness, Lucien, too. Then threw up her hands and whirled away, "I need an army and get a bloody serving girl. How marvellous!"

"I can fight. I can do all sorts of useful things!" Hilde beamed at them.

"I already know how to cook and sew," Lucien said before hoisting an eyebrow, "that only leaves-"

"Enough!" she pointed at Hilde, "You cause me one single problem..."

"I won't, my lady," she said. Then grabbed Renard's hand. Seemingly much to his surprise.

She'd lost Morlaine, she'd lost the men-at-arms she'd hoped the *Markgräf* of Gothen would give her, and all she'd gained in her quest to destroy the Red Company, was a bloody serving girl, and by the way she looked at Renard, a lovestruck one.

She resisted the urge to rap knuckles against her forehead.

Instead, she took several deep breaths of horse-tainted air to calm herself.

Lebrecht chose that moment to return, "Saddle up; we are leaving in ten minutes."

Outside, sounds of iron clattering on stone broke the silence as men led horses from other parts of the stable complex onto the courtyard.

"Good," she just about managed not to spit.

Lebrecht eyed Hilde.

"Who's she?" he asked.

"My new maid."

"Where did the old one go?"

"She decided to leave before anyone tried to burn her at the stake."

"Oh..."

She turned her back and busied herself saddling Styx. The huge stallion eyed her curiously but didn't make a fuss.

"Let me help you with that," Lebrecht said.

Styx tossed his head and whinnied.

"Best I do it, he's temperamental."

"I-"

"I said I can manage; I will see you in the yard, my lord."

"Of course," Lebrecht nodded and hurried outside to where his men were preparing their horses.

"They could be taking us off to the woods to do away with us," Lucien cheerfully offered.

"No," she said, concentrating on buckling Styx's saddle once she'd got it over his huge back.

She knew no such thing. The *sight* was silent on Lebrecht's intentions, leaving her to rely on her more mundane instincts.

He could have killed her atop The Grace Tower if he'd simply wanted rid of her. Why involve others in murder when he could have done the deed quietly and without witnesses?

Of course, a man may have less qualms about giving an order than dirtying his own hands.

After several fumbles, Lucien appeared at her side and started buckling the saddle properly.

Her hands, she noticed, were shaking too much for the task.

After a moment, she stepped away and let the mercenary do it.

Renard had taken it upon himself to give Hilde her mare. It made sense, as it was spare now Morlaine wasn't with them, but it still rankled enough for her to have to force herself not to storm over and demand to know what he thought he was doing.

As she watched, the pair laughed, Hilde bright-eyed and loud, Renard more reserved but almost as bright-eyed. She might have accused him of being happy if she didn't know him better.

"I'll be outside," she barked at Lucien, stomping away and wrapping her cloak about her.

She'd changed into her travelling clothes while they'd waited for Lebrecht. None of the soldiers busying themselves with their mounts paid her any heed. Probably thought she was one of the stable lads.

She pulled up her hood against the drizzle and rested her back against the stable wall.

Half a dozen men were preparing horses with Lebrecht.

The young nobleman held up three fingers.

Presumably, he meant three minutes till they left. She nodded.

She recognised a couple of the men from the fight against Gottlieb. Which meant nothing. They weren't her men, and she would never be the Mistress of Ettestein Castle.

She peered through the thickening murk towards the grey bulk of the fortress, perched above them on its crag.

What would it have been like?

Her eyes found the Sparrow's Tower.

Would it be a worse fate than whatever awaited her in Magdeburg, whatever awaited her at the far end of the Night's Road. Not worse. But it would likely take a lot longer to kill her.

Lucien and Renard led the horses out. Hilde followed with the rest of their gear. Making herself useful. Now nice!

She glowered at the girl. Then told herself to stop being stupid and petty. Which did nothing to stop her feeling stupid and petty.

Hilde wore an apron over her dress and a woollen shawl around her shoulders. The rain would soak the wool within minutes. She'd likely freeze to death overnight.

Part of her thought it'd serve the silly girl right for forcing herself upon her.

Renard grinned at something Hilde said.

Still looking happy.

She muttered under her breath, then went to Styx, now fitted with her saddlebags.

She found her spare travelling cloak and took it to the girl.

"Wear this; you'll catch your death riding in this weather dressed like that."

"Thank you, Ma'am," Hilde found another clumsy curtsey to go with her smile. She smiled a lot. Should you trust people who smile too much? She wasn't at all sure.

"You can ride, can't you?"

"Yes, Ma'am. I grew up on a farm. We had horses..." the smile faded, "...before the war took em. And everything else..."

Hilde wasn't any older than her and would likely struggle to remember the world before the war came.

The girl took the cloak. Renard helped her into it.

She bit her lip as she watched. And her tongue.

"Good... How much has Ulrich told you about what we are doing?"

"Just that 'tis dangerous and I should stay here."

"'tis true. The chances are we will die. By coming with us..." she glanced at the castle again, "...you should stay here."

"I have made my choice, Ma'am. Nothing's gonna change it."

She almost asked why. But she didn't have to. The way the girl looked at Renard was sufficiently eloquent.

Will I ever look at anybody like that?

That didn't seem likely. And not any concern.

"Stay close to me; do as I say," she said to both of them.

Then she hurried away and climbed into Styx's saddle.

Now Lebrecht's men did notice her. A horse like Styx demanded attention. And a strip of a girl perched on his high back even more so.

She stuck her chin up, fixed her eyes straight ahead and desperately tried to look like she belonged atop a warhorse. For his part, Styx tossed his sable black mane and whinnied a couple of times but kept his temper in check. Landing arse first in the puddles would have done little to improve her mood.

"These men know they're disobeying your father's orders?" she asked Lebrecht out of the corner of her mouth when he came alongside.

"They will follow my orders; that's all that matters," he said, patting his own horse's neck to soothe the animal as

Styx took exception to the company.

"And the ones at the gates?"

"We shall soon find out, shan't we, my lady…"

His eyes held hers, then he wheeled away and shouted for them to follow.

Lucien came alongside, Renard and Hilde behind, followed by Lebrecht's men.

"Looks like it's going to piss down all night," Lucien said, eyeing the leaden sky.

She focused on Lebrecht's back.

As they passed through the village and down towards the Gate Towers, she constantly expected a cry of alarm and the thunder of hooves coming down from the castle. She refused to peer over her shoulder for fear of bringing her imagination into life.

Another reason not to look over her shoulder was to see Hilde and Renard. The girl was probably making big moon eyes at him that very minute.

Something, of course, that did not matter to her one jot.

"What do we do if they refuse to open the gates?" Lucien's question dragged her mind back to more pressing concerns.

"Prepare to spend the winter in Ettestein," she glanced at the mercenary, "possibly longer."

"I've been to worse places."

She thought about asking him, but behind her, all she could hear was Hilde chatting away to Renard.

"That girl has no idea what she's letting herself in for."

"None at all," Lucien agreed.

She chewed her lip and stared at the approaching gates; if they couldn't get through them, her worries about Hilde would be meaningless. She wouldn't be going anywhere, just like the rest of them. The girl would be locked inside Ettestein alongside Renard and...

"Coming with us will likely cost that girl her life."

"All gotta die sometime," Lucien sniffed.

The drizzle was hardening to rain, cold enough to turn in time to snow.

Wonderful.

There hadn't been any since they'd arrived at Ettestein, now they were finally leaving...

Or trying to leave.

Two guards barred the gates. Both had been leaning casually on their pikes until they recognised Lebrecht at the head of the approaching riders. Then, they straightened up quickly.

A good sign?

They reined their horses in before the two guards.

Somewhere a dog barked.

She risked a glance over her shoulder. No signs of alarm from the castle, while Lebrecht's men all rested easily in their saddles. Hilde still chatted away as if they were off on some splendid little adventure. Renard noticed her attention and found a pinched smile.

What is it about that girl...?

She edged the stallion forward, and the horse snorted a plume of steaming breath.

"We have orders, my lord..." one of the guards was protesting.

"Now you have new orders. From my father. Do you wish to keep me waiting here in the rain while you go and check with the *Markgräf*? If you do, Gruder, I *will* remember it..."

Gruder exchanged an unhappy glance with his comrade, who'd fixed his eyes to the middle distance in a nothing-to-do-with-me kind of way.

"Of course, my lord, at once."

The two soldiers put aside their pikes and began lifting the bar of the iron-studded wooden gates.

More than those gates stood between her, *Graf* Bulcher, Saul the Bloodless and the Red Company. But she couldn't help but feel she was getting on with the bloody business of vengeance at long last. It would have been good to have a hundred men-at-arms behind rather than a single large-chested maid, but she would make the most of whatever tools the good lord sent her way.

A scruffy one-eared mutt sat in the mud next to Lucien's horse, looking up at the mercenary and barking furiously.

Lucien grinned at her, then twisted around and grinned at Renard, who rolled his eyes. Lucien patted down his pockets, pulled out what looked like a twist of dried meat and tossed it at the dog, who snapped it out of the air.

The gates opened slowly, with a creak and a moan. She might have thought it sounded a little like the tortured warning of a dead man's shade if she possessed a fertile enough imagination. But she already had the *sight;* she didn't want to encourage imagination as well.

"Friend of yours?" she asked.

The mercenary watched the dog lick its chops, bark once more then turn and trot back up towards the castle.

"No..." he returned his gaze to the opening gates before them, "...dogs are too smart for that..."

Finally, Gruder and his friend got the gates open. Other soldiers stood atop the towers on watch. No one called in alarm or questioned why the gates were opening.

Lebrecht wished the men a good afternoon and urged his mount on. She followed, a moment's shadow, and then they were out of Ettestein, for the first time in nearly a month.

The world beyond seemed no different to the world inside the castle's walls.

Except here, she was free.

Although, perhaps, vengeance made it a strange kind of freedom.

They walked the horses away despite her desire to spur Styx's flanks and put as much distance between themselves and Ettestein as they could.

Would the *Markgräf* send men after her? He knew precisely where she would be heading, after all. Who could tell what a man driven half-mad by love might do?

A man driven half-mad by you...

She ignored the thought.

And kept her spurs from the stallion's flanks.

The path wound away gently from Ettestein. She brought Styx alongside Lebrecht's when they lost the castle from sight behind a copse of Ash trees.

"Thank you, my lord."

Lebrecht offered only a twitch of the shoulders in reply.

"Your father will not be pleased with you, will he?"

"No..."

"I hope this does not come between you."

He looked sideways at her, "I am sure he will see the sense of it in time now that he is removed from your spell."

"You think me a witch?" she laughed, perhaps shrilly.

"No more than any other beautiful woman possesses magic."

She didn't laugh at that, though maybe she did glow a little.

"When will you head back to Ettestein?" she asked after a long pause.

"I will see you safely to Magdeburg first."

"Really? There is no need."

"The road is not safe. I would have brought more men, but..."

She turned to him and raised an eyebrow. Atop Styx's high back, she was at Lebrecht's eye level.

"These men are *my* men. I trust them. Gathering more... would have been risky. If word had reached my father..."

"I understand... thank you."

"Hopefully, they won't be needed. But these days..."

Six men rode behind her. It wasn't a hundred, but it was better than just a serving maid. Perhaps she could find a way to persuade Lebrecht to stay longer...

She felt his eyes on him but kept her head turned in case she somehow betrayed that scheming thought.

Renard looked questioningly at her. She gave him a shallow nod and a thin smile by way of reassurance that all was well. He nodded in return and rested a little easier in the saddle of his sag-backed gelding. Next to him, Hilde had, mercifully, fallen silent and was gazing about her as if they were travelling through some exotic land full of wonders rather than a coppice of ash on one side and untended fields choked with dead winter weeds on the other.

Hilde turned towards her. At first, uncertain, maybe even unnerved by the attention, before she found a smile.

Her stomach clenched hard as the realisation who Hilde was broke over her like a freezing wave.

She was the girl she'd seen Saul kill before the church altar during the sack of Magdeburg in her dream. And the word that had seemed so familiar on the dying girl's lips crashed into her with startling clarity.

Ulrich...

Except, of course, it hadn't been a dream.

Hilde was a girl Saul the Bloodless *would* kill.

On the 20th of May, the year of our Lord, 1631, Hilde would be with Saul the Bloodless.

And if they could stay close to Hilde, so would whatever army she could build in the next four months.

She smiled at Hilde.

Perhaps the girl would have a use after all.

Anything was possible...

Part Two

Probabilities

Chapter One

Upon the Road, Principality of Anhalt-Dessau, The Holy Roman Empire - 1631

They reached the village of Durgen an hour after a sunset obscured by gunmetal clouds and rain flirting with sleet, the last colourless light of the day teetering upon the cusp of memory.

"How many people lived here?" he heard Solace ask Lebrecht as he dismounted.

"Thirty, maybe forty... I'm not sure..."

Solace hesitated when the young *Markgräf* held up his hand to help her down from Styx's mountainous back. Then shook her head before sliding down into the mud with a fair amount of grace.

Despite the more modest drop from Plodder's back, he achieved it with no grace whatsoever. But simply not landing on his arse was an achievement these days.

Hilde stayed in the saddle while the soldiers behind her climbed from their horses.

She'd become progressively less talkative during the hours since they'd left Ettestein, he suspected proportionally to how wet and cold she'd become. Fortunately, Solace had given her a cloak to keep the worst of the rain off. When they'd pushed the horses from a walk to a canter, she'd grown pale; when they'd galloped, she held on for dear life as her complexion verged on corpselike.

She looked down at him hopefully.

He offered her his good hand and told himself he was going to keep Hilde's arse out of the mud too.

As it was, she half stumbled and had to grab hold of him. He tried not to wince too much as she squeezed his bad shoulder. Otherwise, it wasn't the worst experience of his life; the way she smiled at him suggested it wasn't hers either.

While she stepped away, Lebrecht waved his men towards the dark buildings around them.

"Make sure there's no one here!" the young nobleman bellowed, standing next to Solace, one hand holding the reins of his own horse.

He led Plodder to them; Hilde followed a couple of steps behind.

"My lady...?"

Solace shook her head. Leave the search to the soldiers; she wanted him and Lucien close by, just in case.

"How long has this place been abandoned?" Lucien wrinkled his nose and peered into the swelling gloom.

Only the occasional snicker and snort from the horses broke the profound silence. Beyond the black oblongs of the buildings, leafless trees clawed at the sky. It felt like the world had died here. Many lifetimes ago.

"Years..." was the only answer Lebrecht offered.

"Where did the villagers go?" Solace asked, drawing her cloak more tightly about her.

"Anywhere safer. Some of them. The rest..." he shrugged, "...war, famine, pestilence, plague... take your pick..."

Even in the grey half-light, it was clear many of the cottages were nought but burnt-out shells. A church loomed over the northern end of the village, its tower stark against the weeping sky.

"Not Magdeburg..." Solace said.

"As safe as anywhere these days," Lebrecht replied, "the city has high walls and soldiers. Too much for any brigands or mercenary bands to pillage."

"But not an imperial army," Solace stared at the church, eyes distant, seeing other things he suspected. Things yet to come.

"They will not take Magdeburg, 'tis too well defended," Lebrecht insisted.

"The Emperor has many soldiers. He will want to make an example," Solace's voice fell to little more than a whisper, the kind reserved for churches, graveyards, and other places where the human voice is an intrusion, "too many have defied him. He wishes to draw a line. One drawn in blood if needs be."

"You sound well informed, my lady," Lebrecht laughed but weakly.

Hilde moved closer to him. She was trembling, and he suspected not only from the cold, damp air. He resisted the urge to put an arm around her. Just.

Solace turned her eyes on the nobleman, "Oh, yes, my lord, I am. I have seen the work of monsters at close quarters…"

Magdeburg would fall. Solace had foreseen it. He shared the hope the people who once lived in this dead place would not be there when the walls fell.

They stood in silence until one of Lebrecht's men, the burly sergeant, Paasche, reappeared.

"No one, my lord. There are the remains of fires. Others have sheltered here, but none recently, I'd wager."

"How sound are the buildings?"

Paasche crumpled his face, "Poor, my lord. Mostly roofless and rotten."

Lebrecht turned to the tower, "The church may offer the best protection from the weather. Churches are built to last."

"Yes, my lord."

Once the other soldiers returned from scouting the village, they led the horses through the silent ruins. Several men lit lanterns, but they illuminated little more than slashes of rain.

As they walked, Hilde's hand found his.

He didn't look at her but squeezed it. She squeezed back. It warmed him deeply.

The church was a ruin too, the stone walls blackened by long dead fires. Beyond a door hanging from its hinges, it smelt of dampness and rot. Someone had locked themselves inside, but someone else had smashed it down. These days, even the lord's house could not always provide sanctuary.

The shadows squatted thick and deep, but it kept the rain and wind from them. He pulled back the hood of his cloak and helped Lebrecht's men ensure nothing worse than rats lurked in the shadows.

The door was wide enough to bring the horses through one at a time. Some hesitated, the men encouraging them with curses, tugs on their reins and slaps on the rump.

Styx eyed his fellows disgustedly and walked through, head high and made straight to the part of the church no longer boasting a roof. He took the best spot, under some overhanging timbers, for himself. Plodder, Lucien, and Hilde's horses came alongside. The others kept their distance from Morlaine's evil beast.

He wondered where the demon was. She couldn't have gone far; perhaps they'd find Styx spirited away when they awoke in the morning.

He missed her company, which he found a curiosity.

There was little dry wood to hand, but they built small smoky fires with what they could salvage and made themselves as comfortable as possible once the horses were seen to.

Solace unsaddled, fed, and rubbed down Styx despite his offer to do it.

"I can manage," she said, running her hand along the stallion's muscular flank.

Styx turned his great head to give him – and he was certain he didn't imagine it – a dirty look. He retreated and found Hilde before the monster could take a lump out of him.

Several of Lebrecht's men eyed Hilde from a distance, but no one spoke to her. None turned eyes on Solace. The ignoring seemed determined and purposeful.

They ate apart from Lebrecht and his men, mostly in silence.

Occasionally, he caught Solace eyeing Hilde. Sometimes without expression, sometimes with a flicker of something he couldn't put a name to.

Hilde kept close. Shoulder to shoulder close. She didn't say much. She'd never been quiet around Lucien before, so he didn't think it anything to do with the mercenary's presence. She avoided looking at Solace, her eyes finding refuge in any spot his lady wasn't.

Once they'd finished eating their meal of road provisions, Lucien offered his waterskin that didn't hold water. No one accepted. They all stared into the meagre flames and the smoke coming in waves towards one or other of them on the whims of the draughts cutting through the ruined church. It was producing a lot more smoke than heat,

After a few slugs, Lucien ambled off to his bed roll.

Solace barely acknowledged him; her eyes moving back and forth between the flames and the church's shadowy door beyond the fire's smoky gauze.

Two of Lebrecht's men kept watch over the only entrance.

He wondered if she was expecting someone but knew better than to ask about her *sight* in front of a stranger.

Eventually, he led Hilde away. She didn't have a bedroll, so he gave her his.

"Where will you sleep?"

"I'll keep guard for a while. And we have some spare blankets. I'll be fine."

When she tried to protest, he knelt beside her and ensured the blankets covered her.

"Thank you," she said as he made to straighten up.

"For what?"

"For letting me come with you."

He smiled, "You didn't give us a choice. And I'm sure you'll soon regret leaving Ettestein's walls."

"I won't."

"If you do, you can go back with Lebrecht and his men."

"I won't," she said more forcefully, then reached out and brushed her fingers against his bad hand.

"Why? Why do you want to be here? With me?"

"Because... I just do..."

In truth, it wasn't much of an answer, but it warmed him more than the fire managed all night.

When he made to stand again, her fingers tightened about his hand.

"She doesn't like me, does she?"

"She doesn't know you. She..." how could he even begin to describe Solace? What they'd faced together. What they'd suffered together. What they would confront together. At the end of The Night's Road, "...is a good person. Trust me on that."

Hilde nodded and let her hand slip away, stifling a yawn.

He stood up and turned away from Hilde, back to Solace, still hunched over the fire, hair a thickening blonde mess atop her head, eyes hollow shadows, mouth downturned, the fire's kiss making her skin glow.

Is she still a good person?

She was no longer the feted young noblewoman of a year earlier; she wasn't the frightened girl who'd put a pistol under her chin and pulled the trigger to escape the demons invading her home. She wasn't the one who'd run away from Saul the Bloodless. She was now... he didn't know. She'd killed. Demons and men. Vengeance consumed her. Driven beyond reason. Driven beyond Sense. Driven beyond... sanity?

He sat on the opposite side of the fire and stared at his mistress.

Who are you now, Lady Solace?

And perhaps, more importantly...

What are you becoming?

*

Part of her didn't like the girl, Hilde. Her easy smile, her constant inane chattering, and, most of all, the comfortable familiarity she enjoyed with Renard despite only knowing him for five minutes.

Part of her liked the girl, Hilde. In a little over four months, she would die in Saul the Bloodless' arms, discarded on the floor of a church grander than this one ever had been, used by monsters for their pleasure, neck ripped open and drained of her lifeblood. Which meant she was bait. She could be tracked and followed to find the Red Company. Possibly. She was a thing to use, the way she'd tried to use the *Markgräf* of Gothen's love for her mother for her advantage, how she would now try to use Lebrecht so she could add his six men-at-arms to her little army.

And a third part detested the other two down to the very depths of her soul.

She hadn't added any more wood to the fire, better to let it burn down to embers overnight. The walls hid the flames and the night the smoke, but by morning, it might give away their presence in a world where it was now always prudent to avoid others.

Renard had left her to settle the girl, Hilde, in his bedroll. Then he came back, looking like he had things to say if he could figure out how you put the right words in the right order. Then he went to stand with Lebrecht's men guarding the door for a while.

Now he was back. Still seemingly arranging and rearranging words in his head.

"This girl, Hilde..." she asked, eyes rising from the dagger she hadn't been aware she'd been sharpening with a whetstone, "...why is she here?"

"She seems... to like me..." he said, brushing the bristles on his chin while avoiding her eye.

"She is going to a lot of trouble for someone she *likes*. Someone she's only just met."

How long had they been in Ettestein? A month, more or less. How well could you get to know someone in a month?

Probably quite well indeed.

If you were a certain type of woman...

Her eyes resisted the pull of the form curled up against the scorched stones of the church wall, upon which gossamer orange light swirled in time with the flames.

She gave her dagger another lick of the whetstone instead.

"I didn't ask her to come."

She kept her attention on the blade.

"I didn't want her to come..." Renard added.

"How much does she know?"

"As I said before. I've told her where we are going is

dangerous. Nothing more."

Her eyes rose as she silently mouthed a single word.

"Vampires?"

Renard shook his head, "No. But she's heard the rumours. The gossip. You know how castle life is?"

She did.

"Rumours? Gossip?"

"About what happened with Wendel. About Morlaine. About you."

"Me?"

He looked uncomfortable again. Renard had always been good at discomfort.

"That you are a witch, my lady. That you cast a spell upon the *Markgräf...*" he smiled, though she thought it hollow.

"If I did, my spell worked a little too well..."

"Men's passions can be dangerous, my lady."

She snorted and poked the fire with the dagger. A cloud of glowing fireflies jumped towards the church's sagging roof.

"It was worth a try."

Renard, she noted, kept his counsel on that.

Her eyes rose to meet his, "You understand I will do whatever it takes to stop them, don't you?"

"Morlaine said-"

"I don't care a shit about Morlaine, she's gone, and I'll damn well do whatever I need to see Saul's head at my feet," the words came out louder than she'd intended. Lebrecht and his men stretched out around the other fire. None stirred.

She leaned forward, far enough for the fire's remaining heat to prickle her skin, "She's spent centuries looking for that bastard and has never so much as ruffled his cloak. She's no bloody expert, Ulrich. Taking her wisdom with plenty of salt is my advice!"

Beneath the tousled fringe of her lengthening hair, beads of sweat erupted on her forehead.

She sat back.

Renard eyed her curiously. Maybe warily. Had he ever heard her swear so much before? She was sure he had. She was no Princess. Not anymore.

"You should sleep, my lady..."

"I'm not tired."

"How are your ribs holding up?"

"They are fine. Good as new."

They weren't. They'd started throbbing after less than an hour in the saddle. No matter. They weren't going to snap again from riding. It was only pain.

"Perhaps-"

"Go, Ulrich, sleep. I will keep watch."

"That is my job, my lady."

"I have no wish to sleep yet. You should rest," she glanced at the soldiers by the door, "we are well protected."

His voice dropped, "You trust *Markgräf* Lebrecht?"

"Yes."

She nodded towards Lucien and Hilde, "Now go, sleep. That is an order."

Reluctantly, he pushed himself to his feet.

"You gave your bedroll to the girl, Hilde?"

"Yes."

"Use mine, then."

Renard pursed his lips. Then, he shook his head, "No, my

lady. You might need it. I have a spare blanket; it will suffice."

She was going to snap at him not to be so pig-headed, but he said goodnight and wheeled away with a troubled expression on his hangdog face before she could get the words out.

He settled down next to Hilde, back against the wall and drew a blanket over his knees.

The next time she checked, he was talking to Hilde, and then the girl lifted the blankets. It was hard to make out in the thin light, but she thought Hilde nodded towards the bedroll.

She pretended to still be absorbed in sharpening her dagger when Renard's eyes flicked in her direction.

Renard was no longer sitting with his back against the wall when she looked next.

Just keeping warm.

Nothing more.

And even if it was, what did it matter to her?

She had his oath, not his soul. And certainly not his heart.

For a long time, she hunched over the ebbing fire. Much of it remembering what it had felt like to share a bed with Renard.

Remembering what it had been like to feel warm. From skin to soul.

What it had been like to feel alive.

She stared into the fire until it died.

Chapter Two

Upon the Road, Prince-Bishopric of Magdeburg, The Holy Roman Empire - 1631

They crossed from the Principality of Anhalt-Dessau, of which Gothen was part, into The Prince-Bishopric of Magdeburg around noon.

Nothing marked the border. The land on one side no different to that on the other. It was as dead and bleak as any winter landscape, though it felt the lifelessness ran deeper than it should. The emptiness was more noticeable than it had been when they'd only travelled at night with Morlaine.

He found the absence of people profound.

Tassau had been relatively untouched by the war until the Red Company arrived. But here, most peasants and villagers had fled to the towns and cities to find protection behind walls and armed men.

They only came across two people. A pair of girls, no more than thirteen and fourteen, collecting firewood as they rounded a bend in the muddy track masquerading as a road.

They'd dropped their bundles of sticks and fled into the

trees as soon as they spotted them.

Out here in the countryside, the sight of armed men offered no protection, no comfort. Only fear.

As their hooves crunched over the wood, two grubby faces watched them from deep within the winter-bare undergrowth, ready to bolt deeper into the tangles of lichen-flecked trees at the first sign the riders displayed any interest in them.

He'd smiled and raised a finger to his temple in salute as he went by. They'd flinched and scrambled backwards as if he'd pointed a pistol.

He'd seen deer less timid and fearful than that pair.

The rain at least had abated by the time they left the deserted village in the grey half-light before dawn. The wind, however, became sharp and spiteful, clawing at cloak and skin. The cold sank deep.

He thought about Hilde's warmth a lot as they rode.

After he'd climbed under the blankets with her, she'd turned her back on him. When he'd done nothing but listen to her breathing, she'd found his hand and pulled his arm over her. After a moment, he'd snuggled up close.

They were both fully clothed, and nothing else had happened.

He'd remembered the times he'd slept with Solace. The first, half frozen in her father's hunting lodge after The Wolf's Tower fell. Naked and teetering on death's embrace. He had been too weak and sick for any excitement to trouble him.

In Madriel, it was a practical matter. They had not embraced, but excitement had troubled him plenty that time. He'd kept his back to his lady so as not to trouble her with it, too.

This time, with Hilde, he had been pressed hard against her bottom and back.

Under such circumstances, even fully clothed, concealing an erection was tricky...

He slept better than expected. On waking, he'd found himself staring into Hilde's chestnut eyes and a faint knowing smile.

There had been little opportunity to talk. Or anything else.

They were on horseback before the sun rose.

If all went well, Lebrecht assured them, they would arrive in Magdeburg by sunset.

Where they would have to figure out a way to avoid the imperial blockade to enter the city.

He didn't think the route they took was the most direct one. He hadn't caught sight of the river Elbe since the previous afternoon. Perhaps Lebrecht feared his father would send men to find Solace. Of course, if the *Markgräf* had, those men would be in Magdeburg before them.

But would he risk sending soldiers to Magdeburg? Gottlieb was likely there as part of the small imperial army blockading the city, and any sizeable force of Gothen troops would be seen as a challenge to the Emperor. Not to mention an act of defiance against the *Markgräf's* liege, the Prince of Anhalt-Dessau, who so far had refused to align himself with Magdeburg.

Of course, men driven by lust, love and passion did not always give much thought to the political consequences of their actions.

He still struggled to imagine the *Markgräf* being driven by lust, love, and passion. He'd struck him as a cold fish. But it was always difficult to know exactly what went on behind a man's eyes.

Lucien chose that moment to unleash a belch of sufficient abrupt violence to send what wildlife remained in the woods fluttering, squawking, and scampering away in alarm.

Most men's eyes, anyway...

They kept the pace modest and wary within the patches of woodland interspersing the fields and open land. Two of Lebrecht's men rode ahead, scouting for trouble, the nobleman and Solace at the head of the rest of their little column. For the most part, it seemed *Markgräf* Lebrecht was far too engrossed with talking to his mistress to pay their surroundings due notice.

Although Hilde chatted often in his ear, he said little himself. Eyes shifting constantly over whatever landscape they traversed. Lucien was noticeably quieter than normal, too. Belches and farts aside, anyway.

Hilde was asking, not for the first time, exactly why they were going to Magdeburg.

He'd told her Lady Solace had business there but kept its nature vague. Given the business involved killing a rich and important nobleman, then waiting for an Imperial army to sack the city, so they could confront the demons drawn to the bloodshed like flies to dog shit on a hot summer's day, he'd thought that best.

Hilde, though, was proving persistent. Or nosey.

He looked up from her latest attempt to wheedle more out of him when the two riders scouting the road came to a halt.

Leaving Hilde with Lucien, he came alongside Solace and Lebrecht.

"Trouble, my lady?"

Their two outriders had stopped under the bare overhanging branches of a giant oak. The woods their rutted track cut through were thick here. A few birds chirped, but the only other sound bar their horses was the wind.

Solace didn't reply, but Styx pricked his ears, his front left hoof pawing the ground as he snorted clouds of steam.

His hand found the butt of one of the pistols attached to Plodder's saddle.

The scouts beckoned them forward but didn't continue themselves.

"Follow me," Lebrecht rode out. He'd already drawn one of his own pistols.

"Should we let the Gothen's go ahead?" he asked.

Solace shook her head and urged Styx on, "Trouble can come from any direction..."

True enough.

He flashed Hilde a reassuring grin. Lucien had come alongside the girl, hooded eyes peering into the silent, dead woods around them.

He saw what had stopped the two soldiers before they were halfway down the rutted track towards them.

Bodies.

"Looks like someone had a bad day, my lord," Usk said to Lebrecht, nodding at the corpses strewn across the road ahead of them.

Four naked bodies lay in the mud.

All men.

"How long have they been dead?" Lebrecht asked.

Usk gave his lord a look that suggested he was considering asking how the hell he should know.

"Usk..." Paasche's gravel-scoured voice floated over his shoulder as the sergeant manoeuvred his mount forward. The road wasn't wide enough to accommodate more than three horses comfortably abreast, and briar thickets spread around the trunks of the trees, hedging them in. It was a choice spot for an ambush.

Usk dismounted reluctantly, whether through concern for his safety or bone-idleness wasn't obvious. Dreyfuss, the soldier with him, gave his friend a quick smirk but continued scanning the undergrowth.

It was much thicker here than where he'd seen the two girls. He didn't think the fact men died here was a coincidence.

He pulled a pistol free and cocked it.

"I don't think they have been dead very long, my lady..." he edged the reluctant Plodder closer to Styx.

"No..." Solace agreed, keeping a tight hold of Styx's reins.

"Still warm, my lord," Usk, crouching by the nearest corpse, confirmed his suspicion.

"How did he die?" Lebrecht called back.

Somewhere in the woods, a bird exploded upwards.

"Crossbow bolt..." Usk pushed his considerable bulk back upright.

"Ambushed, my lord," he said across Solace, "we shouldn't linger here."

Hoof and footprints churned the mud around the corpses. Broken branches and pools of blood, a section of thicket had been trampled down, too. Horses led away or dragged if they were dead. Horse meat was too valuable to leave to rot these days.

His attention returned to the dead.

Human meat, on the other hand…

"We should take them for Christian burial," Lebrecht said, as much to himself as anyone else.

"They're dead," Solace said, "if we stay here too long, we might end up the same way."

Lebrecht couldn't argue with her logic, but the coldness in her voice was as bitter as the breeze.

The pair stared at each other as Usk hauled himself back into the saddle.

"Very well…" Lebrecht sighed, finally breaking eye contact, "…move on!"

The horses picked their way past the corpses. Each was stripped to the flesh. In a time of nothing, everything has value. Save for a man's life.

How much longer till people start hauling away the human meat, too…

He shook the macabre thought away and checked Hilde. She was pale-faced and kept her eyes fixed forward, but otherwise, the sight of the dead didn't appear to have troubled her too much. She'd no doubt seen corpses before, murdered ones too.

Likely of people she cared for.

They all had.

"How many people attacked them?" Hilde asked once he'd

fallen in beside her again.

"Hard to say..."

"Enough to attack us?"

"No."

"You're sure?"

He nodded, "Lucien's ugliness would scare off an army."

She pressed her lips together as if they were still too close to the dead for laughter.

A voice rumbled behind them, "You should know, Lucien Kazmierczak is famed from Gothenburg to Granada for his *exceptionally* keen hearing..."

*

Styx snorted and shook his head when they finally emerged from the woods.

She patted the giant horse's neck.

Whoever killed those four men had probably been too busy hauling away their booty to trouble them, but every bird's song and branch's creak set her teeth on edge.

She kept telling herself she hadn't come this far to have her throat slit by a band of brigands.

The land fell gently from the woods into a shallow valley carved by a modest river lined with alders and hawthorns, likely feeding into the Elbe. The road they followed, two muddy ruts, cut across the valley and up the other side. There were a few clumps of trees and bushes, but the land was mostly open. She doubted brigands would favour such terrain.

"Do you have no care for those men's souls?" Lebrecht asked as they made their way down. Dreyfuss and Usk were still riding ahead.

She thought about the question before shaking her head, "No."

"You have a rare hardness in you, my lady…"

"I care more for the living. Does that give me a flinty soul?"

"All men deserve a Christian burial so their souls may go to God."

"All men deserve food in their bellies too. As do women and children. Yet many do not have even that. Thanks to this war. This war about God. Let the All-Mighty care for the dead if he is more interested in them than the living."

Without looking at him, she could sense Lebrecht's eyes widening.

Did she honestly believe that?

Or was she striking out at Lebrecht to mask the fear she'd felt as they'd ridden through the woods? She'd faced demons and killed some of them. Why should a few petty, half-starved bandits trouble her?

Though she supposed dead was dead, whatever hand struck you down.

"You should be more careful with your words…"

"Will you denounce me for heresy, my lord?"

She turned and smiled at him.

Lebrecht was not her enemy.

And he had six good men-at-arms she had a use for.

Not as useful as his father, but still…

Hopefully, this time, she could figure out a way to manipulate a man to her advantage without driving him mad enough to want to lock her in his highest tower.

Being a manipulative seductress clearly required a bit of

practice.

"No... but, in these times... 'tis prudent to choose our words carefully."

"Of course. But one should always be able to speak openly to a friend..."

She held his eye for a second before her gaze slid away.

Was flirting appropriate so soon after seeing four naked corpses?

Perhaps literature existed for this kind of thing, but she suspected she would have to carry on making it up as she went along.

The road curled around a clump of hawthorns. As they rounded them, the point it forded the stream at the bottom of the valley came into view.

And a carriage that had seemingly lost a wheel trying to cross it.

They reined in their horses once they caught up to the waiting Usk and Dreyfuss.

A knot of men stood about the carriage, which was a fine one; other armed men watched over them. Several muskets swivelled in their direction.

"They don't look like brigands..." Lebrecht said.

"Shall we wander down and see if they shoot at us, my lord?" Lucien asked, coming alongside her.

"Is there another way?" she asked.

"We can ride cross country, find a different crossing... depends on how deep it is," Sergeant Paasche said from Lebrecht's side.

Something tingled. Familiar and uncanny. Her *sight* was trying to tell herself something. As usual, its voice no louder than the breeze.

She walked Styx a couple of paces down the rutted slope.

"I don't think they will cause us any trouble," she said, looking back over her shoulder.

"My lord..." Paasche growled.

Lucien walked his horse past them, "Last one to wet their feet is a nanna in her bloomers..."

She set Styx walking on. The beast had relaxed since leaving the woods. She took his lack of skittishness as an auspicious sign. The stallion's senses were as good a judge of anything as her *sight*.

"You sure?" Lucien asked out of the corner of his mouth.

"They won't cause trouble. So long as we don't give them reason to."

She kept the pace gentle as they approached the ford.

As they came closer, she saw more men were sheltering under the trees. One sat against a trunk, arm bandaged, and eyes closed. Another laid out on the grass asleep. Or dead.

A heavy-set man came to meet them; he wore a soldier's garb, thick leathers and a dented steel helm. He looked like he'd seen a fair few fights and led with his face in most of them. A sword hung from his weapon belt. A pistol, too. He kept his hands close to them as he approached.

"Who are you?" the man demanded.

"Charming..." Lucien said under his breath.

"We're from Gothen, on route to Magdeburg on the *Markgräf's* business. You?" she shouted back.

The man pulled off his helm to wipe a bald pate; despite the coldness of the day, it glistened with sweat.

"The *Markgräf* of Gothen sends little girls to do his business now then?" the man's red and bulbous nose, wrinkled, "Strange days these, right enough."

"No," Lebrecht rode forward, "the *Markgräf* of Gothen sends his eldest son to do his business. And you are blocking our way, my good man."

The man peered at Lebrecht, taking his measure. Lebrecht certainly had the tone, bearing and appearance of a nobleman. Of course, anyone could *say* they were a noble, but calling the wrong man a liar was an excellent way of earning yourself a horsewhipping.

"Apologies, my lord, we've suffered a bit of bother."

"Not just a thrown wheel, either?" Lucien asked, hands resting easy on his saddle's pommel.

"No, friend. Brigands attacked us up in those woods..." he slipped his helm back on, "...knew we should have taken the long way around."

"We found four bodies on the road. Stripped naked," Lucien said.

The man nodded, "They'll be our boys alright. Fuckers came out of the woods from every side, managed to get the carriage out and away. But left some lads behind," he gestured at the tree with the wounded men sheltering under it, "will be leaving some more here too, most likely."

"And you've seen no more of them?" Lebrecht asked.

"Nah, my lord. Them devils don't like to walk in the open like honest men. They skulk in the trees and shoot you in the back for your boots. Bastards," his eyes swivelled back to her, "begging your pardon for the language, 'tis been a trying day."

"Let us hope you've suffered the last of them," Lucien slid from his horse.

"Reckon so, long as we're away before nightfall, we'll be alright."

"Need some help getting that carriage repaired?" the mercenary hitched a thumb over his shoulder, "We've got some hefty lads; they get a bit bored sitting on their arses all day watching the countryside go by."

Lebrecht glanced at her as if to remind her that he was the one in charge. Or thought he was.

"Oh, don't want to be no trouble, friend."

"Well, faster that carriage is fixed, faster we'll all be on our way. 'tis only the Christian thing to do," Lucien grinned back at them, "eh, my lord, my lady?"

The man's eyes followed Lucien's gaze with curiosity; she wasn't dressed like anyone's idea of a noblewoman.

"Indeed," she said, reminding herself to speak with Lucien about his careless mouth later.

Lucien stuck out his hand, "I'm Lucien Kazmierczak, the famed soldier, adventurer, and lover. You might have heard of me."

The man stared at the hand, then wiped his own on his britches before accepting Lucien's, "Captain Miroslav Bosko, famous only in the brothels of Pressburg."

Lucien laughed and slapped Bosko's arm.

"Those two will get on like a house on fire..." Renard muttered with the air of a man who'd just discovered his neighbour had bought a second dog to shit on his doorstep.

Lebrecht leaned in, "It appears we're helping these people..."

"Yes, my lord. One good deed won't cost us much."

Lebrecht wasn't convinced, peering back up at the woods atop the hill several times as he dismounted.

Worried about the brigands or pursuit from his father? Either way, he'd been more interested in burying the dead than helping the living.

It didn't matter. They were going to help; she didn't know why, but since the Wolf's Tower fell, she'd never ignored her hunches and feelings. The *sight* came calling in many guises.

Lebrecht ordered Paasche to take the men, haul the carriage out of the ford and do what they could to fix it. Then he told Renard to watch the road behind them for trouble.

Renard's eyes immediately slid to her.

She nodded.

Alongside Lucien and Lebrecht, she walked down to the stream with Bosko. The road was as much bog as road and the low sky threatened to dump more water on to the land.

Including the wounded, she counted ten men in Bosko's group. Plus whoever occupied the carriage. None were well enough dressed to be one of the occupants. They were all soldiers, save one portly fellow in livery, who she assumed was the driver. Horses had been hobbled to trees and bushes on the other side of the ford; another soldier guarded them.

"Have you travelled far?" she asked Bosko as they walked.

He eyed her. As with most men, he likely believed women had limited uses and asking questions wasn't one of them.

"From Vadia... lost eight men so far. The Lord knows how

many of us will make it to Thasbald."

"A long journey," Lebrecht said.

"A mad one!" Bosko snorted, "But love must win out in the end. Says so in the story books and poems, so it must be true!"

"Love?" Lucien asked as they came to a halt overlooking the water. Up close, the stream was more a small river, swollen and running fast over the gravel and smooth rocks of the ford. The two horses of the carriage were struggling to pull it up the far bank. Lebrecht's men joined Bosko's to lift the back end, where the near side wheel had come away.

"Delivering a bride to her one true love," Bosko snorted a bitter bark.

"She couldn't have married someone closer to home?" Lucien asked.

Bosko rubbed his beard, "You know how... people are..."

She strongly suspected Bosko would have said *nobles* instead of *people* if she and Lebrecht hadn't been with him. Or, quite possibly, something much less polite.

"Would it not be easier to shift the carriage without the blushing bride still in it?" Lucien asked.

"Oh, she doesn't weigh more than a feather. Just a slip of a girl. She'd catch her death from a bit of drizzle..."

With a volley of curses, the coach began moving up the bank. One of Lebrecht's men slipped and ended up momentarily face down in the river, much to the amusement of all.

"Well, Captain," Lebrecht said, glancing behind him again, no one bar Renard, Hilde, and their horses was in sight, "we should have your carriage out in a jiffy and get you on your way before too long."

"That'll be a joy… c'mon lads, put your bloody backs into it!" Bosko gave them a resigned look and began to make his way to the coach, "Excusing your pardon, but if you need a job done right…"

"Captain Bosko…" she said, a question forcing its way onto her lips, although deep, deep down, she already knew the answer, "… may I ask who your lady's intended is?"

Bosko paused, looking back up at them; his sour smile didn't touch his eyes, "She's an incredibly lucky girl…. She's marrying Siegfried, the *Graf* Bulcher."

Chapter Three

Hilde stroked her horse's mane. As far as he knew, Solace had never given the mare a name. Her eyes returned continually to the woods atop the hill. His own traced the two muddy ruts climbing the slope to the tree-crested ridge, too.

The sound of curses mingled with whinnying horses rose from the river behind them, but he didn't turn around. The travellers were no threat to them; if trouble came, it would do so from those woods.

Aside from the trouble standing next to him, of course.

He took a couple of paces back up the road, boots squelching with every step, to run an eye over the land unobscured by horsemeat.

Nothing moved above them bar a few birds. The light was flat, and the shadows in the woods deep. He was certain they were being watched.

Only the fact the brigands had been busy dragging away the booty from their attack on Bosko's party had gotten them through the woods unscathed. Four horses, dead or alive, and whatever the men carried and wore.

A rare piece of fortune.

If Bosko had not been ahead of them on the road…

He resisted the urge to look at Hilde again.

She is going to die because of me…

Another one to add to the list.

He should have tied her up, stuck a gag in her mouth and left her in Ettestein's stables. No doubt she'd be cursing his name every day till Easter, but at least she'd still be alive for Easter. Now.... how likely was it someone would helpfully take the crossbow bolts for them next time?

Despite himself, he glanced over his shoulder.

Hilde was watching him. She smiled as she continued to run her fingers through her horse's mane.

His hair had grown during their time in Ettestein but remained much shorter than a horse's mane. Still, he couldn't help but imagine what it would feel like to have-

He whirled back to studiously stare at the woods.

Still nothing.

The brigands were probably a mix of starving peasants and deserted soldiers. The Empire enjoyed an abundance of both. In open ground, they would have little chance against mounted men-at-arms. Only the surprise of an ambush had allowed them to waylay some of Bosko's men. No doubt they wanted whatever was in the coach, but they would settle for what they had.

At least till nightfall, and they would be on their way long before then.

More shouts and curses from the river broke the chilly silence.

Hopefully.

Hilde left the hobbled horses and came to stand at his shoulder.

"I keep thinking about those men..." she said.

"We couldn't stop to bury them or bring them with us."

"I know."

When he noticed her biting her nails; she quickly stuffed her hand into the pocket of her dress.

"My brothers..."

"What happened to them?"

She let her eyes drift away.

"Nothing good."

He could see she didn't want to say more, and he'd never been much of a one for unnecessary talking. It encouraged idiots. Created the false impression he gave a shit about whatever drivel they might spit in his direction if they got the chance. There was no shortage of idiots in the world. Which went some way to explain the current sorry state of the Lord's creation. So, lots of people he didn't want to talk to.

It turned out, however, Hilde wasn't one of them.

He found he liked talking to her. Which was a curiosity when he thought about it.

But the distant and watery look in her eyes told him, this wasn't the right time to pursue his newfound interest in conversation.

Instead, he rested his hand on her shoulder.

She looked up, then placed hers on his.

Actually, this was much better than conversation.

He was toying with hugging her when her gaze drifted back to the woods.

"We have company," she said, nodding up the track to the crest of the tree-lined hilltops overlooking the shallow valley.

A solitary cloaked figure stood in the lee of the dead winter trees where the road emerged to fall towards the river. Leaning on a spear or staff, he appeared to be staring directly down at them.

Hilde pressed herself closer to him, "One of the Brigands that killed those men?"

"Possibly..." he shrugged, "...probably. Whatever he is, he can't do us any harm."

When Hilde didn't appear convinced, he lifted her chin so her eyes met his.

He did his best to act reassuring and manly. The kind of thing that might make a woman think a fellow gave enough of a damn about her to look after her.

Her eyes widened, and she stepped away from him.

He sighed inwardly.

I'm really not very good at this.

"Ulrich..." she jabbed a finger over his shoulder.

Frowning, he followed the finger all the way until his heart sank.

And completely forgot he tried not to swear around women.

"Oh, shit..."

*

As she watched the three remaining wheels of the carriage spin and turn as men and beasts hauled it up the incline of the far side of the ford, the wheel in her head whirled much faster.

Graf Bulcher's latest bride.

At least he didn't appear to have slaughtered this one's family. Perhaps he was mellowing with age?

She didn't know what he'd done to win this girl. Whatever it was, she'd wager the expenditure on flowers and poetry had been minimal.

Lebrecht was talking to Bosko. She had no idea what about. She'd heard the words, but they wandered off somewhere between ear and brain. Lucien was eyeing her. Significantly.

"Are you the bride's men or Bulcher's?" she asked Bosko abruptly.

The Captain gave her another one of his looks. The kind people reserved for curious beasts from far off lands in a lord's menagerie.

"*Freiherr* Hoss has my oath, Lady Karoline's father."

"And all your men are the *Freiherr's*? None Bulcher's?"

Bosko frowned and shook his head.

"A perilous journey for a bride to make, in the mid-winter, at a time of war and lawlessness?"

Bosko shrugged, "I merely follow orders. As I understand it, the *Graf* insisted Lady Karoline came immediately to marry him. People say he is quite smitten."

People who have never met Graf Bulcher, most likely.

"Has Lady Karoline ever met Bulcher?"

"No. He father arranged the marriage with the *Graf* via intermediaries."

"And yet he is quite smitten?"

Bosko pulled a face, an ill-advised expression given the one he had was unsightly enough to start with.

"The aristocracy..." he glanced at Lebrecht, "...begging your pardon, my lord."

"Quite alright," the young nobleman smiled, "my own

father has done all sorts of peculiar things recently."

"Does-"

"You seem very interested in Lady Karoline's marriage?" Bosko peered at her.

"Oh, I'm a hopeless romantic. I've always dreamed about a Prince of the Empire sweeping me off my feet and marrying me."

Just not one who hired monsters to kill my father and destroy my home.

She kept that thought from her lips but managed to smile sweetly at Lebrecht.

Lebrecht smiled back. And blushed. At least, she thought he might have. They were all somewhat red-faced from the cold.

Save Lucien, who she suspected was red-faced from whatever he kept sipping from his waterskin.

Over the river, they'd finally got the carriage up onto level ground and the men dropped the corner of the carriage. They all either bent over, hands clamped to knees or collapsed to sit panting in the damp winter grass.

The squeal from inside the carriage as the axle missing its wheel hit the ground, carried across the river remarkably well.

Bosko winced.

"Can't you idiots put that down gently?" he boomed.

Nobody, his own men or Lebrecht's, paid him much attention. They were all too busy trying to breathe.

"Is Lady Karoline a scold?" she asked.

"A scold? No! No! She is made from sweetness and light!"

Bosko flashed a smile that was both knowing and

strained.

Still, whatever the girl's faults, she couldn't have done anything to deserve *Graf* Bulcher's bed.

"Pavol! Get that bloody wheel fixed."

A young man with a shock of red hair looked up. He was too far away for his reply to carry, but they all got the gist of it well enough.

Bosko took a step towards the river, "Don't you fucking cheek me, you useless little shit! Get your arse up and that wheel on, or you'll be feeling my boot up your worthless scrawny arse all the way to Thasbald!"

"Morale issues?" Lucien asked before swigging his waterskin again.

"Not at all. The only person these boys love more than me is Lady Karoline..."

Lucien chuckled and offered Bosko the waterskin.

When Karoline's Captain just stared at it, Lucien raised a bushy eyebrow and gave a couple of quick nods.

Bosko took the waterskin.

"Jesus!"

He almost threw it back at Lucien.

When Lebrecht looked between the two men, Bosko shook his head and croaked, "Trust me, you don't want any."

She bit her bottom lip, rolling it back and forth as she watched the carriage. She wanted to question Bosko further. She had a lot of questions. But questions birth suspicion, and notwithstanding the assistance they had given Bosko's party, they were still strangers in a dangerous land.

While Pavol and a couple of Bosko's other men started

working on reattaching the carriage's wheel, she decided she needed to speak to Lady Karoline. A young woman far from home travelling with rough-handed soldiers, she would appreciate a new friend to share the gossip about her impending wedding with.

Perhaps a friend she could persuade to invite to travel with her, to see her new home.

And to meet her husband-to-be.

She touched the bag of demon ash beneath her shirt.

What part of Bulcher should she add to it?

Her hand dropped quickly to her belt.

And she started down the bank to the ford.

Lucien hurried after her.

"I thought Bulcher was in Magdeburg?" he asked once out of earshot of the others.

"So did I."

"It appears he isn't."

No. Karoline wasn't travelling to Magdeburg to meet Bulcher. Presumably, he waited for his new bride in Thasbald. That was just one of the many questions plaguing her. But her *sight* had been wrong. Something had whispered to her Bulcher was in the blockaded, soon to be sacked, city on the Elbe. But he wasn't.

This made her uneasy as she turned it over in her head. But as she wet her boots in the fast-flowing river, realisation struck.

They hadn't run into Lady Karoline by chance.

They were only here because her *sight* had brought her to this spot, travelling towards Magdeburg to deliver her Bulcher. They hadn't found Bulcher in Magdeburg, but the *means* to find him by travelling towards that doomed city. Her sight hadn't gotten it wrong; she had just misunderstood the urge to head towards Magdeburg.

By the time she reached the middle of the river, icy water hissing over the shallow stones of the ford, she'd straightened that part at least within her mind.

After weeks of frustration and disappointment in Ettestein as her ribs healed and she tried fruitlessly to gain an army, at last things had begun to move. She knew where Saul would be, Hilde gave her a link to the monster and now Lady Karoline would lead them to Bulcher.

Vengeance would receive another offering while they waited for the 20th of May.

And if she could *persuade* Bulcher to divulge the whereabouts of the Red Company, they could stop the demons before the night the walls of Magdeburg fell, and the monsters came to feast upon the slaughter and dance to the World's Pain. And the horrors her vision showed her inside that cursed church would never come to pass.

It was almost enough to paint a grim smile on her face as the river sloshed about her ankles.

And then the shouting started.

"Fuck!" Lucien cried.

Twisting around, beyond the ash and hawthorn lining the riverbank behind her she could make out the land rising to the tree-lined crest of hills overlooking the valley.

And the figures swarming down the hillside towards them.

She stood rooted to the spot as if the icy water had frozen her legs solid.

Then Lucien grabbed her hand and pulled her in the

direction of the riverbank they'd just left and the brigands hurtling down the hillside.

When she didn't move, he screamed in her face, "The horses!"

They'd left them hobbled on that side of the river.

On horseback, they could outrun the brigands, but on foot...

She yanked her hand free of Lucien's and sprinted back.

"Hold the crossing!" Lebrecht yelled at his men on the far bank.

Further down the road, Renard and Hilde struggled with the horses. They needed to untie them and take them across the river, but eleven horses were too many for the pair of them to control alone. If any of the startled animals bolted once untied, their rider would be stranded.

Beyond them, a black tide of filthy bedraggled men, and some women, were hurtling down the slope, whooping and hollering like savages.

The prize of the damaged coach must have attracted every half-starved peasant and brigand sheltering in those woods.

Oh, Lord! How many of them were there?

She put her head down and ran.

Better she didn't try to count.

"The horses!" Lucien yelled at Lebrecht as they hurtled past the young nobleman.

She thought she heard him curse as she sped by, and his feet soon pounded over the mud and sodden grass behind her.

Hilde was coming down the track, the reins of a horse in each hand. Renard's and hers. Probably the two least desirable animals in their little herd. Wide-eyed and open-mouthed, it was a close-run thing who looked more agitated and frightened between the girl and the two horses.

"Get them over the river!" she shouted.

Hilde and the horses all put their heads down and ran.

The crack of gunfire pulled her attention back. At first, she thought it Lebrecht or Bosko's men firing at the mob until she saw puffs of white smoke rising above the oncoming brigands.

They were still too distant to hit anything, and running full pelt downhill wouldn't improve anyone's aim, but it was enough to unnerve the horses further.

Renard struggled with one of the Gothen horses, which momentarily reared up. She thought he would take a hoof in the face before he managed to haul on the reins hard enough to force the frightened animal down.

"Get in the saddle!" she shrieked once the beast was under control.

Skidding to a halt as Renard clambered onto the horse's back, she began untying the other horses.

"You too!" she told Lucien and Lebrecht.

The mercenary immediately boosted himself into the saddle, but Lebrecht hesitated, panting, at her side. Perhaps he had trouble taking orders from a girl.

Looking over her shoulder, she shouted, "Get on the fucking horse!"

Lebrecht recoiled like he'd been shot.

After Renard wheeled his mount around, she thrust the reins of the two horses she'd untied into his hand.

"Take them over the river."

"My Lady-"

"Don't make me fucking swear at you, too!" she slapped the rump of his mount.

By the time he was heading off to the ford, Lebrecht was in the saddle of his horse. Lucien had mounted, too.

But he was galloping at the swarm of brigands now over halfway down the hill.

"Come on, you filthy cocksuckers!" Lucien levelled a pistol at the brigands and fired. He was too far away for an accurate shot as well, but he had a lot more target to miss.

Hands shaking, she untied two more and led them to Lebrecht, who stood staring dumbly at Lucien charging the brigands.

"Don't get any ideas..." she warned, thrusting the reins up at him, "...he can get away with such things on account of being an idiot. It doesn't work for the rest of us!"

"You're not-"

"No, of course I'm not. Go!"

Lebrecht nodded and kicked his horse towards the ford; she stepped back as hooves splattered mud, and three more horses headed down to the river.

She looked to see how Lucien was doing.

Some of the brigands had checked their mad cartwheeling runs down the hill. Lucien had swapped pistol for sword and was making a show of waving it about over his head. As he approached the mob, he veered off and galloped parallel to the front of the brigands.

She hoped none of them could shoot, as the idiot was now very much in range, albeit moving fast enough for his cloak and moustaches to be billowing around him.

He knew what he was doing. Didn't he?

Two horses remained.

Styx and one of the Gothen horses.

The Gothen horse whinnied, shuffling back and forth, and trying to pull its reins from the hawthorn tree it had been tied to.

Styx cast a disinterested eye about as if to see what all the fuss was. When he didn't see anything much, he immediately went back to munching some undergrowth he'd evidently taken a shine to.

She untethered Styx and the skittish horse.

If she attempted to climb in the saddle, she reckoned the Gothen horse would likely bolt, so, taking a rein in each hand she started running back through the mud to the ford.

Styx, being Styx, immediately tried to bite the Gothen horse for having the temerity to come close enough to pollute his nostrils.

Which didn't make the skittish Gothen horse any less skittish.

Screaming in Lebrecht's face had got the nobleman to do what she wanted, but she doubted the same trick would work with this pair. Not least because she suspected both were quite a bit brighter than Lebrecht.

Instead, she just tugged on the reins and got them moving again.

She could hear voices above the squelch of mud and the horses' bickering and snickering. The first wave of brigands wasn't far behind her now. Where was Lucien...

He knew what he was doing, she tried to convince herself,

resisting the urge to look.

The others were all on the far side of the river, save for Renard, who was charging back across atop his borrowed Gothen horse.

She wanted to wave him back, but she could see from the thin press of his lips he would ignore it.

And he had a better idea of how close behind her the brigands were.

Not that crossing the river offered much in the way of safety. Lebrecht and Bosko's men spread out along the bank, waiting with muskets and pistols for the brigands. But did they have enough guns to turn back this many outlaws?

Heaven knew what they thought was in that carriage, but it was clearly sufficient to make every emaciated, half-starved brigand in the region pour out of the woods and down the valley despite the guns waiting for them.

Pavol was still working on the carriage. A couple of hefty men, including the giant Usk, were lifting the damaged corner so he could hammer the wheel back into place. It didn't need to be perfect; just hold long enough to get them away from the brigands.

A shot rang out behind her and alarmingly close.

She put her head down and ran harder, a horse on each side.

The sound of voices behind her swelled. Not just voices; screams, shouts, cries, wails, fragments of curses and insults, beseeching pleas to God himself. It was as if a lunatic asylum sat within those dead winter trees on the ridge, and someone had thrown open the doors to allow all the inmates to rush out into the world again.

In order to pursue her.

Styx kept pace with her, but the Gothen horse kept trying to break free, forcing her to pull it back while running as fast as she could.

"Come here, me little bitch!" a voice screeched, almost as loud as Styx's snorting breath in her ear.

She expected to feel a bony hand clamp down on her shoulder, dragging her back into the maw of the mob.

Instead, a dark blur rushed by, flashing silver, followed by a scream.

Now she twisted around.

A headless corpse hit the mud. She couldn't see where the head landed.

Renard slashed his sabre at another brigand. A handful, the strongest or dumbest, had surged ahead of the main group, slipping and sliding down the muddy track towards the ford. They frothed around Renard, grubby hands trying to unseat him, but he kicked the horse away from them; a spear gouged the flank of his mount, but he made it clear and hauled the animal about to face her.

She dropped the reins of the Gothen horse before clambering up into Styx's saddle. The stallion turned in a circle to face the mob as her feet found the stirrups; the beast snorted and pawed at the mud.

If she could see Styx's face, she was quite sure the black monster would be grinning at the mob.

A balding man in a decaying leather jerkin came at her with a rusty sword, the toothless grin stretching a grimy face fit for any asylum.

Styx reared up and a wet, cracking sound accompanied both iron-clad front hooves connecting with flesh and bone.

The man went down fast. And didn't look like he'd be getting up again.

"My lady!" Renard surged past her.

The leading wave of the mob hesitated, chastened by Styx's hooves and Renard's sabre. A wailing woman with leaves and twigs stuck in her knotted hair dashed forward, but only to try and pull the man Styx had kicked in the head back off the muddy road.

Behind the girl, a man in a mud-splattered frock coat with more beard than face raised a pistol and pointed it at her.

She stared at him. Styx seemed to shuffle and quiver between her legs.

Kill me and it's over...

No fear accompanied the thought.

Blackened teeth snarled through wild twists of hair. The brigands surged forward again, emboldened by more of their number catching up with the front. Her fingers tightened around Styx's reins. The stallion snorted steam at the oncoming mob like dragon smoke. The pistol fizzed. Someone screamed. It wasn't her.

Kill me and I'm free...

Chapter Four

He wheeled his horse when he realised Solace was not with him.

Unlike Plodder, it was a warhorse and responded well to his commands, allowing him to control the animal as much with his legs as the reins, which was just as well as every meaningful pull he made with his bad arm sent spasms of white pain surging along the usually numb limb and into his shoulder.

His good hand held his father's sabre. Slickened with blood.

Later, if there was a later, he would add the wide-eyed expression of horror on the man whose head he'd taken from its shoulders to his collection of ghosts and nightmares.

For now, he concentrated on keeping Lady Solace alive.

She sat atop Morlaine's monstrous stallion before the horde of brigands.

Perhaps horde was an exaggeration; there were fifty or so of them. A wretched-looking, half-starved mob more deserving of pity than fear, many armed with no more than farming implements or crude clubs. A few wore the disintegrating garb of soldiers, and a smattering of real weapons gave the brigands teeth.

Enough teeth to kill four of Bosko's men earlier that

morning anyway.

"My lady!"

Some of the brigands were holding back, wary of Styx. The corpse between the beast's hooves with a head of red pulp most likely explained why. But others were surging on either side. One of the brigands, tall and wildly hirsute, was pointing a pistol at his mistress.

He urged his horse forward again but would never reach the man in time. And he wasn't the only one. A crossbow bolt flashed past his face, close enough for the air to kiss his cheek.

Solace remained still, staring at the brigands.

He saw the brigand's pistol fizz. The bastard was only ten paces from Solace!

Old Man Ulrich never liked pistols. He said they always chose the worst possible moment to let you down. An opinion the brigand likely now sympathised with as the pistol exploded in his hand and sent him staggering backwards, clutching his face.

Whatever spell held Solace and Styx in place broke with the misfiring pistol.

The stallion reared again, so high Solace had to lunge forward and throw arms about the monster's neck to keep from flying from the saddle. The brigands scattered before the beast's flailing hooves. One of them, a skinny lad with a pimple-splattered face, didn't move fast enough, and his scream must have carried clear across the valley as Styx trampled him into the mud.

A man came at him with a spear, the brigand's mouth a toothless hollow as he screamed something uncomplimentary about his mother.

His sabre met the spear, little more than a sharpened stick, shattering it to kindling. The heel of his boot did much the same to the brigand's nose.

"Ulrich, with me!"

A black mountain of horse shot past.

Slashing at another pale, contorted face, he hauled the Gothen horse around again. Screaming back at the surrounding faces, not in anger or fear, but pain.

For a moment, hands snatched at his cloak and leg, another pistol fired, close enough for him to smell the gunpowder.

He slashed wildly, connecting with something. Mist sprayed the world red.

Then he was away.

Ahead of him, Styx's beautiful black arse rippled as the stallion galloped through the ford, spraying water in all directions.

He ducked down low in case there were any more firearms or crossbows. Or, more pertinently, any better shots. He gritted his teeth, held on to his ride and, with an even firmer grip, his father's bloody sabre.

If anything else came his way, he didn't hear it, and his horse flew across the river and up the far bank in Styx's wake.

The stallion stopped close to where Usk was helping Bosko's men desperately trying to reattach the damaged wheel to the carriage they were protecting.

The Brigands hadn't pursued them. Perhaps the sight of the levelled muskets and pistols dampened their enthusiasm. Or they were simply waiting for all their number to make it down the hill to the riverbank before charging.

After all, who would want to miss out on such fun?

"My lady?"

Solace remained atop Styx, breathing in time with the stallion.

He moved his horse closer to the demon's mount. For once, Styx made no complaint.

"What do you think you were doing?"

The words were sharp, harshly spoken. Not the way a man should address his mistress.

Solace's eyes were so intent he turned to see what she was looking at, half expecting more brigands pouring down the other side of the valley. But there was nothing. Muddy meadows, then another gentle slope rising to meet a series of rolling hills crested with clumps of barren winter trees.

What lay ahead looked much the same as what lay behind.

A line of thought he decided best to leave alone.

"What do you think you were doing?!" he raised his voice enough for one of the men trying to fix the coach to look sharply up.

He risked edging the Gothen horse closer to Styx. The stallion tossed his head and gave the newcomer a *that's-close-enough* glare.

"My lady?"

When she still did not react, he leant over and placed his good hand on hers. She clutched the reins so tightly he could feel her trembling through her thick leather gloves.

She blinked, gave a little start, and turned her head towards him in the manner of someone shocked to find they aren't actually alone when singing at the top of their voice.

"Ulrich?"

"What were you doing?" he asked again, this time more gently, the lost expression on her face draining some of his anger.

"Saving the horses."

Frankly, others could have done that. But he hadn't meant charging toward a mob of brigands.

"You... just sat there while that bastard pointed a gun at you. If it hadn't misfired, you would be dead!" his voice and anger rose again.

"But I'm not dead, am I?" she leant in so sharply he had to straighten himself in the saddle again to avoid her forehead, "God has a plan for me, Ulrich. A purpose. And for you, too. He isn't going to allow some lowly brigand to put paid to that plan, is he?"

He thought about telling her history was littered with the bodies of great men who thought their god had a plan for them, right up to the point some non-entity perforated them with an arrow, spear, musket shot, sword or dagger. Or they just fell off their horse.

He reached over and eased Solace back to the vertical.

"I hope God is as aware of this plan as you are."

"'tis the second time a misfiring pistol has saved my life, Ulrich. First, in the Wolf's Tower, when despair made me try to take my own life. And now today. What does that tell you?"

It tells me it was one of the few things Old Man Ulrich was right about.

"Never trust your life to a pistol; they're not a reliable weapon."

They both swivelled in their saddles as gunfire broke out behind them, but no tide of dirty-faced brigands rushed the river. Bosko and Lebrecht were just encouraging them to keep their distance with a few warning shots.

"You are a terrible cynic," Solace said, then smiled. The dark intensity faded from her eyes, and she was once more the young woman he knew. The one he both loved and hated.

She leaned in again, summoning him to meet her halfway with a flick of the hand. The Gothen horse shuffled under him as he leant in close enough for Solace's lips to brush his ear.

"But perhaps you will more readily believe in God's plan when you find out who is in that coach…"

*

The mob appeared reluctant to cross the ford.

Their guns would kill some of the brigands as they splashed through the shallow water, their swords would take more as they struggled up the bank and their horsemen would cut a bloody swathe through the ones that made it.

Clearly, the same thoughts were going through the brigands' minds. As it was, their mad charge down from the woods earned them only the badly injured soldier under the ash tree. In the scramble to save the horses, no one had thought to get the wounded Vadian over the river. She wasn't sure what that said about either them or the world.

The brigands slit the poor man's throat and stripped him of his clothes. As she watched at Lebrecht's side, two tangled-haired women were squabbling over the dead soldier's boots. Even with a river between them, they didn't look like particularly good boots.

Not much reward in return for the half a dozen or so brigands they'd killed.

She heard the wet snap of Styx's iron-shod hooves crushing the skull of one of her attackers again.

It had been a curious sound. She couldn't quite describe the noise, though it did put her in mind of a melon hitting the ground from a great height for some reason.

No matter.

She had more pressing concerns.

Lucien had not returned.

"Did nobody see what happened to him?" she'd already asked Lebrecht, now she was asking the same question of Captain Bosko.

The stocky soldier crumpled face crumpled further while his eyes stayed on the far side of the river.

"We were a bit busy," he said.

The trees fringing the river partially obscured their view of the hillside. None of the bits they could see boasted the uncouth mercenary or his moustaches.

"He's a resourceful man," Lebrecht offered tentatively, "I'm sure he is fine."

"He's an idiot," she snapped.

"That idiot probably saved your life," Bosko said, "and,

more importantly, your horses. He distracted those bastards long enough for you to get them over the river. Shame he couldn't do the same for Bernard, mind..." Bosko's eyes flicked to the pale, naked corpse discarded on the far bank for the crows.

"I'm sorry for your man."

"He was done for. A slit throat was a kindness..." Bosko spat into the brown undergrowth.

"Don't blame yourself for his death, Captain," Lebrecht said.

"Blame, my lord? I only blame those bastards over there..." he spun away and stomped off towards Lady Karoline's carriage, "...though if some idiot had thought to put the wounded on this side of the river..."

Lebrecht gave her a pained smile and returned to watching the brigands. Most of them had gathered into a huddled knot, presumably trying to decide how many were prepared to die to seize the horses and Lady Karoline's coach. There didn't seem to be anybody giving orders. A rabble who ruled themselves? Whatever madness would the world conjure next?

"We should make haste for Magdeburg once the carriage is fixed. We could leave now, but that would-"

She cut Lebrecht off, "We're not going to Magdeburg."

Renard's boots scuffed the damp undergrowth behind her. He hadn't said much since she'd told him Bulcher's latest bride was in that coach.

"We're not...?"

"No, we're going to Thasbald."

"We are?" Lebrecht's eyebrow shot up, "Why?"

She supposed there might come a time she would need to tell Lebrecht she planned to torture and kill Lady Karoline's betrothed. But this didn't seem the most opportune moment.

"To ensure Lady Karoline arrives safely. Bosko has already lost half his men; there's a fair chance they won't make it without our assistance."

"Well, yes. But... is that any of our business?"

"As Christians, helping those in need should always be our business, shouldn't it?"

Over the river, someone started wailing. She couldn't tell if it was a man or a woman. Either way, it was annoying.

"Yes, I suppose, but... 'tis a dangerous journey."

She nodded, "But I feel 'tis important we help these people. Will you come with us?"

Lebrecht's expression faltered between a smile and a grimace.

"Are you eager to return to Ettestein and talk to your father?"

"No..."

"Then come with us. I'm sure *Graf* Bulcher will be grateful. And he's an important man, I believe. Perhaps his good graces and gratitude towards Gothen will salve any... *disappointment* your father might have about your recent choices..." she stepped in close to him and held his eye. She considered brushing her fingers against his but decided not to overdo it.

"...and I would be ever so grateful too... my lord..."

Lebrecht swallowed. The cold already flushed his cheeks, but she fancied they reddened even more. He might have an eye for the ladies, as his brother Joachim had warned her when they first met outside Enoch the Miser's farm, but he did not appear quite so comfortable when the ladies started acting... *boldly*.

"Well, I can see that, but my men... 'tis dangerous, they-"

"They are soldiers. Paid by Gothen. After your father, *you* are Gothen. They will do as you tell them to. You have their oaths, do you not?"

Lebrecht nodded.

"Well then," she beamed, "we are agreed!"

"Yes... my lady... but-"

"Excellent! Best you start getting the men prepared. We need to be away the moment Lady Karoline's coach is ready to travel."

"Yes," Lebrecht said, more assuredly this time, before wheeling away to join Paasche and the other Gothens overlooking the ford.

Her sunny smile faded as soon as Lebrecht turned his back.

Across the river, a crow fluttered onto Bernard's corpse. Out of gun and earshot, the rest of the brigands appeared to be arguing. Behind her, Renard shuffled his feet in the damp, rotting leaves.

"I can hear the disapproval in your boots..." she said, not looking over her shoulder.

Renard cleared his throat, perhaps deciding whether to say anything or not. It didn't take him long to make his mind up.

"You tried to seduce the father and almost ended up locked in a tower. Is trying the same trick with the son a good idea?"

'tis a bloody terrible idea, but what else have I got?!

"Seducing? Is that what you think I'm doing?" she asked.

"Whichever word you would prefer, my lady. We are going to try and kill a man."

"You think he would be more likely to help if I told him that?"

"Probably not."

"Well, then."

"But-"

"I need an army, Ulrich. I will do whatever is necessary. The fact I was prepared to give myself to Hendrick of Gothen should demonstrate any lingering doubts you may have about my seriousness are misplaced," now she looked over her shoulder; Renard appeared as miserable as ever, "I need an army. Even a small one. We are not enough to destroy the Red Company. And if Lucien has got himself killed, then we are even weaker than we were. But I trust God will provide all I need..."

Her eyes moved to Lady Karoline's coach.

"Lucien isn't dead," he said, refusing to follow her gaze.

"You think so?"

"He's far too irritating to disappear that easily."

"I hope you're right; we need him."

Renard put himself between her and Lady Karoline's coach.

"Lebrecht, Bosko and their men will not stand with you against the Red Company. No sane man would."

"You would."

"My sanity has been questionable for some time, my lady."

She smiled and put her hand on his arm. The bad one he mostly kept pressed to his side.

"We will prevail, Ulrich. Trust me. I know what I'm doing."

Renard managed to restrain himself from punching the air and cheering.

"We will run Bulcher to ground. I will have justice. And I will find out how he contacted the Red Company. It may be possible to stop them before they reach Magdeburg. So we don't have to be there when the walls fall and the slaughter begins."

And that girl you are growing fond of dies in Saul the Bloodless' arms...

There were several holes in her plan. In fact, it had far more holes than it did plan. Renard at least had the good grace not to point any of them out.

Still, one problem at a time. One bridge. One ford.

And she would prevail. Whatever the odds. Whatever the cost.

She turned back to the river.

On the far bank more slick-feathered crows arrived to feast on Bernard.

Fortunately, she didn't much believe in portents.

Chapter Five

It took another hour to fix the coach's wheel.

All the time, he expected the brigands to come pouring over the river or another horde to roll out of the wood to join the first in an unstoppable wave of filthy banditry, or Lucien to return.

One calamity or another, anyway.

The distinct possibility Lucien lay face down dead somewhere caused a distant stab of guilt for the uncharitable thought. He might be an annoying idiot, but he hoped the fool hadn't gotten himself killed.

He moved from watching the brigands, whose debate about what to do next had descended into a farce of childlike squabbling and fist fights, to sweeping the horizon behind them. The worry the brigands were simply lulling them into a false sense of security while more of their number sneaked up behind them nagged him. Surely, they couldn't be as incompetent and desperate as they now seemed? To realise the enemy who'd filled you with terror an hour earlier was but a bunch of hungry, impoverished buffoons was a bit galling.

In whichever direction he wandered, and to whatever horizon he stared, Hilde trotted after him.

He wasn't sure if he found that endearing or irritating.

She said little and looked worried.

Perhaps he should reassure her all was well.

Except it wasn't. And he'd told her to stay in Ettestein. And he was already trying to keep one woman intent on dying alive.

And why did she keep looking at him?

Like *that*.

He kept pacing.

Time passed.

They finished fixing the wheel. The brigands remained on the other side of the river arguing. If they were trying to divert their attention while their friends snuck up on them from elsewhere, the sneaky friends must have gotten lost. Lucien didn't reappear. Hilde kept looking at him. Solace kept looking at Lebrecht. The young nobleman kept looking at Solace. Things churned inside him without him ever totally understanding what those things were.

"Mount up!" Bosko eventually yelled, to his great relief, "Let's get out of here!"

Three mounted Vadians watched the ford in case the brigands tried to pursue them, but he could already make out small groups trudging back up the hill to their woodland redoubt. Their moment had passed. Without the element of surprise, they were but a rabble.

"How long will it take to get there?" Hilde asked when she finally stopped looking over her shoulder.

They were delivering Bulcher's bride to the *Graf*'s estate in Brandenburg, a place called Thasbald, but he didn't know where it was exactly. Solace rode ahead of Karoline's coach with Lebrecht and Bosko; they followed behind the rattling contraption weighed down with cases and trunks strapped to the roof. No wonder the brigands were so keen to get their hands on it. He wondered what kind of dowry Karoline's father was giving Bulcher to take his daughter's hand and whether it trundled towards the *Graf* along with his wife-to-be.

"I don't know. A week, maybe."

It was as good a guess as any. Given the time of year, the roads, and the war, getting anywhere was a lottery.

Plodder trudged, head down. He'd had to return the Gothen horse to its rider, a jug-eared young man called Harri, who'd acted more like he'd borrowed his sweetheart for a ride than his horse. He was once more in the saddle atop his own sag-backed gelding. Would the nag last another week?

He blew out a frosty breath and gently slapped his bad arm.

Would he?

Hilde started chatting again after a while. The countryside was largely open, and fear of brigands receded. He mainly listened. Though she thought him terribly brave, she'd been scared when he'd ridden to Solace's aid. She was worried about Lucien. She was curious about Lady Karoline, who'd yet to venture outside her coach, and why Solace wanted to accompany the bride-to-be to Thasbald instead of going to Magdeburg and... well, lots of other stuff. He kept his answers vague and short.

Worry, who'd been his friend much longer than Hilde, nagged and gnawed him again.

Sometime in the afternoon, when a little watery sunshine started to break the clouds, they came to a crossroads; by his reckoning, the left-hand road would take them to the

Elbe and Magdeburg. They went straight across, heading north.

No one else was in sight in any direction.

He fancied he could make out a haze of smoke to the west. The chimneys of Magdeburg.

If Solace was right, come the end of spring, that sky would glow beneath the choking black smoke of a burning city. A city with twenty thousand souls inside.

He shivered.

"What's wrong?" Hilde asked.

He turned his eyes to the north.

"Nothing. Just the cold. Makes my arm hurt."

She looked at him sideways, like she didn't believe him.

Hilde didn't say much more for the rest of the afternoon.

The sun finally shrugged off the clouds to hang low and bright above skeletal trees and empty fields. Although dazzling enough to make him squint, the wind whipped away what little warmth it brought.

The road climbed towards a huddle of stone buildings atop a hill. Smoke curled from several chimneys. It was the first living place they'd seen since leaving Ettestein.

A coaching inn.

In normal times, a refuge from the road. But these weren't normal times.

Usk and Harri rode behind them, he told Hilde to stay with them. When he checked with the two Gothen men-at-arms, Usk nodded, while Harri, whose horse he'd borrowed to fight off the brigands, looked like a man who thought he was now owed a ride.

He pushed Plodder forward. The gelding gave a weary,

resigned snort before picking up its hooves.

People meant danger. Which meant he should be close to Solace.

As he passed Lady Karoline's coach curiosity got the better of him and he tried to glance inside, but a curtain hung across the window, as it had ever since they'd found it stranded in the ford.

"My lady..." he said when Plodder caught up with Styx, who whinnied as if hugely amused by something. He didn't know if the stallion was laughing at him or Plodder but was sure it was one or the other of them.

Solace nodded at him, relaxed in the saddle.

"We may have a bed tonight, with a little luck."

He wondered how much of her mother's silver she'd be prepared to pay for that luxury. Nothing came cheap anymore. Other than life.

"This place is safe?"

"Apparently, *Graf* Bulcher kindly advised where Lady Karoline could rest each night during the journey to Thasbald. What a thoughtful and considerate man he sounds, don't you think?"

"Indeed, my lady," he said, ignoring the malicious twinkle in her eye. He thought Bulcher might have taken care not to send his intended through a brigand-infested wood if he was that bothered about her safety, but he kept that to himself. There were too many ears about.

By the time they reached the inn, cloud had swept back in to obscure the sunset.

Wary-looking armed men awaited them.

Bosko called their little column to a halt and rode ahead.

Woodsmoke tainted the air; a robin perched upon a bare branch, alternating between eyeing them and pecking at something in the bark. The wind rustled and pulled with frigid, insistent fingers.

"With any luck, we will rest more comfortably tonight, Lady Celine," Lebrecht said.

Solace had instructed Lebrecht to address her only by her "road" name. He had a feeling Lebrecht would do whatever she told him, hopefully the other Gothen men would do likewise.

He'd have wagered news a woman called Solace was travelling with his bride-to-be might make Bulcher's ears prick up. There weren't many women with that name in the Empire.

Bosko dismounted and, after a couple of minutes haggling, waved them forward. The armed men relaxed and cleared the entrance into the inn's courtyard for them.

The Inn had once been a fine one. Like much of the Empire, however, it now found itself reduced by the times. Wooden planks covered several broken windows, tiles were missing from the moss-softened roof, one wing appeared completely boarded up. An air of neglect and decline hung about the place more pungently than the horse dung.

It was hard to make money from travellers in an age where travelling presented a very real threat to your life.

Which no doubt explained why the innkeeper nodded incessantly, grinning from one hairy ear to the other once Bosko pressed a purse of silver into his bony hand.

One of the inn's men ushered them to a stable complex on the other side of the courtyard. He thrust the reins of

Plodder and Hilde's mare at Harri.

"A beer for you if you put these two to bed."

"Three."

"Two."

The Gothen soldier shrugged, took the reins, and led them off to the stable.

"You should get inside," he said, taking Hilde's elbow.

"No need to fuss about me!"

"You look like a ghost."

She did, too. A day's riding in the cold had robbed her face of colour. Morlaine had rosier cheeks.

He wanted to get Solace out of the cold too but knew better. She wouldn't let anyone else touch Styx; the monster would likely take a finger off if a stranger tried to get that bit out of his mouth.

She stuck close to Lebrecht. Which made him queasy. He didn't like the Gothen lord, nor how he stared at Solace whenever he thought she wasn't looking.

He hurried Hilde inside. Through the door they found a cavernous dining room with huge stone hearths ablaze at both ends.

Only one other patron was in the place, parked in front of the nearest fire, boots up on a chair, tankard in hand.

The man turned around and eyed them, sneering as they approached.

"Ah, you're here at last! You won't believe the fucking day I've had," Lucien flipped the tankard upside down and gave it a desultory shake, "I'm out of bloody beer already!"

*

She wanted to see Lady Karoline as soon as possible.

Unfortunately, she had to settle Styx in first, and Bosko would have whisked the lucky bride-to-be inside long before she finished. Of course, as a *Freiin,* she should have people for this, but the only person she had left was more interested in settling in that girl, Hilde, than helping her.

Styx snorted. It sounded like in derision.

"You're bloody smart for a horse, aren't you?" She scratched the stallion's ear. Styx didn't disagree.

Around her, the men of Gothen and Vadia attended to their horses for the night. Several kept glancing her way. They probably thought she should have someone doing this for her, too. And she shouldn't be dressed like a man, nor riding the biggest horse in their little company.

It was quite possible a few other thoughts were circling, too.

As much as the *sight* unnerved and frightened her, she counted the fact her mother's gift had not also run to reading minds a blessing.

"You shouldn't be doing that…"

Lebrecht stepped in and took the heavy saddle she was struggling with from her arms.

Styx peered over Lebrecht's shoulder as if enquiring whether she wanted this one kicked too. She had checked earlier that no blood and brains were left smeared over the beast's hooves.

"Thank you, my lord."

She found herself shaking her head at the horse. Just in case.

"Don't you have a man for this sort of thing?" he dropped

his load on the nearest free saddle rack.

"I'm not a Princess of the Empire on the road, my lord. I am nobody."

"And I am not a prince!" he beamed, rubbing his hands together.

No, you're something else for me to use because the price of vengeance is not paid in silver...

She shook the thought away and carefully removed Styx's bit and reins. She thought he liked her, but it was still prudent to keep your wits about you around the stallion.

The same as with any man.

"I wanted to speak to Lady Karoline," she said, hanging up the gear.

"Why?"

To see how best I can use her, too.

"I thought she might like a friend. She faces... a daunting journey."

"Indeed," Lebrecht dropped his voice, "I understand Bulcher is a pig."

"I wouldn't let him hear you say that..." she said before she could stop herself.

"He's a powerful man, for sure. I think you are right; if I can curry favour with the *Graf* it might help smooth the waters with Father."

"What do you know of *Graf* Bulcher?" she asked as innocently as any girl might about the man she intended to kill.

"Not a lot," Lebrecht pulled a face, "and nothing good. Truth be told, I don't envy the girl. He must be old enough to be her father, the-"

He might have ended the sentence quicker by running headfirst into a wall, but not by much.

She smiled and concentrated on feeding Styx from the hay bales in the stables.

"Erm..."

"Don't worry, my lord. There is no offence. And your father would not have made a terrible husband."

"Would you have... if he'd provided the men you wanted?"

She looked at him sideways as she worked, "I would do anything to destroy my enemies, my lord. Anything."

She held his eye. Probably a moment too long as she dropped the hay over her feet rather than Styx's trough.

Lebrecht, however, didn't seem to notice.

She would have given herself to the father for a hundred men; would she give herself to the son for six?

He was handsome but not, she suspected, exceedingly bright. Both things in their own way might make the task easier.

"Come," he said when she'd finished with the hay, "I'll get one of my men to rub your horse down."

While Lebrecht barked at the nearest of his soldiers, a sallow-faced, sad-eyed Saxon the others called Swoon, she gave Styx a significant look.

Play nicely, please.

Styx swished his tail and munched.

Outside, dusk settled quickly. They hurried across the muddy, straw-carpeted cobbles past Karoline's coach. A couple of Bosko's men were still unloading trunks from the roof, but the blushing bride was already gone.

"Your lady travels light," she said to the men.

One smiled thinly, the other rolled his eyes. Both looked cold and miserable.

"Do you know anything about Karoline?" she asked Lebrecht as they approached *The Eagle's Claw*.

"Nothing. Though my father has no doubt tried to marry me to her."

"My father did much the same."

"I was engaged to be married."

She raised an eyebrow, "You were? I didn't know."

"Circumstances changed," he opened the door for her, voices billowed out on a warm, smoky breath.

"She decided you weren't pretty enough?"

Lebrecht gave her a rueful shrug, "No, my father decided she wasn't Protestant enough. Her father converted to Catholicism before we were due to marry. Currying favour with the Emperor rather than any crisis of faith... my father decided it no longer a suitable match. A family without principle or backbone was not worth marrying into... he told me..."

Once they were inside and the door closed on the night, she asked, "How did you feel about that?"

"Disappointed. I didn't much care about backbone and principle."

"She was pretty then?"

"Exceedingly, but she converted along with the rest of her family. I assume her father has now found an advantageous Catholic prince to marry her..." his words carried more than an edge of bitterness.

So, your father prevented you marrying the woman you wanted, and now you have prevented him... locking the woman he wanted in a tower?

The sound of laughter, strangely jarring after a day of cold silence interrupted only by death and fear, dragged her mind away from pursuing that thought further.

Familiar laughter.

"I'm sure you will find another, better match soon, my lord..." she said, remembering to hold his eyes and smile coyly before turning away and heading for the knot of men warming themselves around one of the inn's two blazing hearths.

"You're not dead then," she said, interrupting Lucien as he regaled the group with some tall tale. Renard sat next to him, that girl, Hilde, at his side again. Very close at his side.

Lucien hoisted his tankard in salute, "Sadly, for brigands and husbands everywhere, Lucien Kazmierczak has survived to fight and love another day! Hurrah!"

A ragged cheer and more laughter erupted from the onlookers, both Gothen and Vadian, as well as some of the inn workers drawn into Lucien's orbit by his brash charisma. And enormous capacity for bullshit.

He'd likely saved her life with his daft charge, but she still felt vaguely irked. Possibly because he'd left her all day thinking she'd lost him, or maybe just because he was so clearly enjoying himself.

Enjoying himself while the monsters who'd slaughtered her father, taken her brother, killed everyone she knew and destroyed her home walked, and breathed, and laughed too. Probably at her. If they gave her so much as a thought. Which-

"My lady?" Renard asked, standing. Was he offering her his chair by the fire or enquiring about her well-being? A few of the men were giving her curious looks again. Had her mind wandered for a moment. Leaving her gawping like a simpleton? She didn't think so, but...

"I am glad you are alive. But how did you know we would be here?" she asked Lucien.

"'tis a gift, my lady. But I do not give my secrets away cheaply," he hoisted his tankard upwards again, "secrets cost beer!"

More laughter and cheers.

"We will talk later," she said as one of the serving girls took Lucien's tankard and headed to the drawing room to fill it.

Before she could say more, Renard manoeuvred her away from the group.

"Are you well, my lady?"

Ah, he had been enquiring about my wellbeing...

"Perfectly, why?"

"You went... vacant for a moment."

"I did?"

"As if..." Renard looked pained as he struggled to conjure the right word. She saved him the trouble of finding it.

"Really, I am entirely fine. Just tired and cold."

Renard didn't look reassured but indicated his chair by the fire, next to which that girl, Hilde, sat. Now flushed and expectant in the firelight, eyes wide and beguiling as she stared up at Renard.

You're going to die soon...

The realisation hit her like an open hand. She'd seen

Hilde's death already in that desecrated church when the walls of Magdeburg fell, and the demons swept in upon the heels of the Imperial army to feast and slaughter.

Now, the certainty felt palpable.

Why do I not care?

She shook her head.

"Have our rooms been arranged?"

"I believe Bosko has paid for us in return for our help."

"Go and find them."

"Yes, my lady."

Renard gathered up his cloak, said something to Hilde, and then hurried out.

Weariness descended. She ignored it. Instead, she went and found Bosko. The soldier sat alone on the far side of the room before the other fire.

She didn't ask for an invitation to join him.

He turned slow, heavy eyes on her as she eased herself down next to him.

"You sit alone, Captain?"

"I am never alone," he said, gaze returning to the fire.

He'd lost five men today. And they were not the first since they'd set out to take Karoline to Thasbald.

"Don't blame yourself for the world we find ourselves in."

He snorted.

"The world is what it is. The dead are on me, though."

"The dead are on those that do the killing."

He had a saggy, abused face. The kind that looked like the world had taken a dislike to it. It crumpled further as his eyes fell to the tankard in his lap.

"I know Bernard's mother well. She is a... friend. I

promised to bring her son home in one piece."

"'tis not your fault."

"No? If I'd had the sense to move the wounded across the ford before the bast- ... before the brigands attacked..."

"You said he was beyond help?"

That earned her a hollow smile, "We shall never know, shall we? By the time I realised what was happening..." he rapped a knuckle against his balding skull, "...thinking has never been my strongest suit."

She trawled through the usual platitudes you were supposed to trot out in times of grief. All rang as hollow as Bosko's smile, so she kept them locked away where they could do no harm.

When she said nothing, his eyes seemingly struggled to overcome the pull of the bags beneath them as they rose to meet hers.

"Who are you?"

"My name is Celine."

"I didn't ask you your name."

"I am just another refugee from the war, Captain."

"You don't act like a woman fleeing the war."

She offered only a faint smile in return.

"Why do you want to accompany us to Thasbald? You said you had business in Magdeburg?"

"I do. But it can wait. I have a few months before I need to be there."

"But why spend the time out there?" he jerked his head at the door, "'tis no place for a woman."

"Perhaps I am an incurable romantic and the idea of helping a bride reach her intended appeals to me."

"'tis no place for a woman," he insisted.

"Have you told Lady Karoline that?"

Bosko snorted, "I told the *Freiherr*. Several times. Begged him, in fact."

"Seems a strange time to travel; why not wait for the spring?"

"No business of mine..." he turned over his bottom lip, "...but the *Freiherr* is old. I understand he wishes Karoline settled before he goes to the Lord."

She sensed there was more to it, . Those words made Bosko squirm. He was sharing a lie he did not believe. But something else floated beyond her grasp.

"Her siblings are married?"

"She has one brother. Who is still a child. And a sickly one to boot."

Her ears pricked up.

"Tell me about Vadia. I know nothing of it."

"A small barony in the Duchy of Westphalia, relatively untouched by the war."

"Wealthy?"

"More than some, less than others. The war has made everyone poorer. Save the mercenaries."

She turned her eyes to the fire. Vadia sounded a lot like Tassau...

Both had sickly heirs, though Torben's illness was of the mind, not the body. If Karoline's father and brother died, as it stood, the barony would pass to Karoline if there were no other male heirs.

And if Karoline was married to Bulcher...

With Torben incapable of ruling, it was always likely she

would have inherited Tassau as she had no uncles or male cousins.

And if she'd been married to Bulcher...

"My lady...?"

She looked up. Bosko was peering at her. From the furrows in his forehead, she suspected he might have been doing so for some time.

"Captain, I'd like to see Lady Karoline as soon as possible..."

Chapter Six

The Eagle's Claw Inn, Prince-Bishopric of Magdeburg, The Holy Roman Empire - 1631

Lucien seemed determined to get prodigiously drunk.

This wasn't unusual. The mercenary had been in various stages of inebriation for at least half the time he'd known him.

Tonight, however, he was attempting the task with fierce gusto. He was also talking a lot. Again, not unusual, but a particular urgency fuelled his boasting, the words tumbling over each other in their eagerness to escape his mouth.

Lucien's hands were shaking, too. Only slightly, but it was something he hadn't seen before.

If he'd had the chance, he would have asked what happened after the mercenary had ridden off toward the brigand mob, but Lucien was too busy entertaining his audience for him to have a word. No doubt an opportunity would arise later, though, by then, the oaf would be too drunk even to remember who he was, let alone what took place that morning.

Instead, he sat quietly by the fire, nursing his beer. Hilde with him. Until he sent her away. Lucien wasn't the only one getting shit-faced and he didn't know if all the soldiers could be trusted around a woman.

Hilde shared a room with Solace.

She hadn't been keen, presumably because she wanted to stay close to him or Solace unnerved her. In all likelihood, a bit of both.

Eventually, she'd relented. After he agreed to take her to the room.

He didn't know where Solace was. He might have suspected she was working on seducing Lebrecht if the Gothen nobleman hadn't been sitting alone in the corner, staring into the shadows.

The room was modest but comfortable. A room suitable for a lady of some quality and her maid.

"Do you have to go?" Hilde had asked. Eyes big in the way some women's could.

"Yes," he'd nodded, "There's something wrong with Lucien, I should keep an eye on him."

"He charged a mob on his own today; I think he can look after himself."

"Probably, but still..." in truth, he didn't care about Lucien, he just didn't trust himself to be alone in a bedroom with Hilde much more than he did the soldiers downstairs.

He wished her goodnight.

She came over, stretched up and kissed him on the cheek.

Which made him care even less about Lucien.

He told her he'd see her for breakfast and hurried out of the room before he could convince himself a stupid idea was a brilliant one.

In the tavern, Lucien still regaled all and sundry, though

some of his audience had started to drift off. A few newcomers waded into the fray, including the grey-haired old goat who described himself as the Inn's master-at-arms, charged with keeping the peace despite his enormous belly and bandy legs.

"Is he gonna cause me any trouble?" the man asked out of the corner of his mouth as he stood beside him.

"Does telling tall tales and talking bullshit count as trouble?"

"Nope. In fact, 'tis pretty much compulsory. We must make our own entertainment up here."

Lucien slammed the latest emptied tankard on the table and peered up at them.

"Tell me," Lucien asked, "any whores in this inn of yours?"

The master of arms narrowed his eyes. And bristled, "Tell me, friend, do I look like the kind of man who'd work in a place that didn't have whores?"

Lucien held up a hand, "No offence."

"None taken. But I have a reputation to think of."

"I can see you're a fine, resolute, upstanding fellow!"

"I've always tried to do the right thing," the master-at-arms found space under his belly to squeeze his thumbs behind his belt, possibly responding to an entirely different conversation, "Some of the girls will oblige, but they don't come cheap. Fucking war has made everything more expensive. Even fucking."

"Fucking war..." Lucien stared forlornly at his empty ale pot.

The master-at-arms pulled out a chair and slumped into it without reducing it to sticks.

More soldiers started drifting away, maybe not caring to hear more grumbling about how everything was better before the war or possibly to find out how much the girls here charged for themselves.

The grey-haired old man stuck out a hand, "Gabriel Gotz, I keep the peace in this fine hostelry."

Lucien readily accepted the offered hand, "I am none other than Lucien Kazmierczak, the famed soldier, adventurer, and lover. You've probably heard of me."

Gotz scratched his thick beard, "Nope, can't say I have."

"Oh..." the usual look of puzzlement Lucien got when someone told him they'd never heard of him flitted across his face.

"Ulrich Renard," he said, sitting down. Neither man acknowledged him.

"You've got the air of a soldier about you?" Lucien asked Gotz.

"Stamped on my soul. Been tramping from one side of Europe to the other with one bloody army or another since I was a boy. Fucking idiot! Sarah!" Gotz hollered at one of the girls before pointing at himself, Lucien and the fellow with the bad arm who was even less renowned than the famed soldier, adventurer and lover next to him.

Sarah said something not entirely polite in return but did at least wander off in the direction of the drawing room.

"Game lass," Gotz said, spitting on the floor, "be out of here soon if she's got any sense. I tell all the girls, but no one listens to an old fool like me even though I know more of the world than everyone else here put together."

"Things getting bad?" he asked.

Gotz looked over as if noticing him for the first time.

"Bad everywhere, son. We've managed, but with an Imperial army likely to be at Magdeburg in the spring..."

"It'll get worse..." Lucien said.

"Old Suckow..." Gotz nodded towards the still grinning innkeeper, who was at least fifteen years younger than him, "...thinks it'll be great for business. Lots of soldiers looking for beer and girls. Old Suckow likes to think the best of people..." Gotz sucked on one of his remaining teeth, "...frankly, dunno how he's lived as long as he has."

"Never been a soldier, has he?" Lucien groomed his moustaches with grubby fingers.

"Nope. When they reach Magdeburg and put the city under siege, they'll be foraging everywhere for supplies. Maybe they'll pay. But in my experience, *foraging* is just a bullshit term for stealing. They won't be paying for food and beer. Girls neither."

Sarah interrupted them with more ale, which she dumped on the table without a word or a smile.

"Even if they do pay, these girls will be bloody ruined," Gotz said, reaching for his drink with a sigh once Sarah left them.

"I worry about em, I really do. Like a father to them, I am..." the froth crowning his tankard hovered below Gotz's beard, "...well, not *exactly* like a father in every respect; I do get a discount, but I still wouldn't want to see anything bad happen to any of them."

"You are sticking around then?" Lucien asked.

"Fuck that! 'tis every man, woman and pig for himself once the Imperial army gets here!"

"Where will you go?" he asked after sipping his own beer. It was surprisingly decent. Or he really needed a drink.

"Oh, somewhere or other along the road. Been a soldier all my life. Still got a clear eye and a strong arm, even if my legs aren't as good for running as they used to be. Which is a shame, as I was very handy when it came to running. A useful skill to have on the battlefield..." Gotz waggled, wiry, unkempt eyebrows, "...running away."

"Always work to be had soldiering," Lucien agreed from behind his now frothy moustaches.

"Aye. Though the trick," Gotz raised a finger, "is to find a position that doesn't require any fighting. Or marching. Never been keen on the marching."

"Not much marching here, I'd guess," he said.

"Nope. Not much fighting either. If there is any trouble, I point it out to the younger lads and let them do the actual whacking."

"Much trouble?"

Gotz puckered his lips, "Nah, not really. Hardly any guests, which keeps the trouble down no end. Got the Merry Gentlemen over yonder, sometimes a couple of them try to spend their ill-gotten gains here, but they're usually told to fuck right off if they darken the door," Gotz chuckled, "I'm a right hospitable bugger, me."

"Merry Gentlemen?" he asked.

"The bastards you ran into earlier. Been lurking around for a while now. Though, by the sound of it, there's more of them than there used to be. Now Magdeburg's under blockade; there's no one to keep the buggers down. The local lords are keeping their men behind their walls, too.

So, the vermin are breeding like fucking rats."

"Cunts," Lucien spat.

"Couldn't put it better myself," Gotz tipped his beer in the mercenary's direction, "but as I'll be on the road again soon... Shame. But there you go. Cushy numbers are hard to find these days."

"They won't attack the Inn?" he asked.

"Never have. We got guns, high walls and a big fuck off gate. They like easier game."

"Didn't look like it today..." he said, remembering them pouring down the hill.

"Maybe they're getting bolder. Or hungrier. Another reason to be leaving."

"Where will you go?"

Gotz pulled a face, "Wherever the road takes me. Ain't got a wife, family, no children I know of, and every woman I ever laid with is likely to dump her night soil bucket on my head if I rolled up on her doorstep again. I'm not sure how it ended like that, but... I'll find somewhere. Just gotta learn that nothing good lasts. Had a soft number before here, the Prince-Bishop of Würzburg's household guard. No fighting, no marching. Just had to stand around and ensure no cunt threw shit at the Prince-Bishop. Very cushy."

"I'm assuming something went south?" Lucien asked.

"Oh, you assume right. The little arsehole of a Prince-Bishop got himself an enthusiasm for burning witches. An enemy with a sword I can honourably run away from is one thing, tossing women and children on a bonfire..." Gotz took a long, hard pull on his beer, "...have no time for such business."

Gotz's eyes, red and bleary above lavender-tinged bags, flicked between them, "You fellows ain't got a sniff of fanaticism about you, but it can be hard to tell..."

Lucien shook his head, "I worked in Madriel not long ago. Much the same happened there, so I left."

"Good man," Gotz's chins wobbled as he nodded, "I seen some shit in my time. Done plenty of it, too. No one who goes a soldiering can avoid that, but if you have a soul, there must still be a line. I crossed it in Würzburg. But not again. Never again."

"Amen to that," Lucien raised his beer. Gotz clinked his against it.

"What about you, young fella? You old enough to have done things you shouldn't have?"

A long and weighty pause followed, then, "Yes..."

"And how does that make you feel?"

"Like shit."

Gotz sucked on another tooth before telling him, "Then you still got a soul; best you do what you can to keep it..."

He let his eyes drift to the fire.

*

The face peering around the door didn't look like anyone *Graf* Bulcher would be interested in marrying, so she assumed her Lady Karoline's maid.

"Yes?"

"I'm sorry to disturb you, but I wish to speak with Lady Karoline?"

The girl stared so blankly she initially thought she might

be deaf, but after a few facial contortions, the maid slammed the door in her face. The sound of mumbled voices came from the other side before it creaked open again.

"Who are you?" the girl asked in heavily accented German, most likely French.

"I am Lady Celine, a *Freiherr's* daughter, like your mistress, and my men helped protect you from the brigands this morning.

That earned another look so blank she expected the girl to ask, "What brigands?" Instead, the door shut in her face again. More mumbling ensued.

The next time the door opened, she barely managed to hide her irritation behind a smile.

"My lady is very tired, I-"

"Well, I will try not to take too much of her time then," she said, squeezing by the squealing girl before she could slam the door shut in her face again.

The room was the best *The Eagle's Claw* offered, comfortable if sparse. Another girl stood behind a chair next to the hearth; pale and drawn, she looked like a fawn ready to bolt. And she was a girl too; if Karoline was more than fourteen and Solace von Tassau was a gambler, she'd have lost a lot of money.

"There is no need to be alarmed," she said quickly, holding out her hands. Lady Karoline swayed like she might faint if anyone came within half a dozen paces of her.

Thin to the point of skeletal and as pallid as any demon, dark rings weighed heavy under her eyes. Lady Karoline appeared not to have slept or eaten properly in months. If she wasn't suffering from some malaise, the prospect of marrying *Graf* Bulcher was making her look like she did.

"You should not be here," Karoline's maid put a hand on her arm and tried to pull her back.

"Don't touch me!" she snarled, half turning on the woman.

Whatever the maid saw in her eyes was enough to make the young woman recoil as if she'd slapped her face.

Did I slap her face?

No, of course she hadn't.

"Elin, 'tis alright; I can receive a guest," a faltering smile twitched Karoline's pale lips, "I am not too tired."

Elin's scowl suggested her mistress had agreed to have supper with a slavering beast.

Karoline sat down and indicated the room's other chair. Elin hovered, seemingly looking for the heaviest object in the room to grab just in case.

"You do not dress like a noblewoman?" Karoline ventured as she took the offered chair. Sophia had asked her something similar. Did she look so peculiar? She supposed she must. Clothes defined a woman so much more than they did a man.

"'tis better suited to travelling the road."

"I would imagine..." Karoline ran bony hands down her own gown, unfussy but finely cut. It gave her the air of a child trying hard to be a grown-up.

"The war destroyed my home... I currently have little need for frocks."

"I am sorry. This war..." Karoline's voice trailed off, every word seemingly hauled up from some deep, far away place at great expense. The *Freiin* looked exhausted; it would be easy to mistake the tobacco-tinted skin beneath her eyes for bruises.

She stifled a distant pang of guilt for disturbing her. If Bulcher lived long enough to marry the girl, lack of sleep would be the least of her problems.

"I live. I grieve. What else can we do?"

Apart from killing your husband-to-be?

"How can I help you?"

Did Karoline think her here for money? Homeless nobles were no more than better-dressed beggars, after all.

"I'm here to offer you my help."

Another twitchy smile, "Your help?"

"To reach Thasbald safely. To deliver you to your intended."

"Captain Bosko is in charge of my safety if you require money-"

"I don't require money."

Karoline appeared confused. She shuffled and rearranged her skirts.

"Then...?"

"I have men, soldiers. Trustworthy and dependable. I am willing to put them at your disposal for the remainder of the journey. I have already discussed this with Captain Bosko. He is agreeable. But I thought it proper to confirm this with you, as you are in charge."

The idea she was in charge amused Karoline.

"My father placed Bosko in command. I have little-"

"Captain Bosko is a worthy and capable man, I am sure. But you are a Princess of the Empire. As am I, despite my reduced circumstances. We should not lose sight of our position in the world, my lady."

"I suppose..." Karoline didn't look convinced. As a young woman, she'd probably never considered the concept that she was in charge of anything, including her own destiny.

"So, is my offer acceptable?"

Karoline's eyes flicked to Elin, who loitered behind her. Elin was only in her early twenties herself. She found it surprising Karoline wasn't travelling with an older, more worldly woman. But she was glad she wasn't. It would make using her a little easier.

"And you want nothing in return?"

"But one small favour, my lady."

"Ah... I see."

She still thinks I'm after money.

"I wish a private audience with *Graf* Bulcher once we arrive in Thasbald."

"An audience... why?"

"A business proposal. Something my late father wished to discuss with him. Tragic circumstances prevented him from putting the proposals to the *Graf*, but I wish to take matters forward. Our chance encounter upon the road makes it clear to me God wishes me to go to Thasbald and do what my father could not."

"Oh..."

She smiled, innocent and reassuring was what she was reaching for.

"You know how the world is, my lady. As a mere woman, such things are supposed to be above me. I fear the *Graf* may not even entertain them if I were to go to him directly, but, with your good grace..."

Karoline's eyes slid to Elin and back, "Well, I suppose that's the least I could do in return for your help. After we were attacked again today, I feared I would never make this journey alive."

"Lady Karoline, there are many dangers in this world. I will do everything in my power to keep you from the very worst of them..."

Chapter Seven

"I thought you were going to find yourself a girl?"

Lucien peered at him, "I think I missed that boat..."

They were alone, save for Suckow, the innkeeper, who remained by the door to the drawing room on the off-chance Lucien fancied putting any more of his beer away for the night. The innkeeper was still grinning like a village idiot with an interesting new stick. The serving girls had finished for the night some time ago. Whether they had all finished work yet was another matter.

He'd had his fill of drinking hours ago and wasn't quite sure why he wasn't in his bed.

"How'd you know we'd be here?" he asked when Lucien took an uncharacteristically long pause for breath.

"I heard who was in the coach. Didn't take any great leap of deduction our lady would be staying close to her. This is the most likely pissing hole on the road towards Thasbald you'd spend the night in..." Lucien winked, "...I'm clever, right?"

"Dead clever."

The mercenary shrugged off his modesty to nod in agreement.

"Though the way you charged at those brigands wasn't."

Lucien's grin faded, "Needed to be done. Put the wind up the buggers. They would have got to you and the horses otherwise. You, we could afford to lose, but the horses?

Damn hard to replace a decent horse these days."

"You could have died."

"The thought did cross my mind..." Lucien flexed his fingers. When the mercenary captain saw him gazing at the slight tremor running through them, he curled the hand into a fist and let it fall to his lap below the table.

"Did your life flash before your eyes?"

Lucien chuckled, "Would have died with a smile on my face if it had!

But no, I didn't think about life. I thought about death."

"Yours or theirs?"

This time, there was no laugh.

"Mine. Which is something that has never happened before."

"Never?"

"I have fought many battles, some between armies in the field, some between drunks in a tavern. Whatever the situation, whatever the odds, I never thought for a moment I wouldn't walk away, wouldn't be toasting my comrades and enemies, wouldn't drink another keg dry, never make another woman laugh, never fuck another whore, never..." he snorted, "...break another heart."

"You're a confident fellow, aren't you?"

The smile returned briefly, but this one cast a melancholy shadow over the mercenary's face, "You've noticed that, huh?"

"'tis hard not to. You're a terrible braggart and boor."

Lucien laughed and looked more like his usual self. He first pushed his empty tankard across the scored, beer-puddled table and then hauled himself upright.

"I must be getting old; the prospect of drinking till dawn does not appeal to Lucien Kazmierczak."

He followed Lucien to his feet.

"Let's see how many people we can wake up trying to find our beds, eh?" Lucien winked.

"You're not going to sing, are you?"

Lucien shook his head, "I feel no song in my heart."

He nodded at Suckow that his last guests were done for the night. The innkeeper managed to look both relieved and disappointed as he turned a dog-eared towel around his hands.

"Why did you think you were going to die?" he asked as Lucien swayed his way to the door.

"I was charging several hundred rabid dogs armed to the teeth with fearsome weapons."

"There were nearer fifty, most of them armed with rusty farming implements and sticks."

"Your memory is faulty. Lucien Kazmierczak is famed for his excellent powers of recall from-"

"Why, Lucien?"

They halted in the doorway, behind them the clink of tankards as Suckow cleared the remnants of their night's drinking. Otherwise, the world remained mute.

"Because..." he said in a small voice that barely sounded like him, "...I thought I would never see Morlaine again. One lucky pistol shot, one rabbit hole to catch a hoof, one... mistake. I never expected or feared death before because I had nothing to lose. Now I'm afraid I have."

Beer can make a man say things he wouldn't normally. Sometimes, it showed their worst side, and occasionally, admittedly less often, a better one.

Was he seeing the more sensitive man skulking behind the bullshit and bluster, or just an even bigger idiot who thought he'd fallen in love with a monster who drank his blood because she happened to have a pretty face?

He took a rush light from a shelf, lit it, and shoved Lucien through the door into the shadowy corridor beyond.

"How do you know you'll see her again anyway? She thinks we're heading to Magdeburg."

"Oh, she'll find me. I have no doubt."

"We do have her horse," he admitted, the boards creaking as they shuffled unsteadily towards the stairs leading up to the guest rooms.

"Lucien Kazmierczak is a famed lover. Perhaps the greatest in the world! Trust me, Ulrich, she'll cross heaven and Earth to find me again!"

He sighed.

No, he really is just an idiot.

"Greatest lover in the world?"

"'tis true, I swear! Every woman I have been with has told me I'm the greatest lover they have ever known," Lucien peered at him as they mounted the stairs side by side, "they can't *all* be wrong, can they?"

"Does that include the whores?"

"Of course! Given how many men they fuck, they must know what they are talking about."

He paused halfway up.

The margin between Lucien being serious and joking could be a thin one.

"Or they tell you what a man wants to hear in the hope of

a pfennig or two more?"

"Oh, no. Lucien Kazmierczak can always spot a lie. He's famed from-"

"Please shut up."

Lucien's chuckle echoed behind him as he carried on up the stairs, annoyed with himself for entertaining the possibility for even a few seconds that the famed soldier, adventurer, and lover was anything other than a shallow, boorish arse.

*

Fury lit the woman.

Other feelings buzzed around her too; grief, guilt, and a sense of injustice so palpable it strode at her side, spitting malice in her ear.

She was cold, but she was used to being cold.

She was hungry, but she was used to being hungry.

She had nothing, and she'd become used to having nothing, too, though she remembered owning things. Not a lot, but a little. Back in the old days when she'd still been a child, before the lords and princes, bishops and men of fancy words decided the world must be ripped asunder by war.

Before they'd been forced from their homes, before her mother died, before they had been chased away, spat at, and treated like dogs simply for having nothing.

Now her father was dead, too.

Thanks to the bitch on the big black horse.

Hate bloomed within the woman, driving into her, spearing her, impaling her so firmly she thought she'd never be able to rise from the cold, damp grass she hunkered on. That she might as well claw down into the earth and make her own grave right here.

Pa was dead.

Killed by that monstrous horse.

Killed by the bitch who rode it.

At first, she'd thought it a boy atop the beast as she'd pelted down the hill behind her father, only as they'd drawn close could she see it was a young woman with her hair cut short.

What kind of woman did that?

Bitch! Bitch! Bitch!

How she wished they'd stayed in the woods, but Gulver wanted that coach. Full of fancy shit, he'd told them. All piled high on top of it. Enough in that thing to feed them till spring. Some fucking rich shit prancing around the countryside while they starved.

She'd followed him like the rest of them had. Get down that hill quick enough and will have the lot of them before they know what's happening.

Gulver had shaken a fist at the sky above the bare canopy of branches they gathered under, shrieking, "Rich cunts!"

Father had shaken his fist, too, like most others. The few who said it weren't worth it got shouted down. She should have listened to them voices, but empty stomachs and shivers don't always sit well with common sense.

Looking back, she could see Gulver was just pissed they'd let the coach escape in the first place. And his pissiness only got worse when he found out another bunch of riders had gone through while they'd been busy taking the horses and booty from the corpses of the four men they managed to nab in their ambush back to camp.

Jumping buggers on the road was one thing; charging down a hill towards soldiers was quite another.

Maybe if one of the cunts hadn't charged back at them, they would have at least bagged some of the horses for their trouble. But he'd given the hot heads at the front some pause for thought about getting their hot heads chopped off their cold shoulders.

The few brothers with guns and bows wasted shot at that rider, but he hadn't stuck around. He'd galloped off before they could overwhelm him. But he'd delayed them long enough for the cunts below to collect up their horses and set themselves up over the ford.

They'd been a brouhaha about what to do then. Gulver had still been for charging across the river.

She hadn't paid a lot of attention, what with crying over her dead Pa and all, but Gulver had been of the opinion they outnumbered the cunts by enough they could overrun them if they all went fast together.

The dissenting voices pointed out that they'd take a dozen or more lead balls before they got across the river, and nobody were much taken with that idea.

Part of her wanted to pick up Pa's old sword and go splashing after the bitch on the black horse with it. She was angry as a wasp, always had been, but she weren't stupid to go with it, as many seemed to be.

No, she'd get that bitch and the rest of those cunts on their fine horses and whatever rich cunt was in that fancy carriage too. But she'd do it her way. Still angry, but cold

The Night's Road: Book IV – When the Walls Fall

anger worked a lot better than the sizzling kind, in her experience.

So, she stayed still, she stayed quiet, and she waited.

It were bitter, and the ground sodden. There wasn't much cover up here as the road climbed up atop a ridge of hills, rather than staying below, where it often flooded in spring and stayed boggy for much of the year.

The Merry Gentlemen liked sticking to the woods, even when winter stripped the trees naked. Their kind of living weren't best done in plain sight, even in these times when there were few prepared to spare soldiers to keep the roads clear of the likes of them.

Still, thieves couldn't be choosers any more than beggars could.

She'd brought a couple of blankets from the camp, wrapping them around herself as she stretched out on her belly. Weren't helping a great deal with damp or cold, but they were dark and dirty, and the night a cloudy and moonless one, so the chances of any cunt spotting her under them were slim to nothing.

Pa's sword sat next to her. It were old, heavy, and flecked with rust. She didn't reckon she were strong enough to do much damage with it, but she'd brought it along anyway. A bit of Pa to keep close.

The rest lay beneath an oak near the Merry Gentlemen's camp. Maybe she'd go back and bury it tomorrow. Maybe not. Depends how business went, she supposed.

Lifting her head, she peered at the coaching inn again. Another few lights blinked out. That was good. She wanted all the cunts sleeping like babes in their big comfy fucking beds.

She glanced left and right at the others. Friends of Pa's who wanted to put things right. Weren't as many of em as she'd hoped when she set off to trail the cunts here. But there was enough for what she needed doing.

Just a little longer now...

*

Solace's eyes snapped open, and she sat bolt upright in bed.

Shit...

Chapter Eight

Gothen men, Wickler and Usk, occupied two of the other beds in the room, and they were starting to mumble and complain.

He pulled on his britches while Hilde stood over him with a rushlight. By the time he strapped on his weapon belt, Lucien was awake and cursing.

Solace headed for the door, snapping at them all to come with her.

Lucien gave him a quizzical, bleary stare as he sat in bed.

"Nothing good," he explained, pulling on his jerkin as he hurried after Solace. Hilde padded behind him, carrying his hat.

"My lady?" he called after Solace, who banged on every door she passed as she ran down the corridor.

"Does she often do things like this?" Hilde asked.

"All the time," he said, taking his hat from her, "and whenever she does, you can be sure it is something bad..."

Solace wasn't waiting for anyone to come out of the rooms or offering explanations. Which he assumed meant time was of the essence.

"Stay close to me," he told Hilde as he broke into a run after his mistress.

Solace was already hurtling down the stairs. Behind him, doors were opening, voices calling out. He bolted after her, one hand on the pommel of his father's sabre.

Solace might be the one with the *sight*, but he also knew a bad feeling when it slapped his face.

"My lady!" he called once he reached the bottom of the stairs. She was halfway down the short corridor to the inn's dining room. When she ignored him again, he bellowed, "Wait!"

If anybody was still asleep in *The Eagle's Claw*, the cry should have put that right.

Solace skidded to a halt and glared over her shoulder at him, panting like a cornered animal. Her fencing dagger, he noticed, gripped tightly in her right hand.

"What's wrong?" he asked, coming alongside her.

"The Merry Gentlemen are here," she said, eyes moving toward the door to the dining room.

"How do you... oh," it was a question he still sometimes caught himself asking, "...but Gotz has men on guard?"

Solace shook her head to say this was not the time for questions and moved towards the door. He grabbed her arm and pulled her back.

It was his turn to shake his head as she glowered at him.

He moved past her, drawing a pistol and cocking it as he walked.

Solace followed on his heels. He thought about telling her to wait for Lucien and the rest of their company but saved his breath.

As the whole inn above them rattled to the sound of boots and voices, stealth seemed needless, so he shoved the door open and charged through it.

Something whizzed past his ear to thud into the doorframe.

The room was dark and large, only the orange embers of the two fires broke the shadows. There were no windows on the outside wall of the inn, and the ones facing the courtyard let in no light through glass thick with condensation. The front door, however, hung open on to a black rectangle of night.

As he ducked behind the nearest table to avoid further crossbow bolts, he thought there were at least two people in the room. One hunkered by the door, another silhouetted by the furthest fire. Possibly more, but he might as well start with the enemies he was sure about.

He fired his pistol at the figure by the door; the flash illuminated the scrawny figure of a boy frantically trying to reload a crossbow. The one by the fire was a woman, equally scrawny, with wild, tangled hair. Half bent over, shuffling backwards.

The boy fled through the open door with a startled scream.

Solace was next to him. Others poured through the door behind, Lucien for one, judging by the heavy breathing and smell of stale beer that came with them. Light washed the room as men with lit lanterns followed.

"Brigands!" he swapped pistol for sabre.

"Cunts!" a woman howled back.

Caught in lantern light, she stood by the stone hearth with a shovel in her hand, the small kind used to clean a fire.

He couldn't see any more brigands as Lucien and the other soldiers started fanning across the room.

"Scarper while you still can, bitch," Wickler growled,

drawing his sword.

As he stepped forward to put his body in front of Solace, his heel slipped, and he had to reach out with his bad arm to stop himself as he went down on one knee.

When the pain subsided enough for him to pay attention again, the brigand was still screaming abuse at them.

"I'm sorry... truly..." Solace was saying.

"Fucking bitch! Don't come any closer!" the tangle-haired woman swivelled one way, and then the next, towards the men approaching her. The shovel held out before her, glowing with hot coals from the fire.

His fingers brushed the floor. It was wet. He recognised the smell when he raised them to his nose.

For a moment, he was back in the Darkway, surrounded by screams.

"Oil! She's doused the place in oil!"

"Stay back or I'll fry all you fucking cunts!" the woman screeched.

Which was when someone shot her.

*

Light replaced darkness as the glowing coals tumbled from the woman's hand and hit the floor.

Blue flame rushed away from the fireplace in all directions.

"Cuuunts!!!" the woman screamed, staggering backwards before a whoosh of flame consumed both woman and scream.

"Out!" she thundered, "Get out now!!"

Renard was still climbing to his feet after stumbling. She

dragged him the rest of the way and shoved him at the door as fire rushed towards them. The woman – she'd felt pain and heard her thoughts but didn't know her name – had been a busy bee.

Lucien appeared at her side. Judging by his breath, he was the next most combustible thing in the room. She pushed him at the door, too.

"Out!"

Figures moved, some trying to make for the door, some vainly battling the blaze, some screaming as the flames danced about their feet, eager to consume everything.

Between the three of them, they managed to propel each other outside.

"Hilde!" Renard spluttered, half turning back to the inn before the girl threw her arms around him. She'd clearly had the sense to head straight for the door.

She backed away from the inn across the cobbled courtyard.

The downstairs windows were already glowing like baleful orange eyes as smoke started to belch out of the door along with coughing, stumbling figures.

"Is there another way out?"

"There's a kitchen door," someone said.

She bent over, hands on knees, feeling the heat on her face, feeling the woman's hate in her heart.

Bitch killed my Pa!

Saliva flooded her mouth, and she forced it down to stop herself vomiting.

A hand rested on her shoulder; she looked up. Lucien's face creased in concern.

"I am fine. Just winded," she tried to find a reassuring smile, "at least we left most of our gear with the horses."

Lucien pointed a finger.

Across the courtyard flames started to lick through the stable roof.

She swore as Lucien sprinted to the stables.

"The horses!" she shouted at Renard and the others.

The people inside would have been the priority in some worlds, but they were going nowhere without horses.

She ran after Lucien.

Behind her, boots slapped on the cobbles, shouts and cries cut the air. There were plenty of people to deal with the fire, and there was another way out of the inn. There was nothing to feel bad about.

Bitch killed my Pa!

Nothing at all.

The iron-studded wooden gates to the courtyard hung open. She could see at least two huddled forms on the floor in the flickering orange light. Bodies. Gotz's men, she assumed.

How the woman whose name she didn't know had gotten in and killed them, she couldn't imagine.

Resourceful. She had to give her that.

Karoline's coach was parked under a lean-to next to the stables. Two figures were on the roof, tugging at the strapping holding the trunks the Vadians hadn't hauled up to their lady's rooms.

Revenge hadn't solely motivated all the Merry Gentlemen who'd followed the woman whose name she didn't know.

Lucien was already in the stable as she skidded to a halt,

torn by indecision. The horses were more valuable than the people, but Lady Karoline's good favour was more important still.

She squinted back at the burning inn. Although, if Lady Karoline died...

No, Bosko and the Vadians would see to her safety.

"My lady?" Renard was with her, of course. And Hilde, equally, of course. The lunky Gothen man-at-arms, too. Usk? Yes, that was it.

"Help Lucien," she ordered Hilde before stabbing a finger at the brigand-infested coach, "you two, deal with them."

Usk glanced at Renard as if still unsure who he was taking orders from.

"Now!" she screamed so vehemently at the young soldier, who was almost big enough to fit her snugly in his pocket, he flinched.

Neither man looked happy. Renard at leaving her side, Usk at being shouted at by a girl, most likely.

She left them to it and headed after Hilde. As much as she'd like to find favour with Karoline by personally rescuing her dresses, hats and whatever other shit was in those trunks, she was a lot better suited to saving horses than kicking brigands.

And she could claim the credit afterwards regardless.

The sounds of frightened animals and crackling wood came from the stables as Hilde ducked inside.

She'd awoken from her dream just in time. Any longer, and both inn and stables would be completely ablaze. The woman's thoughts and feelings still clung to her like dirt she would have to scrub herself raw to remove. In the past, her *sight* had been whispers in the wind, half-snatched demented conversations, urges, hunches, and uncanny certainties.

Now it came to her less, but it was far clearer when it did. First the slaughter to come in Magdeburg, now this. She could almost have been out there with the woman whose name she didn't know and her little band of brigands.

How many of them had there been? The woman and the boy with the crossbow. The two atop Karoline's coach.

There had been more than four of them in her vision.

Hadn't there?

Rough hands grabbed her as soon as she entered the stable's smoky interior.

Yes. There had.

Chapter Nine

"Feisty bitch, ain't she?" Usk laughed as they ran to the coach.

The head of one of the figures atop the coach shot up in the increasingly orangey light.

He ignored the remark to concentrate on pulling his second pistol free and cocking it without tripping up over his own feet or shooting himself.

"Oi, you!" Usk drew his sword to stab towards the carriage, "Get down!"

One of the brigands gave another hopeful tug on the chains securing Lady Karoline's baggage, as if one more would be enough for him to free the booty and escape with it casually slung over his shoulder.

His mate, who seemed more practical, jumped onto the cobbles.

There was one way out of the coaching inn, the heavy wooden gates to the courtyard. Otherwise, there were high walls and buildings on every side. And currently, he and Usk stood between the brigand and the gates.

The jumping brigand landed on his haunches and came up smoothly. Holding a meat cleaver. Wiry and filthy, a hollow-cheeked face framed by dark, greasy hair sprouting from under a shapeless beret.

"Drop it and you live!" he yelled at the man.

The brigand flashed a toothless smile, "Long enough for you to string us up, right?"

"Your choice."

The man hurled himself at them.

His pistol flared and the brigand doubled over before the cleaver got near Usk's head.

"Obliged," the hulking soldier grunted, finishing the brigand with his blade, sending him down to splash into his own entrails.

The second brigand leapt from the coach in the excitement, landing on hands and knees, he scrambled past them before he was even upright.

Usk, who turned out to be surprisingly nimble for a big lad, shot out his free hand, grabbed the brigand's filthy collar and dragged him backwards with a yelp.

The brigand was a wretched specimen. Face caked in dirt, coat rotting around him and thin as sticks. It didn't seem likely he could be more than sixteen, probably less. The boy's eyes fixed on his dead mate.

"Please..." he whimpered.

"Should slit your gizzard, save us the trouble of hanging a runt like you," Usk loomed over the boy.

It took a moment before he realised the soldier wasn't joking.

"No, we'll deal with him later," quite how, he didn't know, but he didn't want to kill an unarmed boy. Whatever mischief he'd done.

Usk pulled a face like he wasn't overly bothered either way.

The lad remained on his arse, head moving back and forth between them like a scrawny dog hoping for a scrap from the table but expecting a kick.

"Tie him to the coach wheel for now," he said, fumbling the spent pistol back into his weapon belt.

"You tie him," Usk scowled, "bad enough taking orders from your witch."

"Have trouble with knots," he held out his withered arm as best he could, "too much wanking, remember?"

The clouds evaporated from Usk's lumpy, unfortunate face and he sniggered like a mischievous boy sharing unsuitable words with his fellow urchins at the back of church.

"Oh yeah, right enough!"

While Usk dragged the squealing boy over the cobbles to the nearest wheel, he checked around the coach. They hadn't managed to break any of the chains affixing Lady Karoline's baggage to the roof or damage the vehicle as far as he could see and there were no more of the buggers up to no good.

Across the courtyard, Gotz was cursing every man, their slovenly ways, and the virtue of their mothers as he tried to organise a bucket line from the well to the inn.

Fire was a bad business wherever it broke out; once it took hold, there wasn't much chance of saving anything you couldn't carry away from it. He didn't know why the bastards fired the place instead of just thieving. Still, everybody was outside now, and shivering was preferable to burning alive.

His eyes moved from the inn to the sables. Smoke started to twist out from between the roof slats at the far end, but none of the horses had emerged yet.

Why?

He returned to Usk and the boy. The big soldier was picking something out of his teeth. Good to see he was making himself useful.

"How many of you are here?" he asked the young brigand.

The boy didn't answer. But he didn't have to. The shifty but uncertain expression on his grubby face said enough.

"There's more of them in the stables," he yelled at Usk, pulling his father's sabre free.

"Huh?" Usk's rudimentary features rearranged themselves a bit. Nothing else moved.

He shoved the lunk towards the inn, "Get some men!"

"What about him?" Usk tapped the boy's ankle with his boot.

"I'll trust your knot-tying. Go!"

Usk nodded and lumbered off across the courtyard with all the urgency of a man who wasn't quite sure if he needed a piss or not.

He shook his head. The world was full of fools. Old Man Ulrich had been right about that, even if he'd been one of them.

He'd spotted a side door to the stables behind Lady Karoline's coach; leaving the clamour of the courtyard, he slipped through it as quietly as his haste and the door's old hinges allowed.

Inside, the smell of smoke mingled with that of horses, dung, and hay.

He didn't need to worry about noise; the alarmed animals were making enough racket to cover even his clumsy feet.

There wasn't a lot of light, and what there was mostly came from the orange flames at the far end of the stable.

He moved along the paddocks, sabre before him.

Solace, Hilde, and Lucien would have gotten some of their horses out by now; the fact they hadn't, re-enforced his certainty more of the brigands were in here. Trying to steal some of the horses while the inn burned.

Ahead, voices cut through the whinnies, snorts, and snickers. Shadows and shapes shifted. Horses and men.

He edged forwards.

How long would it take Usk to round up some soldiers?

Not long.

But as a tall man had Solace against the wall with a blade at her throat, that might still be too long...

*

Lucien sprawled face down on the floor. Dead or unconscious, she couldn't tell as someone dragged her across the smoky stable to slam her against the back wall.

"Another one!" the man cried; he was tall, though not so far above her the rankness of his breath didn't make her want to heave.

She started struggling, trying to stamp on the man's toes.

Cold metal pressed her throat.

"Still..." another hiss of fetid air stole her breath.

She did as he said.

Others moved behind her captor; she wasn't sure how many.

"We came for their horses, not their women!" someone barked.

The man holding her showed her what remained of his teeth, "Bonus, I sees it as."

"We ain't got time!"

"Shouldn't have torched the fucking stables straight off then. Told you not to!" the man snarled over his shoulder. One hand gripped her throat, the other pressing a blade against her skin above it.

Slowly, she started reaching for her own dagger.

"Just doin' what Madge said," the voice came back.

"Fucking mad bitch..." the man tightened his grip on her throat for an instant.

"The courtyard's full of em, Madge fucked up. Sort the horses, and let's get gone!" a third voice, as panicky as the horses.

"Do it!" the stinking breath man said, eyes reduced to dark narrow slits as he leered down at her.

Some of the horses were out of their paddocks, saddles fitted. They shuffled and moved, agitated by the smoke.

There were four or five of the Merry Gentlemen in the stable. The horses were the most valuable and easiest things to steal here. Having the *sight* was all well and good, but a bit of common sense to go with it would help wonders...

"We can't take em with us," another voice amongst the moving shadows behind the stinking breath man said.

"Course we fucking can! Just throw that one over your saddle, I'll have this one," he roared, hand jumping from throat to her hair as he dragged her away from the wall, "put these two right to work once we're back to camp we will."

Laughter, as much nervous as dirty, rippled the smoky air.

Five. She counted five of them as her captor span her around.

One held Hilde, standing behind her, one hand clamped over her mouth while the other... wandered. The girl's eyes were wide, but fixed on her. Questioning rather than fearful.

What do we do?

Three other men were saddling and gathering horses.

They were nearly ready to go.

The smoke thickened by the minute, the light of the fire at the far end growing ever brighter. Horses were screaming down there, hooves clattering against wood as they tried to escape.

"Got the fucker!" another voice said, "this the one Madge wanted for dinner, right?"

A scrawny, balding man appeared out of the gloom, hauling the reins of a huge black shape behind him. Styx.

"That's the one," the stinking breath man said, "now let's-"

It might have been the sight of a knife at her throat, the swirling smoke, or the prospect of anyone thinking he was dinner, but the stallion decided it high time he took exception to *something* and reared up, flailing hooves caught the scrawny man square in the back, sending him careening forward.

"Get that fucking monster under control!" the brigand holding her yelled as the scrawny man shrieked.

The screams ended abruptly with a crunch beneath Styx's hooves.

The knife eased away from her throat.

Far enough for her to twist away and drive her dagger into his side.

"I already have work to do!" she hissed at him as he staggered away.

Another man came at her, a cudgel raised, "Bitch!" he wailed, but the cudgel fell from his hands before he could swing it, and he dropped to his knees as a figure stepped out of the smoky shadows, blood spraying from his sabre.

"Ulrich!"

One of the brigands tried to make a grab for him, but the hilt of Renard's sword connected with his nose. A wet snap and the man collapsed, holding his face.

Renard brushed past her toward Hilde, who struggled in the grip of her brigand. The man snarled and pushed her into Renard before turning and running.

Or trying to.

He yelped in alarm and went flying to the floor, Lucien's hand around his ankle.

"Fucker!" the mercenary shouted, "You ain't going anywhere."

The stinking breath man staggered away into the thickening smoke, clutching his side. She let him go as Renard tried to untangle himself from Hilde, though the girl didn't seem inclined to release him.

She stepped forward and grabbed Styx's reins. The stallion's nostrils flared, and he tossed his head as if looking for someone else to trample.

"Sssshh..." she put a hand against the horse's face and blew into his nose, "...you did well, boy, really well..."

The beast pawed at the floor, ears pricked, but calmed after a moment or two.

She steeled herself for more brigands at the sound of approaching boots. Instead, the big ugly Gothen soldier, Usk, and half a dozen men emerged from the smoke.

Lucien was climbing gingerly to his feet, judging by the bloody brigand on the floor, he'd been busy. Renard and Hilde were embracing.

"Is everybody alright?" Usk asked, head turning one way and then the other in the manner of a man eager for someone to hit.

"Yes," she said, stroking Styx's mane, eyes lingering on Renard and Hilde, "we're all alright..."

Chapter Ten

Lucien filled one of the discarded buckets from the well.

Then bent over and stuck his head in it.

The mercenary stayed like that for so long he began to consider the possibility it had all become too much for him, and he was trying to drown himself.

Eventually, Lucien straightened his back and let the water pour down his shoulders. He stood like that, shivering in the smoky dawn light before finally taking the bucket off his head and tossing it away.

"Better?" he asked.

"It's an *excellent* cure for a hangover."

"Does it help with a sound beating?"

Lucien glared at him. Or tried to through his bruised and swollen eyes. He'd earned himself a broken nose, his right temple had some interesting new colouration, too. Neither were doing much for his looks or mood.

"I was blindsided," Lucien insisted, not for the first time, "sneaky fuckers!"

"Guess they got the worst of it," he conceded, "after we saved your backside."

Lucien answered with a gob of spit and some muttering.

The boy Usk had tied to the coach was the only brigand they'd taken alive; the others were dead or fled.

They'd lost the three guards Gotz posted for the night. Fools, the old man said, showing no reluctance about speaking ill of the dead. Several horses had died and a few people had nasty, but not life threatening, burns. Otherwise, the only casualty was Suckow, the innkeeper, who'd run back into the burning inn to retrieve his money. He never came out.

"He was a parsimonious old skinflint," Gotz said with a sorry shake of the head, "always told the silly fool money would be the death of him."

They spent the night in the courtyard; at least the inferno kept them warm.

Now, in the grey dawn, most of the inn and the stables were smouldering ruins.

"Where will you go now?" Lucien asked Gotz.

"I'll take my bad luck down the road to share with some other poor sod," Gotz said, rubbing his beard, "came here from Würzburg when I disagreed with my previous employer, as knew Suckow from ages back. Luckily, he ain't the only fool in the world, so dear say I'll find someone else."

"I need men," Solace said.

A bushy and slightly sooty eyebrow shot heavenwards, "You must have a desperate need if you're offering a fat old goat like me a job?"

"I have."

Gotz chuckled, "Don't sweeten the medicine for me, my dear; I have a thick hide, don't take offence easy."

"You can still swing a sword and do what you're told?"

"Can still swing a sword..."

"Good enough."

"Where are you heading?"

"Thasbald. Escorting Lady Karoline."

"Escorting. I can do that..."

She stuck out her hand and raised her own less bushy but equally sooty eyebrow.

He stared at it, sucked at a tooth stump, then took it.

"The same offer applies to anyone else here who needs work," she said, raising her voice and looking around.

"Not sure what the serving girls can do for you...?" Gotz said.

"I can see them to the nearest town."

"That'd be Magdeburg."

Solace stiffened, "No one's going to Magdeburg."

"Nearest place. Couple of em were talking of heading there."

"The city will be under siege soon."

Gotz shrugged, "Not yet. May not happen. They might see sense and back down. Not everyone wants to pick a fight with the Emperor."

"No one's going to Magdeburg," she stared at him and then headed across the courtyard to Lebrecht, who was deep in conversation with Captain Bosko.

"She ain't an optimist, is she?" Gotz asked him.

"No."

The old man went to work on another tooth, "Good. Optimists are far more likely to get you killed."

Gotz winked before sauntering off.

You have no bloody idea...

Hilde returned as he was glaring at Gotz's back. She thrust some bread and milk salvaged from the inn's kitchen at him.

"Eat."

He wasn't hungry but forced it down; other than their road rations, it was all they possessed. Smoke tainted the bread; the milk was warm.

"You saved my life," she said, looking up at him, "thank you."

She'd thanked him constantly through the night as they'd watched the inn burn. Didn't seem she'd tired of it yet.

He swallowed another piece of bread softened in the milk. Once he'd finished eating, she took the chipped mug from him, put it on the floor and slid her hand into his.

He found a smile and squeezed. She beamed like he'd just given her all the silver in the Emperor's vault.

They stood in still, silent regard as the world moved around them. Despite the people and horses swirling about the courtyard as they readied to leave, for a moment or two, all he could see were Hilde's eyes.

You need to stop this soon, before...

He let her hand slip from his.

"We need to get ready..."

"Yes!" she jumped back, "Lot's to do!"

She edged backwards, still smiling, then hurried off.

His own smile lingered for a few heartbeats after her back turned.

He caught Solace staring at him across the courtyard, though her eyes quickly snapped back to Lebrecht.

He walked, not sure where he was going, but standing like a gormless fool amid the surrounding bustle, shock, and grief wasn't helping anyone. Least of all him.

Lady Karoline's coach had been wheeled away from the

burning stables into the middle of the courtyard before it could catch fire.

Bulcher's bride-to-be and her maid spent most of the night in it. Apparently, she was aghast no one had been able to save the luggage taken inside. Judging from the number of trunks and cases still on top, however, she must have plenty of spares of everything.

That was the thing with being rich; the more you owned, the more you thought you couldn't live without.

The young brigand they'd captured remained tied to the wheel. Luckily, someone remembered to untie him before they moved the contraption. Lacking anywhere better, they'd tied him back to it. He didn't know how Lady Karoline felt about that. He doubted it the kind of ornamentation she was used to.

In the dawn light, the boy looked even younger and dirtier.

Tired, watery eyes raised as his boots approached.

The boy was doing a piss poor job of trying not to look scared.

"What's your name?" he asked.

"Hugo... sir."

"No need to call me sir. Anyone given you food?"

The boy shook his head.

"Water?"

Another shake of the head.

He called out to one of the inn's serving girls wandering past, red-eyed and vacant.

"Is there any milk and bread left?" he asked after calling her over.

"A little, I think," she said.

"Fetch me some, please."

"For him?"

"Yes, for the boy."

She gave him a look but went off without further comment. Hopefully, she wouldn't spit on whatever she brought back.

"You going to hang me?" Hugo asked once she'd gone.

"That's what happens to thieves."

The boy sniffed and dropped his eyes.

"But it isn't up to me."

"Who is it up to?"

He shrugged, "The law."

They fell under Magdeburg's jurisdiction here but taking him to the city wasn't an option. No doubt they could find some local lord along the road who'd be happy to dispense justice. Hanging a thief was never a bother.

"How'd you end up with the Merry Gentlemen?"

He turned at the approaching sound of feet. Solace stopped at his shoulder.

"Answer the question, boy," Solace said.

"He's name's Hugo," he told her.

Her eyes fixed on the boy, "My name is Celine."

"You the one that killed Madge's pa?"

She nodded.

The boy shuffled on the cobbles.

"How'd you come to be with the Merry Gentlemen?" he asked again.

"They took me in," Hugo said, voice small, eyes not wavering from his threadbare boots, "was heading for Magdeburg. Last summer. To try and make something of me self. They told me I'd find nothing but misery there..."

"Why were you going there?"

"Plague took my family. I was the only one left, and the landlord turfed me out of our cottage when I couldn't pay no more. Didn't know where to go. So, I just walked. Dunno for how long. Hid from everyone. Lived off berries and stream water. Remember my Dad saying Magdeburg was a fine place, full of rich people. Thought with all that money someone might... help me..."

Solace's lips pressed hard together.

"Ran into the Merry Gentlemen and they gave me food. Gulver, he's sort of in charge, though they said the Merry Gentlemen were all equal and didn't have no need for kings or lords, told me otherwise. Said I'd be better off with them, cos they were all freemen. Said the rich folk never gave away money to the likes of us. Said we had to take it for ourselves, and thieving weren't a sin when the only other choice is starving. Said all the world's ills were caused by the rich folk. Said they started the war. Claimed it was about God, but really, it's all about rich folk trying to grab more for themselves and expecting the poor to do their fighting to get it. Gulver reckons the world's turned upside down now, though, and one day soon, the poor folk will have enough of dying for the rich and will rise up and make a new world where everyone gets a full share..."

"Seems this Gulver has some fancy ideas to justify his thieving," he said.

"Gulver's full of shit. Nice dream, though..."

The serving girl appeared at his shoulder with a chunk of bread and a cup of milk. After looking at each of them, she thrust the food at him and walked away. He managed to keep the cup from falling from his bad hand.

Solace crouched down in front of the boy.

"You promise not to run away if I untie you?"

"If I do, you gonna believe me?"

"No."

"Then why ask?"

"To see if you're the kind that sticks to their promises."

Hugo looked confused, "Will say anything if it keeps me alive for another day."

"Promise me."

"I promise I won't try to run away."

That sounded more shifty than sincere to his ears, but it satisfied Solace enough for her to untie the boy.

Hugo shook his hands, snatched the milk and bread and immediately started gobbling it down. Didn't look like the Merry Gentlemen spent much time teaching table manners.

They stood watching him till he'd finished. Which didn't take long.

"Why did you come here?" Solace asked once Hugo swiped the last drops of milk from his chin with his fingers and sucked them dry.

"Madge..." his eyes darted back and forth between them, "...wanted you dead for killing her Pa. Gulver didn't want no part; most of the others didn't neither. Said it were too risky to go so far from the woods. Especially just for killing. A few came along, mostly cos they thought they could steal some horses rather than the killing, but they agreed to do what Madge said."

"Which was?"

"Burn this place down and all you lot with it."

"And you agreed to help Madge?"

"Madge's mad as the moon, but she done good by me. Took care of me. She were hurting so bad about her Pa..." he shrugged, "...should have stayed with the others. We all know we gonna hang one day. Just always hope it ain't gonna be today."

Solace's lips tightened, and her eyes dropped.

"You the one who killed him, aren't you?"

"He was trying to kill me."

"Gulver reckoned this coach..." he jerked his head backwards, "...was full of silver. That we'd be living like kings if we got the bugger. Is it?"

"Not that we know," he said.

"Didn't think it likely," Hugo sniffed, "but half the Merry Gentlemen are as moon-touched as Madge is... was. She's dead, ain't she?"

He nodded.

"Will the rest of them come after us now?" he asked.

Hugo shook his head, "They don't venture far from the woods."

Solace raised her eyes from her feet, "You ever killed anyone, Hugo?"

"No... I got sharp eyes, fast legs, quick hands. Said I'd make a decent thief, but I'm no fighter."

"But you've seen others kill. Like the men on the gate here and with the coach in the woods yesterday?"

He nodded.

"If we hand you over to the law, they will hang you. Do you understand?"

He'd thought Hugo's face was already as white as it could get, but his skin turned to the colour of sheets beneath the dirt.

"And we *should* hand you over for what happened here."

The boy said nothing.

"But frankly, we haven't got the time to even find out who is the law here now..."

"So... *you're* going to hang me?" Hugo's bottom lip quivered. He blinked several times.

"What choice do I have? People are dead because of you. I can't let you walk away. Who knows what you'll do? I don't want your next crime on my conscience."

"I'm sorry... I..."

"Don't snivel, boy!" she barked.

Hugo swallowed and drew his knees up to hug them.

Solace squatted until at eye level with the boy.

"However, there is another choice."

"There is?" the boy blinked again.

"You work for me."

"Doing what?"

"Whatever I damn well tell you."

"And you won't hang me?"

"No. I'll feed you, clothe you and try to make sure you don't get yourself killed. And in return... you'll serve me. As a retainer. As a servant. As... anything I want."

The boy looked like he had plenty of questions. He also looked like he'd quickly decided he was better off not asking them.

"So, Hugo, with your good eye and fast legs. What do you say?"

There was only one answer the boy could give.

*

Progress was slow.

They didn't have enough horses for everyone, even without the ones lost in the fire.

Renard gave up his mount for two of the Inn's girls and squelched through the mud alongside Hugo. Some of the soldiers had let women climb up behind them to share their rides, though she suspected their motivation was less altruistic than Renard's.

Lady Karoline's coach could have accommodated more passengers, but she didn't ask, and the young noblewoman didn't offer.

Styx could have taken another couple on his broad back, but as the stallion would likely take that as an affront to his dignity, she didn't try.

After an hour, they reached a small village. Most of its cottages were boarded and empty, but the church was still in use, and they left the three bodies of Gotz's men there for a Christian burial after the old man haggled for the best price with the grizzled pastor.

There was a tavern, too, so dilapidated and uninviting even Lucien wasn't tempted by its beer. They'd tried to buy food, but there was none for sale. A few of the serving girls asked about jobs, but the owner just laughed.

They soon moved on, and none of *The Eagle's Claw's* staff opted to stay.

Several of their party kept shooting Hugo cold looks. Lebrecht told her they should hang him before he stole anything. She told him he should try to be a better Christian. Renard warned her the boy would run the first chance he got. She'd said they'd lose nothing if he did. Renard told her not to take her money belt off.

"What do we gain if he *doesn't* run off?" Renard asked.

"He might prove useful."

Renard laughed, "What an army we're building! Whores and thieves. Saul will suffer a few sleepless nights if he gets word of us. Or days."

In truth, she didn't know why she'd taken in the boy. But it felt right. And she listened to her feelings these days.

She thought of Madge a lot as they rode.

Her *sight* had never shown her anything similar before. She'd been inside the woman's head and, as Hugo said, she was as mad as the moon. But mad with grief as well as lunacy. The feelings coursing through the women, hatred, grief, and a consuming thirst for vengeance, were all too familiar. They'd become her travelling companions, as constant and reliable as Renard or Lucien. Madge's anger had led to people's deaths. How many would die because of hers? That was something her *sight* had yet to whisper in her ear.

She felt no regret about killing Madge's father. If Styx had allowed him to pull her from the stallion's back, she'd likely be as dead as him now. No, it was the deaths to come that pricked her conscience.

Perhaps that was why she'd given Hugo a chance.

The possibility of redemption against the probability he'd run away and cause someone else mischief. Or die in her service.

She didn't know.

So, she kept her face to the road and concentrated on moving in time with Styx's long, easy gait.

Graf Bulcher had kindly provided a list of recommended places to stop on the route to Thasbald. Before the war, coaching inns were common along major roads and the next would have always been no more than a day's travel, even at their sedate pace. Nowadays, though...

Luckily, the winter had not been severe. Other than the night the snowstorm forced them to shelter in Enoch the Miser's farm, there had been little significant snow. Luck, however, rarely held indefinitely. The sky was a sharp, frosty blue, but they were far from deep enough into the year to escape more.

The road remained rutted and muddy. Lady Karoline's coach got stuck several times, slowing them down even more.

"If we got rid of some of the shit on top of it..." Lucien grumbled after another inexorable delay.

"I'm sure she has some very important dresses she can't possibly do without," she said, trying to remember the days when little in the world seemed as important as her dresses.

They met few fellow travellers, and those they did consisted of groups of armed men. No one caused any problems, but none offered anything beyond a nod or brief wary greeting.

An air of sorry desolation hung about the villages and farms they passed. Some abandoned, others burnt out. The ones that weren't kept their doors locked and windows shuttered. If anybody was about their business in the crisp January daylight, they quickly ensured they weren't by the time their little column trundled and splattered by.

It took three days to reach the next major town, Burg, further along the Elbe near the border with the Electorate of Brandenburg. The four of them alone could likely have ridden there in a day.

No matter.

The 20th of May was still a long way away. They had plenty of time to kill.

And in the meantime, she had *Graf* Bulcher to kill...

A town of towers and spires; Burg, like Madriel, was awash with refugees. However, if you had money there were inns that could accommodate you. And they had money. She had some, so did Lady Karoline. Which no doubt went some way to explaining Bulcher's interest in the waifish girl.

She hadn't wanted to linger, but Karoline insisted she required time to recover from the simply ghastly ordeals she'd suffered so far. And the best room in Burg's best inn proved itself suitable for the purpose of recovering from ghastly ordeals.

Lucien, Bosko and Gotz took the opportunity to get drunk together. They seemed well-matched. Renard was at her side when she wanted him and with that girl, Hilde, when she didn't.

Each morning of their journey, she'd expected Hugo to have slipped away. Each morning his scrawny bones were still with them. Once settled in Burg, she likewise expected him to disappear into the crowds. He didn't. He kept himself to himself, large eyes watching everything. Perhaps wary someone might wish to even a score with him about the attack on *The Eagle's Claw*, perhaps just naturally wary.

She found herself spending a lot of her time in Burg with Lebrecht. Which wasn't an accident on either of their parts. She even went to the trouble of wearing a dress as they walked along the river, explored the scant fare on offer in the town market and attended services at a couple of the town's numerous churches.

The first sermon was about God's love; the second pastor was more interested in explaining how they would all burn in Hell for one thing or another.

Lebrecht listened with furrowed intent while she wondered if the sins she'd accumulated were already irredeemable. Or was she doing God's work, so received special dispensation?

She had offered herself to Lebrecht's father for fighting men; now, she was attempting a similar trick. Except this time, it seemed to be working. There was no offer of marriage and no request for any army, but Lebrecht appeared content to accompany her to Thasbald in return for... what exactly?

A promise? A suggestion? An understanding?

He made no inappropriate move, even when they were alone and not in a church. Looks tended to linger, words sometimes hung. But nothing that could be construed – she was almost certain – as sinful.

All things considered it was a somewhat chaste seduction.

He displayed little actual curiosity about why she wanted

to go to Thasbald. Did he really think her a kind soul only interested in helping Karoline? That her only motivation was the pursuit of romance? If delivering a fourteen-year-old girl to a monster old enough to be her grandfather counted as romance.

Did he not care? Would he genuinely follow her wherever she went because he was so enamoured with her? A flattering thought that would have thrilled the Solace of a year before no end, but it didn't ring entirely true.

Perhaps Lebrecht was just pretty but dim.

That was more plausible but more worrying. She needed all the help she could find, even from thieves and whores if it was forthcoming. But complete idiots were another matter entirely.

She continued to smile brightly at Lebrecht as she tried to work out what went on behind those rather lovely eyes of his and why he was so willing to follow her without question or protest.

He couldn't really be *that* dim, could he?

Chapter Eleven

River Elbe, Prince-Bishopric of Magdeburg, The Holy Roman Empire - 1631

From Burg, they decided to take barges along the Elbe as far as Wittanberge, which sat across the border in the Electorate of Brandenburg. According to the locals, the roads north passed through marshes and bogs and were often an impassable morass.

Possibly locals who had an interest in promoting river transport, but he was happy enough to sit and watch the blue-misted hills slip by.

They were warned brigands were also active, and since the army of the Swedish king, Gustavus Adolphus, landed in the north, more refugees and mercenary bands had come south.

Most of *The Eagle's Claw's* staff opted to remain in Burg, apart from two of the girls, who'd become friendly with a couple of the soldiers.

Gabriel Gotz not only found a horse in the town but one that didn't sag under his bulk.

"How do you stay so fat when the Empire's starving?" Lucien had slurred one night as they'd attempted to drain another tavern of its wares.

"In truth, despite my best attempts, I've failed miserably," Gotz told him, patting his ample stomach, "I'm half the size I used to be!"

They hired two barges for the journey to accommodate the horses and Lady Karoline's coach. The Vadians took one, the rest of them another. Who paid, he didn't ask.

Thasbald was apparently less than a week by road from Wittanberge.

He was not looking forward to getting there.

The weather was closing in. A flaying wind ripped off the water, while the northern sky swelled with the colours of old, livid bruises.

"Snow..." Gotz has assured him, one boot up on the rail, grizzled face crumpled against the wind, "...might be a while before we get our young lady to her husband."

"You know of *Graf* Bulcher?" he asked, as casually as he could.

"If I were Lady Karoline..." Gotz looked at him sideways, "...I'd be praying for that sky to shit as much snow as the world has ever seen. And then some more."

He nodded but didn't say anything in reply.

Gotz kept staring at him.

"Why is your mistress so keen to help this young lass get to Bulcher, eh?" Gotz asked when he continued saying nothing.

"She keeps her own counsel. I just follow her orders."

Gotz carried right on with the staring. Then he started sucking on one of his remaining teeth like something particularly bothersome had rooted between them.

"But a young slip of a girl is Celine. What is she...

nineteen? Twenty?"

"About that."

"Not old enough to have seen anything much of anything. An old bastard like me, on the other hand, has seen some things. Some you wouldn't believe, some that'd turn your stomach and some that'd straighten your pubes right out..." Gotz finished working on his tooth, "...thing is, I look at that little slip, who isn't old enough to have seen anything much of anything, and I keep thinking... you've seen some *real* shit, haven't you? Maybe I'm wrong. Happens to the best of us..." Gotz leant forward and put his considerable weight on the rail to peer at the grey-brown water below, "...but I don't think so..."

"The world's a bad place."

"So it is! And getting fucking worse by the day," Gotz's eyes narrowed as he turned to him again, "And what happened to your arm?"

"A fall."

"Long drop, was it?"

He only smiled.

"From a lady's bedchamber, perhaps?"

"No... it wasn't."

Gotz shook his head, chuckled, and made to move off.

"Why didn't you stay in Burg with the others?" he asked.

"Most of the others are young, women or young and women. They'll find something to keep bread and beer in their stomachs. But me? I'm a fat old fart. Who's going to give me anything?"

"Lady Celine did."

"As I said, she's a strange girl."

"Actually, you said you thought she'd seen a lot. Not the same thing."

"Well, yes... strange in more ways than one," Gotz pushed himself off the rail and patted his shoulder as he moved past, "don't worry, son, I've never been the curious type. I'm only here because I've got nowhere better to be."

"We're glad to have you."

"I'm sure you are," Gotz ambled away, still chuckling.

He went in the opposite direction and found Hugo sitting on the barge's edge, feet dangling over the side.

The boy twisted, startled, when he became aware of the attention, only to immediately return to gaping at the distant mist-shrouded hills, satisfied no one was about to kick him. Hugo seemed slightly less wary around him than the rest of their hodgepodge company.

"Keeping warm?"

Hugo nodded, eyes remaining fixed on the landscape slipping by them.

On Solace's instruction, he had bought the boy a heavy jacket, a wool-lined cloak, and some sturdy boots in Berg.

"Why spend silver on me?" Hugo had asked their lady later.

"Because you're no use to me if you freeze to death," she replied with a perfectly straight face.

Hugo hadn't looked any less perplexed.

He was increasingly unsure about what went on in Solace's head and had no idea why she liked the boy. She'd asked him to keep an eye on the lad, too. She hadn't elaborated on whether to ensure he didn't steal anything, run away, or get on the wrong end of a beating from someone in their company with a much lower opinion of the thief they'd taken in. A thief partly responsible for several deaths.

Still, he'd survived this far, and as most of *The Eagle's Claw*'s staff opted to stay in Burg, a beating seemed far less likely now.

He stood next to the boy for a while. The barge was basic and offered little protection from the elements. Still, the cold was a regular companion. Probably even more so for Hugo.

After twenty minutes of strained silence, he thought he'd done sufficient eye-keeping to satisfy Solace but before he could leave him to find Hilde, the boy pointed down into the river, "Look."

He followed Hugo's finger to where a floating corpse, white and bloated, stared towards heaven with milky eyes.

A man, middle-aged as far as it was possible to tell, stripped half naked. His eyes were gone, taken by his killers or scavenging birds.

"Should we-"

"No," he said, "none of our business."

He doubted the barge's skipper would stop for a corpse. More likely get oars in the water to move them faster.

He hurried along to the front of the barge.

More bodies.

Half a dozen, all men, all stripped and dumped in the river.

He scanned the riverbank; no buildings, no village, just reed banks fringing the Elbe's low marshy flood plains.

"Soldiers?" Hugo asked, coming up to his shoulder.

"Maybe..."

"Probably sensible to travel by river," Hugo said, eyes fixed on one of the bobbing corpses.

"We can't get all the way to Thasbald by boat."

"Heard things are worse the further north you go," the boy said.

"Yes, I think so."

Hugo's eyes moved from the corpse to him, "Then why's this fancy lord still living up there, and why's he making his bride travel through a war to marry him?"

The boy's questions were good.

But he didn't have an answer to either of them.

*

She'd never been on a boat before and found the experience wasn't much to her liking. It left her both queasy and itchy, and feeling more than a little imprisoned by the band of grey-brown water separating her from the rest of the world.

The land they passed through was largely flat and wet, with great flocks of water birds and endless reed beds. Distant hills broke the landscape, but otherwise the occasional small village, typically no more than a cluster of ramshackle huts housing families eking a living from fishing and drying out reeds, were all that was available to distract the mind and eye.

Their skipper, Jonas, said there were larger communities set back from the river; most of this section was too vulnerable to flooding to allow building on the riverbank, though canals and irrigation had drained parts to create fertile farmland.

She didn't pay much attention. The sky and the future were her main concerns.

Snow started coming in flurries as the boats moored for the night. By morning, the marshes were white, the reeds crisped with frost. The snowfall wasn't as bad as she'd feared, but if it heralded more, they might find themselves stuck in Wittanberge until it cleared.

And every day they could not travel meant another day the world suffered *Graf* Bulcher breathing its air.

She thought of him as some huge, bloated spider awaiting them, cocooning the innocent and living off them. A malevolent monstrosity requiring extermination.

Quite how she still didn't know.

But once Karoline got her alone with the monster, she was sure everything would fall into place.

The future came to her at night while she huddled under coarse blankets, drifting away from the sounds of water on wood, the snorts and snickers of the horses and the occasional, unfathomable noise floating out of the black, endless wetlands.

Fire. Blood. Death. Pain.

Walls falling.

Shaking, cracking, tumbling blocks of masonry crashing to the ground, clothed in flame, serenaded by screams.

Nothing as clear as her visions of Saul killing Hilde in Magdeburg or Madge preparing to bring vengeance down on *The Eagle's Claw*, just phantom voices and flirting images that refused to linger whenever she returned to the waking world. But she knew what they were well enough, all the same.

The World's Pain.

They did not make for a restful night any more than the canvas stretched over the rear of the barge made for a roof.

If she could carve out a way to find Saul from Bulcher's blubbery hide, they wouldn't need to be in Magdeburg when the walls fell. But her *sight* told her she would be there; Torben – or at least Henry Cleever – had said they must be there to stop Saul.

Yet, in spite of all her *sight* whispered, she did not believe the future decided. It was a series of possibilities. No more. Some more probable than others. But nothing was set. Nothing was certain.

Bulcher telling her how to find the Red Company would change everything.

That morning, she found herself irritable and listless.

Everything and everybody annoyed her, so she kept herself to herself as much as possible.

Renard brought her some sweetened herbal concoction the barge's skipper swore kept him young and vital. The decrepit state of the man was enough for her to question its medicinal qualities, but it tasted bearable and, most importantly, it was hot.

She told Renard she was fine when he asked.

And bit down on her tongue when she wanted to add he could stop fretting about her and return to that girl of his.

He lingered, reading her mood.

I should tell him about Hilde, about what I saw.

She sipped Jonas' brew.

About the future.

She said nothing.

Was that really because she thought she could use Hilde to find Saul, or was it more because-

"What do we do when we reach Thasbald?" Renard asked, sitting down next to her.

Nobody was in sight, but *The Friesian* wasn't a big boat.

She let her eyes drift down the river to where the *Anja* sat moored in midstream, wisps of mist softening her lines, as the crew prepared to cast off and continue their journey with the dawn.

"I shall save Lady Karoline from a fate worse than death."

"But how?"

"Leave that to me."

"My lady..." he leaned in closer to her, close enough for his shoulder to touch hers, close enough for his body to provide a momentary warmth, "...what happens after? 'tis not just Bulcher. He will have a household, soldiers... we have no one we can rely on bar each other and..." he added, a tad reluctantly she thought, "...Lucien, no one else knows. Do you think *Markgräf* Lebrecht and his men, Gotz and Hugo, or anybody else will help us after you murder Bulcher?"

She sipped more of the tea. It was growing on her.

"One problem at a time."

Renard blew out a breath to steam upon the morning air.

"It will be much harder to destroy the Red Company if you are hung for murder!"

"Trust me..."

"I'll follow you all the way to the gallows, but..."

"Trust me."

She'd meant to sound more confident and assured than the first attempt, but it came out curt and snappish.

She sighed, "We still have a fair journey ahead of us. I am working on a plan. We will ride out of Thasbald alive with most of our current company. Bulcher will be dead; my father's shade will receive another slice of vengeance. I also hope to learn how we might find Saul before Magdeburg's walls fall. But that is an aspiration, not a promise."

Footsteps on the other side of the canvas stilled their words, when they passed, Renard was staring intently at her.

"I do trust you, my lady."

You shouldn't.

The little niggling voice at the back of her head whispered. It was a voice she was becoming familiar with. And one she was beginning to despise.

You are using everyone else; why not him, too?

"Thank you," she tipped the mug in his direction, "for this."

He shrugged, "Thank Captain Jonas. Or his mother. If he is to be believed."

"How are you?"

The question befuddled Renard too much for him to answer.

She tried again, "Are you well?"

"I think so," he eventually replied.

"In mind, body and soul?"

"My body hurts more than it used to, but somewhat less than it did; my soul is already damned, while my mind... well, that's never been my greatest asset."

A smile curled the corner of her mouth upwards. A real one.

"And your heart? How is that?"

He went back to looking confused.

"It beats... soundly, my lady."

This time, she suppressed the smile.

"That is good to hear."

Standing up, she ventured beyond the canvas awning serving as one of the barge's rudimentary cabins.

The Friesian wasn't well suited to transporting passengers during winter, but she and the *Anja* had been the only vessels available and willing to make the journey downriver.

Snow dusted the deck along with the rest of the world. Still cradling her mug, she checked on the horses corralled in the middle of the barge. There wasn't sufficient space for so many animals, but all the others decided to allow Styx as much room as possible.

The stallion snorted as she approached, drawing her attention to the indignity it currently endured on her behalf.

"Don't worry, boy, I promise you will not have to suffer this for long. We will be back on the road soon..." she reached up and patted his neck. Styx tossed his mane and gave her a look that suggested if he wasn't, there was going to be trouble.

She moved along the barge, nodding and smiling at everyone she encountered. Those smiles, however, were forced and empty. It struck her that only Renard and Styx could illicit a genuine smile out of her these days.

With Lucien, who she found hanging over a rail vomiting,

eye rolls were usually the thing.

"Are you ill?"

"Nah," the mercenary pulled the back of his hand across his mouth, "Captain Jonas kindly shared his brandy to help keep us warm last night."

She held up her mug, "You should stick to his sweet tea, 'tis rather decent."

Lucien shot her a look Styx would have been proud of.

Then thrust his head over the side to further pollute the Elbe.

She patted his back and moved on.

A light breeze sputtered from the south, enough for Jonas to get the barge's sails up and speed their journey north. With the *Anja* in their wake, they were soon pushing forward again.

She found Usk standing at the bow with Swoon and the chiselled, middle-aged Wickler and his seen-it-all eyes, who spent an inordinate amount of time either shaving his scalp or spitting.

"Gentlemen…"

The three men nodded and mumbled, "My lady," in unison.

They didn't know what to make of her.

Which wouldn't do at all.

She needed them to love her. To follow her wherever she led and to lay down their lives for her if she deemed it necessary.

She knew what she wanted of them but getting them to see it that way was another matter.

Usk liked looking at her but would never do anything else,

for he was the type who talked more than did. Swoon seemed faintly embarrassed whenever she spoke to him, while Wickler just peered at her with the same world-weary expression as he did everything.

"Anything to see?" she asked, smiling. Another false one. Her understanding of the world remained limited, but she knew enough about men to know they liked women to smile at them. Particularly if the woman in question was their mother or pretty. Although presumably, for different reasons.

"Birds, snow, water, grass," Usk swept a gauntleted hand at the panorama *The Friesian* nosed through.

"No one's trying to kill us, at least," Wickler said before spitting over the rail into the froth rippling around the barge's bow. Fortunately, the wind was behind them.

Her eyes skimmed the leaden sky. She wrinkled her nose, "Apart from the weather."

The soldiers chuckled. Soldiers liked to moan about the weather. The men of The Wolf's Tower's garrison were always grumbling about it being too cold, wet, snowy, foggy, or windy. And if it wasn't any of those things, it was almost certainly far too hot.

They chatted for a few minutes. She was amiable, smiled a lot and never missed offering a kind word when she could squeeze one in.

They weren't used to a high-born woman talking so freely to them, but she hoped she was winning them around a little as none of them suggested throwing her overboard to see if she floated.

She was about to leave them in search of more hard-handed soldiers to charm when Swoon's smile froze, and forehead furrowed as *The Friesian* followed a shallow bend in the Elbe.

"Jesus..." Usk followed Swoon's gaze. Wickler spat again, though this time into the grey slush frosting the barge's deck.

"My lady..." Usk moved to put his broad shoulders between her and the shoreline.

"I've seen the dead before," she stepped around him, "they do not frighten me."

A small rise in the land, too modest to call a hill, stood where the Elbe turned to their left. A thick necklace of mostly winter-shorn shrubbery ringed the foot of the rise; the top was bare, except for four stakes, each adorned with a half-burnt corpse.

"No," Wickler agreed, "best to save your fear for the living in this world..."

Each body was lashed to a stake, hands tied behind their backs, blackened and charred up to their stomachs. Presumably, enough wood hadn't been piled around them to burn them completely. Trees were at a premium in the wetlands, after all.

A man, a woman and two adolescent boys. A family?

Witches? Heretics? Brigands or mercenaries enjoying themselves?

It was impossible to tell from the river, but whatever the reason, they had not died easily.

"How long ago?" she heard herself ask. Her voice was flat and emotionless—not the voice of a young woman, not even the voice of Solace von Tassau, for that matter.

She looked at Wickler. Older than the other two, he struck her as a man who tended to keep his wits closer at hand than his younger comrades.

He sucked in a deep breath through his nostrils, "Hard to say. No smoke, no smell, but the snow could have dampened that down."

"And whoever did this...?"

"Could be behind the hill, could be twenty leagues away. Whether they're any threat to us would depend on why they killed those people. And if they have a boat, of course."

Despite his words, the soldier decided it an opportune moment to load his pistol.

"Don't think they've been there that long..." Swoon said, two rosy flushes erupting on pallid cheeks.

"Why?" she asked.

"Because the woman's still alive..."

Her head snapped back to shore.

At first, she thought only the breeze moved the woman's long fair hair about her face, until the poor creature lifted her head. The woman's mouth was a dark hole visible through the damp strands of her hair. No sounds reached them across the water, but she seemed to be trying to say something.

How the poor woman could still be alive, she couldn't imagine. Her legs and lower torso were as charred as the others, clothing burned away, leaving only blackened, scorched flesh. While the other three slumped forward motionless, the woman's head continued to flop from side to side, mouth moving silently.

"Should we-"

A sharp retort cut off Swoon's words. The woman's head jerked back before her body slumped forward like the other victims of the pyre.

She twisted around.

Gabriel Gotz still held the smoking musket levelled toward the shore, his mouth a bloodless line visible through the tangles of his beard.

"The only kindness left for her in this world," he said, lowering the gun.

The old man turned away and walked back along the barge's rail without waiting for a reply.

Chapter Twelve

Wittanberge, The Electorate of Brandenburg, The Holy Roman Empire - 1631

"You're going to *Thasbald?*"

A degree of incredulity always accompanied the question, varying from mild horror to the completely dumbstruck.

He quickly developed a kind of hopeless smile cum twitch of the shoulders and moved on as quickly as possible.

Solace tasked him with replacing what they'd consumed since leaving Madriel or lost in *The Eagle's Claw* fire. In Madriel, supplies had been sparse and expensive; in Wittenberge, crumbling behind its centuries-old walls, they were non-existent. Where refugees choked Madriel's streets and squares, Wittenberge felt like a ghost town. Rows of boarded-up shops and empty houses lined deserted street after deserted street.

Those still living in the town were largely those too old or lame to run away from the fighting or go and join in.

They were close to the sharp end of the war here.

George William, Elector of Brandenburg and Duke of Prussia, had tried to stay neutral at the start of the war, but once the armies of Albrecht von Wallenstein overrun the north, he was forced to join the Imperial/Catholic side.

Then Gustavus Adolphus had arrived, officially to aid the protestant cause. A large army of murderous Swedes camped outside the gates of Berlin had helped to persuade George William to see sense and change sides, allowing the armies of Gustavus Adolphus, the Swedish king, transit rights across Brandenburg, along with a couple of fortresses and some other baubles. Consequently, the Catholic armies returned to fight the Swedes and ravage Brandenburg lands.

Which made travelling to Thasbald a very questionable choice.

Inevitably, Hilde went with him on his tramp around the town. She accompanied him everywhere, even under his blanket. Wittenberge had some nice churches *(St. Marienkirche* boasted a particularly impressive clock tower), but little else of note. Not that Hilde minded; she was too busy staring at him to notice much else.

It was very strange.

He'd never met a woman who'd behaved like Hilde before.

The fact someone liked him sufficiently to seek out his company was peculiar enough, that the person doing it was an attractive young woman made the whole business damn right odd.

He'd never been easy around people; even as a child, he'd been happiest alone. As he'd grown older and started noticing women as something other than the creatures his father used to inexplicably devote so much time, money, and effort pursuing, matters had become more complicated.

Whenever he met a woman he wanted to be close to, things ended badly. Even with the ones who hadn't died horrible deaths at the hands of demons. He'd suffered rejection, disinterest, mild amusement, and downright disgust. And some other looks he'd never quite been able to name.

And now here was Hilde.

Who was pretty. Who made him laugh. Who he enjoyed being close to. Who was looking at him. Continually. Like that.

"What?" Hilde asked as they returned to the town's square.

On market day, merchants, artisans, farmers from town and surrounding districts would have filled the square, selling their wares to crowds who'd flocked to Wittenberge from far a wide. Now the square was deserted other than for a couple of dogs chasing each other's tails and a bent-backed old woman pushing an empty barrow over the slush-softened cobbles.

He suspected years might have passed since the last market day.

He shook his head.

"Nothing," he said. Grinning back without quite knowing why.

"What do we do now?" Hilde asked. Still looking at him. Like that.

"Go back to the Inn and report our miserable failure to Lady Solace... I mean Celine."

"Why does she want people to think her name is Celine?"

It wasn't the first time she'd asked that question, and it wasn't the first time he had not given her a complete answer.

"As I said before, she has enemies. Bad ones."

The skin at the top of Hilde's nose creased. Something he found increasingly endearing, but also knew meant more questions were brewing.

"We should go back, 'tis going to snow again," he said.

"Then we should walk more while it's light and not snowing."

"We can walk back to the Inn while it's light and not snowing."

She shrugged and fell in next to him.

He understood her point. The nights were long this time of year, and spending one cooped up in a smoke-filled inn with a bunch of soldiers who'd pass their time drinking and leering at her probably wasn't at the top of Hilde's list of preferred ways to spend the evening.

I wonder what is top of the list?

He could see her still looking at him from the corner of his eye. Like *that*.

She was going to walk into something if she wasn't careful.

In truth, walking alone with Hilde appealed far more than watching Lucien drink himself into a stupor while regaling his new audience with more outlandish and unlikely tales of his magnificence.

But something about Wittenberge depressed him deeply. The deserted streets, broken windows, empty buildings, and air of inevitable decay all reminded him, for some reason, of his father dying in the shit-stained sheets of a flea-infested mattress in the very last of the countless rooms his transitory life had taken him through, with nothing to cling to bar the memory of better days and the bitterness of a thousand might-have-beens.

He was stretching his imagination a tad, but the town felt like it was waiting to die, too, and the flies were already gathering in anticipation.

Besides, he was worried about Solace, and whatever was happening with Hilde (if that wasn't his newly stretchy imagination, too), his mistress remained his first responsibility.

They were heading towards *Graf* Bulcher, and she had, he strongly suspected, no plan other than she would kill him. Bulcher was a powerful lord whose estate sat slap-bang in the middle of a war. The chances of him being lightly guarded seemed achingly slim. So, even if Solace did get her wish and slash the monster's throat, how would they escape Thasbald without a noose around their necks?

That sort of thing caused him sleepless nights.

Currently, she spent most of her days joking with the Gothen and Vadian men-at-arms, closeted away with Lady Karoline laughing merrily like the frivolous girl she very much wasn't or recruiting unsuitable people like Gotz and Hugo to their peculiar little company.

He'd tried talking to her, but frankly, he'd never been much good at talking and felt more than a little helpless.

They were hurtling to their deaths, and there wasn't a bloody thing he could do to stop it.

And he was taking Hilde with them.

"You're looking glum again?" Hilde asked.

Had she spent so much time looking at him (whether like *that* or otherwise) that she could now read him like a book?

If she knew how to read. Which she didn't.

"'tis just the face I was born with. 'tis a burden to have to live behind it."

Hilde giggled, "There's nothing wrong with your face. You are most handsome!"

She might be able to read him like a book, but her eyes were clearly not without fault.

It seemed to him he had two choices. The first was to save Hilde by sending her away before they reached Thasbald. However, a woman alone in this part of the world was at the mercy of all manner of monsters. Most might not be as great as Saul the Bloodless, the Red Company, or even *Graf* Bulcher, but when you ended up just as dead, the distinction became rather moot.

The second was to accept they were all going to die very soon one way or another and make hay with what little time they had together,

It was an option that had become ever more tempting as they'd huddled under blankets on *The Friesian's* cold boards.

Now they were lodging in an Inn, Hilde shared a room with Solace, and the only temptation requiring resistance was not smothering Lucien to death with a pillow to stop the bugger's infernal snoring.

It was enough to make him pine for the freezing barge, which had departed Wittenberge empty along with the *Anja* to continue down the Elbe to the port of Hamburg in the hope of finding cargo to bring inland.

There was, of course, a third option.

They leave together.

He knew he was not much in the way of protection, but Hilde would be a damn sight safer with him than if she were alone.

But then, so would Solace. And she had his oath. The oath he'd broken once and sworn never to break again...

"Still looking glum...?"

He tried to find a brighter face and hurried her along.

Above them, fat snowflakes began floating out of a charcoal and gunmetal-streaked sky.

*

It snowed for three days.

Sometimes lightly, often heavily, but every time she wiped the condensation from a window to check, it still fell. She started to wonder if it would ever stop. Which was silly. Or whether it would snow long enough to completely bury the town. Which seemed much less silly as the days rolled by and the drifts grew deeper.

January became February.

Spring still seemed a teasing promise, but the 20th of May edged closer.

There was still time aplenty. No need to panic yet.

Each night she climbed under the blankets piled upon her bed, she listened to Hilde's breathing across the room and saw her dropping from Saul's arms, drained and discarded. Thoughts of Magdeburg kept her awake; the slaughter she'd witnessed when the walls fell, and the terrible suffering to come.

And whenever she did sleep, her dreams echoed to pain-wracked screams, crackling wood, and the tumbling stone of falling walls. Destruction engulfed not just Magdeburg, but the world itself. Blinding, fiery blossom erupting across the globe, again and again, until they were the only points of light remaining beneath a blackened, smoke-choked sky of eternal night.

Sometimes, in the hinterland between the waking world and the one of dreams, her fingers found Flyblown's mark. It had remained cold since Wendel's fall from the Grace Tower. Keeping its own counsel, or was it quiet because no vampires were nearby?

As she traced the five angry welts, she asked it to take her to the grey hills above the dusty plain, where the sun forever rolled along the horizon and the damned walked in circles through the ash. She pleaded with it to take her to see Torben.

Are you helping me?

Is what Henry Cleever told Renard and Morlaine true?

Did you kill those people at Enoch the Miser's farm like Wendel said?

When Magdeburg's walls fall, will you feast upon the World's Pain alongside the other monsters?

Are you still my big brother, or are you lost to me forever?

Her dreams only took her to a world of falling walls and burning buildings, never to the grey hill where her brother waited.

During the short colourless days and flickering candlelit nights she spent as much time as she could stand with the disparate members of what she already thought of as *her* company.

They have to love me, they have to love me, if they don't

love me, they won't die for me...

That refrain constantly beat in the back of her mind whenever the urge to crawl away and hide in some dark corner, with her eyes screwed shut and hands clamped over her ears, tried to overwhelm her senses.

With Karoline, she became the confidante and loyal friend, giggling about boys and chatting about the kind of inane mundanities she'd once considered so important - hair, dresses, jewellery, manners. Just how a lady should behave. It made her want to scream, but she did it because she needed Lady Karoline to access Bulcher.

With Lebrecht, she became the flirtatious amour, all lingering glances, unspoken promises, and half-parted lips. It felt ridiculous and alien. It made her want to laugh at its absurdity, but she did it because she needed Lebrecht of Gothen and his men to help her kill Bulcher.

She became the jolly comrade with the soldiers, all jokes and banter, though with an added sprinkle of flirtation, when Lebrecht wasn't in sight anyway. It made her feel cheap and tarnished, but she did it because she needed men prepared to fight and die for her.

With Hugo, she became the watchful big sister, offering trust and advice, praise, and stern words. It made her question her judgement. A few days before, the boy had been one of the Merry Gentlemen, who'd slit a throat for a pair of boots, but she did it, in case the boy might one day be of use.

And with Renard... she did nothing but try to avoid him.

Every time she saw him with that girl, Hilde (and it was increasingly rare to see him without his little, busty, ginger shadow), something she couldn't name turned in her stomach.

He appeared happy when he was with Hilde. Or at least less miserable. Hilde fair glowed. She couldn't keep her mind from wondering whether they had-

She hated it!

She should be delighted for him. He was the closest thing she had left in this world to a friend. They had been through so much together and she was asking him to endure more. There was a very fair chance he would die for her. Why shouldn't he enjoy a little happiness when it presented itself?

Even if it was with some shallow, vacuous, illiterate, vaguely irritating peasant girl. With ginger hair! Quite why the bright copper-coloured locks made things worse, she couldn't fathom. But they did.

And in a few months Hilde would be dead.

At Saul's feet.

She could save the girl's life in many ways, yet she couldn't shake the idea Hilde was nothing more than a means to find Saul. Not a living, breathing human being, her only friend cared for. An opportunity. She hated those nasty, unworthy thoughts, yet found herself incapable of stopping them.

Almost as much as she hated how seeing Renard and Hilde together made her feel.

"We could be here for weeks..."

She moved away from the window with a start she tried to conceal behind a cough. As a woman who could see the future, being startled was a particular annoyance.

Lucien loomed over her. An ale pot, inevitably, in one hand. How could he possibly drink so much?

"The snow has stopped," she said, peering up through cheap, slightly blackened glass at the dull, flat sky.

"Hasn't melted though. The roads to Thasbald will be impassable. And when it does melt, they will be worse."

"You have no positive thoughts to share with me, Lucien?"

"The snow might keep all the brigands, renegades, mercenaries, armies and other sundry killers between us and Thasbald indoors."

"I was thinking the same. The horses could get through the snow..."

Lucien's expression suggested he either didn't approve of the idea or needed to concentrate in order to focus.

"Or they might freeze to death," he said, "and even if they don't, the lucky young Karoline's coach certainly won't get through."

"No..." she agreed, eyes returning to the sky.

"You're trying too hard."

"Trying at what?"

"To be a leader."

Her eyes returned to the mercenary, "I am?"

"Be yourself... 'tis the best way to inspire loyalty. Unless you're very skilled at it, men smell falsehood like they would a latrine after one of Lucien Kazmierczak's infamous evacuations."

"I've... never really thought of it like that..."

Lucien grinned, "I am here to help you. As you know, Lucien Kazmierczak is renowned as a leader of men from Bordeaux to Belgrade!"

"There is one problem with being myself, Lucien."

"How so?"

Braving the fumes, she leaned in, "I'm an eighteen-year-old girl."

"Eighteen?" Lucien's eyebrows shot up, "You told me you were twenty?"

"It seems not all my falsehoods are as pungent as... your movements."

"Evidently not. And Lucien Kazmierczak is well known as a spotter of lies. Given his own unwavering integrity and innate honesty!"

She smiled. Indulgently.

"Regardless. I am not a born leader of men."

"I am following you."

"Well, yes..."

Lucien touched her shoulder, "Be yourself, my lady. Trust me, it will be enough..."

With wisdom dispensed, the mercenary belched and wandered unsteadily back into the dark, smoky bowels of the inn in search of more beer.

Chapter Thirteen

Lady Karoline reminded him of a bird; small, nervous, restless. Wary eyes always moving in fear that something bigger might gobble her up. A bird that hadn't eaten for a long time.

He didn't see much of her. She kept herself apart from the rest of their company; only her maid Elin, Solace and Captain Bosko spent any time with her. Whenever he did catch a glimpse, she'd grown thinner, paler, and more sunken-eyed than the last time.

She seemed an unlikely bride.

He'd never met *Graf* Bulcher, but all he knew elicited nothing but pity for the girl.

They stayed in Wittenberge a week. He didn't think Karoline left her room in the *Red Ox* the whole time. When she finally did emerge into the chill sunlight, she hurried into her coach without a word to anyone save Solace, who helped her into the carriage.

Karoline clutched his mistress' hand with such fierceness he expected the bride to yank Solace into the carriage with her.

"Poor girl is terrified," Gotz muttered as they checked the buckles on their saddles. The horses had been cooped up as long as the rest of them and were skittish.

"She has every right to be," he said, stamping his feet. The snow had largely melted, but it didn't feel much warmer, thanks to a ripping north wind.

"The aristocracy are a strange bunch," Gotz patted the rump of the unfortunate beast that would be labouring through the mud under the old soldier's bulk.

"We shouldn't be leaving yet," he wrinkled his nose at the threateningly overcast sky.

"Nope," Gotz squeezed on a helmet so antiquated and dented he'd likely had it for years. Presumably, since he'd possessed a smaller head.

Something about Gotz reminded him of his father, less the bitterness and broken dreams. Still, despite that, he found he rather liked him. Which was somewhat peculiar as he rarely liked anyone.

The old soldier contemplated his saddle with the air of a man resigned to making a long and treacherous climb involving considerable risk to life and limb. Then spat into his gloves.

"But we don't make the decisions; Captain Bosko and our lady are both keen to reach Thasbald. I assume Bosko has orders," Gotz's gaze lingered on him, "as for Lady Celine…"

He avoided Gotz's red-rimmed eyes. The old goat had spent most of the week going beer for beer with Lucien. What a fearsome force Solace was building!

"We should be staying here till spring," Gotz continued, "when the roads will be better."

"And choked with soldiers as soon as the campaigning season starts."

"Soldiers are easier to avoid than the weather. No army on Earth has ever killed more men than winter."

This was true, but he hoisted himself onto Plodder's back

without further comment.

Gotz sucked at a tooth, wrinkled face further, and then heaved himself up into the saddle. The gelding he'd found in Berg was a sorry-looking creature. Perhaps that was one of the reasons he liked the old man; he was the only one in their company atop a more pitiful nag than Plodder.

"Only thing I hate more than fucking marching is fucking riding," Gotz grumbled.

"Saves your legs," he grinned.

"And fucks my arse."

He laughed. A rare enough sight to draw a couple of curious glances his way.

"You don't have to come, old man. *The Red Ox* still has some beer left."

Gotz glanced at the innkeeper standing in the doorway watching their departure, hands turning over themselves in a continual chase. He didn't look happy, though Lennart seldom did. At least he'd survived their stay, which was more than some innkeepers had managed recently.

"Drunk my fill of the piss they serve here," Gotz started sucking on another tooth. He did that a lot; perhaps he was trying to prise the last few blackened stumps out of his gums.

Hilde smiled at him from atop her horse. He smiled back.

"You better be careful of that boy..." Gotz said, leaning across.

Hugo was clambering up to ride behind Hilde.

"Don't think she has much to steal," he said.

"That's not what I meant. At that age I would have sold my brother's soul to the Prince of Hell for the chance to get so close to such a lovely maid …"

"Well, I'm sure-"

"Don't want him stealing your goods, do you?"

"She isn't my *goods*."

Gotz hoisted a bushy eyebrow, "No?"

"No."

"And you're sure she doesn't whore?"

"Certain."

"Pity…" Gotz puffed, "…always been quite partial to gingers."

Aside from Solace and Lady Karoline, Gotz had asked every woman they'd met if she would sleep with him for the right price. And he suspected he'd thought about asking them too on the off chance.

"We're… friends."

Gotz laughed.

"What's so funny?"

"I see the way she looks at you."

"I have no idea what you mean."

He glanced at Hilde, who was staring at him intensely enough to soften steel and harden… other things at thirty paces.

He was already blushing by the time he looked away.

"By God, I wish I was young again…" Gotz's chuckle deepened, "…would have wasted much less of it with that bloody fighting nonsense, I can tell you!"

As the horses shuffled in anticipation, Lennart had one last try at pleading with Bosko and Lebrecht not to go. He'd been telling them the road to Thasbald was too dangerous from the moment they'd arrived; Imperial forces had been clashing with the invading Swedes for months, and neither side seemed too principled in who they killed.

He thought Lennart more motivated by the silver they'd been giving him than their safety, but he, for one, would have listened to him. But then he wasn't in charge. Neither were Lebrecht or Bosko, but Lennart could have pleaded with Solace until he ran out of breath for all the good that would do.

Eventually, their little column clattered away from the *Red Ox* and into the streets of Wittenberge. The handful of blank-faced locals out and about stopped to stare at them; a few held out hands like withered claws to plead for charity, but for the most part, the town was deserted. To the south, the war had emptied the land; here, it emptied the towns too.

The echo of their own hooves and the creaky protests of Karoline's coach were the only refrain to serenade their departure.

A handful of old men resting on even older pikes watched them from the town's ancient walls as they passed through the gates. He hoped for the sake of Wittenberge's remaining inhabitants the war did not arrive on their doorstep, but he hoped even more fervently they did not find it on the road ahead.

*

"Trouble..."

Bosko straightened his back as if the extra height might help him see further.

The smoke curling into the flat white sky before them

didn't seem to mark a huge fire, but Karoline's Captain did not like the look of it.

"Is there an alternative to going forward?" she asked, knowing the answer.

It was proving difficult enough to keep Karoline's carriage moving on the mud-choked road; going off-road would be impossible. Not for the first time, she thought of suggesting they put the girl on a horse and abandoning her damn luggage.

"Might just be burning a witch," Lucien offered what passed for looking on the bright side these days.

"Possible..." Bosko's shoulders sagged as he slumped back into his saddle.

"We have a couple of hours daylight left, at most..." she added.

Bosko chewed his lip, then twisted around to shout back at the rest of the column, "Everything loaded if you please, gentlemen!"

"I'll go," Lucien pushed his gelding forward, "see what I can."

"We'll keep moving slowly," she nodded as if there was any other way they could.

Bosko didn't argue as Lucien galloped off towards the smoke curling above the next low rise. The land was generally flat and seemingly always sodden. If she remembered Tutor Magnus' infernal maps, it stayed that way till the land met the Baltic Sea, a great plain interspersed with rivers, lakes, marshes, and heath.

They were doing well if they could travel an hour without manhandling Karoline's coach out of a bog or quagmire.

"Perhaps we should wait for Lucien..." Lebrecht ventured.

"We're not going to make our next rest stop before dark as it is," Bosko said.

They'd already been forced to spend one freezing, uncomfortable night camped by the side of the road as it was. If Bulcher's map was to be believed, and it had proved accurate thus far, a sizeable Inn sat where the road forded a river a few hours ahead.

She fixed her eyes on the smoke. At least, there used to be.

Besides the dearth of people, they'd come across little evidence of the war since leaving Wittenberge.

However, she expected that to change soon. Yet her *sight* remained silent. Did that mean it was sleeping, or that no real danger awaited?

She rode at the head of their column with Bosko and Lebrecht. Both men had given up telling her she should be sharing Karoline's coach or trying to dissuade her from the idea she was in charge. Lebrecht just spent his time stealing glances at her while she thought Bosko was a little afraid of her.

Five minutes later, Lucien came galloping back down the road; nobody was chasing him, at least.

"There's a hamlet over the rise," he explained once he'd swung his horse alongside them, "and a group of soldiers making merry."

"Whose?" Bosko asked.

"Either one side, or one of the others would be my guess," Lucien said.

"Lucien..." she warned.

The smile faded, "I didn't get close enough to be sure. But they're ransacking the hamlet; a foraging party or mercenaries looking for some extra coin, I'd say."

"How many?" Lebrecht asked.

"Twenty or so, from what I could see."

"We wait for them to finish...?" Lebrecht suggested.

Bosko and Lucien shook their heads in unison, "They're as likely to come down this road as go any other way, and there's nowhere for us to hide," Lucien said, waving a hand at the scattered clumps of leafless trees and bare bushes dotting the surrounding scruffy lowlands. "And even if we could get that damn coach off the road, we'd probably never get it back on..."

"So we go," she said before she knew she would.

"And if they take as much interest in Lady Karoline's coach as the Merry Gentlemen?" Lebrecht asked, wriggling in his saddle.

She shot the men a thin smile, "We dissuade them..."

It took more time than she would have liked to persuade Bosko and Lebrecht no better option existed. She suspected they only agreed when Lucien wayed into the fray to tell them so. And that was more to do with the fact he possessed a penis rather than the colourful questioning of their courage and sense that got them to agree to her suggestion.

As they approached the top of the rise over which Lucien promised them they would see the hamlet, Renard arrived at her shoulder.

"Are you going to tell me I shouldn't be at the front, too?" she asked without looking at him.

"I wouldn't waste the breath, my lady. But if there's a fight, I should be at your side..."

She stopped herself asking about Hilde.

Instead, she concentrated on the approaching hamlet, a humble collection of stone cottages fringed by clumps of trees. A couple of the buildings were on fire, and men milled in the road bisecting the settlement. Twenty or so horses were gathered at the far end of the hamlet, the soldiers' mounts.

A cart with a couple of horses blocked the road; soldiers were busy filling it.

As they grew closer, she saw another group huddled on the damp ground beneath a stone wall, all elderly or children. Threadbare clothes and hollow-cheeked for the most part. Several were weeping, most were stony-faced and silent, and all were clutching somebody they loved. Soldiers, laughing and drinking, stood over them.

A couple of figures lay face down in the mud. Neither dressed like soldiers.

Noticing their approach, half a dozen men, some with muskets, spread out across the road to block their path.

"Let me do the talking," Bosko said, holding up his hand to bring their column to a halt.

A tall man in a fine blue cloak, a wide baldric across his chest from which a sheathed sword swung, pushed through the line to stand in front of them. He stuck his thumbs in his belt and looked them up and down, grinning.

"Talar du tyska, ja?"

She spoke French and Latin in addition to German, as well as a smattering of Spanish, Italian and English, but didn't recognise the soldier's tongue.

"Swedes..." Renard breathed.

A foraging party from one of the Swedish king's armies then. Come to the empire to fight for the Protestant cause. Supposedly.

"Yes..." Bosko, who presumably knew some Swedish, said, "...what is going on here? Why are you blocking the road?"

"The business of King Gustav Adolphus," the Swede said in heavily accented German, "with allowance from your prince-elector."

She walked Styx forward, "What business?"

Bosko and Renard sighed in unison. If rolling eyes made a sound, she didn't doubt she'd hear plenty of clacking eyeballs, too.

"Nice horsey!" the Swedish captain laughed.

She edged Styx, whose ears were dangerously pricked, forward till he loomed over the soldier. The Swede didn't step back, but his smile faltered. Behind him, men shuffled muskets.

"I asked you," she demanded, "what's your business here? Don't make me fucking ask again!"

Styx snorted in the man's face, suddenly enough to make him flinch. Behind him, someone laughed. The officer shot a look over his shoulder, choking the laughter off.

"We collect provisions. For the war. To fight Catholics. For you people," the officer said when he turned back, eyes flicking between her and Bosko as if confused as to why the young girl on the huge horse was asking the questions.

Her eyes drifted to the cart filled with sticks of furniture, bags and sacks, food, wooden cages with chickens, a freshly slaughtered pig. In other words, anything and everything the inhabitants of the little cottages had. She then made a point of staring at the burning buildings, the corpses, and the peasants cowering against the wall before twisting back to stare at the Swedish officer.

"I thought you were here to fight for these people?"

"They stubborn and stupid. We must make lessons of them. Armies not fight with empty bellies, with empty purses. Everybody must give to the cause, one way or other," his smile returned, "you contribute with the nice horsey, ja?"

"No."

"No? But how can we protect you from the Catholics if you won't pay us?"

He pulled off his wide-brimmed hat to reveal long blonde hair, turned it upside down and held it towards her, "You want to keep horsey, give us silver. You must pay the toll to use this road. Same as peasants here. Be nice and pay and we not then have to hurt you stupid people."

A scream from one of the unfired cottages cut through the smoke. A woman's...

The soldier shrugged, hat still outstretched, "You can pay the toll in other ways, pretty..."

She bent down in the saddle, "We'll give you something to let us pass. We don't want any unpleasantness, do we?"

"No, you don't," he smirked, "Horsey, silver, pussy. You choose which you want to pay us with..." he put his hand on her leg, "...I know which I prefer though, pretty..."

"How about..." she lent down low enough to whisper in his ear, "...steel?"

"Huh?"

Grabbing a fistful of greasy hair, she yanked his head forward till his throat met her dagger.

"Don't do anything stupid, or this idiot's war ends here!" she snarled at the Swedish soldiers spread across the road; several now had muskets raised to their shoulders and levelled at her. Hopefully, some of them understood German.

Renard's horse came alongside her, trapping the Swedish officer between Styx and his mount.

"You sure this is a good idea?" he asked through gritted teeth.

Another terrified, sobbing scream rolled out of one of the cottages. The same girl or a different one?

"Damn sure," she pressed the dagger harder against the Swedish officer's throat, "tell your men to lower their weapons. If one of them fires, you're dead. Understand me?"

He made a gurgling noise she took to be a yes and flapped a hand behind him. After a few exchanged glances, the muskets lowered.

"Now get all your men out front where I can see them. Including the ones in the cottages."

More gurgling, but this time nothing much happened. Behind her she could hear her men – if that wasn't too much of a stretch yet – fanning out.

"You," she yelled at the nearest Swede, "get your men out front now!"

The soldier, little more than a boy, ran off, shouting in Swedish.

"This big mistake," the officer snarled at her.

She yanked his head further back and pressed the dagger harder against his throat, "Gotz!"

Asking the old soldier to join her company had been instinctive; now was as good a time to find out if she could trust him as any.

After some puffing and grunting, Gotz dismounted and squeezed between Styx and Renard's horse.

"You'd like me to take this piece of shit off your hands, my lady?"

"Very much."

Gotz yanked the Swede backwards, his heavy blade replacing her thinner one at the man's throat.

"Believe me," Gotz hissed in the man's ear, "I'm nowhere near as nice as her…"

Straightening up, she risked a glance behind; most of the Vadians, weapons drawn, clustered around Lady Karoline's coach, protecting their mistress. Bosko stayed with her; wide-eyed and pale.

"Put a couple of your men in front of the villagers, she nodded at the peasants gathered by the wall. An old woman had crawled away from the rest to cradle one of the bodies. Her wailing cut through the smoky air all the way down to her soul.

"Do it!" she spat, glaring at the Vadian's Captain till he barked at his men.

The Swedes spread out in front of her, a wall of angry and confused faces mixed with some embarrassed ones. Most of them were young, not that callowness was an excuse for anything.

A few more appeared from one of the cottages with the boy who'd run to fetch them. One of the men was fixing his britches as he strode towards her, face flushed red.

"What's the fucking meaning of this?" he demanded, his German better than the well-dressed officer Gotz was looking after for her.

"Go and stand with the rest of your men."

The older man jabbed a finger at her while spitting at his company, "*Varför har du inte dödat den här slynan?*"

Gotz shoved his captive forward a little and shouted something back at the man in Swedish.

The man stared at his comrade, threw his hands out wide, and exclaimed, "*Dumbon!*"

She raised her dagger, pointed at him and then the rest of the soldiers.

The man's square jaw jutted forwards, "Captain Naslund is an idiot. You kill him... then what are you going to do, you stupid bitch?"

"Then I'd kill the rest of you and take your horses and weapons."

"Really?" the man looked amused, "How so?"

She lifted the dagger to point behind him.

Frowning, the man twisted to stare down the road where the Swedish horses were hobbled.

Lucien waved back.

Lebrecht and the Gothens were spread across the road, muskets borrowed from the Vadians levelled at the Swedes.

The dagger moved to the man.

"Now go and stand with the rest. And drop your weapons..."

Chapter Fourteen

Upon the Road, The Electorate of Brandenburg, The Holy Roman Empire - 1631

"Jesus," Hugo gasped.

There were two young women in the cottage's single bedroom.

One curled into a ball on the floor, face to the wall as she cried. The other sat on the bed, hugging knees raised to her chin, glaring at him through strands of blonde hair. Both women were naked. Blood stained the bedsheets.

"No one is going to hurt you," he held out a hand.

The girl on the floor kept crying while the one on the bed stared at him with glassy eyes.

Why should either believe a word he said? He was a soldier and looked no different to the men who'd been raping them.

"Do what you can," he said to Hilde, standing aside to let her into the room.

She nodded and squeezed past them into the room.

He closed the bedroom door after her before leading Hugo back through the ransacked cottage. What the Swedes hadn't bothered stealing they'd smashed to pieces, not that these people owned much to start with.

"We need to check the rest of the cottages..."

The boy nodded, "I can do it."

He didn't like leaving Hilde, there could still be Swedes lurking, but he didn't want the boy poking around alone.

While the Vadians were getting the Swedish soldiers to kneel and surrender their weapons, he crossed to where the surviving villagers were clustered by a wall. Some had risen shakily to their feet, but many remained on the ground where the Swedes had ordered them to stay. They watched him approach with wary eyes.

They were mainly elderly, with a smattering of very young children. The younger adults and older children must have fled, maybe to the nearest city, maybe south. Leaving only those too old, too young, or too stubborn behind.

He told them the two young women needed help and familiar faces.

"Who are you?" a stick-thin, toothless creature demanded, hairy chin quivering as she peered at him.

"Friends... we mean no harm."

"I will go," another woman, red-faced with flinty eyes, set off to the cottage. No one else moved.

"Are there any more Swedes? Any hiding somewhere, any you don't see over there?"

A few shook their heads; most just stared at him as if he were speaking in another language.

Behind him, a woman hugged a corpse, face buried into his chest. His throat had been slit.

He should say something more, do something more. Do anything.

Instead, he turned to one of the Vadians watching over them, "Get them inside once we've checked the cottages; don't want any of these old folk freezing to death."

The Vadian looked at him as blankly as the peasants had.

He didn't wait for any more of a response.

"Why'd they do it?" Hugo asked as they headed to the nearest cottage.

"Because they could."

"But they're on our side. Aren't they?"

"Whose side are we on?" he asked, pushing the door open on another ransacked cottage.

"The Protestants. I suppose."

"The only side you need to be on is your own and the fellows at your shoulder," he gave the boy a serious look, "which currently is me and our lady."

"But the Swedish king came to fight the Catholics, so why-"

"It's war, boy. There are no rules. Everybody is the enemy. And anybody weaker than you is... something to be used."

The only sign of the Swedes in the cottage was a pile of turds sitting in the middle of the rush-covered floor.

Hugo gave him an uncertain look, big liquid eyes almost lost in the cottage's gloomy half-light.

"Have you ever done anything like... this?"

"No..." he shook his head and turned for the door.

I've done far worse...

"Why not? Why are you different?" Hugo asked.

He stopped and looked over his shoulder, "I'm not, and neither are you. None of us know what we're really capable of until the moment comes. For good or ill."

"You'd rape women? Kill old folks?" Hugo's eyebrow shot up.

"Never have," he waved the boy out, "C'mon, we need to clear these cottages."

Hugo trailed after him. The wind snapped at their faces outside, teasing the smoke from the burning buildings across the road.

"Why'd they set the cottages alight?"

"Same reason they killed those old men. To make them give up their valuables."

"They have valuables?"

He pushed open the door to the next cottage with his bad hand, sabre in the other.

"A chicken is valuable these days..."

It was much the same as the last one, less the turds.

"So they killed those people for a chicken?"

"I saw the Merry Gentleman slit a dying man's throat for a pair of boots..."

Hugo dropped his eyes, "I never did anything like that."

Outside, the shouting continued, much of it in Swedish. He checked no fighting had broken out; when satisfied it hadn't, they moved on to the next cottage.

"No? You helped Madge fire *The Eagle's Claw*. Helped her kill the guards."

"Didn't hurt no one! I just kept an eye out and-"

He jabbed a finger at the Swedish soldiers, "I dare say most of them never left home thinking they were going to slit a man's throat for a chicken or rape a woman or burn down a peasant's cottage. But they did."

Hugo trailed him into the next wrecked cottage. This one

had more furniture left in it. All smashed to firewood.

"But I didn't choose to start thieving like they chose to come to war. I ran away cos nobody wanted me!"

A flash of colour brightened the boy's cheeks, draining his anger as quickly as it had arisen. He wasn't even angry with Hugo; it was simply easier to be angry with a boy than the world and the things it made you do.

"Let's just do this; the sooner we're out of here, the better..."

The boy nodded and trailed after him, dragging his boots through the debris.

They checked the rest of the hamlet in silence. All were empty. If any Swedes had decided to get sneaky, they weren't hiding out in the little cottages they'd ransacked.

"What we going to do with em?" Hugo nodded at their prisoners as they emerged from the final cottage.

"Don't know. I don't make the decisions."

"No, our lady does," Hugo said.

"Yes, she does."

Hugo stared at him, "She's been kind to me. Considering. And I am grateful..." the boy's face twisted, "...but there's something right scary about her..."

He patted the boy's shoulder after sliding his father's sabre into its sheath, "Don't worry, she won't hurt you. Thinks she likes you for some reason..." he shrugged, "...women can be odd..."

"Right enough..." Hugo laughed.

"But she isn't scary. She's just driven. That's all."

They walked together back to the Swedish soldiers. Some locals had joined their company to shout and point at the soldiers now they'd disarmed them. Solace was in the middle of things, looking red-faced and flustered.

What's going on?" he asked Lucien, sitting on a wall smoking his pipe.

"Our lady."

"What about her?"

"She wants to hang the prisoners."

His eyebrows shot up.

"She wants them punished for murder, rape, and theft. The locals are, perhaps unsurprisingly, quite keen. Bosko is of the opinion making an enemy of the Swedish army wouldn't be wise; our dashing young lord Lebrecht bends with whichever wind is blowing the hardest. Hence…" Lucien opened a palm towards the crowd, "…the current ongoing frank exchange of views."

"Shit…" he sighed.

Hugo pursed his lips and frowned as he stared up at him, "You were saying something about her not being scary…?"

*

"Murderers!"

The old woman spat at the prisoners. One of them shouted back at her. She doubted the woman spoke Swedish, but it inflamed her enough to scoop up a rock and hurl it.

One of the Vadians, Gerwin, stepped in and prevented her from throwing anything else.

"Get them back!" she pointed at the knot of locals eager to exact revenge on their attackers now they were disarmed and on the ground.

She was pleased to see the Vadian and Gothen men did as she said without recourse to checking with Bosko or Lebrecht. They were learning. It wasn't natural for a soldier to obey a woman, even a highborn one, but she found that if she sounded like she believed she *was* in charge, half the battle was won.

Convincing Bosko and Lebrecht to hang the Swedes was proving harder.

She returned to the two men, far enough away from the prisoners so they couldn't be heard, close enough so she could keep an eye on them. They were evenly matched, man for man, with the Swedes; even unarmed, they could still cause trouble.

"We have no right to execute them," Bosko continued where he left off.

"They killed two defenceless old men, torched several cottages, and ransacked the rest to make these peasants reveal what few valuables they possessed. No gold and silver, Captain, but what scant food they had to see them through the winter. Oh, and I almost forgot, they were taking turns to rape the only two young women in the hamlet. Though, I assume, that was just for fun rather than gain!"

"I am not saying-"

"What do you suggest then? We go to their camp to report the matter to their commanding officer? Where do you think that will get us, eh?" she jabbed a finger at him before Bosko could answer, "I'll tell you; it'll end with you dead in a ditch stripped of your possession and me, Lady Karoline and the other women of our company used for entertainment like those two poor girls in there."

"You don't know that."

"Don't I?" she said, going toe to toe with the soldier, "Believe me, I've seen the monsters in this world, Captain, and there's only one way to deal with them!"

"My lady..." Lebrecht said, one arm wrapped across his torso, the elbow of his other arm resting on it as he bothered the fluffy stubble sprouting from his chin.

"What?"

"The Swedes are not our enemy; we are not at war with them. If we were to do as you wish... there would be repercussions..."

"Yet they can murder, rape and steal without repercussion?"

"It would make us a dangerous enemy," Bosko said, scraping his heel back and forth in the mud.

"We've already made an enemy! What do you think they will do if we let them go?"

"We take their horses and weapons..."

"Well, one thing we agree on then!"

"...by the time they make it to their camp, we'll be long gone," Lebrecht said.

It was the young nobleman's turn to face her anger, "And that is sufficient punishment, is it? For destroying these people's homes, for killing, for raping, for stealing. Is it?! Is it?!"

Heat rushed to her face, smarting in the sharp winter breeze. She could almost hear the echo of her father's palm upon her cheek. Smoke still soured the air, as it had around The Wolf's Tower. Across the road, timbers snapped and crackled, and within the flames' snarl, the ghost of her father's screams taunted her.

Nothing troubled Bosko's battered face. As a career soldier he'd seen this before. Many times. Maybe he'd even done similar things himself. In war, everybody was a casualty, especially old people, women, and children. Lebrecht was softer; he knew less of the world and still possessed some concept of right and wrong. Given enough time, she could probably talk him into doing whatever she wanted. But they didn't have an abundance of time.

There were likely other Swedish foraging parties nearby. If one stumbled on them, they were unlikely to deal with them as easily as these fools, who'd been too busy stealing and fucking to notice her men looping around to the other side of the hamlet to take their horses and backs.

Of course, this was none of her business. She'd sent Lucien and the Gothens to ensure they got past the Swedes without being robbed themselves, not to save this nameless hamlet. They could just saddle up and ride on. They could.

But she couldn't.

There were too many echoes here, too many ghosts.

She whirled away from Bosko and Lebrecht and crossed to the locals standing behind the muskets of four Vadians. Gotz was there too, talking to them, trying to calm the crowd.

"Who will tell me what happened here?" she pointed towards the two corpses, each now with a blanket over them, "I want to know who killed those men?"

The babble of voices hushed, uncertain eyes turned on each other, feet shuffled.

"I will give you justice," she said, voice rising, "but I need you to tell me who here is guilty of the most monstrous wrongs done to you."

Gotz came over to her side when no one spoke up.

"They are scared of what the Swedes will do after we leave..." he said in her ear.

Her eyes swept the crowd. Old men and women, some clutching small children, stared back.

Perhaps they required some rousing, passionate speech about righting wrongs, justice, and standing up for yourself. Of not letting the world grind you down under its heel. Maybe she should tell them about vengeance and the fact it was a god that *always* demanded sacrifice.

Instead, she ran her eyes back and forth across the peasants in their dirty, threadbare clothes, hollow-cheeked and hollow-stomached one and all, before telling them, "I have my own business to attend to. All I can offer you is a choice of swift justice or no justice at all. Show me who the murderers are, or we'll leave them all here..."

Just when she was about to turn away, a woman pushed to the front and past the Vadian men-at-arms. In an extremely competitive race, the woman was the oldest, frailest, and most decrepit of the oldsters making up the bulk of the hamlet's population.

Her face, scarred by ancient pockmarks, boasted more fissures than creases. A few thin whisps of hair the colour of sun-bleached bone, escaped a stained and shapeless cap as she shuffled forward, bent over a knotted stick as twisted as her spine.

"I am Frau Falck. I will speak for us all. My eyes are still good. I saw everything well enough."

"Come, Mother..." she took the old woman's elbow and eased her over to where Lebrecht and Bosko waited in front of their prisoners.

Frau Falck's steps were slow but steady. When she reached the two men, the old woman squinted at each of them in turn with rheumy eyes before planting her stick in the mud, wrapping two gnarled hands around it, and staring down at the Swedish soldiers sitting on the ground. A few glared at her. Most, however, refused to meet the frail old woman's eye.

After turning her lips over her gums, Frau Falck began to speak, her words clear enough to carry over the taunting cackle of flames.

"They came an hour after dawn. Said they needed help to fight the Catholics; Herr Dorfmann told them we were all too old to fight anybody. All the young people left here years ago. That one..." she raised a bony finger towards the Swede's sergeant, Widforss, who'd spoken to her while Gotz held a dagger to their Captain's throat, "...laughed and told us they'd do the fighting. They were here to protect us from the Catholics and our mad emperor, but they required food and silver to do it.

We swore on the good Lord's name we didn't have any silver and precious little food. But they didn't believe us, even when we fell to our knees and begged! They started breaking into our homes and taking everything we have!" Frau Falck's voice wavered, and she pointed at the cart still loaded with the soldier's loot.

"When they couldn't find any silver, any coin and nought

but the few crusts we have to eat they began threatening us. Herr Euler..." her eyes turned to the nearest of the two covered corpses, "he stepped forward and explained, most politely, that we didn't have anything. They told him to shut up. When... when he didn't..." a single tear rolled down her pockmarked cheek. The old woman smeared it away with the back of her hand.

"What happened?" she asked gently.

"One of em... took his musket and hit Herr Euler in the face with it. He went straight down. But he kept hitting him in the head with the musket, then stamping on his head till... till... poor Herr Euler's head just... came apart..." Frau Falck, lifted one shaking hand from her stick to cover her toothless mouth.

She glanced at the silent faces surrounding her, Bosko stared back impassively. Lebrecht wouldn't meet her eye.

"Which one did this, Mother, can you show us?"

The old woman's hand moved from her mouth; she could only half straighten her finger to point at one of the Swedish soldiers.

"Him!"

A thin-faced man with a scratchy beard and long, greasy hair glared back and muttered something.

"He kept laughing and stamping on Herr Euler till they told him to stop. Then him..." a bent, bony finger jabbed at the Swede's Captain, "...said if we told them where our silver and food was hidden, no one else would get hurt. Nobody said anything. Then him..." her gnarled hand indicated Widforrs, "pulled Herr Dorfmann out and pushed him to his knees in front of us. Put a blade to his throat and screamed at us to tell him. We begged them to believe we didn't have anything, but..." her eyes moved to the second corpse, "...he didn't believe us..."

She thought the old woman would dissolve into tears, but she sucked in a deep breath and continued.

"The one who killed Herr Dorfmann, I think he wanted to kill us all, one by one. I don't speak their tongue, so can't say for sure. But he kept pointing at the children, with that big knife of his still dripping with Herr Dorfmann's blood, but the other one..." she indicated Captain Naslund, "...I think he said no. They argued, but instead, they started pulling our homes to pieces, destroying everything. Then, they torched the cottages. Maybe they thought that would make us talk, but they could have done anything. We couldn't magic what we don't have out of thin air for them!"

"Did anything else happen?"

Frau Falck nodded and dropped her eyes, "They took Rosa. Pulled her little one off her and dragged her away screaming. Then young Cilly too. Can't say what happened to em as didn't see with me own eyes, thank the Lord for that," she spat at the prisoners, "but I can guess well enough."

"Thank you, Mother," she said, running a hand down the woman's arm, "you've been very brave."

"Nothing brave about it," Frau Falck shot back, "hang the buggers and be done with it!"

Chapter Fifteen

"Those two are murderers; we hang them!"

He'd moved quietly to Solace's shoulder, Lucien too.

Bosko wasn't convinced, though Lebrecht appeared to be wavering.

"We don't have the right," the Captain said, "and you certainly don't!"

Lebrecht kept eyeing the two covered bodies, particularly the one without much of a head remaining on its shoulders. His own attention lingered on the soldiers the old crone had accused of the killings. Each now had a larger space around them as their comrades shuffled away.

"'tis war, Captain, there are no laws in this land. So, justice is left to us. Lebrecht is a *Markgräf,* I am a *Freiin.* 'tis our Christian duty before God to protect the poor and the defenceless."

"I-"

"What if your father lay dead on the ground with his head beaten to a pulp? Wouldn't you want justice for him?"

Bosko ran a hand through his beard but struggled for an answer.

Solace took a step forward. He didn't know what the Captain saw in her eye, but he seemed to be struggling to keep himself from taking one backwards.

"Do you have a daughter, Captain?"

His eyes widened before he eventually said, "Yes…"

Solace tilted her head, eyes so ablaze Bosko dropped his own gaze to his boots. Then she span away to storm towards one of the cottages.

He hurried after her.

"My lady…"

She neither answered nor broke stride.

"Why are you doing this?"

He knew well enough but wanted to know if she did.

"Justice," she said.

"For who?"

That got him a look.

"This is not about me, Ulrich."

"Isn't it?"

She stopped to glare up at him, her hands, he noticed, trembling at her sides. She curled them into fists.

"I feel these people's pain and loss, yes, because monsters came to my home and destroyed it too, but I am not here to find vengeance by proxy. I am here to give these people the justice they deserve."

In his experience, the poor rarely received justice, but he stowed that thought.

"If you hang those men, it will not be forgotten. I know soldiers, my lady. Vengeance breeds vengeance. Someone will come after you. Maybe King Gustavus Adolphus will send his whole damn army after you if this reaches his ears. Don't you have enough unbeatable enemies?"

"No enemy is unbeatable, Ulrich. If I thought that, I would have stayed hiding in the rubble of The Wolf's Tower," she carried on towards the cottage, her stride lengthening with each pace.

Rather than following her inside, he put his back to the wall and watched the flames dancing within the shells of the cottages across the road.

Looks kept coming his way, though he knew nobody was much interested in him. Despite what she'd told Bosko, Solace had no jurisdiction here, no power, no position, yet she seemed hellbent on bending the world to do her bidding purely by force of will.

He didn't know if that was admirable or terrifying.

The peasants here might have suffered a great wrong, but he doubted hanging the perpetrators would make their lives any easier.

Inside, he could make out the sound of women's voices. He didn't strain to make them out and slapped his gloved hands together as much to ensure he didn't as to keep out the cold.

Minutes passed. People were becoming restless. Bosko wanted to turn the Swedes loose and send them on their way but stayed his hand, either out of respect for the peasants' grief and anger or fear of Solace.

How long the prisoners would sit meekly awaiting their fate was anybody's guess. Most of the Gothen and Vadian soldiers ringed them, but if he were in their shoes, he might decide going down fighting preferable to dangling from the highest available branch.

"C'mon on, my lady..." he muttered under his breath as he fidgeted with the pommel of his father's sabre.

Hugo had asked him if he'd ever done anything like this. He hadn't. But neither had he been in a position to choose or refuse. An untested virtue was a base and worthless metal.

Old Man Ulrich had been a soldier all his life. The old man had done things that haunted him to his piss-stained death bed. He didn't know what they were; he'd never talked directly about them. But sometimes he'd caught him mumbling into his ale, nonsense things, wicked things. The ramblings of a drunk. As a boy, he'd always ignored them, as he'd ignored the sound of his father sobbing into his pillow or crying out in his sleep. Dreams and nightmares, perhaps. Or Memories and ghosts, which could amount to much the same thing.

He'd never asked his father what haunted him. And he'd never regretted that ignorance. But he couldn't help himself from wondering what sins made the old man weep in the small hours of the night and turned his eyes into smoky, inward-looking mirrors.

His attention fixed on the corpses on the ground.

And what things might make him do the same.

If he lived long enough.

Of course, he'd already plenty to feel guilty about despite being only a fraction of Old Man Ulrich's age. He didn't expect to live to see the summer, but if, somehow, he did, would that be his fate? A broken old man haunted by sins he couldn't leave on the road behind him.

The cottage door squeaked on rusty hinges.

Solace appeared, with the young blonde woman he and Hugo had found on the bed. She walked stiffly, clutching Hilde's arm.

Hilde offered him a thin, pained smile. The girl's eyes

followed, and she flinched, tightening her grip on Hilde's arm.

"Rosa," Solace said, "this is Ulrich. He is a friend. A good man. You can trust him."

Rosa managed a nod but refused to meet his eye. The idea there were good men in the world might be one Rosa currently struggled with.

Rosa had put on her cap. Without the long blonde hair concealing her face, as it had when they'd found her, the bruises, already swelling enough to half close her left eye, and split lip, were all too evident.

An older woman stood in the doorway watching them, lips a bloodless line. She nodded at him before closing the door. The second girl must have refused Solace's request to come out and face her attackers.

He fell in behind the three women. A hush descended on soldiers and villagers alike.

Even without seeing Rosa's face, he could tell how painful each step she took towards the prisoners was for her, both physically and emotionally.

A little boy, no more than three or four, squirmed from the clutches of an old woman and came barrelling at Rosa, "Mama! Mama!" he cried.

Rosa pulled away from Hilde to hug the boy; her whole body shook as she buried her head in hair so blonde it was almost white.

The woman who'd been with the boy hurried over, "Come, Carl, be a good boy; come with Nanna!"

Carl kicked and screamed and cried for his Mama as he was half carried, half dragged away.

Rosa almost collapsed into the mud. He wanted to step forward and catch her, but the last thing she would want was a strange man's hands on her, so he left her to Solace and Hilde.

Both women crouched down with her, Solace's forehead brushing Rosa's as she spoke to her in low, whispered tones while Hilde held her hand.

Hilde teetered on the verge of tears herself, and he forced himself to stare at the prisoners instead. Some glared at them with angry and defiant eyes, a few were blank-faced; the majority, just looked scared. Aside from Widforrs and a couple of others, most were barely more than boys themselves; even their Captain was no older than him.

In gentle increments Solace and Hilde eased Rosa upright. She kept looking over her shoulder for her son with red, restless eyes, but Nanna had already whisked him out of sight.

When they reached Lebrecht and Bosko, standing before the prisoners, Solace took Rosa's hand and said loudly enough for everybody to hear, "I will not ask you to recount what has happened to you and Cilly; that is plain for all to see, but I want you to point to each of the men who attacked you, Rosa. Can you do that?"

Rosa stared at her feet. For a long while, he thought the girl wouldn't be able to even look at the prisoners.

Slowly, her head rose, her eyes followed, fingers twitching around Hilde's hand. Rosa's gaze swept across the men sitting before her. Lips trembling, she pulled her other hand from Solace's; it started to rise, then flopped back to her side as if chained to iron weights.

Solace whispered something he couldn't hear. Rosa nodded, sucked in a wet breath before fully raising her chin. Her attention fixed on Widforrs, one of the few staring directly back at the young woman. His face cracked into a leering, wreck-toothed grin as he said something in Swedish and laughed. He swivelled around him like some men do when they think they've said something funny and expect everyone within earshot to laugh, too.

No one was.

Rosa lifted her right hand, then extended a shaking finger at Widforrs.

"Him. He hurt me first... and last..." her hand skimmed across the swollen, discoloured skin around her eye and down the right side of her face, "...and most."

"Move him away from the others," Solace said, looking at no one.

"Bitch!" Widforrs snarled, before spitting at Solace.

Usk moved without hesitation or waiting for confirmation from Lebrecht. When Widforrs swore rather than getting off his arse, the big Gothen man-at-arms smashed his musket butt into the Swede's face; bone cracked, blood sprayed.

The raised weapons of the surrounding Gothens and Vadians dissuaded any Swedes from going to their sergeant's aid.

Usk dragged Widforrs away from his comrades by the collar. The Swede wasn't a small man, but he gave Usk no more trouble than a child would anyone else.

"That one too..." Solace told Usk once he'd deposited Widforrs onto a different patch of mud, indicating the soldier Frau Falck identified as the one guilty of caving in the head of Herr Eulers.

Usk was only too happy. That one, a weaselly-looking man he wouldn't have trusted with a wooden spoon, went more meekly.

When done, Solace's attention returned to Rosa, who pointed out four more men in turn.

"Are these the ones who hurt Cilly too?" Solace asked.

Rosa nodded.

Solace touched her arm, "Thank you."

She nodded at Hilde, who then gently led Rosa away. The locals jumped out of their way as quickly as if she had the plague, most of them refusing to meet the young woman's eye as Hilde took her back.

Solace turned to Lebrecht and Bosko, "These six we hang; the rest you can let go. If you must..."

Lebrecht made to open his mouth, but Solace spoke over whatever he was trying to say, "They are murderers and rapists. There are no excuses. War or not. You saw what they did to that girl. There's another one, just as savagely beaten, but she's too cowered to come out and face the men who hurt her. Do you have any idea how much courage it took for Rosa to come out and do that? You are a Prince of the Empire, my lord; 'tis your *duty* to enforce the law and protect our people. Don't you dare tell me those bastards deserve to live!"

Lebrecht shut his mouth and then shook his head. When Solace continued to stare, he added, "No, they don't."

Her eyes, bright and fierce, turned on Bosko.

"You are not in charge here, my lady," the Vadian's Captain said, "I cannot-"

"You are not in command here either, Captain Bosko..."

A waifish figure emerged from the smoke, pale as any ghost or demon, thin and frail as some of the elderly peasants, "...I am," Lady Karoline said, clutching the arm of her maid, Elin.

Bosko hurried to his mistress, "My lady, you should not-"

"I cannot spend my life inside that infernal contraption!" Karoline's body might be frail, but her voice could cut.

"No, my lady, but-" Bosko fussed about her, more like a maiden aunt than a soldier arguing for the lives of killers and rapists.

"I have heard Lady Celine's words and that of these people..." Karoline turned dark ringed eyes momentarily towards the villagers; she really did not look well, "...and I concur."

"My lady, we-"

"Bosko!" she snapped, "Hang them. And be quick about it. We are late enough!"

"Yes, my lady..." Bosko nodded as he mumbled.

"Then we are agreed," Solace stood before the men they wouldn't soon be looking for a tree for.

He came to her side.

"Gotz!"

"Yes, my lady," the old soldier moved to her other shoulder.

"You speak Swedish?"

"Some."

"Enough to translate as I explain how lucky they are?"

"I think I can make them understand the gist of it."

"Good, tell them those men..." she pointed to the soldiers

Usk had dragged away from the main group, "...are going to be hung for murder and rape. But we will allow the rest of them to go. I will trust the fact *they* did not murder or rape was down to choice rather than opportunity..."

Solace paused to let Gotz speak in hesitant Swedish. She stood too close to the prisoners for his liking, but all he could do was stay at her side and hope the weapons surrounding them were persuasive enough.

"...and I further trust if they find themselves in a similar position in future, they will remember what happens to murderers and rapists. Even in war. Perhaps next time they might even consider lifting a finger to stop it..."

While Gotz translated, she stared at their Captain, who had neither killed nor raped but had the power to keep his men from carrying out the deeds.

Naslund kept looking at the mud accumulated on his boots.

"However, if just *one* of you tries to prevent your comrades from receiving the justice they deserve before God... I will see you *all* hanged."

A few men glanced at each other as Gotz spoke, but there was no other reaction.

Solace glared at them all, then crouched in front of a lad with a shock of red hair and a long straight nose who was probably even younger than his lady.

They'd stripped the prisoners of their weapons and searched them, but he wouldn't have bet a turnip against there still being a few concealed blades between them. He stood at Solace's side, drawing enough of Old Man Ulrich's sabre to show the world a couple of fingers of steel.

"What's Swedish for, *do you understand*?" she asked Gotz without looking around.

"*Förstår ni.*"

The young soldier either refused to meet her eye or hadn't understood Gotz's Swedish.

Solace's hand shot out, grabbed the lad's chin, and lifted his head.

"*Förstår ni?!*"

The boy flinched, and Solace squeezed his chin to stop him squirming away.

"*Förstår ni?!*"

He couldn't see Solace's face or eyes, but what the young soldier could was enough to whiten his skin to dirty snow and widen his eyes so far they could have fallen clean out of his head.

"*Ja! Ja!*" he said, trying to shuffle backwards on his arse through the mud to get away from her.

She rose smoothly to move along the line. He went with her, still showing the Swedes his father's steel.

She squatted down in front of another man, this one older and bigger. Broad shoulders hunched forward, hard features clustered too close together in the centre of a ruddy face under a dented helmet. Although almost big enough to snap Solace in half with his bare hands, once her eyes were level with his, he only wanted to scurry away from her like she was a mad, slavering dog.

"*Förstår ni?*"

The man nodded hard enough to rattle the helmet about his ears.

She moved back and forth along the line, asking the same

question and getting the same response. Sometimes she had to ask more than once. Mostly she didn't. Some said, *Ja* in return; others only nodded.

And most of them, once they'd stared in her eyes, looked somewhere between unsettled and terrified.

What do they see that I can't?

Finally, she stood over their Captain, Naslund. Before him, she didn't crouch.

"You killed no one, you raped no one. But you were in charge. You could have stopped this, but you didn't. I should hang you too..."

Naslund bit his lip and struggled to remain expressionless. He didn't look like a soldier anymore. He looked like a scalded child.

"But I won't. Because unlike them," she nodded at the men she'd selected to die, "I am not a monster. Next time you are faced by the innocent and defenceless, remember this day. And remember, there are always consequences for your actions. Whether in this life or the next!"

With that, she spun away and walked off into the smoke.

He remained for a moment. Eyes skimming the cowered soldiers. She was just a girl, but she'd terrified them. What was she becoming? Someone to admire or something to fear?

The road they travelled together would lead them to a doomed city, where, when the walls fell, they could face Saul and the Red Company again. When Magdeburg's walls fell, the monsters, human and demon, would be unleashed upon the city's inhabitants.

But Magdeburg's walls weren't the only ones that were

falling. Solace's own walls were cracking and teetering, too, but her walls weren't keeping anything out. They were keeping something in. And when *they* fell, he feared what else might be unleashed upon the world.

He hurried after his mistress.

And a dead man's voice whispered in the breeze.

Save her, and you save yourself...

*

It takes a surprising amount of time to hang a man.

Six men, even more so.

A pasture stretched behind the hamlet, it would have been used to graze animals in better days, but all the horses, cows and goats had long since been sold, butchered, or stolen. The Swedes had seemingly killed the local's last pig. The pasture, however, did boast a suitable oak with high sturdy branches.

They emptied the Swede's cart of its loot and drove it under the oak to serve as a makeshift gallows. Hugo proved adept at shinning up the tree to loop rope over the thickest branches.

According to the prisoners, a thousand-strong contingent of King Gustavus Adolphus' army camped a day's ride west, so she sent Lucien and four riders to escort Naslund and the remainder of his men an hour's march south and east of the hamlet, less their weapons, horses, and coin. By the time Naslund and his men made it back to their camp, the hamlet should be far behind them.

She had no desire to watch the hangings but could hardly shy away after arguing for them. The peasants deserved justice as much as any King or Prince. They were too weak and powerless to deliver their own, but she wasn't.

Her fingers toyed with the bag of dust hanging from her neck.

They put the condemned on the cart with nooses tied around their necks. Some made more of a fuss about it than others.

Widforrs fought so hard Usk had beaten him half senseless and could now barely stand. A couple of the younger ones were blubbing and babbling in Swedish. Begging for their lives, no doubt.

"They're boys..." Bosko said, appearing at her shoulder.

"And the women they raped are little more than girls," she said, refusing to divert her gaze from the condemned, "I dare say they begged too..."

"Perhaps a little mercy-"

"They're old enough to fight, old enough to kill, old enough to steal, old enough to rape," her eyes finally met his, "They are old enough to die."

Bosko shuffled his feet. He was more than unhappy about the whole business.

The rest of their company...?

She didn't know. They were doing what she wanted. Nothing else mattered.

Of the coins she'd collected from their prisoners, she'd handed half to the locals, the remainder she would share later amongst (as she was increasingly thinking of them) *her* men. Hopefully, that would help salve any consciences troubled by executing murderers and rapists.

"You should have told me you were going to put your

dagger to Naslund's throat," Bosko said.

"You would have stopped me."

"Damn right, I would have; it was bloody stupid. We would have got past the Swedes without any trouble-"

"If I hadn't," she snapped him off, "they probably would have seen our men circling around behind them. And then there would have been trouble. As it was, all their eyes were on me."

Bosko glared at her. She glared right back till he dropped his gaze.

"Trust me, Captain. Just because I don't have a cock, it doesn't mean I don't know what I'm doing."

"You're a child! You could have got us all killed."

"But I didn't. Because God is on my side."

She had no idea whose side God was on, but claiming divine guidance was often a good way of stifling dissent. It shut Bosko up, anyway.

Widforrs made one final attempt to resist, which ended with the pommel of Usk's sword slamming into the back of his head, knocking the Swede senseless.

Perhaps she should have had their throats slit? It would have saved a lot of time. Something she'd have to bear in mind for next time.

Next time?

She shivered and pulled her cloak around herself.

"How very ruthless..."

The voice had not been Bosko's. The Vadian had stomped off across the field.

"My Lord Flyblown," she greeted the apparition.

The day was grey and sombre, but the figure she found

beside her wore shadows like a shroud.

"You know, once you decided to traipse gaily down this path, you really should have done for all those scoundrels. Mercy is all well and good, but..." he flashed her a white, feral smile, "...it does tend to leave enemies behind."

A knot of peasants had come to watch proceedings and throw insults, though most chose to remain in the hamlet. A grim-faced Bosko was now barking at the hanging detail. Renard and Gotz were nearby. Nobody noticed the tall, pale, sharp-faced creature wrapped in a twilight cloak.

"Are you invisible or just inside my head?"

Flyblown chuckled.

"Have you appeared to pass on more wisdom, or do you simply enjoy grisly spectacles?"

"Oh," he smiled, eyes fixed on their impromptu gallows with keen interest, "I must confess, I've always found there was *something* about a good hanging..."

"Well, given how your advice about seducing the *Markgräf* turned out, perhaps 'tis better if you are here solely for the entertainment."

Flyblown arched an eyebrow, "The advice was excellent! It was the execution that lacked finesse. No pun intended."

They seemed about ready to resolve matters on the cart. The soldiers jumped off to leave the condemned with their hands tied behind their backs and nooses about their necks. Hugo, who sat astride the branch above them, gave an inappropriately jaunty wave to signify everything was tied off and ready to go.

Should she say some words? Some prayers? They had no pastor at hand to deal with such matters.

"He planned to lock me in a tower. Which would have done little to bring about the end of our mutual friend."

Muffled sobs and cries came from the condemned, apart from Widforrs whose knees had given way. He appeared to be getting on with the hanging ahead of his comrades, his face already turning blue beneath the blood.

"And yet here you are? With an army of sorts. And the latest bride of the delightful *Graf* Bulcher to boot. I would say it is all going swimmingly!"

"That's one interpretation."

"The correct one, My Lady of the Broken Tower."

"Why are you here?"

"A courtesy. To see how you are getting along," Flyblown's thin, bloodless lips puckered, "How are you getting along?"

"Well enough."

People were looking at her. Not because of Flyblown but because everything was ready.

"Give the order..." she could see Flyblown staring at her intently out of the corner of her eye, "...no qualms now... don't allow compassion to cloud your judgement or slow your hand."

The pleading and sobbing grew louder. Several of the men were thrashing, trying to extract themselves from the nooses. A dark stain bloomed on one man's crotch.

"It is traditional for the condemned to have their faces covered when they are hanged," Flyblown said softly, "It is not done for *their* benefit."

She swallowed. She wanted to drag her gaze away, cover her ears, and run across the pasture. Contorted faces begged, pleaded, cursed, screamed, eyes bulged, mouths gaped, features transformed into grotesque masks of the damned.

And they weren't even hanging yet.

What am I doing?

"What needs to be done."

"Why does it need to be done?"

"Because you are but a woman, and if you are to lead men, you must be more ruthless than any man. You are beautiful, so they will love you, but that is not enough. Love is just one side of the triangle you need to build to be what you need to be."

"And what are the other two sides?"

"Respect," Flyblown said, "and fear."

"I do not want to be feared..." she whispered.

"My Lady of the Broken Tower, you need to be, otherwise you will not survive that which lies before you. The darkness beckons; you must be ready to face it, to walk into it, to be consumed by it so that you can destroy that which must be destroyed..."

"I don't understand."

"Harden yourself, child. To destroy the darkness, you must become the darkness..."

"Morlaine warned me, the night I met her in The Wolf's Tower, that if I stared into the darkness long enough, the darkness would creep into my soul until one bitter day I become the monster..."

"Morlaine..." Flyblown sniffed, "...well, what does *she* know? Her newfound morality is all very commendable. But do you think that's going to get the job done, eh?"

Bosko mouthed the question *My lady?* from under the tree

about to bear kicking, pissing fruit.

Flyblown's cold eyes lingered on her, "You must always do what you deem is necessary. Regardless…"

"I know…"

Hanging murderers and rapists had not seemed a difficult choice an hour ago. The bodies and burning homes reflected The Wolf's Tower, Rosa and Cilly's bruised faces and tormented eyes mirrored her own pain. She looked at the men responsible and saw monsters.

Now only terrified boys begging for their lives cowered before her.

Flyblown leaned close to her ear, bringing the north wind with his words, "Darkness beckons…"

Darkness beckoned. Darkness consumed.

She nodded at Bosko.

"Do it!"

The Captain barked a command, and Usk, standing by the cart's horse, yanked the animal's harness, leading the beast forward.

And left six men kicking air…

Chapter Sixteen

They rode deep into the night.

The clouds cleared at dusk, and the moon smiled on them from a sharp, crystal sky. How long before Naslund got to the Swedish camp, and how long would it take to find them if their commander was as enthusiastic about matters of vengeance as Solace?

Those were the kind of questions worrying his mind. Though, whether King Gustavus Adolphus' army was more or less of a foe to be feared than the Red Company was debatable. Either way, the constant looking over his shoulder for signs of pursuit proved a useful diversion from the memories of six men swinging under the boughs of an oak tree.

He had seen hangings before. By his reckoning, the first had been a drunken deserter from the retinue of one of the long list of lords and masters his father served during his childhood; he could have been no more than eight or nine.

Yet this one shocked him more. Not so much by the manner of the men's deaths, hanging was a slow and horrible way to die regardless, but because they died at Solace's insistence. She hadn't personally bound their hands, tightened the ropes around their necks or pulled the cart away to leave them kicking air and pissing their britches as their faces turned blue, but if she hadn't been there, they wouldn't have died.

The Swedes may well have tried to extract a *contribution* to their war effort, but their party was as well armed as them; they probably would have let them pass, and certainly so once they saw Lucien and the Gothen men had seized their horses.

Solace would no doubt argue, correctly, that had they ridden on, more of the villagers might have died, and the ordeal of the two women would have been longer and even more appalling.

And yet, and yet, and yet... to send men to their deaths, to watch them beg, and cry and piss themselves, regardless of the wrongs they had done, without flinching, that took a coldness and hardness he hadn't known Solace possessed. For Saul and the Red Company certainly, and Bulcher too. But the rest of the world?

Hilde rode at his side on Plodder, who he'd replaced with one of the Swedish horses, a fine dapple-grey gelding. Solace had given half the horses and some weapons they'd confiscated to the hamlet peasants. She'd also told them to leave as soon as possible and that they had seen no one on the road up from Wittanberge. Even if the Swedes didn't return, somebody would; Imperials, Catholic League, mercenaries, brigands.

It would be a shame to have hanged those men just so the peasants were free to get robbed, raped, and murdered by somebody else.

Whether they would or not was another matter. Aside from Rosa and Cilly everyone else was very old or very young. The able-bodied had already left, and the old tended to be stubborn.

"You're quiet...?" Hilde asked.

His attention returned to her, "I've never been very talkative."

She wrinkled her nose in that way he was finding ever more endearing, "It gives you an air of intrigue and mystery."

"It does?"

She laughed.

The laughter was good-humoured and genuine. The kind that could be spirit-lifting and infectious. But here, this night, with six corpses hanging in their wake, he found it jarring.

Hilde's smile faded.

"Are you thinking about the men we hanged?"

He twitched his shoulders.

"You shouldn't, they deserved to die," she said.

"Probably..."

"There's no probably about it. Men like that..." Hilde spat.

He wasn't sure how different men like that were to men like him. He presumed Hilde saw one; he wasn't so sure he did.

If he's been in that foraging party, would he have done enough to stop his comrades killing those old men? From raping those women? Would he have taken part in the killing? The raping?

War makes you do things, boy, changes you. It takes a man and makes a monster of him...

Old Man Ulrich's words slurred out of the darkness.

He shook the voice away. His father's wisdom was rarely

helpful.

"'tis more Solace that concerns me," he said.

"Why?"

"Those men died because she insisted they did."

"Does a woman being as hard as a man make you uneasy?" Hilde's smile didn't have so much mirth this time.

He'd told Hilde little of what Solace and he had experienced and less of what lay ahead of them. The possibility, perhaps probability, that it was driving his mistress insane was one he couldn't express without changing that.

So, he shrugged again.

"Men like that killed my brothers. If the Lord answered my prayers, I would hang every last one of them."

Hilde never talked about her life prior to Ettestein, he knew that pain, loss, and grief ran through it but never asked. He suspected she hid a lot behind a smile, but if she wanted to tell him, she would. Personally, he thought anguish better buried than shared, but not everybody thought the same.

Hilde lapsed into rare silence.

Thanks to the day's troubles, the moon hung high in a star-scattered sky by the time they reached the inn they intended to spend the night in.

Illuminating the burnt-out derelict shell that remained.

He could almost believe in all the excitement they had gone the wrong way and ended up back at *The Eagle's Claw*.

The smell of charred timber lingered in the silvered air, and beneath that, the faint, greasy hint of roasted meat.

The inn hadn't long burnt down, and people, dead or alive, had been inside when it had. More Swedes? Maybe the handiwork of the ones that ransacked the hamlet?

They decided to press on until midnight, finally making camp for a few hours, where a thicket of trees shielded them from the road. They had seen no signs of life since the hamlet. It was a winter's night, so that was not unusual. But no lights or fires broke the deep, distant dark. He could believe their horses carried them through a land stripped of humanity, leaving the shadows to the monsters alone.

They lit no fires and ate dry rations before making themselves as comfortable as possible on the cold, damp ground. Solace moved around the camp, pressing a portion of the coins they'd taken from the Swedes into each soldier's hand.

Not Lebrecht. Not Bosko. Solace.

When she passed him, she said, without pausing, "I'll take your share off what you owe me for Madriel..."

Every so often, he thought she might have forgiven him for spending some of her silver to get Madleen's daughter into an orphanage. And then she'd do something to remind him she hadn't.

A little later, Hilde came to him without asking, pressing herself against him under the cover of their blankets.

She swiftly fell asleep, head on his chest. Nobody commented. Two girls from *The Eagle's Claw* remained in their company and shared the blankets of a couple of the Vadian soldiers, Hector and Egon. From the sounds of it, they enjoyed other ways of keeping off the chill. Nobody much cared; soldiers were generally more concerned with enjoying what they could from their possibly short lives than morality.

He listened to Hilde's breathing, the quiet nearby coupling, the shuffling footsteps of those on guard duty, the occasional snicker from the horses, the distant, mysterious sighs of the night.

Occasionally, he lowered his face to press it into Hilde's hair, soft and downy on his skin. Each time he resisted the urge to find her breast with his hand and ignored the hardness in his britches.

Why shouldn't you?

A voice that wasn't his father's whispered in his ear.

You're likely going to die soon, anyway.

Indeed, he was. But he didn't want Hilde to die with him, as she surely would if she stayed with him long enough. He should have made her stay in Berg, Wittanberge, or anywhere else along the route. They would be in Thasbald soon, and Solace would move heaven and Earth to kill *Graf* Bulcher. There was a fair chance she'd fail, and they'd all end up like those six Swedes. And even if Solace did succeed, they would be heading to Magdeburg afterwards. To a doomed city, to face a foe they could not possibly defeat when the walls fell, and the World's Pain was unleashed upon the city.

And becoming closer to Hilde would not make it easier to send her away.

So, he carefully slipped a folded blanket under her head before twisting away and turning his back to her. She mumbled but did not wake. He could still feel her behind him, but it made denying temptation less painful.

Instead, he stared into the darkness, hand wrapped around the hilt of his father's sabre, waiting for death to come for him.

And watching Solace sitting alone, silently sharpening her blades again.

He couldn't be certain, but despite the whetstone's constant strokes along the steel, her eyes never left Hilde and him.

*

The landscape grew sparser, emptier. The closer they got to Thasbald, the sharper the wind, the heavier the skies. Thick dark forests, scattered lakes, separated by open heath or marshy wetlands the road took meandering care to travel around. What signs of man they encountered were generally ruined and burnt.

It made her think of Bulcher as some monstrous creature squatting in its lair, sucking the life from the surrounding world.

Once, the crackle of musket fire in the distance broke the silence, but whatever the fight, they saw no more of it.

The villages and inns promised on Bulcher's map were gone. Deserted, abandoned, lifeless. Ash and dust. They came across corpses hanging from trees, they found the charred remains of the dead bound to stakes, twice they went around bodies in the road.

They never stopped to bury them.

This was not a land to linger in.

While in woodland, the cries of a weeping child echoed through the undergrowth.

Lebrecht wanted to go and find them. She told them not to. It might have been a trap. Renard went pale at the sound. Given his ghosts, she'd half expected him to gallop off in search of the child, but he hadn't.

They rode on; the weeping following them for longer than it should have. Perhaps it had been some lost spirit or ephemeral creature floating through the deep, shadowy pools between the pine trees. The plaintive wail scratched and worried at her soul until it faded, leaving only the occasional bird call and horse snort to break the silence.

"You are a hard woman," Lebrecht commented later.

I've left more than one child behind to die before now.

"We have somewhere we need to be," was all she said in reply.

Still, relief took a little of the chill off her bones when the trees thinned to heathland.

One morning, Tomos Usk came to ride beside her, heavy brows furrowed, lintel shoulders hunched.

"My lady..." he said, voice gruff and phlegmy.

"Yes?"

"The men we hanged..."

Her heart sank; she'd hoped everyone had accepted they had served justice to the deserving.

"Yes?" she asked instead, summoning an encouraging smile.

The man-at-arms didn't look at her, his eyes focused on the road. For a long time, he didn't answer. When he did, his voice was quieter, softer than usual.

"I have a little sister, Swenja, she is small and pretty where I am big and... *not*..." he smiled and checked she was listening. She was.

"...we are nothing alike. So much so I sometimes wonder if our mother... found one of us under a bush."

She nodded.

"I used to watch out for her. Because she was small and pretty. Y'know?"

"I know."

"There was this boy. Well, a man, really, a year or two older than me. Jeremias. He took a shine to her, but Swenja didn't like him. Said he smelt like he slept in a night pit, which he shouldn't have because his family had money, but..." the heavy shoulders went up and down once, "... he tried to be friendly with my sister, but she always said no and did her best to keep away from him. One night, she didn't come home..."

"This Jeremias, he did something?"

"He hurt her. Like those Swedes hurt those two women in that hamlet..." his head turned towards her, "...you understand?"

"I understand."

"When she finally came home, she was all bruised, her dress torn, covered in dirt. She didn't want to tell me what happened, but I made her. When she did... I went to find Jeremias."

"What did you do?"

"Beat him senseless. Beat him so hard his face ended up even uglier than mine!" a humourless laugh followed the young soldier's words.

"You killed him?"

The broad shoulders went up and down again, "He was

still alive when I threw him off the bridge..."

"You didn't report him?"

"Report him?" Usk snorted, "his father is one of the richest merchants in Augsburg, a guildsman. He might have got a fine. Maybe they would have paid us to go away. Maybe not. Either way, not the kind of justice he deserved for what he did to my sister. Not for the look he put in her eye, which was even worse than the bruises he left on her sweet face."

"And afterwards?"

"I left Augsburg and became a soldier. I am not clever like you, but I am not so stupid to think they wouldn't have hung me if I'd stayed, regardless of whether he came out of the river alive or dead. That's how the world works. The rich look after themselves and their own. There's no justice for poor people like me and Swenja..." he gave her, a hard, appraising stare, "...that's what I thought till you hanged those bastards anyway."

"I was only doing what I thought right."

Usk nodded, lantern jaw jutting forward, "'tis good enough for me... my lady..."

The day before Bosko calculated they would arrive at Thasbald, they came across a dozen bodies in various states of decay in gibbets hanging from makeshift gallows on either side of the road. A wooden sign hung around each corpse's neck, the word *thief* burnt into it.

"Looks like you're not the only one still trying to uphold the law..." Gotz said as they passed the rotting cadavers, squeaking and rattling in the wind.

"Bulcher's work, most likely, this close to Thasbald,"

Lucien said, looking at her.

She ignored the eyes of both the mercenary and the dead men as she rode on.

That evening, they came upon a large barn, deserted and derelict. Unlike many other ruins they had passed since leaving the hamlet, this one's air of abandonment suggested it had lain empty for years. No other buildings were in sight.

With dusk approaching, they spent their final night on the road within the rotting timbers, which offered some protection from the sharpening wind and hid the smoky fires they did not dare light till full night fell completely.

Lady Karoline, dark-eyed and so pale you could all but see through her, could not be tempted from her carriage even to warm herself by one of the fires when the damp wood finally took hold and started producing more heat than smoke.

"Our last night on the road..." she said to the girl.

"A relief," Karoline managed a smile as she sat huddled beneath furs and blankets on the carriage's bench.

"You will enjoy a more comfortable bed tomorrow night."

"Will I?" Karoline's eyes turned to the window, even though the blind was down against the night.

"I'm sure all your comforts will be taken care of..."

When the girl said nothing, she eased herself onto the opposite bench.

"You do not seem... relieved our journey is nearly done?"

Karoline pulled the furs more tightly about her thin shoulders. Her maid was preparing food, though, from what she'd seen and heard, the girl ate little more than a mouse's portion of whatever Elin put in front of her.

"I..." her eyes settled on the blinded window, "...am rather scared."

"We will reach Thasbald safely."

"I think that is what scares me the most."

When the girl refused to meet her eye, she crossed the carriage, slid onto the seat beside her and found her hand. Despite huddling under a mountain of furs and blankets, Karoline's fingers were icy twigs.

Whenever she'd tried to talk to the girl about *Graf* Bulcher before, Karoline had clammed up, though, she fancied, fear always floated in the pools of her eyes at the mention of her betrothed's name.

"'tis normal for a woman to be uncertain before her wedding."

Now Karoline's eyes did find hers; the skin below them the colour of old tobacco stains, "Is it normal for a woman to be terrified?"

If you are about to marry that monstrous toad, yes...

"He is a rich and powerful man. Why should you be terrified?" she asked...

"I have heard... things..."

"Scullery maids' gossip?"

Karoline shook her head and looked away again.

"You have never met him?"

"No... my father negotiated the match. He told me Vadia needed me to marry *Graf* Bulcher for the common good..." Karoline snorted a laugh, "...my acquiescence was not required."

"The common good?"

Karoline's shoulders twitched beneath the furs, "A financial arrangement, I believe. I am not party to the ins and outs."

"Bulcher is paying to marry you?"

"I have a small dowry for the sake of appearance, but Vadia is not rich. The war... there are debts, I do not know the details, but Bulcher is helping with them..."

Why would he?

Not from the goodness of his heart, that was for certain.

"You do not wish to marry the *Graf?*"

Karoline's only response was bitter laughter.

"Then do not."

"I have no choice, Celine. Unless you know a rich prince who could make my father a better offer. A rich, handsome prince!" After a moment's thought, she added, "A rich, handsome, *young* prince!"

"What do you know of the *Graf?*"

A pale hand appeared from under the furs so Karoline could nibble a fingernail. It seemed her favoured variety of sustenance.

"He is old, rich, fat, hideous, and untrustworthy."

"And yet your father has trusted you to him."

"Yes. Things must be very bad in Vadia, mustn't they?"

She squeezed the girl's hand as a tear slowly welled from her left eye to roll down her ashen cheek, "There are always choices, Karoline. There are always alternatives."

"There are?"

"Oh, yes, there are..."

Chapter Seventeen

Solace gathered them together around one of the fires.

Lucien, Lebrecht, Gotz, Hilde, Hugo and the six Gothen soldiers; Sargeant Paasche, Usk, Harri, Swoon, Wickler and Dreyfuss. Bosko and the Vadians were either asleep or guarding the barn and Karoline's coach.

He stood at her shoulder as his mistress perched on a half-rotted bucket that was the nearest thing they had to a chair. Everybody else stood, sat, or squatted as close to the fire as they could without catching alight. Many wrapped blankets around their shoulders. The night was as bitter as any they'd known since leaving Ettestein. Winter was far from over.

She hadn't confided in him what she wanted everyone for, but she'd been explicit it was only for the ears of their group, so he kept an eye out to make sure the Vadians weren't showing any interest. Currently, none were. The cold discouraged curiosity, and no one seemed inclined to wander over. They had no beer either, which usually helped men keep their distance.

"My name is Solace von Tassau..." though spoken quietly, the words carried clearly enough over the crackling flames, "...some of you know that, some of you don't. There is a reason I have not used it on the road. Tonight, I will explain why. Some of you know my story, some of you don't.

Besides Ulrich, none of you know all of it. Tonight, I will tell you. When done, I will ask a question of you all..."

He shuffled, fiddling with the pommel of his father's sword. Hilde stared at him with dark, intense eyes. Everybody else's attention fixed on Solace. Lucien looked bemused, Lebrecht concerned, otherwise only curiosity played across the fire-lit faces.

"I am the *Freiin* of Tassau, a small barony in Saxony. Or at least it used to be..."

She spoke without hesitation, but she didn't tell them everything. She did not recite his betrayal and dishonour, though the way shame warmed his cheeks and his eyes refused to meet anyone's that might still be evident even without Solace spelling it out. She did not speak of her *sight*, or Torben's. She did not try to burn the demons entering the castle in this version. The Wolf's Tower was taken by surprise, and the first she knew of the slaughter was the sound of screams and Sargeant Lutz pulling her from her bed.

Lucien knew the story and Lebrecht most of it. They listened as raptly as anyone else. She was a fine storyteller. And maybe it was a good story for a freezing winter's night.

He didn't know how long it took her to tell her tale; time moves differently without the sun marking its passing. He kept adding to the fire, and smoke rose in waves from the damp wood each time. However, Solace never coughed, paused, or cleared her throat. Perhaps she'd recited the story so often in her head the words came alive on their own.

She never mentioned Morlaine, finishing the tale with

them leaving the ruined Wolf's Tower once he had healed sufficiently to make the journey to Madriel to commence her quest for vengeance.

At the end, there was one more thing he knew she would add. Whether she should, was another matter. She was playing a dangerous game.

"There is something else you all need to know..." she said, head tilting, skin glowing orange in the firelight, "...the man that hired the Red Company, that sent the demons to destroy my home and murder my father, that wanted to take me and make me his bride..." her eyes rose to sweep across her audience, "...was *Graf* Bulcher..."

Several backs straightened. Men exchanged glances. A few words were muttered under the crack and pop of the fire.

"So..." it was Lebrecht who spoke, "...you knew Lady Karoline would be on the road when we were taking you to Magdeburg?"

"I had some intelligence, though I was not certain."

His lady lied very smoothly; he had to confess.

"And what is your intention in paying the *Graf* a visit?" Gotz asked, smiling darkly.

"To find out where the Red Company is," Solace replied, just as darkly, "and then kill him."

That generated a lot more muttering and exchanged glances.

She held up a hand.

Once the only sound was the fire again, she continued.

"None of you owe me anything. If you want no part of this, we can take our leave of each other with good grace in the morning." Her eyes took in Lucien, Gotz, Hilde, and Hugo, "that includes all of you."

She hadn't looked at him. His loyalty was assured. He would follow her to the gates of Hell if that was where she led. He loved her and hated her, but if he wanted to regain his honour, he was bound to her. And what else did a man have if he did not have his honour?

His own eyes found Hilde's.

You always were a bloody fool.

"Lucien Kazmierczak is renowned from Madrid to Modena for loving a challenge and a scrap almost as much as he is for righting wrongs," Lucien grinned.

Hugo's skinny shoulders went up and down, "I've got nowhere to go..."

"Me neither!" Hilde said, eyes glued to his.

He concentrated on his boots and moved them around a bit.

Gabriel Gotz said nothing.

"You are asking a lot, my lady..." Lebrecht said.

"I am. And I do ask. But I am seeking justice, and I can not find it alone. Justice for my father, who they roasted alive over a fire, for the women and children of Tassau whose blood they feasted on, for all the people of The Wolf's Tower they slaughtered. And for all the people they will kill in the future, for their own Satanic desires and at the behest of evil men like *Graf* Bulcher."

"You have lost friends to the Red Company too," he said to the Gothen men before he could stop himself, "Gottlieb hired them to open the gates of Ettestein for him. A demon called Wendel who could change his face. We searched for him before the attack. Some of you with me. You didn't believe us then. You should believe us now. My lady does not seek justice only for her people, but for yours too..."

"Demons that change their faces..." Paasche shook his head.

"My lady killed it atop the Grace Tower that night. You heard rumours, I am sure?"

"Gossip and rumour," Paasche returned, "half a soldier's life."

"'tis true," Lebrecht said, glancing at his burly sergeant, "I saw the body. An unholy thing that turned to ash and dust within the day."

"I don't doubt your word, my lord, but-"

"I've seen one of those things before too," Gotz said, looking almost sheepishly around the company, "In a tiny puckered-up dog's arse of a place called Reperndorf, fucking a witchfinder, would you believe. Thought her a young raven-haired beauty till she looked over her shoulder..." the old soldier shuddered, "...long thin face, no colour in it at all, but mottled with veins, big black eyes, and this mouth... full of fangs. The ugliest damn woman I ever saw. And I've seen some bad ones... paid to sleep with a few of em too..."

He exchanged a glance with Solace as nervous laughter flitted around the fire.

When it died down, Paasche, who seemed to be talking for the Gothen men, said, "Perhaps 'tis holy work you offer, but walking into a fortress to kill its lord seems an excellent way to get yourself killed... I'm sorry for what you've suffered, my lady, but..."

A couple of the Gothen men nodded along to their

sergeant's words. The others didn't.

"I could say fighting demons is God's work, and if you fall, the All-Mighty will reward you in heaven. But I am a woman, not a bishop. I could say righting a terrible wrong would be reward enough for the risks you would be undertaking," she shrugged, "but I am not an idealist, and few are in this world."

She scanned her audience, eyes lingering on each soldier in turn. Some held her gaze. Others decided the smoky flames more to their liking.

"However, what I can say is this..." she hunched forward, elbows on her knees, voice dropping, "...*Graf* Bulcher is a rich man. Thasbald drips with silver and gold, silks, and precious jewels. I need an army to fight an army. And I intend the *Graf* should pay for it. I will keep half for that purpose; the rest I will split equally with you all. Just as I did with the silver we took from the Swedes."

She sat back, holding her hands out to them, "If God's grace and the pursuit of justice are not enough to persuade you, how does being rich sound?"

The silence hung heavy.

Then Lucien erupted with laughter, bent forward, and slapped his knees.

"Now you're fucking talking!"

*

"Are you sure they are all with us?"

"Not really."

"Is Thasbald dripping with silver and gold?"

"I have no idea."

"How do you plan to take a fortress with only six soldiers, a drunken braggart, a one-armed cripple, a fat old man who is a self-confessed coward, a wet-eared nobleman, a boy and a serving maid?"

"I will think of something."

"Will I get a cut of the silver and gold, if there is any?"

"No."

He nodded and puckered his lips, "You seem to have thought of everything, my lady..."

She laughed, and for a moment, in the new day's awakening light, she remembered how beautiful being Solace von Tassau had once been.

They stood outside the derelict barn as their company prepared to depart. The sky was a startling blue, the world below glazed with frost. A billion diamonds glistened in the newborn sunlight as gossamer tendrils of mist curled upwards like steam from a pot.

Her eyes narrowed against the glare as the sound of her laughter faded.

"We have other weapons..." she said quietly.

"We do?"

"The Vadians for one."

"You think they will join us?"

"I have spent a lot of time with Lady Karoline. Did you think we were discussing embroidery?"

"I know little of women."

Laughter threatened again; she swallowed it.

"She wants to marry Bulcher no more than I did. The *Graf's* head at my feet will be an effective way of curtailing the marriage."

"But it isn't up to her. Bosko has his orders," Renard said.

"That he does..."

"You have that look, my lady."

Her eyebrow raised, "Which look would that be?"

"The one you get when you know something I do not."

"I know lots of things you don't."

"Indeed... 'tis why I am so familiar with that particular look."

She glanced around her casually and not at all in the manner of someone checking nobody was in earshot.

Running fingers through Styx's mane, she leant in towards Renard.

"Bosko is her father..."

"My lady...?" Renard did an excellent puzzled expression.

"I'm sure once he understands what Bulcher has in store for her..."

The already fine, puzzled expression sank deeper into Renard's features, "She told you Bosko-"

"No, she doesn't know."

"Bosko told you?"

She shook her head.

"Then... oh," he whirled a finger before his nose, "your...?"

She only smiled.

He opened his mouth. Then thought better of it and shut it again.

"As a young man, he enjoyed an assignation with Karoline's mother. He is in no doubt Karoline is his child."

Renard added unconvinced to puzzlement.

She didn't have time to explain. They needed to get on the road as soon as possible to make Thasbald before dark.

And she couldn't explain it.

She simply knew.

When she'd been arguing to hang the Swedes, she'd asked Bosko if he had a daughter. He'd said he had.

And she'd known instantly that daughter was Karoline. Known of the affair he'd had with Karoline's mother and the certainty he felt that she was his daughter rather than the *Freiherr* Hoss', and the depth of his love for the girl.

"But-"

"When I poured oil on the Red Company and set it alight, I was right. I was right when I got everyone out of *The Eagle's Claw* when Madge attacked. Every other time I have believed something, I was right. Trust me. Bosko believes he is Karoline's father, and that is something we can use."

"Yet you never knew Gottlieb had hired the Red Company or Wendel wore Pastor Josef's face, or-"

"No," she said, "I didn't. Because I'm not omnipotent. It doesn't work like that. I don't know everything. But when I know something..." she stepped in closer, eyes hardening, "...I *know*."

Just like I know Saul is going to kill Hilde.

Renard didn't take a step backwards, though he acted like he wanted to.

"I am not doubting you, my lady."

"That is not how it sounds."

"We are walking into the lion's den. I would like to walk out of it."

"We will."

"You have seen that?"

She turned away to check the buckle of Styx's harness

again.

"No," she admitted, "but we haven't come this far to die at Bulcher's hand."

"Let us hope God agrees."

"Do you know what day it is today, Ulrich?"

"Our last day on the road to Thasbald."

"Yes," she nodded, tightening the harness with a yank before turning back to him, "'tis also a year tonight..."

Renard's eyes widened.

"A year to the day the Red Company arrived at The Wolf's Tower, we will cross the threshold of the man who sent them. A good omen. I think."

"Or a bad one..." he turned his face to the eastern sky and the brightest light.

"We will destroy them, Ulrich. All of them."

His eyes returned reluctantly.

"Is there nothing left for us in this world bar vengeance?"

"What else should we do? Walk away? Go and hide? Leave the monsters to do to others that which they did to us?"

He said nothing.

"Run or stand, Ulrich? Run or stand?"

"I stand with you, till the end," he said, though so quietly she might have lost the words if the dawn were not so still.

She nodded. That was all she asked for. All she wanted. She turned to lead Styx to where the rest of their company waited, ready to continue along the road.

"My lady?"

"Yes?" she looked over her shoulder.

"May I ask a favour."

"Of course. You can ask..."

"Send Hilde away."

"Why?"

He shuffled his boots, fidgeted with the reins of the Swedish horse he held in his good hand, his features even more downcast than usual.

"I do not want to see her come to harm..."

She looked to the horizon, then swept her gaze along it. Open ground, bracken, heath, a few low, gnarled trees. Nothing else.

"Where would she go? A woman alone...? We've seen what happens to women out here. There is no law anymore. Nowhere is safe."

And behind her eyes, she saw Hilde tumbling from Saul's arms, blood pumping from her neck, to crash upon the cold stone of a church floor. A floor running with blood. A church echoing to a hymn of screams.

Her one friend's name haunting Hilde's dying lips.

"Nowhere is safe," she repeated, keeping her eyes turned to the horizon.

"I know, but..."

"Have you told her to leave?"

"She won't listen to me."

"And you think she will me?"

"If you-"

"No. She'd no more likely listen to me than you. Besides, she knows too much now. You should have made her stay in Berg or Wittenberge."

"I know..." he mumbled, refusing her eye.

"You are... fond of her?" she asked. Casually.

His brows furrowed as if struggling for words.

If so, it was a struggle he lost, as, in the end, he replied with a roll of the shoulders.

Why would he not be fond of her? She crawls under his blankets at night, doesn't she?

The thought stung her, sharp and nasty. And it wasn't becoming. It was no business of hers. Why shouldn't he find comfort with the kind of woman who cast aside her virtue so easily. He was a man. And a soldier. It was what they did, she was led to believe.

But I kept him warm once, does that not-

No. It didn't mean anything.

Nothing mattered but vengeance.

Last night, she'd called it justice when trying to swing the whole company to her cause. It was a better word. Noble. Civilised. It suggested a higher intent.

It just wasn't the right one.

Vengeance fitted her tongue far more sweetly.

She wanted them dead. All of them. Men or monster. Not to balance any scale, not to put the world to right, not for what might happen to the world if she didn't. But for revenge. For her father, for The Wolf's Tower, for Tassau, for her brother, for all those that died.

But mostly for Solace von Tassau, who'd died along with the rest. For the life she'd been denied. For the loves she'd never find, for the friends she'd never make, for the laughter she'd never know.

Her hand tried to wander to the bag of grey dust hanging about her neck.

Wendel had died quick. Wendel had died easy.

Graf Bulcher wouldn't.

And vengeance would be salved. The pain and emptiness consuming the place where Solace von Tassau had once existed would be eased, would be replaced.

She vaulted onto Styx's back.

The stallion tossed his midnight mane and pawed at the frozen earth.

Around them, the new sun melted the frost to rise about them, hazy as ghosts, floating in shimmering, ephemeral banks of mist.

It softened the world, making it otherworldly and unfamiliar. A dream beneath the sharpest of blue skies.

She blew out a plume of breath in time with Styx's.

Renard was still standing, the reins of his own mount in his hand, gazing up at her like he wasn't quite sure who he was looking at.

"Come, Ulrich, ride. Tonight, we dine in Thasbald!"

She smiled then. It felt like sunlight on her skin, though Renard still stared at her, wary and uncertain.

He had his doubts. No matter. She would prevail. Nothing would stop her. Nothing would keep her from vengeance.

Flyblown's mark upon her thigh smarted in agreement.

She turned Styx towards the waiting company. Her company. The smile on her face growing wider, brighter, sharper.

Why should I not smile this day of all days?

Vengeance was coming....

A Dark Journey Continues...

The Night's Road – Book Five

Darkness Beckons

Follow Solace, Ulrich and company's journey as they continue their pursuit of Saul the Bloodless and the Red Company in *Darkness Beckons*, the next instalment of *The Night's Road*, due for publication in September 2024....

In the Company of Shadows

If you'd like to read more dark tales from the world of *In the Company of Shadows*, there are currently two free novellas (available as eBooks only) – *The Burning* & *A House of the Dead* – available. Both are set shortly before the events of *Red Company*. To get your free copies just visit andymonkbooks.com. or scan the QR code below and join Andy's mailing list for updates, news of forthcoming releases and bonus material.

The Burning

The madness of the 17th Century witch burning frenzy has come to the sleepy village of Reperndorf.

Adolphus Holtz, Inquisitor to the Prince-Bishop of Würzburg, is keen to root out evil wherever he deems it to be. His eye has fallen on young Frieda and he fancies she'll scream so prettily for him when the time comes.

Frieda has already witnessed one burning and knows from the way her friends and neighbours are looking at her that she will be next. She seems doomed to burn on the pyre until a mysterious cloaked stranger appears out of the depths of the forest...

The first novella of *In the Company of Shadows* expands the dark historical world of *In the Absence of Light* and the shadowy relationships between humans and vampires.

A House of the Dead

All vampires are mad...

The weight of memories, loss, the hunger for blood, the voices of your prey whispering in your mind, loneliness, the obsessions you filled the emptiness inside yourself with, the sheer unrelenting bloody boredom of immortality could all chip away at your sanity.

And love, of course, one should never forget what that could do to you...

Mecurio has hidden from the world for twenty years in the secret catacombs beneath the city of Würzburg known as the House of the Dead, a place of refuge for vampires away from the eyes of men.

He tells himself it is so he can complete his Great Work without the distractions of the mortal world. But it isn't true. Time is slowly stealing the woman he adores from him and he has hidden their love away in the shadows of the House of the Dead to await the inevitable.

When a vampire whose bed he fled from a hundred and twenty-seven years before, arrives in search of information, he sees the opportunity to do a deal to save the woman he now loves for a few more bittersweet years. But all vampires are mad, one way or another, and when you strike a deal with one you may not end up with what you bargained for...

Books by Andy Monk

In the Absence of Light
The King of the Winter
A Bad Man's Song
Ghosts in the Blood
The Love of Monsters

In the Company of Shadows
The Burning (Novella)
A House of the Dead (Novella)
Red Company (The Night's Road Book One)
The Kindly Man (Rumville Part One)
Execution Dock (Rumville Part Two)
The Convenient (Rumville Part Three)
Mister Grim (Rumville Part Four)
The Future is Promises (Rumville Part Five)
The World's Pain (The Night's Road Book Two)
Empire of Dirt (The Night's Road Book Three)
When the Walls Fall (The Night's Road Book Four)
Darkness Beckons (The Night's Road Book Five)

Hawker's Drift
The Burden of Souls
Dark Carnival
The Paths of the World
A God of Many Tears
Hollow Places

Other Fiction
The House of Shells
The Sorrowsmith

For further information about Andy Monk's writing and future releases, please visit the following sites.

www.andymonkbooks.com

www.facebook.com/andymonkbooks

Printed in Great Britain
by Amazon